THE GIRL FROM WISH LANE

THE GIRL FROM WISH LANE

Anne Douglas

Severn House Large Print
London & New York

This first l...

in Great Bi...

SEVERN ...

9-15 High ...

First world ...

Severn Hoi...

Copyright © 2008 by Anne Douglas.

British Library Cataloguing in Publication Data

Douglas, Anne, 1930-
    The girl from Wish Lane. - Large print ed.
    1. Jute industry - Scotland - Dundee - Fiction 2. Social
    classes - Scotland - Dundee - Fiction 3. Dundee (Scotland)
    - Social conditions - Fiction 4. Domestic fiction 5. Large
    type books
    I. Title
    823.9'14[F]

    ISBN-13: 978-0-7278-7764-2

Printed and bound in Great Britain by
MPG Books Ltd, Bodmin, Cornwall.

One

The factory hooters rang out, sounding like church bells calling the faithful. Instead they were calling workers to the factories and the mills. From all over Dundee folk would be hurrying, so as not to be late. Arrive after six o'clock, when the overseers had locked the doors, and you lost wages. Who needed the call of the hooters when they knew that?

Not Eva Masson's mother, Bel, that was for sure. She had never in her life been late for the mill, where she worked as a spinner of jute, and she saw to it that her other daughter Letty, also a spinner, was on time too. Letty, seventeen, pale and fair, was always languid, sighing and wanting to sink down wherever she happened to be. She kept going, though, with her mother looking out for her.

Ma's always looking out for folk, thought Eva as she made the tea that was all her mother and sister would have until their breakfast three hours later. Though Eva needn't leave the house yet – for she was going to school, not work – she was already dressed in a cotton frock that had been Letty's, with her dark hair scraped back and her face stinging from a rub with a cold flannel. Going to school, she reflected as she stirred the pot, aye, but not for much longer. Today was her

5

birthday. She was fourteen.

Could it be true? Fourteen? A grown-up, or as good as by Dundee standards. Able to leave school and go to full-time work. Tears stung Eva's dark eyes, so like her mother's, as she poured the tea. Her oval face, which held the promise of beauty, crumpled a little. How she had dreaded this day. But then she knew things might have been worse.

Up till now, she'd only worked for one summer holiday and on Saturday mornings, whereas some children were half-timers at twelve, or even younger, and had school in the morning and work in the afternoon all the year round. Bel had never wanted that for her bairns and for that they were grateful.

'Ma,' Eva called, dashing away her tears, 'the tea's ready.'

The Massons had two rooms, which they called a house rather than a flat, on the second floor of Number 12 Wish Lane, a tenement building off the Hawkhill Road. If they'd lived on the third, they would have had to enter by way of an outside staircase and a 'plettie', or stone platform, which were features of Dundee tenements. But their stairs were under cover, and so, thank the Lord, was the lavatory that served the families of the lower floors.

Their house had a living room with a cooking range, a sink and cupboards, a scrubbed table with chairs, and a box bed for the sisters. Adjoining that was a second room, with a brass bedstead for Bel and Frank, a mattress for young

Roddie, the only boy, and a wardrobe and chest of drawers that the whole family shared.

Finding things to wear usually took some time and caused some friction, but still they considered themselves lucky. Two rooms and no lodgers – that certainly put them in the lucky class, when so many families had only one room and sometimes squashed in lodgers as well – usually women on their own, who were willing to pay a few pence just for a place to sleep.

Dundee in 1921, was a 'she-town', a women's city, as it had always been since the coming of the jute industry some sixty years before. Women got the jobs in the mills and factories because they needn't be paid as much as men, and with single women flooding in from elsewhere, and married women becoming breadwinners, men had a difficult time of it. Though a few were still favoured for overseers' jobs in the mills, work for men was hard to find and, if found, was often lost. Such had been Frank Masson's experience.

When he first came back from the Great War, his job with a precision tool manufacturer had seemed secure, but within months the firm had gone under and Frank had become what he'd most dreaded: a 'kettle-biler'. A man who stayed at home while his wife went out to work. He could hardly bear to look at himself in the mirror. He didn't do much kettle-biling anyway. There'd be no women's work for him. Every day he went out, looking for a job.

'This tea do for you, Frank?' Bel asked as her husband appeared in the doorway, his eyes reddened from sleep and his sandy hair on end. 'Or are you wanting Eva to make fresh?'

'That'll do,' he answered, smoothing his hair with his thin hands. 'You off then? You'll no' want to be late.'

'No fear of that.'

Bel and Letty were ready to go, and Bel was already putting on her shawl, though the June day was warm. But she would never have dreamed of going to work in only her blouse and skirt, or of wearing a pinny in the street as other women did.

Just as she liked to spend what free time she had cleaning her house, to try to keep the dirt at bay. She never judged her neighbours, though, if they didn't want to do the same. Some did, some didn't, and she knew it was easier for her, with a smaller family and more space than most. Besides, getting out the carbolic soap and scrubbing brush after a day at the mill was not something everyone could face.

At thirty-six, though no longer considered young, she was still slim and straight, with dark hair in a knot and those fine dark eyes that Eva had inherited. Some said she was stylish enough to have been one of the weavers, who wore hats and gloves to go to work. Would you credit it? How the young mill girls laughed. Hats and gloves to go to the factory, just to weave materials from the jute the mill girls had spun – those same girls they had the cheek to look down on. What a piece of nonsense!

And yet it was true that weavers earned more than spinners, although they were not as skilful, because they were on piece-work and the spinners were not. That rankled with Bel, and made her eyes flash when she thought about it.

'Let's away,' she said now to Letty. 'Eva, you'll wake up Roddie, eh? And heat your dad's porridge? It's all ready.'

As Eva nodded glumly, her lip drooping, her mother gave her a sharp glance.

'Hey, what's wrong wi' you, then? You look like you lost half a crown and found a sixpence – and it's your birthday, and all!'

Eva shrugged. Now was not the time to say what was on her mind.

'We wished you many happy returns, eh?'

'Aye, you did.'

Bel's look softened. 'And I've made you a new dress.'

'Ma! When? I never knew!'

'Ran it up on Jeannie Fraser's machine. Got the stuff in D. M. Brown's sale, but it's nice, you'll like it. You can have it when I'm back tonight. Letty, come on now.'

'I'm that sorry, Evie, I forgot to get you a card,' said Letty, her blue eyes full of woe. 'Trust me, eh?'

'Nae bother. Never expected one.'

Nobody in Eva's circle expected much for birthdays. Cakes with candles, wrapped presents, cards in the post – these were not for them, though sometimes, if parents had jobs and there had been no strikes or sickness, some little treat might be managed. The new dress that Bel had made, that was something special, but as

9

Eva went to waken her brother the thought occurred to her that the dress might be intended for her to wear to work.

Her heart sank. Aye, that might be why Ma had made such an effort. Wanting her to look smart for her first full-time job. As smart as the weavers maybe – as though the mill girls would care what the new lassie was wearing. But that was Ma for you, always wanting to keep up her standards. Even when, if the truth were told, they all ended up looking the same in the mill, because of the dust from the jute and the machines.

Two

'Roddie, wake up!' Eva cried, shaking her eleven-year-old brother's shoulder. 'Come on, I've Dad's porridge to do yet, so no going back to sleep, eh?'

'Am I having porridge?' asked Roddie, instantly sitting up on his mattress in the corner of his parents' room. Small for his age, he was a quick, energetic child, with curly black hair and dancing blue eyes. At school he was considered clever. But then, so was Eva.

'If you want it. But just shift yourself. You ken what you'll get if you're late for school.'

'Evie, Evie, wait!' he called as she hurried to the door.

'Oh, what is it?'

10

'Happy Birthday!'

She gave a smile that changed her face, and ran back to give him a hug.

'Roddie up?' her father asked, sitting at the table, waiting to be served.

'On his way.' Eva pulled the pan of porridge on to the heat of the stove and began to stir it. Her smile had faded and her father, who was not given to picking up on other people's feelings, saw for a moment what his wife had seen.

'Och, lassie, what's up then? You've no' been greeting, eh?'

'No.' She sniffed and kept on stirring the porridge. 'It's just that I'll be starting work, and I wish I didnae have to. I mean, I wish I could've stayed on and gone to the secondary school.'

Frank's eyes were following her spoon; he said nothing.

'I qualified, you ken,' Eva murmured. 'I could-'ve gone.'

'I wish you could've too.'

'Miss Balfour said if I'd gone, I'd have taken the Leaving Certificate and got a good job when I left.' Eva stopped stirring. 'She said there were these bursaries, to help folk like me...'

'We went into that, Eva. Even if you'd got one, it would no' have helped enough.' As Eva set his porridge before him and handed him his spoon, her father slowly shook his sandy head. 'We need your money, you ken. That's what it is.'

Large tears slowly drifted down Eva's face as she made fresh tea and sliced bread, spreading it thinly with margarine, butter being a rare treat in their household.

11

'You understand?' Frank asked in a low voice.

'Aye.' She ate some bread and drank some tea, then went to the door and shouted to Roddie, who came in running, wearing short grey trousers and a much-darned jersey, but with a pair of boots of which he was very proud. He looked from one worried face to the other.

'What's wrong, Dad? What's wrong, Evie?'

'Nothing,' Eva answered, blowing her nose. 'Hurry up with your breakfast, then, and we'll away. It's all right, Dad, I'm no' complaining. I ken we need the money.'

'Aye,' he said with relief. 'That's a good lassie, then. And you could mebbe stay on till school finishes for the summer. Start at the mill then. That'd be July.'

'July,' she agreed.

'That'd no' be so bad, eh?'

'No' so bad.'

As they left the house for school, Roddie's bright gaze was on his sister's face.

'I could be working soon, Evie. I could make some money, you ken.'

'You're no' even twelve yet. You've no' got the lines.'

By lines, Eva meant the birth certificate that would prove a child was old enough to leave school for work.

'Plenty bairns younger than me borrow other people's lines and do half-time. Shifting and that. Like you.'

'Well, you're no' doing it. Ma willnae let you.'

'What's it like?' he asked after a moment.

'Being a shifter? Some lads say it's awful hard work.'

'Can be. You've to keep changing the bobbins from the spindles of the spinning frames. When one's full, you put on another.'

'Will you be shifting when you go full-time?'

'Ma thinks I'll be given some other job. But let's no' talk about it. Come on, I'll race you!'

Off they ran, brother and sister, flying along the pavements towards school, all thoughts of the world of work temporarily gone from their minds.

Three

Toll Road School was built of the same pinkish-brown sandstone as the mills and factories and, like them, was showing signs of wear. The local stone never did wear well, folk said, yet Dundee's central buildings still had the elegance and even opulence of the prosperous times when they'd been built.

Dundee had been prosperous in the past and had built well, and even today, though it had too many mills and chimneys and overcrowded tenements, it was still a fine city. Not only was it the fourth largest city in Scotland, but the one with the best site, looking out over the estuary of the River Tay, which was beautiful by any standards.

Never mind that there had been that tragedy

13

back in 1879, when the Tay's new bridge had gone down into the water, taking a trainload of passengers with it; modern Dundonians did not dwell on that. They had Dundee Law, their landmark hill with its superb views. They had their harbour and their shipping, their whaling industry, and the amazing mansions of the jute barons – jute palaces as they were called – mainly in Broughty Ferry, the city's coastal resort.

'Prosperity for some,' Frank Masson said once, when he and the family had taken a rare bank holiday trip to Broughty Ferry and looked up at the mansions paid for with jute. Or, to be more accurate, the labour of the jute workers. And Bel's face had darkened as she'd gazed at the great house of Joseph North, who owned the mill where she worked.

'See all thae turrets and windows and things, and a garden as big as a park,' she murmured. 'You'd think a man with a place like that could pay us women a decent wage, eh?'

'Rich folk dinna stay rich by spending money,' said Frank.

'But think of the cleaning you'd have to do, if you lived there,' Letty murmured.

'As though you'd have to do it!' Roddie scoffed. 'If you lived there.'

'None of us ever will,' said Bel.

Who knows? Eva thought. *Maybe someday one of us might? Maybe me?*

That was a joke, of course, just for herself. Or else, a dream.

A dream that would never be realized, she knew

now, as she turned into the school gate marked 'Girls' and watched Roddie running in through the boys' entrance to meet his friends. This was the day she must begin to think about saying goodbye to school and all prospects of a good job, for even if she did stay on until the end of term, there wasn't much of it left. These last days would mark her farewell.

'Eva, happy birthday!' cried her friend Katie Crindle, a girl with a round, rosy face, big brown eyes and glossy brown ringlets. You could tell just by looking at her, Eva always thought, that she wasn't the child of mill workers. Could tell, somehow, that her dad would have a little business – it was a stationer's, in fact – and that her ma would stay at home and clean the flat over the shop and put a nice cloth on the table and make lovely teas. What would it be like to be her? Eva wondered. For she was clever, too, and would be staying on to do her Leaving Certificate.

I'd never swap my folks for hers, Eva thought, smiling at Katie, her best friend. *But I wish Ma could have a flat like Mrs Crindle's and be able to stay at home. And I wish Dad could sell paper and pens for a living and no' have to worry about finding a job.* As for herself, if she were Katie, she'd be staying on at school and thinking about becoming a teacher. That was Katie's ambition, and would have been Eva's, too, if the world had been different.

Katie had a little package for Eva, which turned out to be two pocket handkerchiefs with lace trimming and the initial 'E' embroidered in red chain stitch. Was that not a sign that she was

15

different from other lassies?

'Oh, Katie,' Eva whispered. 'These are grand, eh?'

'I'm no good at sewing, but Mum saw me right,' said Katie in her soft voice that had little hint of the Scots dialect spoken by Eva and her family, or 'Dundee', the unique mixture of Irish and Scots spoken by many of the city's workers.

'And there's a card as well,' Katie went on. 'Dad let me have it from the shop.'

The card had roses and a kitten on it, and a long verse on the subject of friends being ever true, which Eva thought was beautiful. It was her only card that year, unless Letty got one for her in her dinner hour, but she was able to tell Katie about the dress her mother had made for her, and could see in Katie's eyes that she was surprised and pleased.

'Will you wear it tomorrow?' she asked. 'So's we can all see it?'

'I think I might keep it for best. Ma thinks I should wear it for ma first day at work, but it'd just get all dusty.'

'When d'you start?'

'In July.'

'At North's?'

'Aye. In the low mill, I expect – that's where they prepare the jute.'

'I wish you could've gone to the secondary school, Eva.'

'Canna be helped.'

'It's a shame, so it is.'

Eva was spared having to make further reply by the sound of the school bell, and the pupils

16

immediately lined up for the march into the hall for assembly.

Nearly my last one, thought Eva as Miss Piper, the headmistress, bustled on to the platform, and was ashamed to find that her eyes were pricking with tears again. Some of the other leavers were glad, she knew, to be departing, as they thought of school as a prison, but Eva had never seen it as such.

Young as she was, she knew it was the key to change – the only way of getting away from the life her parents had – and already there was a little bitterness in her heart that she must let it go. But that door was closed to her, through no fault of her folks or herself – perhaps through no one's fault at all. She couldn't believe that that was true, though. Someone, somewhere, must be to blame for poverty.

Four

Eva and her classmates were settling in for their first lesson, with the boys on their side of the room scuffling and laughing, and the girls on theirs still whispering and giggling, when their teacher, Miss Balfour, rapped the desk with her ruler.

She was a tall, slim young woman, with delicate features and sharp blue eyes behind metal-framed spectacles. It was said she came from

Edinburgh, and certainly she didn't speak Dundee or Scots, but then few of the teachers did. What her pupils sensed from her was her keenness for them to do well, whether they had boots or no boots, whether they came from a crowded tenement or a pleasant little house. She was, therefore, respected and even admired, and didn't have to use her ruler too much, or the strap.

'That's enough,' she called now. 'Everyone settle down, please, and we'll do our mental arithmetic exercises before we open our books. Five sums each and we'll start with Katie.'

'Doesnae seem worth doing all this, eh?' Ada MacGill, a gawky girl with thin blonde plaits, whispered to Eva as Katie stood up. 'I mean, when we're leaving so soon.'

'D'you want to leave, Ada?' Eva asked behind her hand.

'Och, no! But I canna stay. I canna go to the secondary.'

'Nor me.'

'You girls, stop talking!' Miss Balfour said sharply. 'Eva, you can be next to answer after Katie.'

'Yes, Miss Balfour.'

When Katie had rattled off five correct answers, Eva rose readily – she never minded these little mental arithmetic exercises – but before Miss Balfour could continue, the door of the classroom opened and the headmistress appeared. Silence fell.

Miss Piper, who was unusual in being a woman and head of a school, was one of those fortunate teachers who never needed to demonstrate her authority. It was just there, as much a part of her as her small grey eyes, sharp nose and bouncy little figure, and no pupil at her school ever sought to dispute it. Subordinate teachers felt it too, Miss Balfour being no exception. As soon as the headmistress came in, she grew a little pale and hurried forward to greet her.

A large man was with Miss Piper, dressed in a fine dark suit that showed the crackling white collar and cuffs of his linen shirt. He had probably been a good-looking man once, even if now rather old – at least fifty – but obviously well-to-do, judging from the gold watch chain across his waistcoat and the gold pin in his tie. *He must be one of the nobs from the big houses*, thought Eva. But what was he doing in Miss Balfour's classroom?

'Everyone pay attention – this is Mr North,' Miss Piper called in ringing tones. 'He is the owner of North's Mill and is looking round the school. Some of you might know his name.'

Oh yes, they knew his name. And Eva Masson knew his house.

'Stand up and say "Good morning, Mr North",' Miss Balfour whispered.

'Good morning, Mr North,' they chorused obediently, rising to stand at their desks.

'Good morning, children.' The gentleman looked along their ranks, smiling. 'Though as some of you will be leaving to go to work soon, maybe I shouldn't call you children. How many are going to work in my jute mill, I wonder? Let's see a show of hands.'

As a number of girls put up their hands, Mr

19

North seemed pleased, and Miss Piper permitted herself a rare smile at his pleasure.

'So, how many can tell me what is this jute we work with in the mills?' Mr North asked.

More hands went up, one being Eva's and another Bob Keir's, a rival of hers. All the bright pupils in Miss Balfour's class liked to outdo one another whenever possible.

'Please, sir, it's a plant fibre,' said Bob before Eva could speak. He was a cheeky-faced boy, with black hair and brows to match, and was considered particularly big-headed by his classmates. Not that they told him so, he being taller and heavier than they, for like many Dundee children of poor parents, they were undersized for their age.

'Comes from India,' Bob added, throwing a triumphant glance at Eva, whose brow had darkened. Whether or not Mr North caught the look, he smiled approvingly on Bob.

'Bengal, as a matter of fact, but that's very good, very good indeed. And what do we make with it, then?'

Again, Eva was ready to speak, but Bob beat her to it. 'Sacks and matting, sir. And carpet backing, and rope and string – all sorts o' stuff like that.'

'Very good,' Mr North said again. 'I'm pleased you know so much about it. Jute's been the saving of this city for many years, since an English fellow thought of bringing it over. What's your name, laddie?'

'Bob Keir, sir.'

'And are you going to work in my mill?'

20

'No, sir, I'm too big to do shifting and there's no other vacancies at North's. Only want lassies.'

'Bob, that's enough,' Miss Piper cut in swiftly. 'Aren't you going to train as a mechanic with Berry's Mill, anyway?'

'You'll do well there,' Mr North commented, his tone cool; Berry's was one of his many rivals.

'I wanted to take ma Leaving Certificate,' said Bob. 'I wanted to be a teacher.'

At that there was a certain ripple of amusement around the room that quickly died at Miss Piper's look. Bob Keir, a teacher? Who did he think he was? Eva and Katie exchanged glances.

'That's interesting,' Mr North murmured, studying Bob's defiant face before turning to the headmistress. 'I'm finding all this very informative, Miss Piper, but perhaps we should move on now?'

'Certainly, Mr North.'

'My thanks to you, Miss Balfour.'

'My pleasure, Mr North.'

'Goodbye, boys and girls,' he said from the door. 'I'm glad to have spoken with you.'

'Goodbye, Mr North,' they chanted, and as Miss Piper escorted the guest away, Miss Balfour gave a sigh of relief and told everyone to sit down.

'Back to work,' she said, and in a low voice added to Bob Keir, 'Bob, you did well.'

Eva, taking out her arithmetic book, heard his reply.

'It'll no' do me much good, though, eh?'

'What do you mean?'

'I mean I've still to be a mechanic, whatever

I do.'

'It will be good to have a job, Bob. But who knows what will happen?' Miss Balfour hesitated. 'Never give up hope, is my advice.'

At dinner-time, when Eva sat down outside to eat her piece with Katie, she pondered on her teacher's words and what they could mean. 'Never give up hope.' Hope of what? Of getting what you wanted? She knew how pointless it was to think of that.

Katie was knocking her arm. 'Eva, look!'

'Where?'

'At the gate. That big motor. It must be Mr North's.'

Several children were already gathering, to stare in wonder at the long, highly polished car that had drawn up outside their school. A man in a peaked cap was at the wheel and from a seat at the back a boy was looking out. A handsome boy, perhaps a year or two older than Eva, who wore no cap over his short fair hair and whose eyes, even at a distance, she could tell were light-coloured. Blue? No, grey. And they were looking at her.

For what seemed a long time, they exchanged looks. Then Mr North came out of the school with Miss Piper in attendance, and the boy half-smiled and shifted his gaze away. A few moments later, after an exchange of handshakes and some tentative waves from the children, the car moved off. Mr North and his son were gone.

'Come on,' said Katie. 'Finish your piece.'

Eva ate her bread and jam without replying.

'Is anything wrong, Eva? You're awful quiet.'

'Just wondering what that laddie in the motor thought of us folk at the gate.'

'Why would he think anything?'

'Some have no' even got shoes,' Eva said in a low voice. 'And there he is in a motor like that. He'd think himself lucky, eh?'

'You and me have shoes,' Katie murmured uneasily. 'Maybe we're lucky, too.'

As Eva only stared at her, she blushed.

'Well, I am.'

'Some mothers go into debt to buy shoes, you ken.'

'I did say I was lucky,' Katie said defensively.

She was, too, Eva thought. But not as lucky as the boy in the car.

Five

When Bel came home from work at six o'clock, she presented Eva with her new dress. It was blue with a Peter Pan collar, a dropped waist and full skirt, and she thought it the best dress she'd ever had. Also, it was hers alone, had never been Letty's, and that made it even more precious.

After she'd tried it on and twirled around to let everybody see, she hugged her mother hard, and Bel's lip trembled a little as she thought of her young Eva being fourteen and ready for work.

'I wish I could've got you a cake, pet, but Letty

23

and me picked up a currant loaf on the way home, and a few jam tarts. I've some cold ham and all, so we can have a nice tea, eh?'

'Ma dress is enough for me,' Eva told her. She smoothed down the skirt and retied the belt, and thought suddenly of the face of the boy in the motor and of his eyes resting on her. If only she'd been wearing this dress then ... A sensible voice in her mind said it would have made no difference at all. But, all the same, she wished she'd been wearing the dress at the time.

'I'm going to keep it for best, Ma,' she announced. 'I'm no' wearing it for the mill.'

'Why, I thought you'd want the lassies to see you looking nice.'

'In all the dust?' asked Letty, sitting at the table and fanning herself with a handkerchief. 'Eva's right, she should keep it for best.'

'I was only thinking of the first day. I ken fine what the dust's like.'

'I think one o' you could put on that kettle,' said Frank. 'Here's Roddie and me gasping.'

'You could've put it on yourself for once!' cried Bel, but he gave a wry grin.

'Now you ken well I'm no kettle-biler, Bel.'

'That's for sure!'

Her eyes glittered and she tossed her dark head, but the kettle was put on, the tea made, and everybody settled down to the little celebration. Eva, still admiring herself in her dress, felt grateful to have as much as she had, and happier than she'd been for some time. At the back of her mind, though, she knew the happiness wouldn't last.

24

After her birthday the time began to fly, bringing the end to her school career ever nearer. The weather was sultry, making her head throb and sometimes seeming to bind a tight band round her chest so that she felt she could scarcely breathe. But maybe that wasn't the fault of the weather. Maybe it was just the thought of starting work at the mill.

One evening, when they'd finished their tea of boiled bacon pieces with a lettuce – Bel's concession to the high temperatures – Eva said she and Letty should sit outside on the step.

'You should get some air,' she told Letty. 'You've been inside all day.'

'Some o' the lassies are away promenading,' Letty remarked, yawning. 'They say I should go along.'

Promenading – strolling round the town, seeing what was happening – was one of the favourite occupations of the mill girls when they had finished work, just as it had been in earlier years. Even though there was the cinema to go to now, and dances too, they still liked to go out and look folk up and down, flashing their eyes, showing off their independence.

But Bel's face was thunderous. 'Promenading? Whatever makes you think I'd let you do that, Letty? Some o' thae girls are shameless, so they are. Where do they go when they're promenading, I'd like to know? Pubs and such would be ma guess.'

'They're not all like that, Ma. You ken that very well.'

'True, but how can I be sure which ones you'll be with? Better no' to go at all.'

'Och, they just like to gossip,' Frank said easily. 'And it doesnae cost anything, eh? Talking of fresh air, I think I'll walk out maself. Want to come, Bel?'

'And me just back from work? You ken fine I've too much to do.' Bel, pale and sweating, her dark hair lying in damp tendrils on her brow, looked so weary that Eva was filled with guilt and jumped to her feet.

'You go with Dad, Ma. You need fresh air and all. Letty and me'll clear up.'

'Where's Roddie?' asked Letty. 'He could give a hand.'

'Och, let him play,' said Bel fondly. 'He's out with his pals. Mebbe I will get ma shawl then, if you want to walk out, Frank.'

'Promenading?' he asked with a grin, then put his arm round his wife's waist and said he was only joking. 'Anyway, you'll no' need your shawl, Bel. It's like an oven out there.'

Bel was just about to declare that she would wear her shawl or not go, when there was a tap at their door and she clicked her tongue.

'Hope that's nobody come borrowing. I've no' much in the cupboard anyway, and the milk's turning wi' the heat. Who is it, Eva?'

'It's Miss Balfour,' she whispered, astonished.

Instant panic descended as Miss Balfour was invited in, with even Letty being galvanized into hurrying plates from the table to the sink, and Frank offering a chair and Bel dusting it. Eva, though, just stood still and turned pale. Miss Balfour, here in her home? What was wrong?

But Miss Balfour, who seemed strange in a pale-blue dress she never wore for school, seemed calm. She smiled apologetically.

'I'm so sorry, Mr and Mrs Masson, to call without notice. Things all seem to be happening rather quickly and I've a number of parents to see.'

'Something wrong?' asked Bel fearfully.

'Oh, no, nothing wrong at all. Quite the reverse. Well, I hope you'll think so.' Miss Balfour opened her bag and took out an envelope, which she put into Bel's hand. 'This is a letter from the School Board. It will explain that Mr North of North's Mill is very kindly offering to fund some secondary school scholarships, for certain pupils at Toll Road Public and other schools in the area.'

Eva's hands were beginning to tremble and she held them fast together. Scholarships for certain pupils? Which pupils?

'Are these like thae bursaries we heard about before?' asked Bel. 'There were no' many, we were told, and they just covered school expenses and that.' She shook her head. 'No good to us.'

'There have always been bursaries for children who can progress to secondary school, but these are different. They will be funded by Mr North, not the authorities, and will be more generous.'

'And does Eva qualify?' asked Frank, his eyes on the letter that Bel had not yet opened. Her own dark gaze was still fixed on Miss Balfour, while Letty's had moved to her sister.

27

'Oh, Evie, I bet you do,' she whispered.

'She does.' Miss Balfour smiled. 'Eva and four others from my class are to be offered North bursaries. All have qualified for secondary school, but can't at present take up places.'

'Because their folks need their wages,' murmured Bel.

'Exactly. And it's a great shame, because Toll Road Secondary is a Higher Grade school, where pupils can work for the Leaving Certificate. Which means, you see...'

'A good job at the end o' school,' muttered Frank. 'Aye, we know about the Leaving Certificate.'

'Well, you see how important it is, then. That's why Mr North's plan is so different. He's had the idea of making his awards compensate the parents, so that they can afford to let their children stay on at school.'

While Bel and Frank exchanged glances, Miss Balfour turned to Eva, who was still clasping her hands together as though she couldn't let them go. 'Eva, I think I'm right in saying you'd like to stay on, wouldn't you?'

'Oh, I would! I want to be a teacher! But I never thought ... I canna believe ... I mean, why's Mr North doin' this?'

'Aye, what's in it for him?' asked Frank. 'He's never been known for giving money away. Never pays ma Bel here a living wage.'

Miss Balfour hesitated. 'He has been very generous to the city, to be fair. Donated money for hospital buildings, for instance. But some mill owners provide schools for half-timer children

28

on their own premises and Mr North hasn't done anything like that.'

'So he's doing this instead,' said Bel. 'Paying us what the lassie might earn?'

'That's right, though the details are not complete yet.' Miss Balfour fiddled a little with the clasp of her handbag. 'First, you see, you have to give your approval. Nothing can be done without that.'

Eva's eyes suddenly seemed enormous. 'Ma?' she whispered.

'Nae bother, pet,' Bel said quickly. 'I think it'd be grand for you to stay on at school. I mind you've been clever since you were a wee bairn. Walking quick, talking quick, never any trouble with your letters or figures – if anybody deserves help, it's you.'

'Oh, Ma!'

'Miss Balfour, I give ma approval,' Bel said firmly. 'So that's settled.'

'Is it?' asked Frank. 'I dinna agree.'

The silence that fell was oppressive until Bel broke it.

'What are you on about, Frank? What's no' to agree over?'

He shrugged a little, not wanting to meet his wife's eyes, or his daughter's.

'Well, in ma view, it'd all be a waste o' time. If it was Roddie we were talkin' about, that'd be different, but Eva's a lassie. She'll only get wed.'

'Who says I'll get wed?' asked Eva, trembling.

'You will, pet, you will. And married women canna be teachers. Canna be professional folk, eh? They're no' the breadwinners, so they've to

29

give their jobs up.'

'And very unfair that is!' cried Miss Balfour, then lowered her eyes. 'But not all women marry, Mr Masson.'

Spots of red glowed on Frank's cheeks and he lowered his own eyes. True, Miss Balfour had not married. What could he say to that? 'It'd all be a waste o' time,' he repeated doggedly. 'And I'm no' keen on taking charity. I think it's better for folk like us no' to get involved.'

'Frank, I'm ashamed o' you,' Bel said with scorn. 'Here's this wonderful chance come for Eva and you want us to say no? Never! Whatever they want us to sign, we'll sign. It's come too late for Letty, but we can do this for Eva and we will.'

'No need to worry about me,' murmured Letty. 'I'd never have wanted to stay on at school.'

'Aye, maybe,' said her mother. 'But it's never suited you being in the mill. And the weaving shed's no' much better – just as noisy, and all.'

'I never wanted to be a weaver, Ma. And how would I look going to work in hat and gloves? I'd feel an idiot, so I would!'

The atmosphere eased as everyone laughed – even Frank, even Miss Balfour, before she rose to make her polite goodbyes.

'I'll leave the letter with you then, Mr and Mrs Masson, and you can discuss it again. But be sure to let us know your decision within a day or two. Things have to be set in motion before the end of term.'

'We'll let you know, all right,' Bel told her, opening the door to the stair. She lowered her voice. 'And I think you know what the answer will be.'

'I'm very glad,' Miss Balfour whispered. 'For Eva's sake. You'll be doing the right thing, Mrs Masson, to accept this offer. And I think I can tell you that the terms will be satisfactory.'

Miss Balfour smiled again and shook Bel's hand. 'I'll find my own way out, Mrs Masson. No need to come down the stair.'

'I'll come down the stair,' cried Eva, darting out of the door. 'I'll see you out, Miss Balfour.'

Six

Still very pale, Eva escorted her teacher down the stair, her eyes glistening, as though with tears. Even so, she couldn't seem to keep from smiling.

'I canna think what to say, Miss Balfour. I'm all shivering like I've got a temperature. Seems I'm in a dream.'

'It's no dream, Eva, and as your mother says, you deserve it. You're bright, but you also work hard, and we've been looking for people who do that.'

'You think ma dad'll agree, though?'

Miss Balfour smiled. 'I think your mother will persuade him.'

They had reached the front door, where a horde

of children were playing in the heat of the evening. At the sight of Miss Balfour, with her pretty dress and straw hat, her spectacles and handbag, they raised their small grubby faces to her and held out their hands.

'Spare a copper, Miss? Gie's a ha'penny, eh?'

'Hey, hoppit!' cried Eva, the colour flooding her pale cheeks. 'What'll ma teacher think o' you?'

'It's all right,' Miss Balfour murmured. 'Let me give them a penny or two.'

'Och, if Ma could see you!' cried Eva as her teacher opened her bag and the children pressed closer. 'She'd never let bairns beg like this!'

But Miss Balfour was already pressing coins into the nearest hands and watching as the fingers closed over them like talons over prey.

'Poor things, Eva, poor things – where's the harm in giving them something?'

'Away they go,' said Eva with a sudden grin as the children made off, whooping and screaming. 'Straight to the sweetie shop on the corner – it'll be open, always is. You'd never do to live in Wish Lane, Miss Balfour.'

'You mean I'd soon be bankrupt?' The teacher laughed. 'No, I'm not quite so foolish; I'd learn to draw the line.' But as she turned to go, her face grew serious. 'There's a lot that should be done though, Eva, and it doesn't mean just giving a few pennies. I think you'll come to understand that one day.'

Eva made no reply. She stared down the street, where the tenements seemed to merge together in the hazy, warm air. Where there were no trees or plants, no colour or pleasantness to delight the eye. Where women leaned from windows, some gossiping in what they called a 'hingy oot', others too tired even to talk. Did an educated lady like Miss Balfour not realize that if you lived in Wish Lane, you knew anyway what needed to be done? If you weren't born knowing, it came to you soon enough.

'Don't worry, my dear,' Miss Balfour said again. 'Your father will want the best for you. And he's not going to be the loser, you know. That's the point of the whole scheme. Now, I must go. I've still to see Mrs Keir and other parents this evening.'

Mrs Keir, Bob's widowed mother. She had two other sons, both at work, but would she want Bob to stay on at school? 'I wanted to be a teacher,' he'd said, and everyone had thought it funny. Maybe it wouldn't seem so funny now.

'Miss Balfour,' Eva said hesitantly. 'Mind if I ask you – when you said "Never give up hope" to Bob, was it this scheme you were meaning?'

'Well, I had an idea something was afoot. There had been talk.' Miss Balfour straightened her spectacles and began to move away down the dusty pavement. 'But I'd have said it anyway, Eva. It's a good motto to follow, you know. I've followed it all my life.'

Some of the children were returning from the sweetie shop as Eva paused at the front door of the tenement. Amongst them was Roddie, who was staring at the sticky faces around him and laughing.

'Look at them!' he cried. 'They've gone mad! Who gave 'em the money, then?'

'Miss Balfour,' Eva said importantly.

'Miss Balfour!' He stared. 'She came here? What for?'

'Never mind. I'll tell you later.'

'Wish I'd been here. She might've given me a ha'penny or two. These bairns've bought liquorice pipes and Pomfret cakes, and aniseed balls and sherbert and I dinna ken what else – look at their faces!'

'Better no' let your mothers see you,' Eva warned the children, who were blissfully crowding the steps and keeping silent because their mouths were full. 'You'll be in trouble if they think you've been pestering folk for coppers, eh?'

'Aye, put your faces under the tap before anybody sees you,' added Roddie. 'Are you away up the stair, Evie?'

She nodded, wiping her brow with her hand. 'Come on, I'll tell you what's been happening.'

With Roddie behind her, still shaking his head over her news, Eva slipped into the living room where her parents and Letty were still sitting as she had left them.

'What an age you've been, Eva!' cried Bel, rising. 'You've had time to go halfway across the town and back. And is that Roddie with you?'

'You were supposed to be going for a walk,' Eva said, not daring to look at her father, who was sitting with his arms folded and his eyes cast down.

'And I was going promenading,' remarked

34

Letty.

'That's enough about promenading!' Bel was opening a bottle of lemonade. 'Who wants some o' this?'

'I'd rather have a pint,' muttered Frank.

'Well, have one, then,' said Bel grandly. 'Go on, go to the pub. Take the money out o' ma purse. We've something to celebrate, eh?'

'Have we?' asked Eva, shivering again as though it were cold.

'So your ma says.' Frank's expression was hard to read. 'She's the one who says what's what.'

'You ken fine I'm right about this,' Bel murmured.

'Aye, well, we'll have to see, eh?' He picked her thin purse from her bag. 'I'll take ma beer money, then?'

'I says to take it.'

His smile was crooked. 'Makes me a real kettle-biler, eh? Takin' money from his wife's purse because he's none of his own.'

'Oh, Frank!' Bel bit her lip. 'I'll ask again at the mill tomorrow – see if they've anything...'

'Waste o' time. Only person could walk into work at the mill tomorrow is Eva. And she doesnae want to.'

'She'll be ending up with something good, Frank. That's the idea o' staying on at school.'

'Then she'll be saying what's what, eh?' Frank laughed, while the women of his family stared at him and Roddie gazed at the floor. 'Och, I'm away to the pub.'

'Dad!' cried Eva, running down the stair after him. 'Dad! Wait!'

He turned to look at her, jingling Bel's coins in his pocket. 'What?'

'Dad, did you say I could? Did you say I could go to the secondary school?

'You're the clever one. Have you no' worked that out yet?'

'But you want me to?'

His face relaxed and suddenly he put his arm around her. 'Och, lassie, if it's what you want, we'll see how it goes. No greeting now. What've you got to greet about?'

'Nothing,' she said with her face against his shoulder. 'I reckon I'm the happiest lassie in the world.'

'I'd no' go so far as to say that.'

'Dundee, then.'

'Wish Lane, mebbe.'

'Wish Lane,' she agreed. 'I've got ma wish, anyway.'

Seven

When all formalities of the bursary scheme had been completed and she knew she would be moving to the secondary school in August, Eva felt she wouldn't mind having to work at the mill in the holidays. True, she would be on her feet for long hours, in dust and noise, and earning only a few shillings a week, but when the new term started at Toll Road Secondary, oh joy, she would be there. Along with Katie and all those others whose parents could afford to let them stay on, as well as Bob Keir, Ada MacGill, George Webster and Hughie Harper, who, like herself, would be there thanks to Mr North's generosity.

True to form, Bob Keir seemed resentful of that and on the last day of term sneered at Mr North for fancying himself as Father Christmas, at which the other bursary holders berated him. As far as they were concerned, Mr North *was* Father Christmas. He'd given them the best present they'd ever had, and if Bob didn't want it, they asked, why had he accepted it?

'I'm taking it for Ma,' Bob declared coldly. 'I want a good job so's I can look after her. But she should be paid enough to let me go to secondary anyway.'

'Well, she's getting ten shillings a week for you now,' said Hughie Harper, who was so small he was almost stunted. He rubbed his narrow eyes that needed glasses. 'She'll no' be complaining about him.'

'Have to be grateful for what we have,' Ada told Bob loftily. 'Canna expect more.'

'From a jute baron that lives in a jute palace?' Bob's eyes flashed. 'Could expect a lot more, I'd say.'

Eva had fallen silent, wondering if she was being selfish in thinking only of her own bright future. What about Ma and Letty and all the others who wouldn't be sharing in her good luck? Well, she reasoned, some of the young girls wouldn't want it anyway. In the mill and in the weaving factory some girls sang all day, happy to be at work, in spite of the heat and the noise; they wouldn't be grateful for being offered further years of study at school. Even so, they should have better pay and conditions. It could never be right that so many should get so little, while folk like Mr North had so much.

When she grew up, Eva promised herself, she'd work for change. She wasn't sure what she'd do but, somehow, she'd do something. It would be only fair.

Later on, when the group went to say their goodbyes to Miss Balfour, Eva felt apprehension for the first time, like a cold little hand touching her spine. Supposing she didn't do well at the new school? Would she be asked to leave? Would the weekly allowance be taken away?

'No need to look so anxious, Eva,' Miss Balfour said quietly. 'No need for anyone to worry. You're all going to succeed, I promise you. Now, we'll say goodbye, but only for the holidays. Remember, when you come back, I'll still be here, if you ever want to see me.'

She shook their hands and wished them well, not only at school, but in their various summer jobs. But whatever she said, they knew they were saying more than goodbye for the holidays; this was goodbye to childhood. When they came back to school, it would be for secondary education, something they'd never expected to achieve. Even Bob had to admit that they'd been lucky.

All the same, when they came out and looked

across at the great chimneys of the mill opposite, George sighed.

'Wish we could've had a proper holiday, eh?'

They didn't know anybody who had proper holidays. Not the sort by the sea in lodgings, with bathing costumes and spades and pails. But they knew that George didn't mean that sort of holiday. All he meant was a few weeks of not having to go to work.

'I'll no' mind about going to the mill,' murmured Eva. 'As long as I know it's no' for ever.'

But, on her first morning at the mill, when she was up and making the tea and listening to the factory hooters, she couldn't help feeling nervous about it. Even if it wasn't going to be for ever.

Eight

As it turned out there was another piece of luck to go with Eva's: Frank had found a job. Not much of a job, admittedly – packing cartons at the jam factory was not what he'd been trained for – but it was something to do, and brought in a weekly wage. The only snag was that he had to leave before Roddie, which meant that Roddie now had to get himself ready for school.

'I can, I can!' he cried. 'Anybody would think I was a babby. I can manage.'

'Aye, but will you damp down the stove and

leave everything tidy?' groaned Bel, standing over him as he washed his face at the sink. 'Think I'll no' have a minute's peace, worrying what this place is like when I'm away!'

'You'll be back for your breakfast,' said Frank easily. 'Leave the laddie alone, Bel, and get yourselves to work. Eva'll no' want to be late on her first day.'

'No,' sighed Eva, standing at the door with Letty. 'Can we go?'

In the street, Bel gave Eva a sharp glance and told her she looked as pale as Letty, who was lagging a little behind.

'No worrying, eh? I mean, you've worked at the mill before, so you ken fine what to expect.'

'I'll be doing different work now, though. What d'you think it'll be, Ma?'

'Canna say. You'll have to see the gaffer. He'll tell you soon enough what he wants. Still wish you could've worn your good dress, though. But Letty's right about the dust. You'll have to wear an apron, anyway.'

Bel looked back at Letty. 'Come on, Letty, keep up!'

'She's tired, Ma,' Eva murmured. 'Didnae sleep well.'

'Was she coughing?'

'No, just breathing funny.'

'I'm wondering if it's the asthma,' Bel said, her voice low and worried. 'Jeannie Fraser says it might be. Like her Kendrick's got.'

Eva thought of poor little Kendrick Fraser, so often on his mother's couch, coughing and wheezing, with his eyes all shadowed and his

40

face cheesy-white. Sometimes, when the attacks were very bad, he had to go to the infirmary, but what could they do? No one had found a cure.

'I'm sure Letty's no' as bad as Kendrick,' she said confidently. 'She does wheeze a bit, but she's better than him.'

'I might take her back to the doctor.'

'That'd be best. Then you'd know for sure what was wrong.'

But Bel looked dubious. Doctors, in her experience, didn't always know themselves what was wrong.

They had reached the mill, which was of course familiar to Eva from her previous summer jobs there. She knew that it had once been a flax mill, for Dundee had always been a textile town, making good linen, and that jute had only replaced flax because it was cheaper.

Though the products were different, jute being much coarser than flax, the mill itself was probably not much changed. Preparation of the jute was carried out in the 'low mill', while the spinners and winders worked in another section called a 'flat', and in a separate shed or factory, where every woman had her own loom, the spun jute was woven into finished products.

Noise from the machines sounded everywhere – such that the girls could hardly hear each other speak and sometimes had to use sign language to communicate – and in the low mill and the flat, there were also fumes from the oil that was used to soften the jute. And then there was the dust. Dust from the fibres and machinery – dust that was a part of life. It might have worried Bel, except that at work she knew she could do nothing about it.

On that first morning, she left Letty at her machine in the spinning flat and took Eva along to see Mr Rettie, the overseer, in the low mill, which was already filling up with workers. Apart from a few men sorting the jute, most of the workers were women. The younger ones were laughing together and casting their eyes over Bel and Eva, some calling out in a friendly way to Bel, others simply staring.

Todd Rettie, a narrow-chested man in his thirties with a beaky nose and a solemn gaze, was not known for his good humour, though Eva thought he could not be any worse than Mrs Fleck, the little woman in charge of the shifters. Eva hadn't told Roddie about her, but she was a slave-driver, and Eva was glad to be out of reach of her sharp tongue and her hard hand.

'Here's ma girl, Mr Rettie,' Bel said loudly because of the noise. 'Here's Eva.'

'Aye, she's the wee shifter, eh?' He gave a genial smile. 'Remember you, lassie. Ready to be full-time now, eh?'

Full-time? Mother and daughter exchanged worried glances.

'Why, no, Mr Rettie,' Bel said hastily. 'She's only working for the summer.'

'Summer?' He frowned. 'Is she not finished with school, then?'

'No, she's going back at the end of August, just like last year. What's different?'

'The lassie's fourteen, that's what different. I

42

thought she was a full-timer. I was going to start her training.'

'I told Mr Boath she'd only be wanting temporary work, and he said it'd be all right. And he's in charge o' taking on folk.'

'In charge!' Mr Rettie repeated contemptuously. 'Doesn't know one end o' the mill from the other. It's folk like me do the work, Bel. It's folk like me and the other gaffers that have to train these folk he takes on.'

'Yes, Mr Rettie, that's true. But Eva's worked here before and there's been no worry.'

'As a shifter, Bel, as a shifter.' Mr Rettie's gaze moved to Eva who returned it bravely. If there was going to be trouble, she'd better face it. Just as long as she could still earn something to take home. Just as long as her ma was not upset.

'How come you're going back to school, then?' Mr Rettie asked her. 'You'll not earn much there.'

'I'm going on to secondary, to study for ma Leaving Certficate.'

Leaving Certificate? There was a murmur from some of the women, who had been edging nearer, at which Mr Rettie looked threatening.

'Hey, you lassies, this is none of your business. Should've started work by now, and if there's any more interfering, you'll be getting your pay docked.'

As the women melted away to begin various tasks, Mr Rettie turned back to Bel. 'She'd better just make herself useful then, Bel. Run messages, do a bit of shifting, pick up ends dropped by the spinners – that sort of thing. I'm not

43

wasting time training a lassie who's not staying, I'm telling you. Now, you'd better get back to work yourself, or you'll be losing money too.'

'Aye, but where's ma girl to go now, then?' asked Bel, standing her ground. 'Somebody'll have to tell her what to do.'

'Better go see Mrs Fleck. Ask if she can fit her in for shifting today.'

'Oh, please, not shifting!' Eva was surprised to hear her own voice speaking up. 'I can do other jobs, Mr Rettie. I'll learn quick, I promise!'

He stared at her, seeing the earnestness of her manner, the pleading in her dark eyes, then turned to Bel and found another pair of dark eyes pleadingly fixed on his.

'Let her try the work here, Mr Rettie. It's right what she says – she learns quick and she's clever. That's why Mr North's helping her to do her certificate.'

'Mr North?' The gaffer stared. 'Whatever are you talking about?'

'He's given some of the clever bairns scholarships,' Bel said proudly. 'And Eva's one. He's helping 'em to stay on at school – it's a new idea.'

'Helping? You mean, with money?'

'Aye. So much a week for us, Frank and me, so's we can manage.'

'So much a week, for the lassie staying on at school?' Mr Rettie shook his head and whistled. 'What a thing, eh? But I suppose Mr North knows what he's doing. Usually does.' He laughed as he continued to look from mother to daughter with something like respect. They could see it

44

was going through his mind that these two must be clever, all right, to get money out of Joseph North. 'All right then,' he said finally, 'we might as well get some proper work from your girl, Bel. You get along now, and I'll send somebody to start her on her way. Whisht now, away you go!'

With a last quick glance at Eva, Bel hurried away to her own work, as Mr Rettie jerked his finger at a young woman standing by one of the machines.

'Berta!' he called. 'Come and show this lassie round. I'm away for ma tea.'

Nine

The girl who came strolling across had a look that Eva recognized. With her high colour and strong features, she could only be one of the bold-eyed mill girls that could be seen around town when work was done. One who liked to go promenading, and maybe drinking. One who would sing songs to young lads to make them blush, as Letty had described to Eva when their mother wasn't listening. That was what some of the young mill girls were like, everyone knew, and this Berta would be one of them.

'So, you're another o' Bel Masson's girls?' she asked, after eyeing Eva up and down. 'You're no' much like your sister.'

'No,' agreed Eva. 'She's like ma dad.'

'And you're like your ma.' Berta's full lips curled. 'Clever. Thinks she knows everything, your ma. And isnae even a member o' the union.'

Eva, who knew her mother and Letty were both members of the Jute and Flax Workers' Union, stared. 'She is then. So's ma sister. Why'd you say that?'

'Niver see 'em at the meetings.'

'Ma's got too much to do. And ma sister's no' well.'

'Plenty like that,' Berta said contemptuously. 'Or say so.'

Eva turned a deep, painful red. 'I thought you were going to show me round?'

'No' worth it if you're no' staying, eh? Whit's all this about a certificate? If you get it, whit'll you do with it?'

'I'm no' sure yet. Mebbe train as a teacher.'

'A teacher? Oh my, are we no' grand, then?'

'I said I wasnae sure what I'd do.'

'But you ken fine you dinna want to work in the mill?' Berta gave a hoarse laugh. 'That's just as well, ma dear, because your certificate'd be no use. The machines are the clever ones here, and we lassies'd be as good as you!'

'Give over, Berta!' cried an older woman who'd been listening. 'Leave the lassie alone!'

'Aye, she's only a bairn,' put in a slim girl with a fair plait hanging down her back. She put her hand on Eva's arm. 'Take no notice, pet. Berta doesnae mean it. Just her way, you ken.'

'I do mean it!' Berta retorted. 'I mean everything I say. Why should I hae to waste ma time

46

wi' this girl o' Bel Masson's playin' the lady, eh? Should hae been a weaver!'

'You tell the gaffer that then,' said the fair girl. 'He'll give you what for, disobeying his orders!'

'I'll tell him you could do the job better, Mavis Craik. He'll no' get mad with me, you ken.' Berta gave a knowing grin. 'Him and me's good pals.'

Mavis Craik hesitated, her mild blue gaze resting on Eva's still-scarlet face. 'Aye, well if you think he'll no' mind, I will take the lassie around.' She smiled. 'Want to come with me, Eva?'

'Please,' said Eva promptly. 'It'd be kind of you to take me.'

Berta gave another laugh. 'Nae bother, is it, Mavis, for a saint like you?' As Mr Rettie came back to the low mill, she sauntered over to him and whispered in his ear.

'Will you look at that hussy?' one woman murmured. 'Talk about brazen, eh?'

'And him a married man wi' six bairns,' someone else whispered.

'That'd niver stop Berta Denny. Takes what she wants, does Berta.'

'All right, Mavis?' the overseer called across, as Berta moved triumphantly back to her machine. 'Berta wants to get on here.'

'Fine, Mr Rettie,' Mavis answered, and smiled again at Eva. 'Come away, then, everybody's happy.' Eva stayed silent as she followed the girl across the mill floor. 'Are you all right, Eva?' Mavis asked, and Eva gave a start.

'Sorry. I was wool-gathering, as Ma says.' She

shook her head. 'Why'd Berta say ma mother's no' a member of the union? She's always been a member o' the Jute and Flax.'

'No point in worrying over what Berta says, pet. To tell you the truth, she's no' that bad. Aye willing to help if your machine goes wrong, or anything o' that sort, you ken. We all try to help, if we can. That's the nice thing about the lassies here.'

As she listened and smiled, Eva thought that something about Mavis reminded her of Letty. It was not just her looks, though they had similar colouring, but her manner – so gentle – and also, though Eva didn't like to dwell on it, a certain frailty. Mavis even seemed to breathe the same as Letty, and held herself as wearily, as though she found it too much of an effort to stand upright for long.

'This way,' she said now. 'I'll tell you what we do – if you can hear me over the machines? Sometimes think we'll all be deaf before we're old, eh?'

It seemed that what they did, in simple terms, was turn the fibre of the jute plant into something the spinners could spin and the weavers could weave. To this end, they sorted it, sprayed it with oil to soften it, and carded or combed it into slivers that were then drawn out on a special frame. The roving machine then wound these on to bobbins for transfer to the spinning frame.

'And that bit I know about,' said Eva, when Mavis started to talk about roving. 'That's when the shifters work to change the bobbins. I was a shifter, you ken.'

'I know, I remember you. I remember seeing you come to work with your ma and your sister. How is Letty, then?'

'No' so well. Breathes badly.'

'Same as me. Mill fever, some call it. From the dust, the doctor reckons.' Mavis shrugged a little. 'Plenty of us get it.'

'Is there nothing they can do?'

'If there is, they've no' told me. Just have to get on with it, eh?'

Eva was silent, thinking of Letty. 'It was nice o' you to show me round,' she said after a moment. 'I think I know what happens now.'

'Aye, you're a quick wee lassie. Some never get the hang o' things.'

'But it's right what Berta said – the machines do all the work?'

'No, there's plenty o' skill needed for spinning and winding. I bet you'd be good there, Eva, like your ma. Only you'll be back at school. Wish I was you.' Mavis gave a little laugh that ended in a cough. 'No, that's a joke. How'd I manage back at school? Canna add two and two!'

Mr Rettie said he'd set Eva to work after the breakfast break, maybe on the carding machine, where she could work with Mavis. But for now, she'd better run away to her ma. The breakfast break was not that long.

'Well, how did you get on?' Bel asked eagerly, as she and Eva hurried back home, with Letty following. 'Who showed you the low mill, then? No' that terrible Berta Denny? Oh, what a piece o' work she is! Mavis, was it? Well, that's good.

49

She's a sweet girl, Mavis. No' strong, mind, but lovely natured.'

'She says it's the mill makes her sick, Ma, and there's nothing anyone can do.' Eva glanced back at Letty, struggling to keep up. 'Maybe you should take Letty to the doctor's – see if she's the same as Mavis.'

'Aye, I'll see what I've got in the tin,' said Bel, who had savings in old cocoa tins carefully labelled 'Rent', 'Coal', 'Groceries', 'Doctor' and so on. 'Like I said, with your dad earning again, we should be all right. Now, let's see how that laddie's left the place, eh?'

Everything was in order, except that Frank and Roddie had finished all the porridge and had forgotten to put the pan into soak. No porridge for the women then. At first, Bel's face was long, but then grew bright.

'Tell you what, we'll have eggs. They'll no' take long to boil.'

'Oh, Ma, that'd be a treat!' cried Eva.

'Well, it's your first morning. A treat'd be nice. And for Letty, too. You sit down, Letty, we'll get things ready. If only we'd a bit more time, eh?'

All too soon, they were on their way back to North's Mill, but feeling better than expected after their soft-boiled eggs and bread cut into fingers. Even Letty looked better, with a little colour in her cheeks, and Eva was cheerful, thinking that at least work in the low mill wasn't like the shifting, and wasn't going to last for ever. That was something to be grateful for.

All the same, when she went to bed that night,

50

she wrote the day's date on a sheet of grocer's wrapping paper – all she had for making notes – and marked it with a small cross. Then she slipped it into her work bag without letting Letty see it. One day gone. Fifty-one to go. Somehow, that did seem for ever.

She wondered if she would see Mr North's son again while she was working at the mill. As she lay waiting for sleep, the memory of the boy's grey eyes lingered in her mind and kept her awake, but she didn't mind. It gave her something else to think about, other than all those days of work ahead.

Ten

Gradually, as the warm, sticky days of July progressed, Eva began to grow used to her routine. Well, as folk said, you could get used to anything – even the noise of the machines, even the dust.

It might be harder to get used to Berta Denny though. Mavis might claim she was good at heart, but Eva still kept well out of her way and her cronies – the large-mouthed, hard-eyed girls she went promenading with, and drinking too, it was said. These were the ones Bel criticized, but as Letty had said, not all the 'promenaders' were the same. Most were just pleasant, easy-going girls, proud of their independence, and willing to help their friends, if need be.

Eva couldn't see why their ma should't allow Letty to go out to see the town sometimes. Eva was too young to go herself, of course, but poor Letty had nothing in her life but work and resting from work; she deserved a bit of fun sometimes.

'No, no,' said Bel, when Eva suggested it again. 'Letty's no' up to it. I'm just waiting to get another shilling, to take her to the doctor's.'

It was always a problem, finding the money for the doctor, even though they were on what was known as his panel and could pay at a reduced rate. Treatment was free, in fact, for those needy enough to qualify as Poor Law patients, but the Massons were thankful they hadn't come to that yet.

Sometimes Frank wondered why there shouldn't be a government health scheme, so that nobody need worry about doctors' bills any more. After all, they had an old-age pension scheme now, thanks to the Liberals. If the fellows in charge really wanted it, they could do it.

'All talk, that is,' said Bel, and continued to put what she could into her cocoa tins.

Like everyone else at North's, Eva looked forward to Saturdays, when they worked only half a day at the mill, and even more to Sundays, when they didn't have to go to work at all. Not that Sunday was a day of rest, for that was the day Bel finished her cleaning, with Eva's help – Letty's too, if she felt up to it, though Frank and Roddie, of course, were never involved.

There were not many religious types in Wish

Lane, but if anyone complained that Bel shouldn't be cleaning on the Lord's day, they got short shrift. 'Cleanliness is next to Godliness,' she would say, and so silenced those few who might care enough to notice what she did.

Usually by afternoon, the girls were free to go out to get some fresh air, as their mother ordered, though there wasn't much that was fresh about the air around the tenements. They might go to a park or over to Dundee Law, or perhaps to the Tay, where they could watch the ships and admire the bridge. Ocasionally, Eva would go off on her own to meet Katie.

She knew that Mrs Crindle wasn't happy at first about her daughter's friendship with a girl from Wish Lane, and in a way could understand why. After all, if you looked at it from her point of view, what would Mrs Crindle see? Bairns who wore no shoes all summer, who rarely had a bath, who had to go to work aged twelve because their folks could barely survive otherwise?

Katie had explained to her mother that Eva was different. She'd never said so, but Eva knew she had, or she'd never have been allowed to see Eva out of school and Eva would never have been invited to tea, which she was on certain red-letter days. Although Katie had only seen Eva's home once, she must have told her mother that Mrs Masson kept it tidy and that the family did have baths, because she'd seen the tub sitting by the stove and all the clean clothes drying on the rack.

'Fancy,' Eva could imagine Mrs Crindle commenting, and maybe asking her husband – the plump, balding man who kept the stationer's shop – if he thought it'd be all right for their Katie to play with Eva Masson.

He must have said yes, for not long afterwards had come the first invitation to tea, which Eva, much younger then, had always remembered. The visit to the flat over the shop had been her first experience of how other folk lived: the comfort, the carpets, the easy chairs, the books – and the bathroom! Her eyes had been enormous when Katie had ushered her in to wash her hands before tea, for she'd never seen a proper bath before, with taps and all, or a wash basin with a jar for toothbrushes and face cloths and sweet-smelling soap.

When I grow up, she'd promised herself, *I'll have a bathroom like this, and I'll get one for Ma and Letty, too.*

Katie had even suggested that Eva might like to have a bath herself ('Go on,' she'd urged, 'it'll be all right, you can use ma towel.') but Eva had been too shy. Taking all her clothes off in someone else's house? She couldn't imagine it. Besides, she didn't know how to work the taps.

'Maybe one day,' she'd murmured, but was really thinking that one day she'd not need to use Katie's bathroom, because she'd have one of her own.

One Sunday, in late July, she was asked again to tea at Katie's. She wore her new dress and sat down to the three-cornered sandwiches, scones and fruit cake that Mrs Crindle always provided. Later there would be cake to take home, although Eva knew that Bel would look glum at receiving another woman's baking. 'But of course, it's kindly meant,' she would manage to say, so as not to seem too ungrateful. But she never praised it.

When they'd finished tea, Mrs Crindle congratulated Eva on being selected for one of Mr North's bursaries. She thought it was a wonderful idea that deserving children should be given their chance, and she wished Eva all the best.

'Aye, you're a clever lassie,' Mr Crindle told her, dabbing at his moustache. 'Would you like some paper?'

Eva's eyes lit up. 'Oh, I would! Please.'

'I've a couple of exercise books here you can have then. A discontinued line, as a matter of fact. No reason why you shouldn't have 'em. I know you girls like to write in your own books, eh?'

Eva was in raptures. Paper was an ordinary, everyday thing for most people, but at home it was in such short supply. Now she had two exercise books of her own to fill in as she liked. Her smile was so radiant when she thanked Mr Crindle that he seemed quite taken aback, and his wife bit her lip.

Poor lassie, she thought, *so pleased with so little*. And the insight of the moment told her as much about the world of the tenements as all she'd ever heard about its poverty.

'I'll get you some scones and cake to take home,' Mrs Crindle said, jumping up from the table. 'Give your mother a rest from baking, eh?'

If only that was all Ma had to rest from, thought Eva.

55

* * *

Back home at Wish Lane, as Bel grudgingly set
out the scones and sliced the cake Mrs Crindle
had sent, Letty told Eva that she would be going
to the doctor's next evening. Their ma had
enough to pay the doctor now.

'I'm no' taking ma clothes off, though,' she
whispered, and Eva smiled, remembering her
own reluctance that time when Katie had suggested her taking a bath.

'Doctors are different from ordinary folk,' she
told Letty. 'They have to see you, to find out
what's wrong.'

'Might no' be anything wrong,' Letty said
gallantly, and Eva hastily agreed. Might easily
be nothing wrong. The doctor would say soon
enough.

Letty had said she would like Eva to go with her
and Bel to the doctor's, and though Bel said
she'd only take up space in the waiting room, the
three of them made their way to the evening
surgery together.

Dr Gibson's waiting room was very small, with
plain wooden chairs around the distempered
walls and scuffed linoleum on the floor. Someone did polish the floor occasionally, but always
forgot to clean the one window, which had
become so layered with grime that it looked like
there was perpetual fog outside. Neither Dr Gibson nor Miss Angus his receptionist, who only
worked in the mornings, ever noticed this, but on
the rare times Bel came to the surgery, she
always said she wished she'd brought her wash-

56

leather with her.

'I'd let some light into this place,' she'd murmur. 'Could do with it.'

It was indeed depressing to enter the waiting room and see the people sitting on the chairs positioned close to the walls, their heads sunk on their chests, their eyes fixed on the linoleum. Only when the doctor threw open his door and shouted 'Next!' did their heads jerk up and their eyes rapidly flit along the other patients, making sure that no one was trying to take someone else's turn. 'Aye,' they'd mutter to one another, 'you have to remember to count up who was here before you when you first came in, else you'll be here till the cows come home.'

Eva could tell that a number of hearts sank when she and Letty and their mother walked in. Three more to watch out for, eh? Perhaps she shouldn't have come after all, but Letty's blue eyes were so woebegone and her breath coming so fast that Eva was glad she had. Her sister needed all the support she could get. Meanwhile, Bel was busy checking who was before them and as soon as she had memorized all the faces, began to thumb through the few magazines lying on a table before the empty fireplace.

'Takes your mind off waiting,' she murmured, picking up a well-read copy of a woman's magazine. 'These stories are no' bad.'

But Eva knew her mother's eyes were reading the same lines of type over and over again as they waited for the moment when the door would open and it would at last be Letty's turn.

* * *

57

'Next!' the doctor called eventually, and Bel stood up, frowning at a man who'd half-heartedly jumped up too, and marched Letty into the surgery.

'Shall I come?' whispered Eva, but Dr Gibson, portly and kindly, shook his head.

'If you're well, lassie, you stay where you are. I'll see this young lady here.' And with that the door was closed.

All eyes seemed to be on Eva, who took her seat again, feeling the patients' unspoken resentment that she had taken up space when she wasn't ill, even though no one actually needed her chair. As she pretended to read the magazine her mother had put down, she knew she was perhaps being silly and folk weren't thinking anything of the sort. But that was the atmosphere of the waiting room for you – it made you feel anxious and in the wrong.

How slowly the time passed. Surely Letty and her ma had been in the surgery longer than most? Eva took another magazine, flicked through it and put it back. Looked again at the hands of the big old clock on the wall and saw that only five minutes had passed since she'd looked at it before. And then finally the surgery door opened, her mother and Letty came out, and Dr Gibson had already shouted 'Next!'

'Eva?' said Bel, gently pushing Letty before her. 'Let's away home.'

'Well?' cried Eva, when they were outside on the pavement. 'What did he say?'

Bel's dark eyes flickered. She cleared her throat. 'You were right. Letty's got the same as

Mavis.'

'Mill fever?'

'Aye. Cotton worker's lung. That's another name.'

'Oh, Letty!' Eva grasped her sister's arm, but Letty's face was calm.

'It's just wheezing. Plenty lassies get it.'

'Not all,' said Bel as they began to walk on. 'The doctor says you've to be – what's the word, Letty? Sensitive. Sensitive to the dust from the jute. Or the cotton, or the flax.' Bel shook her head. 'I'm not. Seemingly Letty is.'

'And it's just wheezing?'

'Oh, let's no' talk about it!' cried Letty. She pulled her arm free from Eva's hand. 'I've had enough of it.'

'That's foolish talk,' her mother told her sternly. 'You have to face facts. If you keep on breathing in that dust, you'll get really ill. You'll get asthma. Chronic lung disease. You'll no' be able to work at all.'

As they kept on through the warmth of the summer evening, all three were silent, Bel staring straight ahead, her eyes large with unshed tears, the girls drooping at her side.

'Ma,' whispered Letty at last. 'What'll I do?'

Bel took a hankie from her bag and blew her nose. 'Leave the dust,' she said shakily. 'Leave the mill.'

'Leave the mill?' Frank cried when Bel had finished telling him what the doctor had said about Letty, and what he had advised.

'The doctor says Letty has to leave the mill?

Bel, that's a piece o' nonsense. There must be plenty lassies working with mill fever, eh? It's well known it goes with the job – for some, anyway. But nobody gives up. Not that I've heard.'

'We canna let her get worse, Frank.'

'But do folk get worse? I mean, it's like I say, it's a fact o' life. Some fellas get it too, but they keep going.'

'The doctor says Letty's bad. He says her only hope is to get away from the dust. That's enough for me, Frank.'

His eyes sharpened with anxiety, and went to Letty, who was looking down at her plate. 'Aye, well,' he said after a pause, 'if that's what he says...'

'It's what he says.'

'Must be plenty other jobs,' Roddie chipped in. 'Letty needn't work at the mill.'

'Nobody asks what I want,' Letty said in a low voice. 'I can do ma work well, everybody says so. Why can I no' stay at the mill and see how I get on? It's right what Dad says – plenty lassies keep going.'

'No' you,' Bel said firmly. 'I've never liked you in the mill; I always knew it didnae suit you. I thought mebbe the weaving shed might be better, but now I want you away from jute altogether. We'll find something else.'

'What, though? You tell me what, Ma! All the lassies work with the jute!'

'No,' said Eva. 'Ada MacGill's working at the jam factory.'

Bel frowned. 'Another factory. It wouldnae do.'

'There'd be no dust, though.'

'But awful hot,' said Frank. 'I canna see Letty managing there.'

'How about the place that makes cards?' Roddie suggested. 'Birthday cards and that. You colour 'em in. One o' the laddies I know has got a sister who works there.'

'The paint'd no suit,' his father told him. 'Fumes, you ken.'

'Why, there's nowhere!' cried Letty, jumping to her feet and bursting into tears. 'There's nowhere for me to work! What can I do?'

'Ah, pet, no need to cry!' Bel put her arms around her and held her close. 'We'll find something, course we will, and then you'll get better. We'll start looking tomorrow.'

'Canna think where,' Letty sniffed.

'When one door shuts, another opens, your gran used to say,' Bel said confidently. 'Now, let's clear away, eh?'

A door opened for me, thought Eva. *Let's hope there'll be another one opening for Letty.*

Eleven

In the days that followed, however, Letty found no open door. Every job the Massons thought of seemed to have a snag. Shop assistant? Letty said she couldn't 'give change' and that she'd be in a terrible state behind a counter. Domestic service? There'd be dust involved, as bad as at the factory, and what lady would take her on, wheezing as she did? Apprentice dressmaker? Now, everybody knew Letty was no good with a needle, and jobs of that kind were rare, anyway.

The situation seemed hopeless until an advertisement in the evening paper seemed to leap out at them in letters a foot high, and Eva, thrilled, read it aloud.

'"Young lady assistant required for J. Crindle's stationery shop in the High Street. No experience necessary as training will be given, but must be personable, with a good manner. Please apply by letter with recent reference as soon as convenient."' As she lowered the paper and looked around at the watching faces, Eva's eyes were shining. 'Crindle's!' she cried. 'That's Katie's dad's shop! Letty, it's grand. It'd be a lovely place to work – you'll have to apply. Come on, I'll help you.'

'Aye, but we've nothing to write on,' cried Bel, leaping to her feet. 'Did Mr Crindle no' give you some paper, Eva? Will you get it, pet? So's Letty can write her letter?'

'I've a pen somewhere,' muttered Frank. 'But no ink. Eva, Roddie, where's that wee bottle o' ink we had once? Dinna say we've to buy ink, as well?'

'I saw that ink in the cupboard,' said Roddie, his eyes as bright as Eva's. 'I ken where it is, I'll get it.'

'No need to bother.' Still as a statue and very pale, Letty stood in the centre of the room as her family buzzed with excitement around her. 'I'm no' applying.'

The silence that fell was like a blanket, dowsing enthusiasm as though putting out a fire. All eyes were on Letty, who slowly began to flush, and then to cough. She put her hand to her lips.

'There'd be no point,' she said quietly.

'Oh, because it's a shop!' Eva cried. 'You're worrying about giving the change again, eh? Look, I said I'd help...'

'It's no' just the change. Mr Crindle would never take me, anyway.' Letty pointed to the newspaper still in Eva's hand. 'What's it say he wants, then? A "young lady assistant". Am I a young lady? I'm a mill girl. I'm no' even a weaver. I'd never get the job.'

'Letty Masson, you're a very foolish lassie!' cried her mother. 'You're as good as anyone in this town, and if Mr Crindle asks for young ladies to apply, it's just a way o' putting things. Means nothing.'

'That's right,' agreed Frank. 'And I'm surprised to hear you running yourself down like that, Letty. Girls in Dundee have aye had their proper pride, eh?'

'Letty only meant it'd be how other folk would see her,' Eva put in as Letty stood with her eyes cast down. 'She knows she's as good as anybody else.'

'Well, I should think so,' said Bel. 'But let's get that paper, eh? Letty, you write that letter and see what happens. Canna do any harm, eh?'

'Eva'll have to help me, then.' Letty shook her fair head. 'I've never had to write a letter before. I mean, who would I have to write to?'

For some time, the sisters worked together at the kitchen table, trying to think how to present Letty in the best light.

'I canna think what to say,' Letty sighed, and certainly it was no easy matter to decide what to put in and what to leave out.

'No experience necessary,' the advertisement had stated, but then experience of other work might be important and there was no getting away from it: she was a mill girl. *Ma and Dad can say what they like*, thought Eva, chewing her pen, *but they know, just as Letty knows, what sort of picture those words bring to mind*. The bold-eyed lassie promenading, eyeing folk up and down, drinking maybe, and singing bawdy songs. Would Mr Crindle realize that Letty was not like that?

'Better no' mention your health until he sees you,' Bel advised, when asked. 'No point making too much of it.'

'It's why I'm leaving the mill though,' Letty said sagely. 'It *is* the point, eh?'

'Aye, but why say so?'

'Ma's right,' said Eva. 'You have to make out all you want to do is work in Mr C's shop, and that you know you could do the job.'

'Oh, Lordy!' cried Letty. 'I just wish it was true!'

In the end, the application – mostly put together by Eva – was copied out neatly by Letty and the two girls eventually sat back with sighs of relief.

'All we need now is an envelope,' said Eva. 'Ma, have we got any envelopes?'

'I've a few in ma drawer. Used ones.'

'No used ones. We need a clean one.'

'Have to get one tomorrow, then.'

'I'll get one,' cried Roddie. 'No' from Mr Crindle's, though.'

'Letty can get one from the post office in her dinner hour.' Bel opened up the range and pushed the kettle over to boil. 'I dinna ken why, but I feel as tired as though I'd just done ma shift. It's all this worrying, eh? We could do with a cup o' tea.'

'No' finished yet,' said Frank cheerfully. 'You've forgotten something, Letty.'

'What?' She sat up straight in her chair, her eyes wide. 'What've I forgotten, then?'

Her father picked up the newspaper and pointed to Mr Crindle's advertisement. '"Please apply by letter with recent reference" it says here. You've forgotten the reference.'

'Oh, no! What'll I do?' Letty looked frantically from her mother to Eva. 'I've no reference. Never was asked for one at the mill. Where can I get one? Dinna say school. I'd never dare ask Miss Piper!'

'Why, you can ask Mr Rettie!' cried Bel. 'He'll give you a character reference. You've aye been a good worker, never missed a day even when you've no' been fit. We'll ask him tomorrow.'

'And then it'll be all round the mill that I'm trying to leave,' murmured Letty. 'I didnae want folk to know.'

'Och, nobody'll take a bit o' notice. Lassies go

65

in and out o' the mill all the time. Why, some try every mill in the town and then end up in the jam factory! What's it to anybody if you want away, then?'

'I'll ask Mr Rettie to keep it quiet all the same, Ma.'

As the kettle began to sing and the Massons sat back, relaxing after the effort of making out the application, Frank lit a Woodbine and blew smoke. 'Wonder why Mr Crindle wants a lassie for an assistant, then?' he asked thoughtfully. 'Why no' a young fella?'

Bel laughed aloud as she made the tea. 'Frank, you're no' thinking. It's obvious why he wants a lassie, eh? He can pay her less than a young man. Fancy you needing to be told that!'

'Why do women always get less than men?' asked Eva. 'How can that be fair?'

'The men are supposed to be the breadwinners.' Bel passed Frank his tea and stirred in his sugar. 'In fact, half the women at the mill are the breadwinners, anyway.'

'Let's no' go into that,' he muttered. 'But another thing – why does old Crindle need an assistant in that shop o' his, do you think? Has there been a rush on stationery?'

'Just as long as he does need an assistant and Letty gets the job, I'm no' worrying,' said Bel.

'I'm worrying,' Letty sighed. 'In case I do get the job.'

'Oh, you're no' still on about that change?' cried Eva. 'I tell you, it'll be as easy as pie. There'll be a cash register, anyway.'

But at the thought of handling a cash register,

Letty took no comfort at all, and seeing her fair head drooping and her hankie at her lips, her family felt like drooping with her. The prospect of seeing her successfully installed into Mr Crindle's stationery shop seemed increasingly remote.

Letty had never imagined that applying for a job would be so hard. First, there were those hours spent over the letter; then the copying out, holding her breath in case she made a mistake, which had brought on her wheezing. Then she had to approach Mr Rettie for a reference.

'A reference?' he asked, incredulous, when Bel and Letty found him in his little office. 'Why, Letty, what d'you want a reference for? In all ma years, I've never been asked for one. Where are you going, then?'

'She's applying for a job at Mr Crindle's,' Bel told him swiftly. 'Dinna spread it, though. I mean, she might no' get it.'

'The stationer's, you mean?' Mr Rettie continued to look amazed. 'Leaving the mill, Letty? What's brought this on?'

'Girls are always leaving the mill,' said Bel.

'But Letty's never complained, eh?'

'Mebbe she should've done, then. She's got the mill fever.'

Mr Rettie's eyes flickered over Letty's averted face. 'Who says?'

'The doctor. He says she's to find other work, or she'll get worse.'

Mr Rettie lowered his voice. 'You're not planning to speak to anyone about this?'

'You mean Mr North?' Bel's lip curled. 'And how would I do that? I never see him.'

'No, but this business of mill fever – it's – well, to tell you the truth, it's a bit of a sore point. Some folk don't think it exists, that's the thing, and Mr North, he's not keen on having employees going round saying they've got it. I wouldn't advise talking about it.'

'You ken fine there's plenty o' lassies here have got the wheeze and the cough, Mr Rettie. You canna make something go away by saying it doesnae exist.'

He hesitated, then cleared his throat. 'Well, as long as you're not taking it any further, I'll be glad to give Letty a reference. When d'you want it for?'

'As soon as possible,' declared Bel. 'If that's convenient.'

'Dinner-time, then.'

'That'd be grand. Thanks, Mr Rettie.'

'Thanks very much,' said Letty, reaching gratefully for the door.

'You get it?' Eva asked, catching her mother and sister as they returned to the spinning flat.

'He'll have it ready by dinner-time,' Bel told her.

'That's good, then we can take it round to Mr Crindle's.'

Letty looked horror-stricken. 'I'm putting ma letter in the pillar box, Evie. And dinna say any more, folks'll hear.'

'If you're going round to Mr Crindle's, you'll have to smarten yourselves up a bit,' said Bel.

'You're covered in dust.'

'I'm no' going round.' Letty, flushing, hurried away to her work, aware now of curious eyes upon her, while Eva, after exchanging glances and a shrug with her mother, went back to her carding machine.

'All right?' mouthed Mavis, whose eyes were sympathetic, rather than curious.

Eva smiled and nodded. She would have liked to tell Mavis about Letty's job hopes, and vowed she would, as soon as things were settled, for Mavis herself should be thinking about a move. Even now, she was breathing badly and her face had a stretched, shining pallor that revealed the effort she was making just to keep going. Poor lassie. Oh, surely, if Letty escaped the mill, something could be done for Mavis?

At dinner-time, Mr Rettie, as good as his word, gave Letty her reference. Bel, with the rest of the workers, had already departed and only Eva remained, hovering in the doorway.

'Thanks again, Mr Rettie,' Letty said in a low voice. 'It's kind o' you, so it is.'

'Hope it'll suit.'

Mr Rettie studied her for a moment. 'Is it true you've not been well, then?'

'It's ma breathing,' she said after a pause.

'Might not be the mill, you ken.'

'No.' Bravely, she looked up. 'But it might be.'

'Aye. Well. I hope you get on all right, then. I've said you were a good worker. Very conscientious.' He hesitated. 'You've been happy here, eh?'

'Yes, Mr Rettie.'

69

'Plenty lassies are, in spite of what some folks say.'

'Yes.'

He began to move away. 'Good luck then, Letty.'

'Thank you, Mr Rettie.'

'Let's have a look, then,' Eva said as she and Letty left the mill. 'See what he said about you.'

'It's in an envelope.'

'No' sealed, though. Come on, you'll have to have a peep.'

'Well, it's me to read it, no' you.'

'All right, just get on with it.'

They stood together in the street as Letty took the one sheet of paper from the envelope.

'Why, he's said some nice things about you, Letty. Look here!'

'I did say I wanted to read it maself, Evie!'

'Well, you can. I'm only saying, he's been nice.'

' "Good worker ... conscientious ... quick to learn",' Letty smiled. 'I'd no' say that, eh? But "excellent time-keeper" – that's right, wi' Ma after me, like she is! And "excellent sickness record" – maybe he thinks there's nothing wrong with me then? It's true I've no' been off much.'

'Should've been.' Eva pointed to the last sentence. 'But, see there, he says he "can recommend Miss Violet Masson to any new employer and is sure she will give satisfaction". Is that no' grand?' Eva patted her sister on the back. 'Mr Crindle'll be impressed. Let's take this straight round, with your letter.'

70

'No, Ma's right, I'm no' tidy enough. Anyway, I just want to put the letter in the post. It'll be easier.'

'If you deliver it yourself, he'll know who you are.

'Your sister, you mean?' Letty shook her head. 'It'll no' do a bit o' good, Evie. He'll see straight away I'm no' like you.'

'He'll see you're no' like Berta Denny, that's the point. I mean, there's all sorts o' mill girls, eh? Some'd be right for the shop, and some wrong.' Eva gave Letty a long, serious look. 'We've got to make Mr Crindle understand you'd be right.'

'Why are you so keen to get me into this job?' Letty asked. 'You'd think it was all that mattered, me leaving the mill.'

'I want to see you settled before I go back to school, that's all. Then I needn't worry.' Eva smiled briefly. 'Suppose I'm selfish, eh?'

'Selfish?' Letty shook her head. 'No' you, Evie. I think if anybody's selfish, it's me. Everybody's trying to help me and I'm just wanting to stay at the mill and keep things easy. But I ken the job at Mr Crindle's would be right for me, and I promise you I'm going to do ma best to get it. Just hope I do.'

Eva squeezed Letty's hand. 'And so do I. Let's get back home and see if Ma's heated up that soup she made, else we'll be starving.'

'And I'll put ma letter in the pillar box, eh?'

'I thought you just said you wanted this job?' Eva shook her head. 'We'll take the letter to the shop tomorrow.'

71

Twelve

'You'll just have to wear your old gingham dresses to go round to Mr Crindle's tomorrow,' Bel told the girls fretfully that evening. It had not been her turn to use the tenement's communal drying green, and so she had not had a chance to wash their good ones. 'Run back at dinner-time and get rid o' the dust, anyway.'

'What are you worrying about?' asked Frank. 'Old Crindle will know Letty's no' going to be covered in dust when she works for him.'

'*If* I work for him,' Letty said patiently. 'I'm only putting ma letter in tomorrow.'

'Want me to come with you?' asked Bel. 'You're no good at speaking up for yourself.'

'If you speak for her, Ma, that's just what Mr Crindle will think,' put in Eva. 'I'll just tell him she's ma sister, then Letty can do the rest.'

Her mother fixed her with a dark, thoughtful gaze. 'You could've told Katie a bit more, eh?'

'How d'you mean?'

'Well, she's Mr Crindle's daughter. And your friend.'

'I'm still no' sure what you want, Ma,' Eva said, knowing quite well what her mother wanted.

'You to put in a good word, o' course! Tell her Letty'd be good at the job. And needs it.'

'And then she's to tell her dad?' cried Letty. 'Look, I'm no' keen on that.'

'Why not?' asked Bel. 'It'd only be a word, you ken. Just to let Mr Crindle understand what a good worker you are.'

'Mr Crindle can read the reference.'

'Aye, and that'll be best,' put in Frank. 'You canna go involving a fella's lassie in this, Bel. Letty wants to manage by herself.'

Bel shrugged and turned aside. 'All right then. It was just an idea, eh? I thought Letty could do with some help.'

'You'd never have said that about Eva,' said Letty.

'I would, then. I'm sure, when it comes to getting jobs, everybody could do with a bit o' help.'

'I am nervous,' Letty said after a pause. 'I wish I'd no' got to go tomorrow.'

'Remember you said you were determined to get this job,' Eva told her.

It was a relief when dinner-time came round the next day and the two sisters could run home, change out of their dust-covered clothes, put on their gingham dresses from Bel's wardrobe, and hurry round to Mr Crindle's shop.

'Why am I making all this fuss?' Letty panted. 'I mean, I'm only handing in ma application.'

'It's important, though. Might get you an interview, if things go right.' Eva put her hand on Letty's arm. 'But slow down, eh? You'll no' want to be coughing when you get there.'

'That's true.'

They slowed their pace but reached Mr Crindle's shop in the end, and stood outside for a moment, hearts fluttering, breath coming fast.

'Wonder why Mr Laggan's shut?' Eva murmured, staring at the greengrocer's shop next door to the stationer's, which bore a large 'Closed' sign and had its blinds drawn. 'Think he's ill?'

'Please, let's go in,' said Letty, who was very pale. 'Just want to get this over.'

'In we go, then.' Eva's smile was jaunty, but it was all she could do to stop herself taking Letty's arm. *Better not*, she told herself, as she opened the shop door and heard its bell ring. *Better not let them think she needs me.*

Letty walked in to Eva's favourite shop, with its special smell of paper and ink, its range of boxes and packages, and shelves displaying everything from pens and pencils to leather-bound blotters, autograph books, and snapshot albums. There were stands of Dundee-made greeting cards, fancy wrapping paper, ribbons, invitation cards, wedding stationery and little boxes for sending out cake.

Despite her anxiety for Letty, Eva was still charmed by the shop, but she was somewhat taken aback to see that Mr Crindle himself wasn't there. Mrs Crindle stood behind the glass counter, and next to her was Katie.

'Eva!' cried Katie, after several stunned moments.

'Hello,' Eva said at last.

'Eva, what a surprise!' Katie came round the counter. 'Did you want to buy something?'

74

'Katie!' exclaimed her mother. 'Maybe Eva's just come to see you.'

'We ... we were looking for Mr Crindle,' Eva said, beginning to collect herself. 'This is ma sister, Letty.'

'Why, I don't think we've met,' cried Mrs Crindle, shaking Letty's hand. 'Though I knew you had a sister, Eva, of course. Are you at North's, dear?'

From being quite pale, Letty's cheeks were now scarlet. 'Aye, I am, but ... is Mr Crindle no' here, then?'

'He's just next door, at Mr Laggan's. It's all very exciting, isn't it, Katie?'

'Dad's buying Mr Laggan's shop!' cried Katie. 'We're going to sell typewriters!'

'Typewriters?' The sisters exchanged glances.

'Yes, we're expanding,' Mrs Crindle said proudly. 'Typewriters and office supplies are all the thing these days, with so many firms needing them, you know, and when Mr Laggan said he was retiring, we decided we'd take on his shop and branch out. That's why we need an assistant. There'll be too much for me to do to help out, especially as we hope we're going to do well.' She gave a little tinkling laugh. 'What was it you wanted to see Mr Crindle about, my dears?'

Eva turned to Letty, who appeared to be speechless. 'Letty?' she whispered. 'Tell Mrs Crindle, eh?'

'I ... I want to apply ... for the job.' Letty's voice was cracking a little, and she gave a quick cough. 'As assistant, you ken.'

As Katie's mouth dropped open, her mother's

smiles faded. She seemed stunned. 'As assistant,' she whispered. 'Yes ... yes, I see.'

'I've got ma application here,' said Letty, keeping her eyes on the glass counter. 'I was going to give it to Mr Crindle.'

'I'll see he gets it.'

'Has ma reference and all.' Letty swallowed hard. 'It's no' a copy.'

'Don't worry, dear, he'll be sure to return it.'

'We did want to see Mr Crindle,' Eva said, as Mrs Crindle took Letty's envelope. 'Just for a word.'

'Well...' Mrs Crindle looked at Katie. 'Go fetch your dad then,' she murmured.

'Sit down, Letty,' Eva said in a low voice, for Letty was beginning to wheeze. 'Here's a chair, see, at the counter.'

But just then Mr Crindle hurried in, a tape measure round his neck and Katie at his side, and Letty said she was all right, and that they should be going anyway.

'Why, Eva, what's all this, then?' asked Mr Crindle, smiling. 'You're a bit young for the assistant's job, aren't you?'

'It's ma sister who's applying, Mr Crindle. This is Letty. She's seventeen.'

'Ah,' said Mr Crindle.

He was very kind, very fatherly, as he shook Letty's hand and said he'd look at her application with pleasure, but of course nothing could be decided until he'd had talks with all the lassies who'd applied. He was going to ask everybody to come in the following Saturday.

'Me as well?' asked Letty tonelessly.

'If you can manage it. Two o'clock in the afternoon, all right?'

'You could come then, Letty,' Eva said quickly.

'Aye, I could,' she agreed.

'That's good, so we'll see you on Saturday.' Mr Crindle opened the shop door. 'And thank you for applying, Miss Masson.' He gave his kindly smile. 'Goodbye to you both, then.'

When the girls were back in the street they looked at each other, and Letty sighed.

'That's that, Evie,' she murmured. 'I'm no' going to get that job.'

'You canna tell. Wait till Saturday.'

'Did you no' see the look on Mrs Crindle's face, when I said I was applying? She didnae know whether to laugh or cry. A mill girl, thinking o' being their assistant! What a joke. Even your friend had her mouth open wide enough to catch a fly!'

'Maybe I should've told Katie about you applying. She must've thought it funny I never said anything.'

'I didnae want her involved.'

'But Katie'd want you to get the job, Letty.'

Letty shrugged.

'Well, you'll have to wait and see what happens,' Eva said stubbornly. 'You canna say how you'll get on, so let's think no more about it, till the time comes. Let's just go back to work and have our piece.'

But Letty shook her head and said she wasn't hungry.

Walking slowly, they did not speak again until

77

they'd almost reached the mill, when someone called their names and they turned to see a red-faced Katie running towards them.

'Oh, Eva, why'd you not tell me about Letty? I could have spoken to Dad all nice and quiet, but I never knew anything about it!'

'It was me, Katie,' said Letty. 'I didnae want you involved. Didnae seem right.'

'There would have been no harm.' Katie wiped her brow with her hankie. 'Oh dear, I've got a stitch from trying to catch you.'

'It's all right, Katie,' said Eva. 'We're just going to have our piece.'

'I'll not keep you. Just wanted to tell you that I did say something to Dad. Hope I did right?'

The sisters were silent, waiting.

'I just said – you know – that Letty would be a very good worker and a very nice person to have in the shop. And that she really needed the job, because the mill wasn't good for her and she had to find something else. That's true, isn't it?'

'Oh, yes,' Eva agreed after a pause. 'Letty'd be telling your dad that anyway.'

'Yes, well, that's what I thought. So, I was right to say that, wasn't I?'

'Did you say I was ill?' asked Letty quietly.

'Oh, no! Not ill. Just not suited to the mill. He understood anyway. Look, there's no need to worry. Honestly!'

But Katie's own eyes were worried enough, as the sisters could see for themselves before she left them.

'A mill girl with mill fever,' Letty sighed. 'Just what he's looking for, eh?'

Thirteen

There were only a few days to get through before Saturday, but they seemed endless. All of the Massons were affected – even Frank, even Roddie, who liked to think they were above getting 'worked up' like females, but were just as anxious as Bel or Eva for Letty's ordeal to be over. As for Letty herself, she remained pale and silent, whether at work or at home, and kept her eyes almost permanently down.

'It's such a piece o' nonsense, us worrying like this,' Bel said one evening. 'I mean, there'll be other jobs, eh? Anybody'd think Mr Crindle's was the only one going!'

'It's the best one, that's the thing,' Eva murmured. 'It'd be just right for Letty.'

'Aye, but it's true what your ma says,' said Frank. 'There'll be other jobs. No need to go greeting over this one, eh?'

'And we've all forgotten Eva,' said Bel. 'It's her big day next Monday. Back to school?'

'I'd no' forgotten.' Eva gave a faint smile, for she'd barely had time to think about school, with all that was happening with Letty. *At least*, thought Eva, *we'll no' be expecting success for Letty on Saturday*. Certainly not Letty herself, who seemed to have retreated into a state of calm hopelessness.

* * *

Two mornings before the interview, however, a change came. The sisters were walking to the mill as usual, with Bel hurrying in front, occasionally looking back to tell Letty to take her time, when Letty suddenly asked Eva a question.

'Evie, you know Mr Crindle's going to sell typewriters?'

'Aye, what of it?'

'Well, I couldnae sleep in the night...'

'I ken that, I heard you moving around.'

'And I got to thinking – the assistant might have to know something about 'em, eh?'

'Mr Crindle would never expect that. No need to worry.'

'I'm no' worrying. I was thinking I could ask Miss Hanna in the office, if she'd just let me see how her typewriter worked. Then I could say I was interested, you ken.' Letty's large eyes were defensive. 'It'd be no lie. I am interested. I've always thought it was grand to see all thae letters coming out when Miss Hanna presses the keys.'

For a moment Eva was speechless. 'Why, when did you see Miss Hanna typing?' she asked at last, for very few women from the spinning flat had occasion to enter the office where the clerical staff worked.

'Sometimes Mr Rettie's asked me to take in the post,' Letty told her. 'And when I first started, Miss Hanna often sent me out for stamps and I'd bring 'em back to the office.'

'Fancy. And that's when you saw her typing? You never said you were interested.'

'No' much point till now. Think it'd help, Evie,

to say?'

'Aye, I do. I think it's a good idea. But will you dare speak to Miss Hanna?'

'Why should I no' speak to her? She's nice. Gave me a cup o' tea once. And a biscuit.'

'Fancy,' said Eva again, still amazed at this different side to her sister. Letty having ideas? Letty willing to speak to one of the office staff? Rather ashamed of her own surprise, Eva caught at her sister's arm and pressed it.

'You speak to Miss Hanna then. Canna do any harm. Might do a lot o' good.'

'Hey, was that your sister I seen goin' into the office then?' asked Berta Denny, sauntering towards Eva as the noise of the machines stilled and the girls began preparing to go for their dinner. 'No' thinkin' herself a secertary now, is she? Oh, you Massons, whit'll you be up to next?'

'She's just going to speak to Miss Hanna about something,' Eva answered coolly. 'Not that it's any of your business.'

'I'll say so!' cried Bel, sweeping up in her shawl, her dark eyes glowing with anger. 'We might ask you what you'll be up to, Berta, eh? 'Cept we'd no' want to be told. You get yourself away for your dinner now, and stop interfering in our affairs.'

'You stupid old woman!' shouted Berta, her colour rising. 'Who d'you think you're talkin' to? Tellin' me whit to do! You're lucky we're no' outside, or I'd hae given you what for!'

A murmur went up from the watching mill

81

girls, some shocked, others – Berta's cronies – grinning and clapping, but Eva was already firing herself up to defend Bel.

'How dare you speak to ma mother like that?' she shouted at Berta. 'How dare you threaten her? I'll report you, so I will.'

'What's all this?' Todd Rettie asked as Berta, her face hot and moist, clenched her fists and made a move towards Bel and Eva, who did not waver. 'What's going on?'

'Ask Berta,' Bel said calmly. 'She was all set just now to take me outside.'

'For God's sake, Berta, what are you playing at?' With his hand on her shoulder, Mr Rettie forced her to step back. 'You canna behave like this. You know what Mr North thinks o' fighting. You'll be out o' here before you can say knife.'

'They started it,' Berta said sullenly as she jerked his hand from her shoulder. 'Is that no' right, girls? You saw, eh?'

'They did not start it,' Mavis said quietly. 'Mr Rettie, I heard Berta threaten Bel. It was wrong, it was uncalled for.'

'Aye, it was,' other voices chimed in, and though Berta's friends shouted disagreement, it was clear that the fun was over and that Mr Rettie was not going to take Berta's part.

'Away for your dinners!' he called. 'All o' you, or I'll shut the lot o' you out and that'll be your wages lost. Bel, I'm sorry if there's been trouble you didn't start, but you'd better go as well, and your girls with you. Where's Letty?'

'Here,' said Letty walking between the machines from the office at the back of the spinning flat. 'What's happening?'

'Nothing!' cried Berta. 'Nothing at all. I'm away.'

'Berta, you wait for me – I want to speak to you,' cried Mr Rettie, hurrying after her as she stormed ahead, and suddenly there was silence.

'Well, what a drama!' murmured Bel, pulling her shawl around her. 'We'd better hurry, girls, if we want our dinner. Letty, whatever were you doing in the office?'

'Learning how to type,' she answered with a smile. 'No, that's a joke. But I know a wee bit about a typewriter now, thanks to Miss Hanna.'

'You can tell me whatever's going on when we get back,' Bel called over her shoulder, slightly exasperated. 'We'll have to look sharp and just have bread and some cold meat I've got left. No time for anything else.'

'So Miss Hanna helped you?' Eva asked Letty when they got home.

'Aye, she did.' Letty seemed quietly pleased. 'She said she was just going to change the ribbon, and she showed me how she did it and let me have a wee go – look at ma fingers!'

'Oh, Lordy – all ink!'

'I'll need Ma's carbolic, eh? But she was that friendly, Evie, asking me why I was interested and all o' that, and then she said I'd do well and wished me luck.'

'You seem happier, Letty. Are you no' so worried?'

'No.' She smiled wryly. 'Just scared stiff.'

'Come away, you lassies, and give me a hand,' called Bel. 'Letty, whatever is that you've got on your fingers?'

'It's a long story, Ma.'

'Better get scrubbing when you're telling it then, eh?'

'Ma,' said Eva suddenly, as a new fear came into her mind. 'D'you think Berta Denny would-'ve hit you, if you'd been outside?'

'Berta Denny? No! She's all bluster that one. She'd never have dared to touch me.'

'She does have fights sometimes, I've heard.'

'Aye, when she's been drinking. A lot o' lassies like her pretend to be men, eh?'

'But she'd no' go for you?'

'I'm telling you, she'd never dare.'

Eva and Letty slowly began to spread margarine on the bread they'd sliced, while Bel carved up what was left of a small joint of mutton.

'Oh, what long faces!' she cried. 'Now take a tip from me and spend no time worrying over folk like Berta Denny. She's all talk.'

But neither Eva nor Letty had their mother's confidence where Berta was concerned, and could not forget her threats so easily.

Fourteen

Saturday finally came, and with it Letty's interview and Eva's last day at the mill. Long before the hooter went, Eva was awake, watching the light change at the window, listening to noises elsewhere in the tenement – listening also to Letty's difficult breathing. Knowing she was awake, too.

'Your last day,' Letty whispered at last.

'Aye, though I suppose I might do some holiday work.'

'You're no' part o' the mill, though. You'll never be a mill girl.'

Eva was silent, afraid to talk of her hopes that Letty herself might not be a mill girl for much longer.

'Wish it was time to get up,' Letty sighed. 'Wish I could get this day over.'

'Well, I can hear Ma next door, so your wish is coming true,' Eva told her with a laugh. 'One wish, anyway.'

The evening before the whole family had taken baths, Frank and Roddie going out to the Corporation Baths, while Bel and the girls used the tub before the stove, modestly retiring to the bedroom when it wasn't their turn. Afterwards, they washed their hair and sat by the window, waiting for it to dry in the still warm air, finally brushing and braiding it for bed.

'They say some lassies are cutting their hair these days,' Eva remarked. 'Be easier to dry, eh?'

'If it's worth looking like a laddie,' Bel retorted. 'Canna imagine women with short hair.'

The girls couldn't imagine it either, but stretched and yawned and thought how pleasant it was to be so clean. But, as Letty pointed out, once they were back next day in the dust of the mill, they might as well not have bathed at all.

'And I've to look smart by two o'clock. How'll I do it?'

'Have a quick wash when you get back, pet,' her mother told her. 'And your good dress is all ready, eh? No need to worry what you look like. You'll be the bonniest there.'

'Oh, Ma! I bet they'll all be bonny.'

'You'll be best,' said Bel.

Now there was only the morning to get through, but how long it seemed! At least there was a different feeling in the mill for Eva today. Excluding Berta and her friends, of course, the girls were being very nice to her and wishing her all the best, and that gave her a pleasantly warm feeling she hadn't expected. Seemed they liked her, after all, though when she told Mavis of her surprise, Mavis herself was amused.

'Now, why should the lassies no' like you, Eva? You canna judge us all by Berta, you ken.'

'No, thank the Lord! Oh, but Mavis, I'll miss you, eh? You've been so nice to me.'

As Mavis blushed and shook her head, Eva longed again to tell her about Letty, but the secret wasn't hers and again she kept the words back.

'Mebbe you'll work a bit in your school holidays?' Mavis suggested. 'I'll still be here.'

'D'you never think o' finding another job? You ken this dust is no' good for you.'

'What would I do? And it's no' so bad, Eva. I'm used to it, eh?'

'The doctor says Letty has to leave,' Eva told her, deciding that she could at least say that. 'He might tell you the same thing.'

'No, no.' Mavis smiled. 'I dinna go to the doctor's.'

Finally the end of the longest morning arrived. The waves of relief that accompanied the start of the weekend always sent the workers home in high spirits. Never mind that the married women might be only swapping one sort of work for another, there was a different feeling about Saturdays for everyone. An illusion that, for a little while, people's lives were their own, and not the mill owner's.

But as they left the crowd of women streaming from the works entrance, with their mother striding on ahead as usual, Letty was drooping again.

'I'll no' want anything to eat, Evie. It'd stick in ma throat, so it would.'

'That's just nerves, Letty. But you'd better have something, or you might feel faint.'

'Faint? Oh Lordie, you think I might feel faint?'

'No, no. You'll be fine...' Eva's voice trailed to silence and she slowed down so abruptly that the girl behind her bumped into her and gave her a shove, with a good-natured warning to get out of the way.

'What's up wi' you, hen? Seen a ghost?'

Not a ghost. Mr North's motor. And leaning beside it, while the whistling chauffeur cleaned the windscreen, was Mr North's son.

In the early days of her summer job, Eva had thought Mr North would always come to the mill in his car and had looked out for it – had looked out for his boy as well, though that she didn't care to admit, even to herself, for it would be foolish, so it would. All the same, she'd once asked Mavis about the car and Mavis had told her, with a smile, that the boss never came to the mill before ten and always left before four.

'So, you'd never see him, Eva. He keeps out of our way, you ken.'

'Saw his laddie once,' Eva said casually. 'Outside school. I suppose he never comes here?'

'Och, no! We dinna see Mr Nicholas. Or his sister.' Mavis laughed and coughed. 'Canna imagine Miss North setting foot in the mill, or even the weaving shed!'

'Never knew Mr North had a daughter. Is she pretty?'

'So they say. But they go away to school, you ken, that lassie and her brother. Boarding schools somewhere. Dundee's no' good enough, eh?'

Fascinated, Eva stored all these snippets of information away in her mind, though hearing them had only brought it home that she was never likely to see Mr North's son again. Nicholas. At least she'd been told his name.

Yet, here he was, waiting outside the mill, the first time she'd seen him since that day outside the school. It seemed strange to see him on her last day at work. Like saying goodbye, when she'd never even said hello.

As she walked on down the street, she couldn't help feeling excited, though she kept telling herself that to feel excited was a piece of nonsense. But Letty and the girls from the mill were excited anyway, looking at the grand motor car and the fair-haired boy still leaning against it.

Only to be expected, thought Eva glumly. When did the mill girls ever see anyone like him? In fact, with his looks and his clothes – pristine white tennis shirt and flannels – he rather resembled his father's car. Something so different from all they knew, he and the car might have dropped into the street from the moon.

He seemed oblivious to all around him, all the whispers and nudges and eyes riveted on him. Until his own eyes met Eva's. Grey eyes, dark eyes, and Eva's heart was thumping. She felt everyone around her must be watching, wondering why the boss's son was looking at her. But there was no ripple of interest, no whispers that she could hear. Maybe there was nothing to see at all, for Nicholas North hadn't smiled this time, hadn't shown that he even remembered her.

She wondered if he looked down on her, thinking she was just a mill girl. She knew there was nothing wrong with working at the mill, but still she wished she could just have told Nicholas North that she was in fact staying on at school and taking her Leaving Certificate. She felt sure she would lie awake when she went to her bed that night, regretting that she hadn't been able to let him know.

'Evie, come away,' Letty murmured, putting a thin hand on Eva's arm. 'I've to get maself ready, dinna forget.'

'Sorry, Letty.' Eva flushed. 'I was just looking at the motor car.'

'Like everybody else. But Mr North's coming now. They'll be driving away.'

'Mr North?' From beneath lowered lids, Eva

glanced back to see the mill-owner approach his car and his son, carrying a briefcase, as the chauffeur ran round to open the doors.

'Come on then, let's catch up wi' Ma.'

Fifteen

Time to go. There was only one clock in the Massons' house – a solid piece with an oak case and a pleasant chime for the hours. It stood on a shelf over the range and was by way of being Frank's inheritance. It was all his father had had to leave him, except for the armchair Frank sat in every day, but few folk he knew received more. And the clock was worth having. Old Mr Masson had paid five shillings for it from a second-hand shop, and always suspected it had come from a pawnshop. It might even have been in a fine house once. Anyway, it kept good time, and all eyes were on it now.

'Half past one,' remarked Bel. 'Letty, I'd be walking along, if I was you.'

'It'll never take half an hour to get to Mr Crindle's, Ma,' said Eva, who had been silent until then while they'd had something to eat.

'Best be early, eh?'

'I want to go,' said Letty hoarsely. 'And I'm all ready, anyway.'

She stood up and faced them, a thin figure in a navy-blue cotton dress made by Bel, with Bel's own grey jacket borrowed for the occasion, and a straw hat with a blue ribbon.

'How d'you think I look?'

'Grand!' cried Roddie.

'Perfect,' said Eva, forgetting her own concerns as a great rush of feeling for her sister squeezed her chest and made her want to cry. Poor Letty. Her older sister who always seemed the younger. If only Eva could run to her and put the job at Crindle's into her hands like a present wrapped in Crindle's paper and tied with a Crindle bow.

'You'll do,' her mother told Letty crisply. 'Pity your dad canna see you, but he'll try to get back early, to see how you got on.'

Letty put her hand to her lips. 'I wish you wouldnae talk about it, Ma.'

'And I wish you'd face facts. You'll have to get on somehow, eh? One way or the other?'

'Who's coming with me then?' Letty asked after a pause.

'Why, nobody. It's you who's got to do the talking.'

'I'll go with you!' cried Roddie. 'I'll stand outside and wait for you.'

'And I will,' said Eva.

'Could do that,' agreed Bel. 'But away you go then, Letty. Look willing, eh?'

'Look keen,' put in Eva.

'I am keen,' said Letty faintly. 'But I'm all churned up inside. I canna think what I'll say.'

'You tell Mr C. about the typewriters,' Eva urged. 'Be sure no' to forget.'

'I feel that bad, though. I might forget everything.'

'When you get there, you'll see, it'll be fine,' said Bel. 'Whatever happens, it'll no' be worth crying over.'

With a last despairing glance at her mother, Letty, followed by Eva and Roddie, made her way down the stair and into the street.

'Anybody'd think she was going to have her head chopped off,' Roddie whispered to Eva.

'She's just nervous. You'd be the same if you were going for a job.'

'I'm nervous anyway,' said Roddie, jumping from one pavement flag to the next. 'Now look, if I dinna step on any o' these lines, Letty'll get the job, eh?'

It's going to take more than that for Letty to get the job, thought Eva, *the way things are going*.

There was no one waiting outside Mr Crindle's shop when they arrived. No smartly dressed young ladies exchanging glances, ready to look down their noses at Letty. No mothers, brothers or sisters encouraging them to go in, show willing, look keen. Letty's blue gaze moved to Eva.

'Must all be inside already. I must be late.'

Well, they had no watches, but Eva knew Letty wasn't late.

'Early, more like. Go on in, Letty, before they come. Then you'll feel better. We'll wait here.'

'Aye, we'll wait here,' agreed Roddie, eyeing the display of stationery in the shop window. 'Listen, I'd no' mind working in a shop like this. Looks good, eh?'

'Just let me get ma job first,' said Letty.

'In you go, then,' said Eva, 'and good luck!'

'Aye, good luck!' cried Roddie, as Letty finally got herself into the shop and the door closed behind her.

'She'll be all right,' he murmured to Eva. 'I never trod on a single line.'

Once she'd seen Letty on her way, Eva's thoughts reverted to Nicholas North. She felt like she was like two people, one questioning the other. 'Why him,' asked Number One voice, 'when she'd never taken the slightest interest in the boys at school? Even when they'd looked at her, as Nicholas North had looked at her?'

'Couldn't say,' answered Number Two voice. It was true he was handsome, with a wide brow and a straight nose and fair hair that shone. He was also the boss's son and from a different world from hers, but that didn't count. She wasn't one of the mill girls, staring at him because he was different and as grand as his dad's car.

Nor was she ready to join the silly lassies at school who were always giggling and blushing over the boys, and boasting in whispers that they were going to the Greenmarket Fair with so and so, or the Saturday pictures if they could find the coppers. Eva, Ada and Katie had always been so scornful of girls who went on like that: they had better things to do.

And that was still true, Eva decided, walking up and down outside Mr Crindle's shop while Roddie amused himself rolling a marble along the pavement. She still had better things to do than think about Nicholas North, even if it was true he'd caught her fancy somehow. Why, she was going to the secondary school on Monday! All this nonsense would have to stop then. She'd not have time for anything but work; she had to do well, to justify her bursary and Miss Balfour's faith. And she *would* do well – that was a solemn promise.

'Here comes Letty!' cried Roddie.

She was on the step outside the shop door, her face drained of colour, her eyes strangely glittering.

'Oh, Evie, Roddie, you'll never guess...'

'What? Guess what?'

They were standing close, willing her to go on, but she was breathing fast and fluttering her hankie at her lips.

'Letty!' cried Eva, taking her by the shoulders. 'Will you speak to us?'

'It's all right, it's all right...' Letty pulled herself from Eva's grasp. 'Thing is ... I've got the job.'

Roddie let out a great whoop and began dancing round his sisters.

'Did I no' tell you, Evie? Did I no' say Letty'd get the job? When I never stopped on the lines?'

'Oh, hush!' cried Eva. 'I want to hear what happened. I want to hear every single thing. Letty, why are you no' excited? Why are you no' over the moon?'

'I am,' Letty answered simply. 'But I canna understand it. I mean, why me?'

'Were the other girls there? At the interview?'

'No, they came this morning. And it wasnae an interview – more like a wee talk. Katie was minding the shop, and we were in Mr Crindle's

94

office – me and Mr and Mrs Crindle, and they kept looking at me and then each other and shaking their heads – it was all that strange, you ken.'

'Did you tell 'em about the typewriters? Did you answer all their questions?'

'Aye, I remembered about the typewriters and I think they were pleased. And I answered all the questions.' Letty shook her head, pushing back her straw hat from her worried brow. 'Maybe I did well, eh? Better than I thought?'

'You must've done,' Eva said slowly. 'They must've liked you, anyway, and why not? Oh, come on, Letty, it's grand news, eh? It's a marvel! Shall we run home and tell Ma?'

'Aye, let's run home!' cried Roddie.

'No, I've to go back in. We've all to go back in. I just came out to tell you, eh?' A sudden smile lit Letty's face. 'Ma good news.'

There was a wonderfully light and pleasant atmosphere in the stationery shop when the Massons trooped in, with Katie bouncing up to hug everybody, and Mr Crindle looking affable, and Mrs Crindle smiling graciously as she served a lady customer.

Yet Eva could somehow understand Letty's bewilderment. It did seem strange that, out of all the applicants, the Crindles had actually chosen her sister. For even though she was fiercely loyal and could see all Letty's good points, in her heart she'd never believed the Crindles would see them too.

Why worry though? Eva asked herself. Letty had got the job. That was all that mattered. Still, it was strange...

As Mr Crindle shepherded Letty into his office to be given more details of her employment, Mrs Crindle finished serving her customer and asked if Eva and Roddie would like to go up to the flat for lemonade and one of her cherry cakes.

Roddie was up the stairs like a flash, but Eva, an idea forming in her mind, hung back to look into Katie's large beaming brown eyes.

'Was it you?' she asked softly. 'Was it you who got Letty the job?'

'Me?' Katie widened the brown eyes. 'I told you all I said, Eva. Why Letty needed to get away from the mill, and that. It was all I could do.'

'You made them feel sorry for her?' Eva was flushing brightly. 'For all of us?'

'No! Well, yes, in a way.' Katie put her hand on Eva's arm. 'But Dad would never take anybody on just because he was sorry for 'em, Eva. He always says he's a businessman.'

'We live in Wish Lane though.'

'What's that got to do with it?'

Eva gave a little shrug. 'I'm no' complaining, Katie. I think your folks've been very good, to give ma sister her chance. She'll no' let 'em down.'

'They know that. In fact, it's not quite what you think. Letty did well in her talk with Dad. He was quite impressed with her.' Katie nodded her head. 'Yes, it's true, so don't be worrying. Look, you run up to Mum. I've got to mind the shop.'

Back at home, Bel surprised everybody by bursting into tears when she heard Letty's news.

'Ma!' her children cried, shocked, and Frank blinked and shook his head, but she only laughed and wiped her eyes.

'I'm just that relieved, eh? Oh, I canna tell you – the weight off ma mind, that Letty's out o' that dust! And it looked like we were never going to manage it, with nothing being suitable and the days going by, and then Mr Crindle's job coming up, but he might have been seeking somebody different, you ken...'

'Bel, Letty's got the job,' Frank said firmly. 'No need to go on about what might have been.'

'Aye, but it's such a grand job, Frank! Eighteen shilling a week! I mean, that's generous!'

'I'll give it to you, Ma,' Letty said earnestly. 'Just like I gave you ma mill money.'

'Well, there'll be a bit more for you to keep, pet, because you'll have things to buy. Have to look smart, you ken, when you're dealing with customers.' Bel, all smiles again, was back to her confident self. 'Next Saturday, let's away to the store and pick out some stuff for a nice skirt and blouse. I've the tin money, I can spare it.'

'And what's for our tea now, Ma?' asked Roddie. 'I think we should have something special.'

'I was just going to send you round to the pork butcher's for some of their wee pies. We can have 'em with mash, eh? Oh, and get half o' butter as well. Will you go with him, Eva?'

'Ma, you'll no' forget the cakes Mrs Crindle gave us?' asked Eva. 'She's been so kind.'

'Kind is right,' her father agreed. 'I mean, giving Letty a job *and* a bag o' cakes! Seems like you've fallen on your feet there, lassie.'

Letty, smiling proudly, was taking off her mother's jacket and smoothing its lapels. 'I'll just hang this up for you, Ma. Thanks for letting me borrow it.'

'Your lucky jacket, eh?' Roddie said, rattling marbles in his pocket. 'But I brought you luck, and all.'

'Letty made her own luck,' Eva declared, not of course saying a word about Katie. Anyway, it seemed to be true that Letty had sprung another surprise and done well in her talk with Mr Crindle. She'd found her courage again, after all.

'I'll come with you for the pies, Evie,' Letty murmured. 'I'd like the walk.'

'Are you no' too tired?' asked Bel, taking coins from her purse. 'You've had a long day.'

'No, I feel well.'

'That's what a bit o' good news can do,' said Frank cheerfully. 'Best medicine, eh?'

Sixteen

After they'd left Roddie scuffling outside the house with a boy he knew, the sisters set off down Wish Lane, Evie swinging a basket, Letty holding the money.

'Are you happy, Evie?' Letty asked quietly.

'Me?' Eva laughed. 'You're the one should be happy.'

'But you did say you wanted to see me settled before you went back to school. And here I am, settled. If I do well.' Letty's mouth quivered a little. 'Mr Crindle said he was sure I would, but if I canna do the work...' She broke off, and Eva squeezed her arm.

'You'll do well, Letty.'

'Aye, or else I'll have to go, eh?'

'You're settled, Letty, that's what you are. You said so yourself.'

'I did.' Letty began to smile. 'I am. So, are you glad then? No need to worry. I never wanted you to worry, anyway.'

'I've no need to worry.' Eva was laughing again, but then her dark eyes grew large. Her laughter died and her look on her sister was suddenly apprehensive.

'I've just thought, Letty. On Monday I'll be at the new school. Doing arithmetic with Mr Dyce and all kinds o' new teachers.'

'Well, you knew that, eh? I thought you were looking forward to it.'

'Aye, it's what I want. But now it's coming so close, I feel a wee bit scared. They say Mr Dyce is awful hard.'

'He'll no' be hard with you. You're clever.'

'Supposing I canna keep up?'

'You'll do well.'

'Just what I said to you!'

Their youthful laughter rang out as they turned the corner into the street where Elder's, the pork butcher's, stood. A pale young woman trailing a child by the hand turned to look after them and sighed.

'Ken what we are?' Eva asked.

'No, what?'

'Lucky. Both of us. I've left the mill. You'll be putting your notice in.'

'Putting ma notice in,' Letty said dreamily. 'Wait till I tell the lassies!'

They laughed again, but at the door of Elder's, where Letty checked over the money her mother had given her, they grew serious.

'I wish we could do something for Mavis,' Letty whispered.

'I'm going to do something for Mavis,' said Eva.

'When?'

'When I can. I'm going to do something for them all, at the mill.'

It was grand talk, and Letty knew Eva meant it, but what could she really do? Still, it made them feel better, just to talk. As though there was something to look forward to, something they could really change.

'Hey, have you no' bought the pies yet?' cried Roddie, gasping as he reached them, running. 'I'm starving, so I am. Let's in and buy 'em, then!'

'No shoving,' ordered Letty, entering the shop. 'I go first; I'm the one with the money.'

'And that's the way o' the world,' said Mr Elder, grinning from behind the counter. 'Money always leads, eh? Now, what can I get you?'

Their tea that evening was certainly special, though not because of what they ate, enjoyable though it was. It was special, memorable even,

100

because of Letty and her success.

No wonder they could scarcely stop smiling, even to eat their pork pies and Mrs Crindle's excellent baking. And when they'd cleared away and tidied up, nobody wanted to go out or do very much, except sit thinking over the news of the day and taking pleasure in it. Even Roddie seemed content to read his comic, only occasionally looking away, not saying anything.

Maybe, thought Eva, *he's wondering if he can get out of working at the mill the way we have, Letty and me.* And she wound her hands together and prayed that that could happen. *Please Lord, may Roddie not have to go shifting for Mrs Fleck*, she voiced in her head. Aloud she said, 'Listen, d'you remember it's Sunday tomorrow? We've all got the day off!'

'Plenty to do, Sunday or no Sunday,' Bel said comfortably.

'Ah, no!' they protested. 'Let's have a rest for once!'

And a rest they had and felt the better for it, except for Eva who had butterflies in her stomach and just wanted Monday to come and be over.

In fact, it was fine and warm, and picnicking by the sea was such a wonderful contrast to their usual toil, they felt their world had for a little while turned pleasantly upside down. Letty in particular could hardly believe that life could suddenly appear so rosy, while Eva forgot to be worried about Monday and Mr Dyce – forgot, too, that Nicholas North lived at Broughty Ferry. Until they all looked through the railings at his

101

father's house, and then she remembered she hadn't thought of him since the day before.

It was a relief that nobody seemed to be about in the grounds of the house, for how she would have blushed if Nicholas had appeared and seen her looking through the railings! In fact, by the time they were on their way home, their perfect day over, Nicholas had once again gone from her mind, to be replaced by thoughts of Monday morning and Mr Dyce.

'Ma, I've to get ma things ready for school tomorrow!' she cried in a panic when they reached the tenement in Wish Lane.

'They're in the wardrobe,' her mother told her calmly. 'I got 'em ready yesterday when you were with Letty.'

'Oh, Ma!'

'Stop worrying – you ken fine you'll do well, a clever girl like you.'

'That's what everybody says,' Eva said seriously. 'But nobody knows how I'll get on.'

'You've just got the butterflies. Folk are always like that before they get started.'

'I was,' Letty murmured. 'And I was all right.'

'There you are then,' Bel told Eva. 'You'll be the same. Why, you enjoy school, eh?'

Eva nodded. It was true; she'd just got the butterflies. Just wanted Monday to come, that was all. And be over.

Seventeen

Monday morning came, all right, and with it the mill's hooter, but Bel and Letty were already up when it sounded and Eva had made the tea.

'There's a good lassie,' said Bel, hurrying about as usual. 'And looking that smart! Better wear ma pinny over that dress, before you start the porridge.'

'I wanted to look smart today,' Eva murmured, pouring the tea. 'For ma first day.'

'Canna see Mr Dyce and all thae teachers caring what you look like,' said Roddie, who had appeared without waiting to be woken. 'As long as you're good at your work eh?'

'Well, I care what I look like,' Eva retorted, making a great effort not to start worrying whether or not she'd be good at her work. 'Letty, are you no' drinking this tea?'

A strangely bright-eyed Letty obediently drank her tea and began to pin up her hair. Though she had coughed in the night as usual, she looked well, borne up by the excitement of telling the girls at the mill her news. The very thought was making her flutter inside, as though she had the butterflies again. But at least they were pleasant butterflies – not the sort she'd had before talking to Mr Crindle. Not the sort poor Eva would be having until her first day was over.

'Ready?' asked Bel, finding her shawl. 'Frank, we're away!'

'Aye, I'm here.' Frank came out of the bedroom buttoning his shirt and kissed Bel briefly on the cheek. 'Letty, you've got your letter with your notice?'

'Course she's got it,' said Bel. 'She's dying to see everybody's faces when she hands it in.'

'Wish I could see 'em,' Eva murmured. She had tied her mother's apron round her slim waist and was busy stirring the porridge, finding that these routine actions were calming her nerves. 'I'd send ma love to Berta, only I think I'll send it to Mavis instead. She'll be pleased for you, Letty.'

'Aye, she will.' Letty suddenly pulled Eva away from her stirring and gave her a hug. 'Ah, Evie, good luck at school. It'll be all right, when you get there.'

'Sure it will,' said Bel, hugging Eva herself. 'Now we've to be gone, Letty – canna risk being late when you've to hand that letter in!'

Later, on their way to school, it seemed to Eva that Roddie was hanging back and she told him sharply to hurry up, because she mustn't be late.

'We're in time,' he told her. 'You're just worrying again.'

'I am not! But it'd be awful, if I was late on ma first morning.'

'Tell you, we're all right. Anyway, I wanted to ask you something.'

'Be quick, then.'

'Is there any chance, d'you think, that I might

104

get one o' thae things that you've got? That Mr North gave you?'

Eva turned to look at her brother's strangely serious face. 'You mean the bursary?'

'Aye, that. Could I get one? When I'm your age?'

'You're a clever laddie; I think you'd qualify. You'd have to work hard, though, you ken. Show you really want it.'

'I do. I want to be like you.'

'And no' work in the mill? There's no' so many men work there, anyway.'

'I mean, have a career. A job you canna be thrown out of, the way Dad was.'

'A teacher?'

Roddie shook his head. 'Something with figures. I'm good at numbers. Office work, mebbe.' He grinned suddenly. 'Accounts, eh? Would I no' be grand, wi' ma paper cuffs and all?' He grew serious again. 'Course, I ken I'll have to do part-time shifting when I'm twelve. I want to help Ma.'

Eva was silent until they came in sight of the Toll Road school.

'Mebbe Ma'll no' want you to. She's got a bit more money now.'

'I'd no' mind. As long as I could stay on at school like you.'

'Work for it, Roddie.' Eva's look was fierce. 'Work as hard as you can. And get what you want, eh?'

'Aye,' Roddie agreed and, catching sight of one or two friends outside the elementary school, cast aside his serious mood and darted off to join them, leaving Eva to hurry on to the separate building that was Toll Road Secondary. The place of her dreams it had been up till now, but as she reached the schoolyard and caught sight of Ada and Katie, all she could feel were those butterflies.

'Oh, Eva, are you no' smart?' cried Ada. 'All dressed up for our first day!'

'Just wanted to cheer maself up.'

'As though you'd need to do that,' Katie exclaimed. 'Why, you're glad to be back at school, aren't you?'

Glad to be back. Eva stood still, looking round at the pupils milling around, waiting for the bell to ring. Hughie and George were looking rather pleased with themselves, as befitted pupils of a Higher Grade secondary school, and Bob Keir was kicking a ball to some other boy with his usual confident air. He, of course, would not be worried about moving up, but Eva's gaze returned to Hughie and George. They weren't showing any signs of strain, yet she was sure they would be feeling it. Seemed they, like Ada and Katie, were concealing it well.

But so am I, thought Eva. *No one would know I've got the butterflies.*

For why should she or any of them be worried? They could do the work, they knew they could. It was just that, apart from Katie, they had Mr North's money in the background to remember. They had to prove themselves; that was the point.

Glad to be back. Oh, she was, she was!

And as a tall girl came out and rang the bell for assembly and they all moved from the yard to the hall, something happened. The butterflies in Eva's chest fled. Her nerves vanished. And even when she saw Mr Dyce, with the headmaster they didn't know and other strange teachers on the platform, she thought he didn't look too bad. Aye, he was a bit of a stickler, though not hard on those who tried to do their best, as Miss Balfour said.

What mattered was that they were on their way. They'd been given the key, and they'd be opening the door. Back at school, with their future unfolding wonderfully before them, Eva knew they'd been lucky, and breathed in that feeling of luck as though it were as real as the smell of disinfectant and caretaker's polish that filled the hall.

This is for me, she thought, *this is where I'm happy*. And she joined in the opening hymns of the morning with such strength of voice that Katie glanced at her in surprise, and Bob Keir grinned along from the boys' rows.

Eighteen

Eva and Katie were together on the old Esplanade by the Tay, sitting on a bench looking at the bridge and the small ships passing on the water. Basking in autumn sunshine, taking a break as they could so rarely do. It might be their lunch hour, but so often at the Teachers' Training Centre they had to work through it. Who'd have thought student teachers would have to work so hard?

'Slave-driving' some called it. 'Try a day or two in a jute factory!' was always Eva's response.

Anyway, she loved what they were learning to do. Everything that was laid down in the curriculum: Physical Exercises, Instruction in Hygiene, the Principles of Teaching, including Psychology, Ethics and Logic, Voice Training, History of Educational Theories, Primary School Subjects and – best of all – Teaching Practice. It was with this last that she felt most at home. Most relieved that she had made the right decision. Teaching was for her, so much was true. Even if sometimes she did feel exhausted.

But not as exhausted as she would have been at North's.

The year was 1926. One to be remembered for

Britain's first General Strike, back in May. Workers, including mill-workers – including Bel – had come out in support of the miners, whose wages had been reduced by the coal owners. Nine days they'd stayed out and watched the strike collapse, until recalled to work by the Trades Union Congress, though they were still in sympathy with the miners who'd stayed out and were still out, growing hungrier by the week. They'd have to go back soon, Eva thought. Think of the bairns! But when they did go back, would it be for more money, or less?

Looking at the wide stretch of water, with its distant view of the sea, and of course its railway bridge, Eva felt she should have been enjoying the air and the scene. Usually, she did. Usually, she took pleasure in the chance to unwind by the Tay, which always seemed so calm in spite of its activity.

A train was crossing the bridge now, cheerfully back at work. A few months ago it wouldn't have been running; its crew would have been on strike.

'All for nothing,' she murmured, finishing a cold meat sandwich and shuddering a little over the tartness of the pickle. For a shilling she might have had a meal in the canteen, but a shilling was a shilling. Her grant didn't stretch very far.

'What is?' asked Katie.

'The miners' strike.'

'Oh, yes. Probably.' Katie had taken out an apple and was polishing it with a paper napkin. She could have afforded the shilling for the canteen dinner, but preferred to take packed lunches, always beautifully made by her mother. 'Dad says it's wrong to withdraw labour. Without good reason, anyway.'

'Getting your wages cut seems good enough reason to me.'

Katie's strong teeth closed over her apple. 'I'm not saying I don't feel sorry for the miners,' she said after a pause. 'Especially the children.'

'Everybody's thinking of them.'

The girls were silent, their eyes fixed on the water. The train had crossed the bridge, leaving a trail of smoke to mix with the clouds, but there were still the vessels to watch, moving towards the harbour and the sea, and all the activity of the estuary to take their minds off other people's troubles.

Now nineteen, both girls were slim, with hair newly bobbed and short skirts, but where Katie was pretty, with her freckles and vivid colouring, Eva was something more. She'd always had the promise of beauty, and now the promise had been fulfilled.

And though the female students were not encouraged to mix with the males, that didn't stop the males from casting burning looks at the oval-faced, dark-eyed Miss Masson and her redheaded friend, and asking them out for cups of tea and currant buns. So far, that was all. But what young woman trainee teacher could risk more? It would be a terrible waste of time to get involved with men, as Katie had once pointed out. 'We have our careers to think about and they'd be over before they started, if we fell in love.'

'We can fall in love, just not get married,' Eva

had retorted. 'I call it disgraceful, when men can do as they like.'

'I suppose they are the breadwinners, when they marry.'

'A lot of women I know are married and bread-winners as well.' Eva laughed. 'And they've never been asked to stop work.'

'Ah, you know it's different in the mills,' said Katie.

'Oh, yes, always different in the mills.'

'Only because men don't want what the mill girls do.'

'But if they want the same work as women, they have to have it and the women stay at home?'

'As I said, the men are the breadwinners,' Katie said patiently. 'It's no good trying to change the world, you know.'

'Why not?' cried Eva.

They were silent for a while until Katie, trying to change the subject, said how thankful every-body was that the new Tay bridge hadn't fallen down like the old one all those years ago.

'Remember McGonagall's poem?' She began to recite: '"Beautiful Railway Bridge of the Silvery Tay / Alas I am very sorry to say / That ninety lives have been taken away ..."' Oh, Eva, what a terrible poem. But so sad!'

'Aye,' Eva murmured. 'Sad for everybody. Even the man who built the bridge – you have to feel sorry for him.'

'Died of a broken heart, they say.' Katie frown-ed. 'I don't see how anyone could do that, really. I mean, however miserable you were, how would your heart know?'

Eva's dark eyes widened. 'Sure, your heart'd know, Katie! Mine would, I bet.'

'Be careful, then,' cried Katie, laughing.

Eva laughed, too. 'No need to worry. I've no plans to get my heart broken.'

They stood up, brushing crumbs from their short skirts and gathering their things together, because it was time to go.

Nineteen

It was warm, walking back through the streets to the Teachers' Training Centre, a post-war building close to Dundee's University College. Heat struck up from the pavements through the soles of the girls' black-strapped shoes, and the smoke and steam issuing from the mills they passed made Eva's spirits sink. She hated to think of her mother – or anyone, for that matter – still working in such heat and noise. Poor Mavis Craik, for instance, was said to be off work, ill again.

Thank goodness Letty was out of it, and still so happy working for Katie's father. Quite the professional, too, demonstrating and selling the typewriters, as well as stationery, though not married yet and her all of twenty-two.

'Aye, I'm an old maid,' she'd say. 'And likely to stay so, eh?'

Nobody ever mentioned the young man she'd

been courting when she was twenty – certainly not Letty. A closed book, that was, the pages never to be turned.

'Oh, my!' Katie exclaimed now, pausing to dab at her brow with her handkerchief. 'Isn't that your admirer there, Eva? Surprised he didn't come seeking you at the river.'

'Admirer?' Eva wrinkled her brows. 'Who are you on about, Katie?'

'As though you didn't know! Bob Keir, of course!'

'Oh.' Eva smiled a little. 'He's no admirer, Katie. Just a friend – same as he's yours.'

She knew she was not being entirely honest there, for Bob and Katie were like chalk and cheese, Katie being so true blue like her parents, Bob being distinctly red. Not a Communist, but so much a Labour man, so passionate for social reform, you could almost see the flames of his feeling surrounding his dark head. Feeling for her, though? Well, Eva didn't know about that.

Ignoring Eva's remark, Katie narrowed her eyes at the slightly built young man standing next to tall Bob at the entrance to their college.

'Hughie Harper,' she murmured. 'I bet they've both been to the pub.'

'Well, they're journalists, Katie. Journalists always go to the pub.'

'Time they signed the pledge, then. I'm sure they can't afford to drink.'

'In moderation, it's OK.'

'Not if they were student teachers. They'd not have time to go drinking in their lunch hour.'

113

'Or the money,' said Eva.

But neither Bob nor Hughie had taken up teaching in the end, since the profession now expected men to be graduates before they began teacher training, which they were not. As Bob had pointed out, even with grants, they couldn't have afforded the extra years at university, and didn't see why they should.

'If you lassies can enter with the Leaving Certificate, why no' us?' he'd demanded, reasonably enough.

It didn't seem fair, though it was well known that the teaching profession in Scotland would have preferred all entrants to be graduates, even though the status of women was never likely to change. Promotions would always go to the men, while women, graduates or not, couldn't even keep on working after marriage.

Here was more fuel for Bob's fire, if he wanted to change recruitment policy, but in the end both he and Hughie had considered themselves well out of teaching. On leaving school, they'd been taken on as junior reporters by a small left-wing newspaper that had recently been founded and they couldn't be happier.

'How would I have got on in a school, then?' Bob asked once. 'What headmaster would've let me bend the ears of the bairns, eh? I'd have been out on ma ear inside a fortnight!'

'Me too,' said Hughie, still slender but now of average height and wearing horn-rimmed glasses that made him look as clever as he was. Already he, like Bob, was showing talent as a reporter and revelling in his new life. 'No regrets, eh?

Even if we're no' paid much.'

'Money's no' everything,' Bob declared. 'It's working for what you believe in that counts.'

Which was true for Ada MacGill, who was blissfully happy and fulfilled, working for very little as a nurse in Edinburgh, while George Webster had followed a calling nobody had expected and departed for China to train as a missionary.

'Would you credit it?' his fellow pupils had cried. 'George, of all folk? When's he ever been one for the kirk? And now off, spreading the word o' God in foreign parts. What next? Well, it takes all sorts, eh, to make the world go roond?'

'Have to admire a guy like that,' had been Bob's comment.

But now, on this sultry autumn day, the admiration in his eyes was for someone quite other than George Webster.

'Thought I'd catch you at your dinner-time,' he told Eva at the door, fixing her with eyes that were a mixture of yellow and brown. Tiger eyes, Eva called them, though Katie said not to be silly; they were just hazel.

'Where've you been?' Bob asked now, sparing Katie only a brief nod.

'We went down to the Tay,' Eva murmured. 'Had a sandwich by the water. Why d'you want to know, anyway?'

'Wanted to remind you about the meeting tonight.'

'What meeting?'

'Eva, I told you last week. A fella from the Miners' Union is speaking at the Mercat Hall about doing more to help the miners. We canna just leave 'em to rot, out on strike.' Bob's brow had darkened. 'You said you'd come.'

'I want to come, Bob, but I've an essay to write for our ethics tutor. I should've done it before, but we're that pressed for time, you see.'

'That's true,' Katie put in coolly. 'And we have to keep up. Can't just do what we like, you know, Bob.'

'So you have to write on ethics!' he said contemptuously. 'Where's the ethics in cutting men's wages, then? That's what you should be studying.'

'Canna expect everybody to feel like you, Bob,' Hughie said quietly. 'The lassies've got their own work to do.'

'Eva does feel like me,' Bob snapped. 'We've got the same ideas. Is that no' true, Eva?'

She nodded. 'It's true. I want change, sure I do. All I'm saying is I might have to miss the meeting tonight.'

He put his hand on her arm. 'If you get the essay finished, will you still try to come, though? It'll no' matter if you're late.'

'She doesn't want to have to worry about it,' Katie said firmly. 'Work comes first.'

'Katie, I'm no' asking you, I'm asking Eva.' Bob slid his hand down to Eva's. 'I'll look out for you,' he said softly.

After a pause, she shook his hand free. 'I'll do what I can, then. No promises.'

His face broke into smiles. 'That's all I ask.'

Hurrying to their next lecture, Katie found time

to whisper to Eva. 'Doesn't that fellow irritate you?'

'Bob? He's no different from usual.'

'Anybody'd think he'd a right to tell you what to do. He has a nerve!'

'To be fair, he did tell me about that meeting last week and I did say I'd go.' Eva bit her lip. 'Should've finished that essay before now. Still, I've got the notes.'

'Oh, you're not going to kill yourself trying to finish it before the meeting!' Katie's usually mild brown eyes were stormy. 'Eva, you must see something in Bob that no one else can see.'

'You heard what he said,' Eva answered swiftly. 'We have the same ideas. That's all there is between me and Bob.'

'Hope that's true,' said Katie.

Twenty

Unlike most of their fellow students, who were from elsewhere and had to stay in hostels, Eva and Katie were able to live at home, and at the end of the day they sometimes walked back to Katie's together so that Eva might collect Letty from work.

Home for the sisters was still Wish Lane, but a year or so before there had been a move from their old house to one on the ground floor of Number Twelve. This had the advantage of a partitioned bedroom, so that Roddie, a suddenly tall sixteen-year-old, could at last be separated from his parents.

'About time,' Bel had murmured, and the sisters had exchanged glances but, of course, said nothing. It couldn't have been easy, they knew, for their ma and dad, with a great grown laddie in their room. But there was no need to dwell on it. Few couples in tenements expected a room of their own where they could make love in private. Such luxury!

For Eva, the move had meant that she had somewhere to study, as Roddie had graciously allowed her to use his half of the bedroom. A godsend, indeed, even if she sometimes had to share it with Roddie himself, who was still at school and needed to study too.

'I'm going to do as well as you, Evie,' he would say, and showed every promise of doing just that, after he too had gained one of Mr North's bursaries. But what he wanted to choose as his career was still uncertain. Everyone agreed that he could do anything he liked, as long as it didn't need two good hands, for one of his had been damaged in his shifting days – and not by accident.

'Dinna ask me ever to forgive her,' Bel had cried when they'd heard the news that Mrs Fleck, the spiteful little woman in charge of the shifters, had trapped Roddie's left hand in the machine – to 'stop his blethering', as she'd said.

But three of his fingers would never be the same again, and after an enquiry, Mrs Fleck had been given the sack, so some good had come of

Roddie's pain. He had also been awarded a small sum in compensation, now held in a post office account that he regularly checked for interest, usually laughing and saying he wasn't likely to get rich on what the PO gave him.

'But I will be rich one day,' he promised. 'And I'll have a house at Broughty Ferry.'

'So will I,' said Eva, laughing with him. 'And Ma, we'll invite you and Dad over to have afternoon tea!'

But Frank had said he wasn't interested in Broughty Ferry or afternoon tea; all he wanted was to get back to the work he used to do. It was true he'd progressed from packing cartons at the jam factory to working in the processing plant, but it didn't compare with his old job.

Ah, if only I could give it to him, thought Eva. *That'd be worth more than any house in Broughty Ferry.*

Still, things weren't so bad. Calling at Mr Crindle's for Letty, Eva took pleasure in seeing how well she was looking these days – free from wheezing, her face full of colour, even a little plumper. When Eva and Katie joined her at her counter, she wasn't quite ready to leave since she had a customer, and the customer was Hughie Harper.

'You again, Hughie?' asked Katie. 'What are you doing here? Letty should be on her way.'

'It's all right,' Letty said quickly. 'Hughie was just wanting a new notebook.'

'Canna be a reporter without ma notebook,' he said with a grin. 'Letty knows which one I like.'

119

'Does she?' murmured Eva, noting her sister's bright eyes and the smile trembling on her lips. 'Get most of your stuff here, do you, Hughie?'

'Sure. It's a grand stationer's. You tell your dad that, Katie, eh?' Hughie laid a coin on the counter. 'No need for a bag for the notebook, Letty. I'll just take it, eh?'

'If you're sure.'

'Aye. Thanks.' He put the notebook in his pocket, straightened his glasses on his fine nose, and smiled round at the watching young women, taking care to finish with Letty. 'If you're walking back to Wish Lane, I might as well walk with you, eh? It's on ma way.'

'I'll just get ma hat and coat,' said Letty, while Hughie waited, whistling, and Eva and Katie looked at each other until Mr Crindle came out from the back and said he'd lock up.

'Time you were away, Letty. Katie, your mother's getting the pie out – better go on up, eh?'

He smiled at Eva, then Hughie.

'Buying another notebook, Hughie? Or is it pencils this time?'

'Soon get through ma notebooks, Mr Crindle,' Hughie answered, flushing a little, and Mr Crindle smiled.

'You get through as many as you like, Hughie. It's good for business.'

Though outside in the street the air was still warm, the light was changing, for this was autumn. The long 'white nights' had passed and soon, when October came, they'd be scuttling along against the wind and thinking about fires.

But not yet. For now the three young people could take their time, with Eva walking a little ahead of Letty and Hughie, and only occasionally glancing back and smiling to herself.

When they reached Number Twelve, however, Eva stopped to wait for her sister and called goodbye to Hughie, as did Letty. When they entered the small entrance hall together, Eva took her sister's arm.

'Hey,' she whispered, 'why've you never told me about Hughie Harper, then?'

'Told you what?' asked Letty, lowering her eyes.

'Well, just how often does he come into Crindle's for stationery? He must be the best equipped reporter going. And how often does he walk you home when I'm not there?'

'I dinna ken what you're talking about, Evie.' Letty hesitated. 'There's nothing between Hughie and me. I'm too old for him.'

'You're no such thing! You're twenty-two, he's twenty. What's two years?'

'I think he's only nineteen.'

'No, he's older than me. Stayed back a year at school, you ken, after he was away for so long with the rheumatic fever.'

'That's still two years, though.' Letty shook her head. 'Fellas niver like being younger than the lassies.'

'Hughie isn't "fellas", he's just Hughie, and he's sweet on you, Letty, anybody can see.'

'Well, I'm no' sure I want to get involved.' Letty moved towards their door. 'Let's go in, Evie, eh? If Ma finds us standing here, she'll

121

think we're daft.'

'She mightn't be back yet.'

But Bel was back and already frying sausages, while Frank read the evening paper and Roddie sharpened his pencils.

'Are you girls no' late?' Bel cried. 'Did Mr Crindle keep you, Letty?'

'She just had one last customer,' said Eva.

'Aye, just the one,' said Letty, taking off her hat.

Neither she nor Eva mentioned his name.

Twenty-One

Bel, now forty-one, looked tired that evening. A new vertical line between her dark brows and the shadows beneath her eyes made her look her age, even though she was her usual animated self as she dished up the meal and called the family to the table.

Her life is taking its toll, thought Eva sadly. Women at the mill did not age well. How could they? It was a place for the young and strong who could withstand the strain of the work and the surroundings. Yet older women had to keep on working; they had no other choice.

How soon would it be before Eva could offer Bel something more? When she had a good salary, surely she could help with the outgoings – the rent, the coal, the messages. Maybe Ma could move on to something easier? Finishing her sausages, Eva sighed. She knew too well, it would be years before that could happen.

'Everything all right, Eva?' asked her mother, who never missed a thing, especially not one of her children sighing over sausages.

'Oh, yes.' Eva smiled brightly. 'Just got to do some writing before I go out to a meeting.'

'A meeting? What meeting? Something to do with college?'

'No, it's at the Mercat Hall. Somebody from the union is talking about more help for the miners.' Eva hesitated. 'Bob Keir wants me to go.'

'Nan Keir's laddie?' Bel pursed her lips. 'She's an old misery, she is. You'd think nobody'd ever had to struggle 'cept her.'

'Did lose her man,' Frank put in. 'It's right enough that widows have to struggle.'

'Aye, but she gets her money's worth out of it. Forever on at her boys to do what they can for her, making 'em guilty if they spend a copper on themselves.'

'Never noticed Bob Keir looking guilty,' Roddie observed. 'He's too full of himself, eh?'

'Bob cares about helping people,' Eva said quietly. 'Nobody more so.'

'So, when do you see him then?' Bel asked. 'He's on that newspaper, eh? No' where you are.'

'We just meet accidentally sometimes.'

'Accidentally,' Letty repeated, sliding her eyes to Eva with a meaningful glance. 'Heard that before.'

'I'll clear the table.' Eva leaped up. 'Then I'll

get on. Roddie, I'll borrow your room.'

As she rushed away with the dishes, her family's eyes followed, then Frank returned to his chair and Bel herself sank down for a moment.

'We'll wash up,' Letty told Roddie. 'Come on, I'll wash, you can dry. Eva's busy.'

And as Roddie, for once, took up the tea towel, Bel never said a word.

An hour later, Eva's essay was done. Not entirely to her satisfaction – she liked her work to be the best she could achieve and this was hurried, which probably showed – but it would have to do. Already, it was almost eight o'clock, and she'd be late if she didn't leave now.

No need to dress up. She combed her hair and powdered her nose, pulled on her brown jacket and her hat, checked herself in Bel's mirror and made for the outer door.

'Bye everybody! I'm away.'

'Shall I come?' asked Roddie.

'You've your homework to do,' said Bel. 'But Letty could come with you, Eva.'

'No thanks!' Letty made a face. 'Meetings are no' for me. I'm going to wash ma hair.'

'Dinna be late back, then,' Bel told Eva. 'And if there's a collection, put a sixpence in from me, for the poor miners. Wait – I'll get ma purse.'

'Nae bother, Ma, I can spare something for us both,' said Eva, hoping she could, and ran.

When Eva arrived at the entrance to the Mercat Hall in the Nethergate, gasping after her run, a couple of ushers told her that the meeting had already started and there wasn't much room. She'd have to squeeze in where she could.

'That's all right,' said Bob Keir, suddenly appearing. 'I've saved this lady a seat.'

Taking Eva's arm in his usual masterful way, he guided her into the packed hall.

'Knew you'd come,' he whispered. 'Once you'd sorted the world out, eh?'

'I'll be quite happy to sit at the back,' she said hastily. 'Don't want to disturb folk.'

'That's all right, we are at the back,' he told her easily. 'I guessed you'd be late – in fact, you've missed the first speeches. Mr MacPhail's up now. But nae bother. You're here, and that's all that matters.'

As she slid into her seat next to him at the back of the hall, Eva thought only the fervent voice of the miners' representative filling the hall would keep Bob quiet.

Twenty-Two

Josh MacPhail, the union man, spoke well. He was a small, unsmiling figure on the platform, and his soft Scottish voice held his audience as though on strings, raising them up, letting them down, using all his power to enter their hearts, to seek their help.

Sympathy strikes hadn't worked. Let no one

think mining folk weren't grateful, but other people's sacrifices weren't going to make the employers give in. Only the miners' withdrawal of labour might do that – and so far it hadn't happened. Now the winter was coming, strike pay was running out, and the families were just about starving. What was needed was money. Cash. Something – anything – to feed the bairns and keep the fight going. He didn't like to ask, didn't like to stand before them, cap in hand, but what could he do?

There was silence when he sat down, then applause and emotional cheers, as the chairman of the meeting shook his hand and announced that tea and biscuits would now be served, followed by a retiring collection.

'Retiring collection,' muttered Bob, who'd been sitting very still. 'That'll no' go far. What's needed is big money. Subs from the jute barons, fellas like yon North, your ma's boss. They could keep the miners' bairns fed for months and never notice the difference, eh?'

'Some do give a lot to charity, Bob, to be fair. And Mr North paid for our bursaries.'

'Aye, but did he ever increase your ma's wages? OK, some of 'em care more than others. But there's a hell of a lot who just like giving things and putting their names on forms, eh? The miners'll no' get a look in. Know why?' Bob's tiger eyes were beginning to flame and his voice was rising. 'Because the mill owners are capitalists, that's why. Businessmen. Just the same as the pit-owners. They refuse to pay the workers a living wage. That's what we're up against, Eva.

That's why you've got to join us.'

'I just wish there was something we could do.'

'There's plenty we can do,' Bob began as a dark-haired young woman came moving through the lines of chairs, a cup of tea in her hand and a familiar look of scorn in her cold eyes.

Oh, no, thought Eva with sinking heart. *Berta Denny.*

Only she was no longer Berta Denny but Berta Loch, having married Arthur Loch, a jute sorter, some time before. Eva hadn't seen her for years and didn't want to see her now, but Berta was already eyeing Bob with interest and moving closer.

'Well, if it isnae the young lady teacher joinin' in with us ordinary folk, then! What a surprise, eh? And who's this handsome pal o' yours, Eva? No' a teacher, is he?'

'My name's Bob Keir,' Bob answered coldly. 'And I'm a reporter, if it's anything to do with you.'

Berta put out her hand and favoured him with a smile. 'Berta Loch,' she told him. 'And that's Missus. Of course Eva's friends are to do wi' me! She used to be a mill girl at North's, same as me, but mebbe she keeps that dark, now she's gone up in the world. Are you folk too grand to go get yoursels some tea, then? There's rock cakes as well as biscuits, if you hurry!'

'Will you excuse us?' asked Bob, taking Eva's arm again. 'I have to speak to Mr MacPhail. I'm reporting on this meeting.'

'And a verra good meeting it was, too!' Berta flashed, her smile suddenly vanishing. 'We're all

127

on the same side, eh? Why treat me like nobody, then? I'm givin' tae the miners same as you!'

'Of course you are,' Eva said hastily. 'And you're right; we're all on the same side.'

'Aye, it's good of you to contribute, Mrs Loch,' put in Bob. 'Every penny counts, you ken. Nice to meet you, then.'

'Yes, nice to see you, Berta,' Eva murmured and gladly allowed herself to be hauled away, while Berta stared after them, her brows drawn together, her expression dark.

'Phew, what a tartar, eh?' murmured Bob. 'How'd you get mixed up with her, Eva?'

'She told you. I was at the mill.'

'Aye, but you must've crossed her somehow. She seems to have got her knife into you.'

'All she's got against me is that I stayed on at school. But she doesn't like Ma, either. Doesn't like our sort.'

'I'd no' worry about her. Canna do you any harm.'

'No, I never see her.' Eva spoke confidently, but it was some time before she could forget the look in Berta's eyes as they rested on her, or stop wondering at the hostility she had fostered in the other woman's heart.

'Let's get some of that tea,' said Bob, when he'd completed his brief interview with Josh MacPhail. 'Think there are any rock cakes left?'

As it turned out there were no rock cakes, but there were plenty of shortbread biscuits and Bob ate several as they drank the strong tea served by the party faithful and looked about at the audience.

128

'Just like I said,' Bob muttered. 'There'll no' be much in the collection box from this lot. They canna afford spare coppers from the look of 'em, never mind real money.'

'They're the sort to give what they can, though.'

'Aye, but we need some proper fund-raising, eh? Sales and raffles and such. Somebody with a big name to give a benefit concert. Somebody to rattle tins under the jute barons' noses.'

'Better come down to earth, Bob.' Eva was looking in her purse. 'I've only got sixpence for Ma and the same for me to put in the box. I feel so bad.'

'Ah, come on, if everybody gave sixpence, we'd be well away.'

She looked up at him, smiling a little, and saw that the focus of his interest had subtly shifted, away from the troubles of the miners, and on to herself. Suddenly self-conscious, she said she would take their cups away.

'Och, leave them,' said Bob. 'Let's away.'

'The meeting's over?'

'Aye, you missed half of it, remember? Got your sixpences? Let's put something in the collection box and go. I'll walk you home.'

Twenty-Three

Strolling beside him, her arm once again in his, her feet tapping in time to his heavier tread, she felt uneasy. What was on his mind? If it was what she feared, she hoped he wouldn't tell her.

In fact, he surprised her. When they reached Wish Lane, he drew her to a halt beneath a street-light, and looked for a long moment into her face.

'You'll know me again,' she said lightly, trying not to show her nerves.

'I was thinking that you'd changed.'

'Changed?'

'Aye. Since you went on that teaching lark.'

'Teaching lark?' She laughed. 'That's not what we call it at the Training Centre. But what do you mean, I've changed?'

'Grown away. From Wish Lane.'

She frowned. 'That's not true, Bob. I'm still part of Wish Lane.'

'You wanted to get away, and you are getting away. I'm no' criticizing, just commenting. I mean, even your voice is changing these days. No' so Scots, never mind Dundee.'

'Why, you don't talk Dundee yourself, Bob! A lot of folk don't and we never did.'

'I'm just saying you'll soon be losing your

Scots, now you're on the teaching course. In no time, you'll be sounding like Miss Balfour.'

In the light from the lamp, Eva's eyes widened. 'Miss Balfour? I could never sound like her, Bob! Whatever are you thinking?'

'Ah, come on now!' He caught her hand. 'I've said I'm no' criticizing. It's the way they'll want you to talk as a teacher. Sure, you'll pick up the English, the way you learn about ethics or what-not on the course. And when you do all of that – well, you'll be bound to grow away from Wish Lane.'

'I've not grown away from home,' she said quietly. 'I'd never do that – however I talk.'

'That's good, Eva, that's good. And you'll never stop wanting the same as me?'

'I still want what you want, Bob. Changes in ordinary people's lives. I said so today. Thing is, I don't know how to make the changes happen.'

'Join us. Join the party.'

'That wouldn't be enough. It's Ma I want to help, and all the workers in the mills. Girls like Letty. She's well now, but there's plenty still sick. But what can I do? I don't work at the mill; I'm not in the union.' She gave a wry smile. 'Berta is. She's a leading light. She could end up doing more for Ma than me.'

'I know her kind. Enjoys marching around and throwing bricks at mill-owners' houses. Does no good at all.' They began to walk on, arm in arm again, until they reached Number Twelve. 'No, Eva, it's your kind that'll achieve something,' Bob murmured. 'No need to worry – you'll get there in the end, just like I will. But I've got ma

131

way mapped out already, starting with the local elections.'

'You're going to stand?'

'I am. Soon as I'm of age. Will you vote for me?'

'If I had a vote. I hope you're not thinking I qualify for the thirty-year-olds' vote?'

He laughed. 'Never! But they say all women will be voting soon.'

'And I should think so, too. Why should you men have a vote at twenty-one and not women?'

'That's the old fiery Eva speaking, eh? Remember how we used to be rivals, back in Miss Balfour's class?'

'We were all rivals then.'

'All us big heads.'

'You were the big head, Bob. Still are.'

'Need to be. What I was going to say ... we're friends now, eh?'

'We're friends.'

'So, we can see each other sometimes? No' just at meetings?'

'Well...'

'Well, what?'

'It's just that there's so much to do on the course, I never get much time to spare.'

'Everybody gets some time off. I'm no' suggesting much.'

'All right, then. Yes, I'd like to see you, Bob.'

'That's grand,' he said easily. 'We can just have a bite to eat together some time. Or maybe go to the pictures. What d'you think?'

'As long as we can go at weekends. I have to work in the evenings.'

'Me too. Weekends and all, but I'll do ma best.'

They studied each other's faces for a moment, then Eva said she'd better go in. 'Thanks for saving me a seat at the meeting.'

'Nae bother. I'll be in touch, then.'

'Aye, I'll look forward to it.'

'Do you no' mean, "Yes"?' he called with his old cheeky grin.

'Oh stop it, Bob!' She shook her head at him, but managed a smile before disappearing into the house and closing the door, after which, without waiting, he walked smartly away.

Bel was still up – and Letty, who couldn't go to bed anyway until Eva came in – but Frank and Roddie were away to their partitioned room and there were just three cups on the kitchen table.

'Got the kettle on,' said Bel, rising tiredly. 'How was the meeting, then?'

'Fine. Sad, though, hearing about the miners.' Eva pulled off her hat and unbuttoned her jacket. 'I put your sixpence in the collection, Ma.'

'I'll let you have it, then.'

'Nae bother. But listen, guess who I saw there? Berta Denny! I mean, Berta Loch.'

'Wouldnae be a show without her,' muttered Bel. 'What was she up to, then?'

'Wanting to be introduced to Bob Keir.'

'Always wants to be introduced to anything in trousers.'

'I'd never want to see Berta again!' cried Letty as she made the tea. 'But you're late, eh, Evie? Was it Bob kept you, ranting on about this and

133

that?'

Eva sat down at the table and began to drink her tea. 'Know what he said? I'd soon stop talking Scots, never mind Dundee.'

Bel's weary eyes opened wide. 'He said that? What a cheek! We dinna talk Dundee, anyway. No' what I'd call Dundee.'

'I told him that, but he thinks I'll end up talking like Miss Balfour.' Eva turned her gaze on her sister. 'Is that no' a piece of nonsense?'

'Well...' Letty hesitated.

'Well, what?'

'Well, it's true; you do sound a wee bit like a teacher sometimes.'

'Eva's going to be a teacher,' said Bel. 'She ought to sound like one. And teachers dinna really speak like us, eh?'

Eva studied the tealeaves in her cup, then raised her eyes to her mother's. 'I suppose you're right, but I never thought I'd end up sounding different.'

'No need to worry about it.' Bel stood up, yawning. 'I'm away down the landing, and then to ma bed.'

When she had left them, Letty said quietly, 'Ma is right, Eva. If you're going to be a teacher, you should sound like one.'

'Should I?' Eva put their cups in the sink. 'All I know is I'm all at sea. Bob says I've always wanted to get away from Wish Lane and I have, but now I feel bad about it, as though it's wrong to feel that way.'

'Ah, you're no' thinking straight.' Letty put her arms around Eva's shoulders. 'Plenty folk have wanted to get out o' Wish Lane and places like it, eh? It's what they dream about, to get something better. I'm sure Roddie does.'

'Think so?'

'Aye. And it's what Ma wants for him – and you.' Letty smiled. 'No' me. All she wants for me is a wedding ring.'

Eva's expression lightened. 'Might come, Letty. Might come. And soon.'

But Letty refused to be drawn on the subject of Hughie Harper, and when their mother came back, the sisters kissed her goodnight and began to get ready for bed.

Twenty-Four

Two weeks passed before Eva heard from Bob again, but before that, Hughie Harper had taken the plunge and asked Letty to go to the pictures. She couldn't believe it and kept asking Eva if she should go, although, of course, she'd already said yes.

'Why ever not?' asked Eva. 'He wouldn't have asked you if he hadn't wanted you to go.'

'Aye, but...'

'But what?' Eva groaned. 'Och, you're not still worrying over those two years, Letty? I tell you, they're nothing!'

'So you say.' Letty studied her face in the mirror in their mother's share of the bedroom.

'Think I look all right?'

'Lovely.' Eva laughed. 'And scarcely a day over twenty!'

'No need to tease, you ken.'

'Well, you just stop making trouble for yourself and have a good time.'

'Will you lend me that scarf you got for Christmas, then? It'd go with ma coat.'

'Take anything you like. And put on a wee bit of lipstick, eh? You're very pale.'

'I feel pale. I'm that nervous.'

But when Hughie came to call for her the following evening, Letty was so flushed and excited she needed no make-up, and as Bel said when she'd left, fluttering like a bough in the wind, she could've been seventeen.

'Does ma heart good, to see the way she looks now,' Bel murmured, settling down under the light at the table with a basket of darning. 'When you think how she used to be, eh?'

'We got her away from the mill in time, Ma.'

'No more burnt fingers,' her mother said, shutting one eye and attempting to put wool through a needle. 'Och, this light's no good, eh? Or is it my eyesight? Think I'll have to get a pair o' reading glasses. They say you can get 'em at Woolworth's. You just read the card and they tell you what to buy. Shouldnae cost much at Woolies, eh?'

'Here, I'll do it for you.' Eva threaded the darning needle and handed it to her mother, adding in a low voice, 'And I know what you mean about the burnt fingers.'

Everyone in the family – as well as a number
136

of neighbours, in fact – knew about Letty's burnt fingers and the snobby travelling typewriter salesman who'd been responsible. What a rat he was. Came into Crindle's, took her out for weeks on end, made her feel wonderful and then, when she brought him home, never asked her out again.

'Och, we weren't good enough, o' course,' said Bel, weaving her needle in and out over a hole in one of Roddie's socks. 'As though he was that grand himself! I took against him from the minute Letty brought him in. All smooth talk and soft soap, and his eyes going over all we'd got and deciding it wasnae much. Poor lassie, she never saw him again. He found somewhere else to peddle his typewriters, and good riddance to bad rubbish, I say.'

'Me too. But there won't be the same trouble with Hughie, Ma. He knows how we live, all right.'

'Aye, but he's got problems of his own.' Bel finished darning and turned Roddie's sock right side out, to check her handiwork. 'Always a sickly laddie he was, you ken, and his dad died with the consumption. Will he be the right one for Letty, with all she's been through?'

'He's looking a lot better now than he ever did at school. I think he'll be fine for Letty.'

'Funny little mother he's got,' Bel went on, scarcely listening. 'Now, she's no' so fit herself, you ken. Worked at Berry's Mill for a bit, but gave it up and took in sewing to make ends meet. There's never been much money to spare in that house, I'd say, but that's nothing against Hughie.

All I want is for him to care for Letty – if she cares for him.'

'Ma, you should see the way he looks at her, you'd have no more worries!' Evie threaded Bel's needle again. 'And I think he's going to do well. I've been reading his pieces in the *Dundee Key*, and they're good. Really snappy and witty'.

'Better than Bob Keir's?' asked Bel, with a sideways glance at Eva.

'Different. Bob's writing is like him. Swings a big hammer. But those two laddies are both clever, I'd say.' Eva moved to the door of the bedroom. 'I'd better get on, Ma. Got work to do.'

'Aye, you need to get that done. It's important.' Bel hesitated. 'I mean, for you to do well.'

'No need to tell me!'

'So, will you be seeing Bob Keir again, then?'

'I might.' Eva swung the handle of the bedroom door.

'But you'll no' want to be distracted, though.'

'I won't be letting Bob Keir distract me,' Eva said firmly.

When Letty came back, looking just as flushed and just as young as when she went out, the whole family was at home and four pairs of eyes immediately locked on to her radiant face. They had been to La Scala picture theatre in Murraygate, and had had a wonderful time.

'What was on, then?' asked Frank.

Letty stood with her finger to her lip, while Eva hid a smile. Don't say she couldn't even remember what she'd seen! But her sister was making a valiant effort not to let anyone believe that.

138

'There was one long sad thing – think it had somebody famous in it...'

'Oh, that tells us a lot!' cried Roddie, laughing.

'Well, I didnae ken who she was and we missed the beginning,' Letty retorted. 'But then there were some short things, with comedians, now, what were their names? Och, I canna think, but they were just fooling around, the way thae fellas do.'

'You enjoyed it, anyway?' asked Bel.

'Oh, I did.' Letty took off her coat and hat and unwound Eva's scarf. 'It was grand. We had an ice cream as well.'

'Lucky you.' Roddie gave a theatrical sigh. 'Hughie did you pretty well, eh?'

Letty sank into a chair and looked around with some embarrassment at the watching faces. 'Why's everybody looking at me, then?'

'We're no' looking at you,' said Bel, rising. 'But I'm just thinking, it's nice you're no' too late home. That laddie's got some sense, eh?'

Letty made no reply, only sat fingering Eva's scarf and smiling to herself, probably thinking, Eva guessed, that Hughie Harper had a lot more going for him than sense.

Later, when the sisters were alone and preparing for bed, Eva said in a whisper, 'You were really happy with Hughie then, Letty?'

'Oh, Evie!' Letty's sigh was as extravagant as Roddie's. 'I was. I felt – I dinna ken – completely at ease. As though things were just right between us.'

'That's grand, Letty, that's how it should be. So they tell me.'

Letty, now in her nightdress and brushing her hair, smiled. 'Are you saying I know more than you, Evie? But you've been out with fellas, eh?'

'None that made me feel things were just right.'

'How about Bob Keir?'

'Folk keep asking me about Bob Keir. He's just a friend. No, I mean it. Anyway, I don't want to find the right person yet. Not for years, in fact, because I'd have to give up work.' Eva folded her clothes and put them on a chair. 'The last thing I want is to get married. I'm different from you, Letty.'

'It's a wee bit early to talk about marriage for me. Shall we put the light out now?'

'Are you going to see Hughie again?' Eva whispered into the darkness.

'Next week,' Letty whispered back. 'It's the first time he can make it, since he's to work at the paper most evenings.'

'I bet he'll soon be saving up for that ring we were talking about.'

'He hasnae much money. I'd no' be expecting a ring.' Letty laughed quietly. 'I mean, if we got that far.'

'Letty, you're on your way,' said Eva.

Two days later, Bob Keir was at the entrance to the Training Centre as Eva and Katie were leaving for their lunch break. It was October and no longer warm enough to sit outside. They were thinking of going for coffee and rolls at a cheap little café in Commercial Street. Now here was Bob, standing with his large figure blocking their

140

way, and perhaps expecting to be included in their plans. But he made it clear he only wanted a word with Eva.

'Got some complimentary tickets for the variety show at the King's,' he said in a low voice as he drew her away from Katie. 'Saturday night. Can you make it?'

'Well, I...' she began, but his hand closed over hers.

'Sure, you can. I'll come to Wish Lane at seven o'clock. Starts at seven thirty. That suit?' He hardly waited for an answer, but walked away, waving his hand, smiling briefly at Katie. 'Saturday night!' he shouted from a distance, and was gone.

Eva, feeling Katie's brown eyes cold upon her, gave a shrug. 'That's Bob Keir for you, eh? Thinks what he says goes.'

'Obviously does, for you,' Katie remarked.

'Only if I want it to. I did say I'd see him sometimes.'

'Very dangerous, if you ask me.'

Eva stared. 'Whatever do you mean?'

'Well, things can snowball, you know. Before you know it, you'll be involved. And we're not supposed to be involved with young men, are we?'

'Who's involved? I don't want to be involved. He knows that.' Eva buttoned up her jacket and began to walk on. 'He feels the same.'

'I wonder,' said Katie.

Twenty-Five

Snowball. That was the word to come back into Eva's mind when she met Bob Keir on Saturday night.

Oh, but look at Bob, standing on the theatre steps! So tall and solid in a thin overcoat and trilby hat, his gloveless hands holding their tickets, his face breaking into a smile as she joined him, but not exactly radiant. Didn't look like a man looking for love.

I am right, thought Eva, relieved again. *There is no danger of involvement.* Bob was too sensible for that, and as she'd already decided, too young and too set on his career to want to settle down. And as the same was true of her, she could afford to forget Katie's warnings, her mother's too, and just enjoy an evening out with a friend. After all, complimentary tickets were not to be turned down, even if a variety programme was not her favourite entertainment.

Bob, however, was someone who was prepared to throw himself into the spirit of the show, loudly applauding the magician, the ventriloquist, the dancers, the comics, and even the wobbly soprano and overweight tenor, while Eva kept giving him sideways glances and smiling at his pleasure.

'Good programme, eh?' he asked in the interval, when they had ices. 'And good seats, as well. Especially as we didnae have to pay for 'em.'

'Do you often get things given to you at the paper?' Eva asked.

'Only now and again. We're only small, you ken, and the wrong politics for some. But one of our lads took a front-of-house job at the Royal and he sent a few tickets round.' Bob finished his ice and took out a packet of Woodbines. 'To tell you the truth, ticket sales have been low. Folk are feeling the pinch, one way and another.'

'That's true most of the time in Dundee.'

'Worse at the moment.' He offered a cigarette but she shook her head. 'I think we're on our way to a slump.'

'Oh, don't say it, Bob!'

'Aye. I thought we'd be OK when we got a Labour prime minister, but look what happened! Ramsay MacDonald didnae last five minutes and now we've got the Tories back.' Bob lit his Woodbine and shook his head. 'No hope for the miners and no' much for us. You should join the party, Eva, I keep telling you; we need all the help we can get.'

'I have to qualify before I do anything else,' she told him firmly. 'That should be next year, but then I've my probationary time.' Her dark eyes grew large as she looked into the future. 'By the time I get the parchment – that's the Teaching Certificate – it'll be 1929. Bob, can you believe it? I'll be twenty-two!'

'Wonder where I'll be then?'

'You want to move on, Bob?'

143

'One day, maybe. But I'm happy enough where I am just now.'

'And Hughie too, I suppose?'

'Oh, sure. He's found what he wants to do, and he's good at it, too.'

'Did you know he'd taken Letty to the pictures?' Eva asked after a pause.

'No!' A great grin creased Bob's face. 'The sly devil then! Since when's he been sweet on Letty?'

'I think he's been looking out for her at Crindle's for some time.'

'Very pretty girl, your sister. And thank God, she's so well.'

'Amen to that,' said Eva, half expecting a compliment to come her own way and hoping it wouldn't. But Bob only rose to his feet. 'There's the bell; we'd better go back.'

When they came out of the theatre, a stiff breeze was sending dry leaves scraping down the pavements, but at least it was a fine night. They could walk back to Wish Lane instead of running against the rain.

'That was lovely, Bob,' Eva told him. 'I really enjoyed it. But you needn't take me home, you know – it's out of your way.'

'Of course I'm taking you home.' With his usual commanding style, he tucked her hand into his arm. 'As though I'd let you go back on your own!'

'Modern girls don't need to be treated like porcelain. We can look after ourselves.'

'Look, you lassies may be cutting your hair

and trying to look like men these days, but the fact is you're not men.' Bob smiled and pressed Eva's hand. 'Mind, I'm no' complaining.'

'You think I look like a man?' she asked, rather nettled at the idea.

'No,' he said softly. 'You're nothing at all like a man. And I'm still no' complaining.'

At his tone, she felt a small thrill of unease and, without looking at him, took her hand from his arm and began to fuss about putting on her gloves.

'Better hurry, Ma doesn't like us to be too late.'

Whichever way they took back to Wish Lane, they came to mills. Mills squeezed in wherever a suitable space could be found. Mills of all sizes, some several storeys high with weaving sheds attached, some quite low. All with chimneys and gates and rows and rows of windows, which were, at this time of the evening, dark. So many mills. As she and Bob walked by, Eva's spirits sank, but then they always did in the neighbourhood of the mills. And Bob's sudden change from stalwart friend to flirting man had depressed her anyway. If he asked her out again, she decided, she would not go.

'You're very quiet,' he murmured, taking her arm again. 'Mills depressing you?'

'Depressing places, aren't they?'

'Well, they're work places. Women are glad of thae mills.'

'That doesn't mean they should be paid low wages and risk their health.'

'Eva, you're preaching to the converted. I know conditions have to be improved. I'm only saying that at least the jobs are there.'

'Sorry, Bob. I know you understand.'

He smiled in the darkness. 'You and me always understand each other. That's why I like to be with you, and hope you feel the same about me.' When she made no reply, he stood still, and so did she. 'You do feel the same, Eva? You want to see me again?'

'I don't think there's much point, Bob. You said once you'd your way mapped out. Well, mine's mapped out, too.'

'I never said my way didnae include being with friends.'

'I just want to concentrate on my studies.'

For some time he stood still, looking at her with a long sombre gaze she did not return.

'I'm thinking you've got this wrong,' he said at last. 'I'm no' trying to take you away from your studies. I'm all for women having careers, especially clever lassies like you, and I ken fine you'd be wasted as a housewife. All I want is for us to meet sometimes, go to the pictures, have a meal, talk about the things that matter.' He raised his hands and let them fall. 'But if that doesnae suit, OK, we'll say goodbye.'

Suddenly she was contrite, not wanting to hurt, and at the same time, feeling relieved. He wasn't expecting too much. 'Bob, I never meant...'

'No need to say what you meant. You've made it pretty plain.' He began to walk away from her. 'Come on then, let's get you home.'

'Bob!' She ran after him. 'I've said I'm sorry. Don't be angry.'

'Who's angry? You've a right to say how you

want to spend your time.'

'I'd like to see you again – honestly, I would. Let's no' part like this.'

'Here's your street, Eva. It's late. Your Ma'll be looking out for you.'

At her door, they both stopped again, and Eva, her shoulders hunched, moved to open it when Bob put his hand on her arm.

'Eva?'

'Yes, Bob?'

'You'd really like to come out with me again?'

'I've said so.'

'Well, if we understand each other now, shall I get in touch again?'

'I want you to.'

For some moments, they gazed into each other's faces, then Eva stretched up and kissed Bob's cheek.

'Goodnight, Bob.'

'Goodnight, Eva. And no need to worry – I'll no' misunderstand that.' He grinned. 'Very nice, though.'

Twenty-Six

While Bel and Katie watched disapprovingly from the sidelines, Eva did meet Bob from time to time and, now that her mind had been set at rest, was happy about it. Work on the course continued to be hard, even gruelling, and to snatch a few hours away with someone like Bob gave her the relaxation she needed. Only Katie among her colleagues knew about him, and Katie, whatever her views, would be too loyal to speak of him to others.

Letty, of course, was delighted that Eva had a 'young man', in spite of Eva's patient denials that he was not her young man in the sense that Letty meant, and never would be.

'Aye, maybe,' said Letty, 'but I think it's nice that you've somebody to go out with, whatever you say.'

'And then it gives Ma something else to think about, apart from you and Hughie,' Eva commented shrewdly, and Letty's smiles faded.

'I dinna ken what she's got against Hughie, Eva. I thought she'd be pleased about him.'

'She is pleased and she likes him, too. It's just that he looks so thin, you see.'

'Slim, no' thin.'

'Slim, then. She's worried in case he's unwell.'

'He's quite well. Quite strong, whatever he looks like. Just because his dad died o' consumption doesnae mean he will.'

''Course not.'

'And whatever happens, I'm no' giving him up. It's for me to choose the man I marry, no' Ma.'

'I tell you, she likes Hughie,' said Eva, marvelling at Letty's strength of mind these days. 'I'm wondering how Mavis is,' she said suddenly, being reminded of poor Mavis Craik's health by thoughts of her sister's. 'Must ask Ma.'

'Never said lately.'

'D'you think we should go round and see her? I mean, at home. I don't fancy going to the mill.'

'Oh, no!' Letty pretended to shudder. 'Might see Berta!'

They agreed to call on Mavis very soon, for they already felt guilty over not calling before, but on a cold, rainy night in November, when Eva met Bob, a different guilt settled over her.

The news was that the miners' strike had collapsed. Nobody could save them from a humiliating return to work for less money than they'd had before, and somehow Eva, like so many others, felt that she should have done more.

'Now what could you have done?' asked Bob, as they stood together in the High Street, rain dripping from his cap and her umbrella. 'You're no' a pit owner. You're no' in the government.'

'I know, but I just feel that we should've been able to help – do something.' She shook her head. 'Sounds silly, eh?'

'Sounds like other folk I've heard. But nobody could do anything. The miners had to feed their bairns. It was as simple as that.' He heaved a long, deep sigh. 'But the bitterness will last, Eva. You'll see. It'll go down the years and put back all that's been done for better conditions. The bosses hold the cards. The workers never get to play.'

They'd planned to have one of their cheap meals at a small café nearby, but hadn't the heart for it and just went walking in the rain. Until Bob groaned and said he could do with a drink.

'I suppose we could go to a pub?' Eva asked doubtfully.

'Are you joking? Your folks'd kill me if I took you to a pub.' Bob stood in thought. 'Tell you what – we could go to a hotel. Get a drink in one of the bars where women can go. What d'you say?'

'Now it's you who's joking, Bob. How can we afford to go to a hotel?'

'Ah, to hell with it! I feel like spending what I've got tonight. Come on.'

Twenty-Seven

Entering the cocktail lounge of the Post Hotel in the Nethergate, they felt they were in a different world from the rain-swept streets they'd left, one whose concerns were very different from theirs, whose people were very different from them.

'Nae bother,' muttered Bob. 'We can sit down here and have a drink and not give a damn. I meet folk like this lot all the time and believe me, they're no better than anybody else, they just think they are.'

'I only hope there's nobody from the Training Centre here, or I'll be in trouble,' Eva murmured, keeping her head down but managing to look around at the same time.

'Of course they'll no' be here! This is a toffs' meeting place, especially young toffs.' Bob gave a bitter laugh. 'All the little jute barons and baronesses, eh? Spending Papa's money. Look at

150

'em all, nattering away!'

'Shouldn't we order something to drink?'

'Aye, what'll you have?'

She laughed and blushed. 'I've no idea. Not used to drinking.'

'A sherry, then. And I'll have a whisky.'

When a long-faced waiter had brought their drinks and a small dish of salted nuts, they sat back, appreciating, in spite of themselves, the warmth and comfort of their surroundings. Eva, though still consumed with guilt, couldn't help eyeing the clothes of the women, wondering how much they'd cost and whether she'd dare to tell them at home all she'd seen. Better not. Letty would be fascinated, but Bob had been right, her folks would not be too pleased to think of her drinking with him, whether in a pub or a good hotel.

As they sat, making their drinks last, more and more young people came crowding into the lounge, shaking rain drops from their hair, greeting friends with cries and laughs and even little shrieks, and lighting cigarettes before they'd even ordered drinks, so that the air was thick with smoke.

'Come on, that's enough,' muttered Bob. 'Let's away to the café and have something to eat. You ready?'

'Oh, yes,' Eva answered, but she was making no move. Her eyes were fixed on the distance, her lips a little parted, and Bob, after glancing at her for a moment, followed her gaze.

'You know somebody over there, Eva?'

'No. Who would I know?'

'You seemed to be recognizing somebody.'

'Well, that young man with the fair hair – I think I've seen him before, that's all.'

Bob narrowed his eyes. 'The one next to the girl with the fur? I can tell you who he is, if you like.'

'Oh?'

'That's Nick North. I've seen him around at things I've had to report. You've probably seen him at North's Mill, seeing as his dad owns it.'

'He never comes to the mill.'

'You do know him then?'

'I saw him as a boy.'

'He's no' a boy now.'

No, he wasn't a boy now. A tall, handsome young man, that's what he was, and one with an air that spelled 'Privileged' as clearly as though written in large letters on the back of his well cut jacket.

From where she was sitting, Eva could only see his profile and the shape of his blond head, and though scarcely aware of the way her thoughts were taking her, was longing with all her heart for him to turn round so that she might see the grey eyes she'd almost forgotten. Almost. Perhaps she had never really forgotten Nicholas North. Perhaps he'd always remained, held securely in the back of her mind, with only one look needed from those grey eyes to bring him to the fore again.

But he never turned round. Just kept on looking into the faces of those near him. The girl he was with looked a little younger than Nicholas, and not unlike him. Was she, perhaps, his sister?

Privilege oozed from her, in the way she held herself, her coat with its flattering fur sliding from her shoulders, and the way she drew on a cigarette in a long holder and looked coolly about her, from beneath her cloche hat, as though no one present was of any interest at all. Not even Nicholas.

'Bob, let's go to the café,' Eva said decisively and stood up, now hoping perversely that Nicholas North would not turn round. She didn't really want to know if he would recognize her again.

'Had enough of the idle rich?' asked Bob.

'Quite enough.'

'Well, it'll be good to have something at the café. Get rid of the smell of the sherry, before your Ma smells it.'

It seemed to Eva, as they ate their pies and peas in the café, that Bob's eyes were lingering on her rather more than usual.

'You certainly took your time looking at young Nick North,' he remarked at last. 'Are you sure you didnae know him?'

'Young Nick!' she repeated. 'I'm sure he's older than you, Bob.'

'So you did know him?'

'I said I'd seen him as a boy. He came to our school once – that time his father told us about the bursaries.'

'Funny thing, I never saw him.'

'He was waiting in the car.'

'And you've always remembered that?'

Eva put down her knife and fork. 'What are all these questions? We've got other things to think

153

about, apart from Mr North's son.'

'You're right. We've wasted enough time on folk who dinna matter.' Bob leaned forward. 'Now, why do you no' think about joining the party, Eva? This is the time to show your loyalty and where you stand. How about it?'

'All right, I will.' As he began to smile and tried to take her hand across the table, she shook her head. 'I'll only pay the sub, though. I won't be an active member till I finish my course. You do understand?'

'Aye.' He continued to smile. 'That's fine – as long as you sign up.'

'About the course,' she said hesitantly. 'I've a stack of work to get through before Christmas, and teaching practice as well. You won't mind if we don't meet for a while?'

His face fell. 'How long's a while?'

'Well, until after Hogmanay, maybe.'

'And then you'll be thinking the end's in sight and you've got even less time to see me. Am I being given the brush off, Eva?'

'No, it's not like that at all. But you see how I'm placed? It's vital for me to pass; everything I've done would be wasted if I failed.'

'Aye, I understand.' He sat back, his face sinking into lines of weariness, and ran a hand over his brow. 'Nae bother, Eva. You do what you have to. But we can surely meet over the holiday? See the New Year in?'

'Yes,' she agreed. 'Let's do that.'

Later, when they reached her front door, unusually, they exchanged kisses. Nothing roman-

154

tic, just brief embraces, lips touching cheeks, for both were subdued and in need of a little contact.

'You're all right,' Bob whispered. 'No smell of sherry. You didnae have much, anyway. Better no' mention it, though.'

'They'll all be talking about the miners, I expect.'

'Aye, poor devils. The interest will be on them.'

In the light of the street lamp he gave her a long, considering look, and she began to wonder if he would have liked to say something else.

'Don't dream of Nicholas North,' for instance?

She did, though. Or at least, she thought about him before sleep came, and then dreamed such silly stuff, she couldn't remember it when morning came. For a day or two his presence lingered in her mind, but then the pressure of work grew, and gradually he returned to the back of her mind.

Twenty-Eight

A few days before Christmas, Eva and Letty finally managed to visit Mavis Craik. They felt bad about not calling before, though it was true that Eva had been away to Lochee for teaching practice most days in December and what free time Letty had seemed to be taken up by Hughie. Still, they should have found a way to call earlier and promised themselves they'd do better in the New Year.

Bel was able to provide things to take, for she, unlike many Scots, liked to celebrate Christmas, and always saved up to buy the fruit for mincemeat and the puddings she boiled in the washcopper in the basement. A spare pudding was therefore found for Mrs Craik, and a batch of mince pies was wrapped up straight from the oven, before the sisters set off one evening.

'There you are, girls,' said Bel, packing a carrier bag. 'I think these'll be welcome, though I say so maself. Dinna forget to remember me to Mrs Craik and give ma best to poor Mavis. She's no' been in to work for some time. Just comes when she can.'

'We've got some lavender water for Mavis,' said Letty with a sigh and a look of apprehension, wondering what state Mavis would be in when they saw her.

Mavis's widowed mother, Mrs Craik, opened the door to them when they arrived at her ground-floor rooms in a Blackness tenement. She was a thin little woman with faded fair hair and reddened blue eyes; very like Mavis in her diffident manner, and just as sweet-natured, anyone could tell.

'Oh, what a lovely surprise to see you!' she cried. 'Mavis'll be thrilled!

From the communal passage lined with oil cloth, she showed them into the little living room where Mavis was lying on a single bed in the corner. Everything was very clean and tidy, the stove black-leaded, the table without crumbs, the chairs in place, and there was even a vase of small chrysanthemums at the window.

'She's no' so good today, you ken,' Mrs Craik whispered as their eyes went to Mavis. 'Just has to take each day as it comes.'

'Ma, I can tell them how I am!' Mavis, her voice a thread, was beginning to struggle up against her pillow. 'Eva – Letty – oh, it's grand to see you!'

They asked her how she was and said how lovely it was to see her too, but as they took the chairs Mrs Craik pushed forward, they fell silent, stunned by Mavis's looks.

She was so pale, and her face so small. Like an elderly woman's, in fact, the cheekbones prominent under stretched, shining skin, the eyes smudged with shadows. Every breath was a wheeze, and she held her hand to her chest, but somehow she managed to smile and shake her fair head.

'Dinna look ... so scared. I'm ... no' always ... as bad as this.'

'Sometimes she gets in to work,' Mrs Craik murmured as she helped her daughter to sit up and put a shawl around her shoulders. 'They're very good – niver mind when she comes, or doesnae come – and she likes to do what she can.'

'Very good?' Eva repeated. She took Mavis's thin hand. 'Would you say that, Mavis?'

'Well ... I ken it's the mill that got me ... like this. But it's no' the same for everybody, you ken.'

157

'There's talk o' plans to clear the dust,' put in Mrs Craik. 'I expect one day they'll do it, and that'll be an end to folk getting bad, eh?'

But not in time for Mavis, Eva thought, glancing at Letty, who was reminded to take out the things they had brought.

'Lavender water!' Mavis exclaimed, coughing. 'Oh ... that's so ... refreshing!'

'And one o' your ma's plum puddings!' cried her mother. 'And mince pies an' all! Oh, that's so kind, that is. Mavis, is that no' good o' Mrs Masson, then? Think you could eat a mince pie, pet?' In one of her asides, she added, 'Niver has much of an appetite, you ken. But I've got the kettle on the boil. I'll make us all a nice cup o' tea.'

Over the tea, the sisters, who had refused mince pies but accepted ginger biscuits, talked of what they were doing – of Letty's work at Mr Crindle's, of Eva's studies at the Teachers' Training Centre – while Mavis, who now appeared too weary to talk, gazed at them with admiring eyes.

'You lassies have done well away from the mill,' Mrs Craik said thoughtfully. 'Maybe if Mavis...' She stopped and jumped up to pour more tea. 'No point in looking back, eh?' Her voice trembled a little. 'What's done is done.'

If only I'd worked harder to persuade Mavis to move on, thought Eva, her heart so heavy it seemed a physical burden. As her tragic eyes met the sick girl's, Mavis stretched out her hand.

'I was the one ... who ... wouldnae go,' she gasped. 'Nobody's to blame ... but me.'

Before they left, Mavis's married sister, Freda,

158

came down from her flat up the stair and smiled a greeting before asking her mother if there was anything she could do. To look at her was to see Mavis as she might have been, for Freda was blonde and bonny, and had never had a cough in her life. But then she'd never worked in a mill.

'Grand help, Freda is,' Mrs Craik told the sisters. 'Always looks in on Mavis when I'm away doing ma bit o' cleaning for Mrs Mac-Gregor.'

'Aye, but I'm lucky, see, with ma man in work,' said Freda, plumping Mavis's pillow. 'Earns good money and all, so I stay at home with the bairns. It's nae bother to help Ma.'

'We'll come again soon,' Eva whispered, bending over Mavis. 'Maybe Hogmanay?'

'Aye, we'll wish you all the best for 1927,' said Letty. 'Hope it'll be a better year than this one, anyway.'

Mavis only smiled and nodded, and after making their farewells to Freda, Mrs Craik took the sisters to the door.

'It's done her good, you coming,' she told them. 'Cheered her up, I can tell.'

'Mrs Craik, can't the doctors do anything for her?' Eva asked earnestly. 'I mean, in the hospital?'

'Oh, she goes in, comes oot – they canna cure her. It's like I say, we take it one day at a time.'

'Well, we'll come again soon,' Eva said after a pause, and when Mrs Craik had hugged them both and closed the door, the sisters stood together in the December darkness before finding the will to move away.

'That could've been me,' Letty said in a small, choked voice. 'Lying there.'

'Better no' to think of it.'

'I was lucky. Why should some be lucky and some not, Evie?'

'Ma would say it's the way of the world.'

'No, you made it happen, you and Ma. Got me to apply for Crindle's. That was ma rescue. We should've rescued Mavis.'

Too unhappy to speak of it, Eva only muttered that they should hurry home; the wind was like a knife.

'But we'll definitely go back to see Mavis at Hogmanay, Evie? Whatever else happens?'

'Why, what should happen, then?'

Letty pulled down her hat and shivered in the wind. 'Hughie and me are thinking o' getting engaged.'

'Letty! Why, that's wonderful!' Eva threw her arms around her sister. 'But why'd you never say? Why'd you never tell me before?'

'Wanted to wait till it was sure. Havenae told Ma and Dad yet.'

'They'll be glad. Happy for you. I am.'

'As long as Ma doesnae go on about Hughie's health.'

'No, she'll be happy, I tell you. This is the first good news we've had for ages.'

'But I canna stop thinking about Mavis,' Letty said, her voice so low in the wind, Eva could scarcely hear her. 'We'll go back at Hogmanay, Letty. That's a promise.'

They kept their promise and did return on New

Year's Eve, when they found Mavis rather better; able to sit in a chair and taste Bel's Christmas cake, drink a wee toast, not just to the New Year, but to Letty's future happiness. It had done their hearts good to see her so pleased, so animated, over the news that all the parents had given their blessing and that Letty and Hughie were engaged.

'Am I really one o' the first to know?' she had asked, her eyes sparkling. 'This'll make me get well, eh? To dance at your wedding, Letty.'

They knew there would be no dancing for her, but surely her little recovery was a good omen. A good omen for them all, in 1927. As they returned to Wish Lane, where Bob and Hughie were to first-foot and join the family party, Eva and Letty thought it might be.

But only a week later news came to the mill that Mavis was dead.

'How?' cried Eva stormily. 'She was feeling better. How could she die?'

'Seemingly her heart had grown tired,' Bel said soothingly. 'She'd struggled for so long, the strain was too much, and one night she just ... slipped away.'

'It's for the best,' Frank murmured as his two girls wept. 'She couldnae get better, you ken. Best no' to suffer any more.'

'She shouldn't have had to suffer in the first place,' said Eva, but her anger had died. Later, when she was with Bob, it would no doubt return, and they would talk of what they might do in the future to set their world to rights. But for now, she needed to grieve.

Twenty-Nine

The funeral had been arranged for a Saturday afternoon so that the mill folk could attend, and when the day came the Massons took their time getting ready. Bel was wearing her black shawl and a large black hat over the coil of hair she had vowed never to have cut, while Letty and Eva had each bought a new black cloche hat to go with their everyday coats and Frank and Roddie had put on armbands.

'At least we've done what we can to look right for Mavis,' Letty murmured, pulling on her new hat.

But Eva wondered if Mavis would have cared what they wore anyway. Probably, all she'd have wanted was for them to say goodbye – and spare her a thought or two.

'There'll be good turn out,' Bel declared, taking a turn at the kitchen mirror. 'Mavis was a very popular girl.'

'Got on with everybody,' Letty agreed.

'She did, because she never gossiped and never found fault.'

'No' many like that,' Frank remarked.

'Aye, and they say even Mr North was wanting to attend.'

'Mr North?' Frank stared. 'Why, he'd never've known Mavis! Why'd he want to go to the funeral?'

'Yes, why?' asked Eva. 'I don't think it's right. He never did anything for her when she was alive.'

Bel pursed her lips. 'Folk were saying because of her illness. Wants to show sympathy, eh? Sweeten up the union, in case they're thinking o' trying to get compensation.'

'There'll be no compensation if no' everybody falls ill,' Frank said with certainty. 'Stands to reason; they'll no' be able to blame the dust.'

'But it is the dust!' cried Eva.

'Only affects certain folk, is what they'll say.'

'Mr North isnae coming, anyway,' said Bel, glancing at the clock. 'He's got the flu. Time we were off.'

'Think you'll be warm enough in that shawl, Bel? It's no' looking promising.'

'Might snow, you mean?' She looked out of the window at the dark, lowering sky. 'Och, I'll be fine. Dinna expect sunshine in January.'

Who wanted sunshine, when they were mourning someone like Mavis?

Bel had been right about the turn out; the kirk was packed. Mostly with girls from the mill, though there were weavers there too, and the overseers, including Mr Rettie and Mr Boath, as well as a number of unfamiliar faces, probably Mrs Craik's friends and relations.

'Berta Loch, and all,' Letty whispered to Eva. 'And that's her husband, eh? Can you remember him?'

He looked so small and shy, Eva wasn't sure whether she knew him or not, but then her mother was knocking her arm.

'Look who's here, then! Must be representing his dad.'

'Who?' asked Letty, turning her head.

But Eva already knew. And as the tall, fair-headed man in a long black overcoat walked slowly up the aisle, her face began to burn. It was a relief that she could bow her head when poor Mrs Craik, supported by her daughter and son-in-law, moved to the front of the kirk and was followed by the undertaker's men carrying the coffin. Everyone rose to their feet and began to sing the opening hymn. No one was looking at Eva.

She herself was ashamed to be thinking of Nicholas North at such a time, her only consolation being that her thoughts of him were not romantic, but angry. What gave him the right to attend the funeral of someone he didn't know? Of someone who shouldn't have been ill at all, but who, when she was, should have had some interest taken in her by the management?

Some mill-owners did care, did take an interest in their employees, but though Mr North had instituted the bursary scheme that bore his name and Eva gave him credit for that, he'd never been one to take much interest in his workers. So, attending Mavis's funeral was exactly what Bel had said, just a sweetener for the union, a show of sympathy that was too late. And as Nicholas North had obviously only come because his father'd made him, his sympathy was even less sincere.

How she managed to contain her feelings, Eva

didn't know, but her face was still flushed and her hands trembling when the service came to an end and the congregation began to file slowly from the kirk.

'Lovely service, eh?' people said, standing in groups outside and shivering in the cold air. 'And didnae the minister speak well?'

Eva couldn't remember one word, but warmly agreed, until her eye strayed about and fastened on Nicholas North standing with senior staff members of the mill. Immediately he moved away.

'Very kind of Mr North to lay on something at the mill,' Mr Rettie was murmuring to Bel and Frank. 'Poor Mrs Craik couldn't be expected to do anything for this crowd.'

'Lay on what?' Eva asked Letty.

'Did you no' hear? The minister said. There's to be tea and sandwiches in the mill offices. Everyone's invited.'

'Best get along now,' said Frank. 'Before the snow comes.'

But he and Bel were caught up in conversation with a neighbour, Roddie had spotted a boy he knew, and Letty had joyfully run to meet Hughie who had come looking for her in the street. For a moment, Eva was alone.

'Forgive me,' said a man's voice close by, 'but haven't we met?'

She turned, and met the grey eyes of Nicholas North intently gazing at her. Weren't grey eyes usually cold – cold as January? These were warm.

'I don't think so,' she answered tightly, feeling

165

her colour deepening further.

'I'm sorry – I thought we had. Perhaps I should introduce myself – Nicholas North.'

His voice was as she'd expected it to be. Educated. Standard English. Not Dundee. She could have laughed at the thought.

'I'm Eva Masson,' she said in a low voice.

'You're not from the mill?'

'My mother works at the mill. I'm at college.' *Why am I saying this?* she asked herself. *Why am I not walking away, telling him nothing?*

'University College?'

'No, the Teachers' Training Centre.'

'Oh, yes, I know it. That must be interesting.'

A long pause followed. People were moving away, setting off for the mill and refreshments, while the hearse and the family mourners had already left for the private burial. *Please God, let me move too*, Eva prayed. *Why don't I move?*

'You were a friend of Miss Craik's?' Nicholas murmured.

'Yes. A good friend. She was a lovely person.' To Eva's horror, hot tears filled her eyes and began to spill down her cheeks. 'I have to go!' she cried. 'I have to be with my family.'

She could see her parents moving towards Letty and Hughie, who were both looking downcast, and, gathering all her courage, she ran from Nicholas North and did not look back.

'What's wrong?' she cried, wiping the tears from her face. 'Letty – Hughie – what's wrong?'

Bel's face was as bleak as the wind. Frank was shaking his head.

'What's wrong?' Eva cried again, and Hughie took off his glasses and rubbed his eyes before putting them back on again and fixing her with a look of rueful resignation.

'The paper's closing,' he said quietly. 'Bob and me – we've lost our jobs.'

Words to strike a chill to the heart at any time, but on the day of Mavis's funeral they were particularly depressing.

'I think I'll no' go back to the mill for thae refreshments,' Bel said, seeming to sink beneath her large black hat. 'I just want to get home.'

'Aye, me too,' Frank muttered. 'These things are a misery, anyway.'

'I feel so bad,' said Hughie, holding Letty's hand. 'I mean – I asked Letty to marry me and I said I had a job, and now I've lost it.'

'As though it was your fault!' cried Letty, pressing his hand and staring intently into his face. 'What's it matter about your job? You can get another one.'

'Of course you can!' cried Eva. 'You're good, Hughie. Anybody who reads your pieces will know that.'

'Sure they will,' put in Roddie, who had left his friend at the sight of the dejected looks of his family. 'And there's plenty o' newspapers to write for, eh?'

Hughie shook his head and made no reply.

'Let's away,' cried Bel. 'Let's get the evening paper and see if there's any vacancies.'

'I already know there's nothing,' Hughie told her. 'I'll have to write round to editors, see if they'll take me on.' He cleared his throat and looked at Letty. 'Might mean moving away, you ken.'

'Moving away?' Letty's face quivered for a moment, then appeared to right itself. 'Nae bother. We'll just get married and I'll go with you.'

'Oh dear Lord,' Bel sighed. 'Let's just go home.'

As they turned away together, the first snow began to fall, and Eva, walking beside her father, kept her head down. She did not look back.

Thirty

'It's no' as bad as it seems,' Bob Keir managed to tell everyone, even though his mother retired to bed for two days when she heard his news, and Hughie's mother burst into tears every time he said he might have to move away.

'No, I mean it,' Bob told Eva. 'I'm no' getting ready to shoot maself because the *Dundee Key*'s failed. It was never going to survive for long – I always knew that.'

'You never said so, Bob.'

'No, well, I'm no' one for depressing talk. But with the competition there is here and the scramble for advertising, it never had much hope.' He poured himself more tea in the café where Eva had agreed to meet him once again, and gave a confident grin. 'It was only a stepping stone, anyway.'

'Stepping stone to what?'

'Better things, of course. I've already applied to a Glasgow paper. There are folk on that who share ma views.'

'Glasgow,' Eva repeated thoughtfully.

'It's no' that far,' he said cheerfully. 'You'll no' be getting rid of me, if I go there. Wherever I go, come to that.'

'Looks like you're going to be pretty busy from now on,' she said after a pause.

'Meaning you are, I suppose?'

'Nothing's changed on the course.'

'Ah, Eva, have a heart! Here's me out of a job and you're too busy to see me? You're all I've got to cheer me up.'

'You just said losing your job was not as bad as it seemed. You don't need me, Bob.'

He hesitated. 'OK, it's no' a question of need. I like to think I can see you some time. Will things be different when you've finished the course?'

Eva was silent, gazing down at her plate. What was happening? Bob shouldn't be talking like this. They'd had it all out. She'd explained. He'd understood. And here he was, moving the situation round, so that he could look forward to a future with her that she did not want.

It was true they seemed right for each other – they had so much in common. With her head, she could see why he thought that. With her heart – well, her heart didn't come into it. Her career was what mattered. He'd said he didn't want her to give that up, that he was all for women having professional work, while all the time it was clear he wanted something else for her. And that was something permanent with him.

'Can we leave this for now?' she asked at last. 'Who knows where we'll be, after I've finished my course? I'll have to look for a job and it could be anywhere. Just like yours.'

For a moment his eyes shone with fierce understanding, but then their brightness died. He gave a shrug and picked up the bill the waitress had left.

'Let's go, Eva. I'll pay this.'

'Let me, Bob. Let me pay ma share.'

'For God's sake, I can still afford to buy a pot o' tea and a couple o' haddocks. You know you've no money to spare.'

'I've the grant.'

'And I can guess how much that is.'

Walking back to Wish Lane in the chill January air, neither spoke and Bob did not take Eva's arm.

I've done it now, thought Eva. *I've hurt him, and I never wanted to*. It was for the best, of course, but she didn't feel any the happier for knowing that.

'Do you think Hughie will find a job?' she asked to break the silence, knowing the question to be meaningless. How could Bob answer it?

'Expect so,' he said coldly.

'This has come at the worst time for him and Letty. Just when they'd like to be planning their wedding.'

'They've got each other.'

'Yes, but it's hard, not knowing what's going

170

to happen.'

'Let's no' talk about Letty and Hughie, Eva.'

'You mean, let's not talk at all?'

'No, I mean let's talk about us.'

At her door, they faced each other. 'I'm sorry if I've upset you, Bob,' she said quietly.

'No' your fault. You were always honest with me.' He smiled briefly. 'Maybe I wasnae always honest with you.'

'We're still friends?'

'More than that.'

'Bob, please...'

'I'm no' giving up on you, Eva. Just now, you're so stuck into that course o' yours, you canna really see straight. When it's over, you'll see things in a different light.'

'When it's over, I'll be starting on my career.'

'Aye, and I'll no' be stopping you. I've said that before, but you never believed me. All I want is to see you and have you care what I do. Maybe give me support.'

'And you'll do the same for me?'

'I will, Eva. We're two of a kind, you and me. You know that. We need to see each other, be part of each other's lives.' He put his hands on her shoulders and looked into her face. 'I'm no' offering marriage. It's no' for you, the way things are, and I've ma way to make, but we'll stay close, keep in touch – that's all I ask.' He kissed her gently. 'Is it too much?'

She felt too weary to argue and too afraid, she knew, to hurt him again.

'All right, let's keep in touch, Bob. But I must have time for my studies.'

'That's understood.' His eyes were shining again, but with a new triumphant light. 'I'll be after jobs, anyway. I'll no' be nagging you. We'll just see how things go. That all right?'

'That's all right.'

He held her hard for a moment, then released her and touched her face with his cold hand.

'I'd better go in, Bob,' she murmured. 'Goodnight, then.'

'Aye. We'll say goodnight.' His hand dropped. 'But, Eva – thanks, eh?'

There was an atmosphere of excitement simmering in the house when Eva walked in, as heavily as though she had the world on her shoulders.

'What's up?' she asked, sensing the mood.

'Oh, Evie!' Letty cried. 'Hughie's been called for interview. To the *Clarion*! Would you credit it?'

'It's an Edinburgh paper,' Bel said with emphasis. 'If he gets the job, that's where he'll be going, and taking our girl with him.'

'I hope he does get it,' said Frank. 'He'd do well to get on a paper like that.'

'When's the interview?' asked Eva, holding her hands to the warmth of the stove that Roddie had opened up for her.

'Tomorrow!' Letty replied. 'Oh, I'm so nervous! But it shows they liked the pieces he sent, eh? I mean, they'd never waste time seeing him if they didnae think he'd be any good?'

'No point going into all that,' said Bel, clearing cups from the table. 'No point talking till you know what's going to happen.'

'Oh, Ma, Letty's got to talk,' Eva said, suddenly smiling and putting her arm round her sister. 'I'll bet she keeps me awake all night, talking about this!'

Certainly, Letty did talk about Hughie and his prospects far into the night, but she quite forgot to ask about Bob, and Eva was careful not to mention his name. Even when her sister slept and she lay awake, she tried not to think of him, so that she might eventually sleep.

The following evening, when Eva returned late from college, it was to find Letty twirling round the living room with a laughing Hughie. He'd just returned from Edinburgh, where he'd been given the job at the *Clarion*.

'Aye,' said Bel mournfully, 'they're already making wedding plans.'

Thirty-One

'Wedding plans,' said Katie as she went for lunch with Eva. 'Oh, it's so lovely! I'm so happy for Letty!'

'We're all over the moon – except Ma,' Eva told her as they put up their coat collars and pulled down their hats.

'Surely she wants Letty to marry Hughie?'

'Not to go to Edinburgh. And Hughie's mother

173

will be the same. Probably crying her eyes out by now.'

'And my dad'll be in despair. What's he going to do without Letty, then?

'What am I going to do without her? We've never been apart, you ken.'

'But you have to think of her and Hughie, Eva. They're so happy, nothing should spoil it.'

'Nothing will. Shall we go to our usual place?'

'Yes, and let's run, out of the cold.'

But Eva, instead of running, stood inexplicably still. Very still, as though playing statues, while Katie looked back in wonder and the wind buffeted them both.

'Eva?'

'It's all right. Just ... I think I see ... someone I know.'

She was watching a man in a long black over-coat who was crossing the street towards them. Over his fair hair he wore a black trilby hat and as he reached them, he touched it.

'Miss Masson, isn't it? I don't know if you remember me? Nicholas North. We met the other day.'

'At Mavis Craik's funeral.' Her lips were so stiff, she could hardly say the words.

'I'm afraid so.' His gaze went to Katie, whose brown eyes were like saucers.

'Katie Crindle,' she said at once, and he put out his hand to shake hers.

'Of Crindle's Stationers?'

'That's right.'

'A very good shop. We get all our stationery there.'

As Katie blushed and smiled, Eva said coldly, 'Mr North, we have to be going.'

'Oh, look, I was just passing – thought I'd...' Under his black hat, his face was youthful and nervous, his grey eyes anxious. 'Ask if you'd have lunch with me,' he finished, and turned quickly to Katie. 'Miss Crindle too, of course.'

'How did you know I'd be here?' asked Eva, ignoring Katie's astonished stare.

'I didn't, for sure, but you told me you were studying here. I thought there was a good chance you'd be free for lunch.'

'We've no time for proper lunches, Mr North. We just have something quick. It'd never suit you.'

'Something quick is all I have time for myself, actually.' He gave a brief smile. 'In fact, I often only have a sandwich at my desk. Shall we find a café?'

'I've things to do,' Katie said valiantly. 'Please don't worry about me, I needn't come.'

'I needn't.' Eva's gaze was on the pavement. 'Thanks all the same, Mr North, but we'd better leave it for now.'

'Oh, please. It won't take long and I just want to talk to you – explain...'

'Explain what?'

'Please, may we go? We can talk over lunch.'

His voice was very soft now and persuasive, his eyes still anxious, so that in the end both young women allowed themselves to be escorted away, down the street towards a café of his choice.

Of course, it was actually a restaurant, a more

expensive place than they would ever have chosen. They'd passed it often enough, seen the white tablecloths and vases of flowers, the haughty waiters, and the clothes of the patrons. Not for them, that was for sure.

'I'm sorry, we usually go to a little place off the High Street,' Eva told him firmly.

'Oh, but we needn't have a full lunch here,' Nicholas said quickly. 'They'd be happy to do soup and an omelette.'

'You said you usually have a sandwich at your desk.'

'I do.' He gave a sudden boyish grin. 'Just had the idea of giving you both something more interesting. But, the High Street it is.'

Thirty-Two

Is this really happening? Eva asked herself as the three of them found a table in the crowded little café where she and Katie usually bought a light snack. *Are we really sitting opposite Nicholas North in his immaculate white shirt and dark suit, his beautiful overcoat slung amongst a pile of others on a wobbling stand, his hat dangling among caps?*

She'd been crazy to agree to come and still didn't know why she had. Maybe if Katie hadn't been there, she'd have found the courage to hold out, but Katie was a thrilled spectator to the whole encounter. If they hadn't accepted this lunch with Mr North's son, she'd never have got over it. Certainly she couldn't take her eyes off him. What on earth was she making of it all?

A very young waitress set down their orders – cheese rolls for the young women, a meat pie for Nicholas.

'Wint tea to foller?' the waitress asked hoarsely, eyeing Nicholas as though he were some strange specimen from the deep.

'May we have coffee?' he asked politely.

'Coffee?' she repeated worriedly.

'Tastes like the tea,' Katie whispered. 'Only the tea's better.'

'Tea then,' said Nicholas. He looked enquiringly at the girls. 'And something else to eat?'

'We sometimes have cake,' Katie told him. 'There's seed cake, Madeira cake, or Russian cake. We like the Russian cake.'

'Tea and Russian cake for three, please.' Nicholas sat back in his chair, letting his eyes move around the café and return to Eva.

'I'm sure I've seen you somewhere before, you know.'

With slightly shaking fingers, she sliced her cheese roll. 'You once saw Katie and me at our school. Toll Road School, that is.'

'Saw me?' exclaimed Katie. 'I don't remember!'

'Mr North was sitting in his father's car.'

'I remember,' Nicholas said quietly. 'A long time ago.'

'Your father'd just told us about his bursary

scheme,' Eva went on. 'Did you know about that?'

'Of course. I thought it a very good idea.'

'Eva got one,' Katie put in. 'She stayed on at school; she never had to go to the mill.'

Eva raised her head and looked into Nicholas's eyes. 'I did go to the mill. In the holidays.'

'Maybe I saw you there once.'

'Maybe you did.'

There was a pause as Nicholas ate his pie and said it was good.

'Surprised?' asked Katie.

'I suppose I am.' He smiled, then became serious. 'But talking of my father – he does care, you know. About people. I mean, there was his bursary scheme you've mentioned, Miss Masson. And when you saw me at your friend's funeral, I guessed you thought I shouldn't be there. But that was another of his ideas. He wanted to show his sympathy.'

'Too late,' said Eva. 'Mavis never knew about it.'

A dark red flush rose to his cheekbones, but then subsided. He opened his mouth to speak, but their waitress appeared with a tray of tea and three slices of Russian cake, and he said nothing.

'Wint your bill?' she asked. 'Eh've got it ready. Pay at the desk, eh?'

'Shall I be mother?' asked Katie, pouring the tea, and from her bright face and the way she was lowering her eyes, Eva knew she was feeling embarrassed at the turn the conversation had taken. Maybe nothing should have been said, but for Nicholas to say something was the reason for this lunch. Wasn't it?

In silence, they drank the tea and the so-called Russian cake, which Nicholas said he'd never had before and seemed to be a mixture of other cakes of anonymous flavours. Not bad, all the same, was his verdict.

'We'll have to go,' said Katie, her eye on the time.

'Of course.' Nicholas stood up and, taking a handful of shillings from his trouser pocket, left them under his plate, at which the girls stared.

'That little waitress will think she's come into money,' Katie remarked.

The colour rose to his face again, but he only said he would pay the bill and get their coats.

Outside the café, they thanked him and said they must hurry, couldn't afford to be late. Of course he understood, but insisted on walking back with them, suiting his long stride to their shorter pace.

Katie, who could always be relied upon for small talk, asked him if he was at university, at which he gave an apologetic smile.

'I'm afraid I'm not academic. I did a business course instead. Now I've just begun working for my father at the mill.'

'And you enjoy it?'

'I do. It's my job to meet buyers, deal with orders. Try to increase sales, though they're not too bad, considering that some mills here have had to go on reduced hours. Can't rest on our laurels, though. There's always competition.'

'From India?'

He nodded. 'That's certainly a place we have

to watch.'

Oh, listen to them, thought Eva. If only she could have chatted like that, about business! But her head was whirling; she no longer knew what should be in her mind.

At one time, to have had Nicholas North seek her out, talk to her, take her to lunch, would have thrilled her beyond measure. But how could she feel thrilled now, by someone whose appearance at Mavis's funeral had caused her such anguish? Who probably couldn't understand that his father might have done so much more for Mavis when she was alive?

The awful thing, though – the really terrible secret – was that to have Nicholas walking beside her filled her with an excitement she couldn't deny. Excitement and guilt, a terrible combination. Maybe she should be glad that after today she probably wouldn't see him again. After all, she had her studies to think about. *I am glad about that*, she told herself. *I am.*

And then they came in sight of the Training Centre and she saw Bob Keir standing at the gate.

Despite his height and physical presence, there was something forlorn about him standing there, clapping his arms against the cold, waiting for her, as Eva knew he was, and now about to see her walking up with Nicholas. Her heart sank when she saw that he had indeed seen them as they moved towards him, accompanied by Katie, and that his arms had fallen to his sides and his face had become like stone.

'Eva?' he asked, as though he might have been

mistaken.

'Bob?'

His tiger eyes went from her to Nicholas, then back to her.

'You've been out? I came to see you. Somebody said you were away with Katie.'

'Well, I'm here,' Katie put in coldly, not pleased at being considered invisible.

'We just went for a sandwich, Bob,' Eva said, glancing hastily at Nicholas, whose face showed no expression. 'This is Mr North – I think you know him?'

'Havenae actually met,' Bob answered shortly. He nodded at Nicholas but did not put out his hand. 'Bob Keir of the *Dundee Key*. And how do you know Miss Masson, may I ask?'

Nicholas hesitated, as though he would have liked to say that Bob may not ask him anything at all, but after a moment he replied that they'd met at Miss Craik's funeral.

'Ah. Poor Mavis's funeral. A victim of the mill. Did you know that, Mr North?'

'Bob, we have to go in now,' Katie said crisply. 'We've a lecture on child development.'

'And I'm asking Mr North a question.'

'And I'm not answering,' Nicholas said shortly. Taking off his hat, he bowed slightly to Eva and then to Katie. 'Thank you for your company, Miss Masson – Miss Crindle. I'll be in touch.' He replaced his hat and looked at Bob. 'Will you excuse us, Mr Keir? I think we'd all like to get back to work.'

For a long, tense moment, Bob looked at him, then he shrugged. 'Aye, well, it's good to have work to go to, eh?'

Giving a last glance at Nicholas, Eva touched Bob's hand. 'I'll see you soon, Bob. I'm sorry we missed you.'

'Goodbye, Bob. Goodbye, Mr North, and thank you again,' Katie called, and taking Eva's arm hurried with her through the gate. But Eva turned back and made her own goodbyes.

After the two girls had gone, neither of the young men spoke until Nicholas finally turned to leave.

'I'll say goodbye too, Mr Keir. I'm afraid I haven't up till now read the *Dundee Key* – think I should?'

'Och, yes,' Bob answered, recovering himself somewhat. 'But no' for ma work. I'm going to be writing for a Glasgow paper in the future. That's what I came to tell ma friend, Miss Masson.'

'If you're going to Glasgow, she'll miss you.'

'It's no' so far away. She'll no' need to miss me.'

'I see.' Nicholas began to walk away. 'Goodbye then, Mr Keir.'

But Bob only raised his hand, and continued to stand four square where he was on the pavement, as though he were the victor of some sort of battle. It was only when Nicholas had disappeared from view that a look of pain replaced his truculent expression and he turned away.

Thirty-Three

'See you soon,' Eva had told Bob, and she knew she would. Even if she hadn't felt she owed it to him to talk to him, he would be round to find her. Perhaps when she came out of college at midday; perhaps in the evening when she was hurrying home; sometime he would be at her side, asking about Nicholas North.

'He's going to bully you,' Katie warned her when they were collecting their notebooks for the lecture. 'Steamroller all over you, unless you make it plain that you've to be free to do what you want.'

'I know, I know.' Eva was glancing at the young women at the lockers near her who were rather obviously eavesdropping. 'Can we no' talk about this later?'

'I mean, why shouldn't you have a bit of lunch with Mr North, anyway?' Katie asked, lowering her voice. 'Most girls would want to.'

'Aye, I daresay.'

'How did it happen, then?'

'What?'

'How did he come to ask you?'

Eva's eyes met Katie's and saw that they were not so much curious as wary. As though she was strangely baffled by someone she thought could never surprise her at all.

'You heard him, Katie. He wanted to explain about Mavis's funeral.' Eva looked round and saw that they were alone. 'Look, everyone's gone, we'd better hurry. The professor will no' let us in if we're late.'

'I still don't see why he'd make a special visit to you, to talk about it,' Katie murmured, breathing fast as they hurried towards the lecture hall. 'Seems a funny thing to do.'

'He was passing, that's all.'

'Passing!' Katie paused a moment to laugh. 'Well, I think he's attracted to you, Eva. I think you'll hear from him again.'

'No, I won't.'

'Why not? He did say he'd be in touch.'

Eva only hurried on, forcing Katie to run to catch her.

'Why not, Eva?' she gasped, as they saw their colleagues ahead. 'I tell you, he likes you. He was only being polite, asking me to have lunch, and I must say I felt a complete gooseberry.'

'Have you forgotten?' Eva asked, as they reached the lecture hall door. 'I come from Wish Lane.'

That evening, Bob surprised her by not meeting her from college, but coming round to the house and hammering on the door.

'Heavens, Bob Keir, what d'you think you're up to, knocking like that?' cried Bel on the doorstep. 'Has something happened?'

'Got good news, Mrs Masson. Got a new job.'

'Well, that's grand, but there's no need to scare us all to death, eh? I suppose you'll be wanting

184

in? Thing is, Eva's busy.'

'She'll want to hear ma news, though.'

'Is it Bob, Ma?' asked Eva, appearing at the door. 'Oh, it is.' Her eyes in the gaslight were apprehensive. 'You'd better come in.'

'I thought you were writing something?' her mother asked.

'I can spare a few minutes.'

'Get your hat and coat, then,' said Bob. 'We'll take a wee walk.'

'Where's this job you've got?' Bel asked him as Eva went for her coat. 'Edinburgh, eh, along with Hughie?'

'No, it's Glasgow. The *Glasgow Monitor*. Just heard this morning.'

'You've done well, then. That's a good paper. But what'll your ma do without you?'

'I'm no' going to the North Pole. She'll see me often enough.' As Eva came out to join him, looking at him from under her hat with her great dark eyes, Bob's expression melted. 'And Eva will,' he added hoarsely.

'Eva, you're no' to be long,' Bel said, into the silence. 'You ken what you're like when your work's no finished.'

'I won't be long, Ma.'

There was no snow, but the cold air was piercing. As they walked, keeping close together for warmth, the frost on the pavement crackled beneath their feet, while in the high dark sky, a few stars glittered.

'Do they make you feel small?' Bob asked, jerking his head upwards. 'That lot up there?'

'Yes, they do.'

185

'Me too. Sometimes, I look up there and I think, to hell with all of us, eh? We'll soon be gone and thae stars'll still be there. Why worry?' He laughed and pressed Eva's arm. 'Never works, you ken. I always think I'm the most important thing in the universe.'

Eva said nothing. She was waiting.

'Are you no' going to ask me about ma new job?' he asked after a moment.

'Oh, yes! I heard you telling Ma. Bob, it's grand, it really is – you've done well. I never even knew you'd been for an interview.'

'A pleasant surprise then, is it? To hear I'm on the move?'

'I am pleased for you, yes, I am.'

Suddenly he stopped, held her arms and turned her towards him. 'Let's stop all this,' he said tightly. 'You know why we're out here now. I want you to tell me why that fellow came to see you today. And why you went with him, "for a sandwich".' He mimicked her voice. 'What's he to you, Eva?'

'Nothing. He's a stranger.'

'You were taking a great interest in him the other evening, then. Putting your eyes through him, I'd say. And it isnae true he's a stranger, is it? You said you'd seen him before. Have you always looked at him like that?'

'Bob, listen, he came to Mavis's funeral, supposed to be showing sympathy, and I thought it was wrong. It was just something put on, because nothing was ever done to help Mavis.'

'That's certainly true,' Bob muttered.

'Well, we were talking...'

186

'You and him?'

'After the service. And he must have guessed how I felt, because he came up today and asked me – and Katie – to have lunch and said he wanted to explain why he was at the funeral.'

'And did he? Explain?'

'Well, it was like I said; he was trying to show sympathy.' Eva hesitated. 'I think maybe it was genuine on his part, Bob. His father's the one to blame, not him.'

'Oh, sure, it'll never be him.' Releasing her, Bob turned to go back. 'Truth is, Eva, you canna hide it.'

'Hide what?'

'What you feel for him.'

The words hit her like a blow. All that she'd been trying to conceal, even from herself, was as clear as glass, it seemed to Bob.

Answer him, she cried inwardly. *Say something!*

'How could there be anything between us?' she asked, shuddering in the cold. 'Him and me? His father's a jute baron. I worked in his mill.'

'He's attracted to you. Another one that canna hide his feelings. And you're no' in the mill now.'

She felt too chilled and too strung up by emotion to answer Bob's arguments, have him send his fearsome probe further into her heart.

'I must go home, Bob, I'm too cold – I'm frozen.'

He sighed and held her for a moment, rubbing her shoulders, putting his own cold face close to hers.

187

'Aye, we'll go back, then. Walk fast, hold on to me.'

At her door, inside the stairway where there was some relief from the outside frost, they stood apart.

'Will you let me know?' she asked. 'When you move to Glasgow?'

He shrugged and looked away, leaving her to find the courage to speak about Nicholas again.

'Whatever I feel for him, Bob, nothing will come of it.'

'Know what sticks in ma throat?

'What?'

'All this time, you've been telling me you'd your course to think of, only your course, and that was all that mattered. But for him, I bet you'd give it up tomorrow.'

A brilliant colour rose to her brow and anger gave her the spirit to defend herself. 'You're wrong! I'd never give it up, for him or anyone else. It's for me, it's what I want to do, something I can be proud of, and you don't know me at all if you think I'd give it up!'

'I know you better than you know yourself, Eva. Did I no' say that you'd changed? Is this no' proof? To fall for a fella like him? To be so dazzled that you canna see straight?' He moved away from her, no longer looking at her. 'I'm no' even sure you want the same things as me any more. Still want to help the workers, Eva?'

'A rich young man takes me for a sandwich, and you read all this into it?' she cried. 'You're hitting out because I've hurt you, and I'm sorry. But if it'll make you feel any better, I can tell you

188

that I'll never see Nicholas North again!'

'Yes, you will. Oh, yes. But maybe you'll no' see me. Goodnight, Eva.'

'Good luck in Glasgow!' she cried, bursting into tears.

But as he let himself out, he made no reply.

Thirty-Four

'A blessing in disguise,' was Bel's verdict on Eva's break with Bob. Now Eva could get on with her studies and he wouldn't come bothering her. He would never have been right for her anyway, even if she'd had no studying to do. Especially with that mother of his, who'd be trouble to any daughter-in-law, anybody could see.

'Ma, I was never going to be her daughter-in-law,' Eva said patiently.

She and her mother were alone, for Frank and Roddie had gone to a darts match, while Letty and Hughie were spending the evening with Hughie's mother. There was a small roll of fine blue tweed – a remnant bargain from D. M. Brown's sale – lying on the table and Bel, wearing her new reading glasses, was studying it.

'For Letty's wedding costume,' she'd told Eva. 'I'm thinking I might splash out and get the dressmaker to do it. Tailoring's no' ma style.'

'Ma, you'd be fine.'

'No, Miss Simpson'd be better, and she doesnae charge much. Have to do the best we can for Letty.'

'Canna believe she'll soon be wed.'

'Aye. March or April they're thinking of.'

A tear had come to Bel's eye, but when she'd taken off her reading glasses and seen the pensive look on Eva's face, it wasn't long before she'd heard all about the split with Bob. Well, not quite all – Nicholas North's name was not, of course, mentioned – but Bel had as usual been swift to give her views. As for Eva's point, that she never would have been Mrs Keir's daughter-in-law, Bel was glad to hear it.

'I'm no' meaning to nag, Eva, but you've got such a grand chance here, I canna bear to think you'd ever let it go.' Bel laid aside her glasses and rubbed her eyes. 'Sort o' chance I would've given ma soul for,' she added in a low voice.

'I know, Ma. And you should've had it.' Eva pressed her mother's worn hand. 'Nobody knows better than me how lucky I've been.'

'And you work that hard, pet, I shouldnae speak, but men can change everything, you ken. Sweep a lassie off her feet – make her forget what she might do.' Bel shook her head. 'Next thing, it's all over, she's married wi' the babby, and that's her. No life but his life.'

Eva rested her head on her hand and stared down at the table. She could feel her face growing hot and red as her mother revealed thoughts she'd never put into words before – words that touched a nerve in Eva. If Nicholas North were to come into her life, try to sweep her off her feet, how easily she might let him do it. How easily she might fail her course, and be left with nothing. Not even the marriage and family other women might have, for they would never be offered. Not to her.

'I'd never give up my chances,' she whispered. 'I know what's at stake.'

'Aye, you're a sensible lassie. You'll have your career, Eva. You'll go far.' Bel rose to her feet, smoothing down her apron and smiling. 'Och, but take no notice o' me. I canna think what's got me moaning, eh?'

'I believe it's true what you say, Ma. Except that Dundee women are different. I mean, they do call this "she-town", eh? Where the women go to work and the men depend on them, often enough?'

'Aye, and that suits the lassies fine. But they're only in the mill, like me. You'll be a career woman, Eva. That's the difference.'

'I know,' said Eva.

Some time later, one of the office staff came looking for Eva. She had a small, pinched face with brows that met in disapproval as she put a letter into Eva's hand.

'This came for you, Miss Masson,' she announced coldly, as though to make it plain that it was not her job to act as postwoman for students. 'Don't your friends know your home address?'

'Why, I never get any letters anyway!' cried Eva, staring down at the stiff white envelope. 'Sorry, Miss Renfrew.'

'Who's it from?' asked Katie as the young

woman from the office stalked away. 'Oh, I'm being nosey. Forget I asked.'

The writing on the envelope was unknown to her, but it was a good hand, firm and straight, and the envelope itself looked to be of excellent quality.

'That's my dad's best range,' exclaimed Katie. 'I recognize it. Oh, Eva, do you think it's from him? From Nicholas?'

Somehow, even before she took out the single sheet of writing paper, Eva knew that Katie's guess was right. It was from Nicholas.

'Yes, it's from him.

'Private, then. Look, I'll leave you.'

'No, wait.' Eva raised enormous eyes. 'Katie, he wants to meet me.'

'You've read the letter already?'

'It's no' very long.'

'Long enough.'

Oh, yes. Long enough to turn Eva's world upside down. And already, every word of it was in her memory. Perhaps might always be.

There was a printed address at the top of the page, the sort of thing that well-to-do customers paid to have done at Mr Crindle's.

Garth House, Broughty Ferry, was where Nicholas North lived, and beside the elegantly printed letters of the address was a telephone number. Imagine having your own telephone! But Eva couldn't see herself ever trying to call it. Oblivious to Katie, who was watching without speaking, she read the letter again.

Dear Miss Masson,

I've looked for you outside your college, but have never seen you. I'd really like to talk to you again, and wonder, would it be possible for us to meet?

If I were to come to your college gate next Saturday afternoon, could you be there? Please send me a message if this is not possible. If I don't hear from you, I'll come at three.

Here's hoping!
Yours sincerely,
Nicholas North

'So, when does he want to meet you?' asked Katie with sudden impatience.

'Saturday afternoon, at the gate, at three.'

'Lucky there's no hockey this week, then. Bet you'd have given it a miss, anyway.'

'No, I wouldn't.' Eva folded the letter and replaced it in its envelope. 'I have to do what's right here.'

'You'd give up a meeting with Nicholas North for a hockey match? Eva, you'd be crazy!'

'It means everything to me to pass this course. I'll have no career without it.'

'You'd not need a career, if you married a jute baron's son.'

The blood rushed to Eva's face. 'Now who's crazy?' she cried. 'You know that's impossible for me!'

Katie, taken aback, placatingly put out her hand. 'Eva, I didn't mean anything. It was just a joke.'

'Och, yes.' Eva gave an uneasy smile, as her colour faded. 'Sorry.'

'Anyway, you are meeting him, so that's all right, isn't it?'

But Eva didn't know if it was and didn't want to discuss it. She just wanted to hug the thought of the meeting as tightly as she'd hugged dreams in the past. To put from her mind the truth, that there was no future for her with this man who had moved from her dreams into reality. However things went between them, all she had was her career, and she must safeguard it. In the meantime, for a little longer, she would dream her dreams.

Thirty-Five

There was no problem for Eva about what to wear on Saturday, as she only had one outfit that could be described as smart. This was a dark red woollen jumper suit she'd saved up for, which had a V-necked top and a short skirt and had done duty for every special occasion for some time. With it, she could wear her black cloche hat and new lisle stockings, but only the same old shoes and same old coat.

Couldn't be helped, she thought, as she dressed in Roddie's slice of a room, and the fact was she'd other things on her mind than how she looked. Not just Nicholas North, either, but what to tell her ma about where was she going that Saturday afternoon. What could she say? Not the truth, anyway. Oh, Lord, no.

Wearing her coat belted over her giveaway two-piece, she casually moved to the door. 'Ma, I just have to go back to college for a bit – need to look something up in the reference books.'

Her mother, who was rolling out dough for scones, raised her eyes. 'Well, that's me on ma own then, eh? Everybody away doing something or other,'cept me.'

'I can help you when I get back, Ma.'

'Och, nae bother. You've to get your work done. Dinna be late, though. Hughie's mother's coming for her tea.'

Eva's heart sank, but she smiled and nodded. 'I'll be on time.'

As she ran out, her heart thudding, her father's clock on the shelf chimed the quarter to the hour.

Hurrying through the Saturday crowds in the town, she thought she'd be too early, but her nerves forced her on and she couldn't seem to slow her pace. What of it, anyway? If she was early, she could slip into the Training Centre, where there were always folk about; it was never closed until evening.

Three o'clock, he'd said he would be at the gate. Of course, he might be early. More likely, late. Maybe he wouldn't come at all. That did halt her for a minute or two. Might be for the best. Then she could go home with a clear conscience, change out of her best outfit that was already sticking to her, help her mother make a few scones and buns...

He was there. Grey eyes looking up and down the street for her. Fair hair blowing in the winter breeze, for he'd taken off his hat.

'Miss Masson!' he cried. 'You came!'

He seemed different, she thought, from when he'd met her with Katie. More at ease. He was smiling, anyway.

'Did you think I mightn't?' she asked as they shook hands.

'I wasn't sure. But you hadn't said no, so I was hopeful.'

'The thing is – I'm very sorry – but I have to go back soon. Somebody's coming to see us.'

'I see.' His smile was wavering. 'Well, I just wanted to talk to you – apologize, in fact.'

'Apologize?'

'For embarrassing you – with your friend.'

'You mean Bob? It's all right, you didn't embarrass me.'

'Might have upset him, though, I suppose?' When she made no reply, his eyes searched her face. 'But maybe we needn't talk about him? Look, can you really not stay? I have the car.'

'Car?' Her colour, already high, burned more deeply at the information so casually given. The only people she knew with motor cars were a couple of tutors, and it was only with them that she had occasionally been given a lift. 'You've got a car?'

'It's parked round the corner. I thought we might have driven out – had tea somewhere.'

'Oh.' The vision of herself and him, driving into the country and stopping at some wonderful little place for tea, was almost too much to bear when it couldn't happen. 'I wish we could've done that, Mr North.'

'My name's Nicholas,' he said softly. 'And are you saying we can't?'

She would have given anything – anything – to have told him she wasn't saying that at all, but could only keep silent. After a moment, he took her arm and said never mind.

'Another time, Eva. You'll let me call you Eva? Come on, let's at least get out of this wind.' He smiled down at her as they walked on together. 'That's the good thing about a car – you can always get out of the weather. If it has a top, of course.'

No words came to her until they'd rounded the corner and she saw the red sports car parked at the side of the road. Small boys were already inspecting the well-polished bodywork and the shining chrome lamps, but luckily could not get inside, for the top Nicholas had mentioned was already in place.

'Scoot!' he cried, throwing pennies, and turned to Eva as they scattered. 'What do you think of it then?'

'It's beautiful,' she whispered. 'I've never seen anything like it.'

'My pride and joy, I'll have to say. Best present I ever had.'

'It was a present?'

'Twenty-first.' He laughed a little. 'But I'm twenty-two now and I said they needn't give me anything else. Here, hop in.'

How different the world seems from here, she thought, sitting in the passenger seat and looking through the windscreen. But then, Nicholas had been different from the rest of the world ever since he'd been born. Different, at least, from her world.

'How long have you got?' he asked.

'About an hour. An hour and a half, maybe.'

'Why, that's ages! Not long enough to go out of town, but we could still have tea.'

She shook her head. She didn't want tea.

'I don't, either. Tell you what, let's just drive down to the Tay. Look at the water instead of a street.'

Her eyes lit up. 'That'd be grand.'

'Away we go then!'

With a roar of the engine, the sports car leaped away, then quietened smoothly into a pleasant drive through the town to the Esplanade, with Eva ready to wave her hand, the way she'd seen Queen Mary do on a royal visit back in 1914. Not that she could really picture Queen Mary in a sports car. Nor could the Queen have possibly felt the way she did now. No one could.

Thirty-Six

So often, to sit and look at the water and its quiet traffic, or to raise her eyes to the bridge, would calm Eva's spirit. Not on that Saturday afternoon, though, in Nicholas North's car, with Nicholas himself sitting next to her and reaching for her hand.

'I wasn't exactly honest the other day,' he said in a low voice. 'When I said I was just passing. I suppose you guessed that, did you?'

She gave a smile. 'Well, I couldn't be sure.'

'After we met at your friend's funeral, you never thought I might look you up?'

'No.' She could be quite sure about that. 'Never.'

'Well, I wasn't honest at the funeral, either.' He gave a short laugh. 'I said I thought we'd met before, when I knew we hadn't. But I'd seen you.'

'Outside my school?'

'Yes. Where you said you'd first seen me yourself.' His gaze on her was unmoving. 'When you told me that, I couldn't believe it. I mean, after all these years, you'd remembered me.'

'Well, you remembered me,' Eva answered, trying not to show that everything around her seemed to be spinning, and she with it.

'That's the point. We both remembered. In fact, I can tell you just how it was. You were standing with another girl – the one with red hair I met the other day...'

'Katie.'

'Yes, Katie. But all I really saw was you. You and your great dark eyes looking at me. I knew I'd never forget them.' Gently, he turned her face to his. 'I never did.'

I must hold on to this, thought Eva. *I must believe it's happening.* But could it be?

'We saw each other again,' she murmured. 'Do you remember? Outside the mill?'

'Of course I remember. It seemed so amazing. I was waiting for my father again, standing by the car, and then suddenly there you were. The girl from the school. The girl with the dark eyes.' Nicholas shook his head. 'Why didn't I try to get your name then? I wanted to, but in no time you'd passed me, and it was too late.'

'Did you think I was a mill girl back then?'

He hesitated. 'Why, I don't know. I suppose I must have done. I just knew I wanted to speak to you and I didn't. Went and played tennis.' He laughed. 'Very badly.'

'I wanted to tell you that I was going back to school. With your father's bursary. I lay awake that night, thinking how I wished I could've said.'

'Did you? Lay awake?' He smiled and laid his hand against her cheek. 'I bet I did, too.'

'But then we had to live our own lives.' Eva turned her face aside. 'Pretty different lives, too.'

'I never forgot you, though.'

As she had never really forgotten him, even though the memory had faded, like bright materials in the light.

'I saw you again, not long ago, when you didn't see me,' she told him after a pause.

'Saw me again? Where? How could I not've seen you?'

She told him of the rainy evening when she and Bob had gone into the Post Hotel's cocktail bar and seen Nicholas come in with other young people.

'You were in the bar at the Post?' A shadow crossed his face. 'With Bob Keir?'

200

'It was the time we'd heard about the miners having to end the strike. Bob was upset and wanted a drink, but we couldn't go to a pub. So we went to the hotel – that was the only reason. Not our sort of place, of course.'

'I wish I'd seen you. I wish you'd spoken to me.'

'As though I could! Anyway, you were with other people. There was a pretty girl with fair hair; I saw you talking to her.'

'That would be my sister, Willow.'

'Willow?' Warm, comforting relief enwrapped her. She'd been right, the girl was his sister. One thing less to worry about.

'Unusual name, I know.' He smiled. 'But that's my sister. Her real name's Winifred, so she changed it.'

'And everyone calls her what she wants?'

'Oh, yes. People usually do what Willow wants.'

Eva was smiling, charmed, until she caught sight of the time on his wristwatch.

'Nicholas, I have to go! They'll be waiting for me! Will you take me back to the town? Anywhere will do.'

'You're really leaving me?' She nodded and he sighed. 'All right, I'll take you home. Where is it, then?'

'Wish Lane.' With sharpened eyes, she watched his face, but saw no change of expression. Of course, he would know the sort of place where she would live. 'You needn't take me there, though,' she said quickly. 'It'd be better not to.'

'Why d'you say that?'

'Can we go, Nicholas? I'm worrying about the time.'

'It's all right.' He pressed her hand. 'Just tell me where you want me to take you.'

'The Nethergate, please. That'd do fine.'

When he drew up at the kerbside in the busy central street, she tried to open the catch of the passenger door, but he leaped out and opened it for her, giving her his hand to help her climb from her seat.

'May I see you again?' he asked, bending his head to hers.

'I've got to work.'

'Work?'

'I mean, study.'

'You must get some time off. Say next Saturday? Same time, same place?'

'No, no, it's too difficult.'

For a long moment, as passers-by pushed by them, most casting interested eyes at the striking little sports car, Eva and Nicholas stood without speaking, she knowing she should go, he sensing her strain.

'Look, I understand,' he said at last. 'I know there are problems. But now that we've really found each other, we can't just say goodbye. I'm not going to let it happen.'

It thrilled her to hear him talk that way, but of course she knew it was meaningless. He probably knew it, too, if he really did understand the 'problems'. She didn't try to reply, but as she began to walk away, he called after her.

'We'll see each other again soon! We'll find a

way. Trust me.'

But she was already hurrying home.

'Wherever have you been?' Bel demanded when Eva appeared in the doorway of the living room and saw the interested faces round the table. 'Here's Mrs Harper waiting to see you.'

'Got held up,' Eva whispered. 'Hello, Mrs Harper.'

Hughie's thin little mother gave an uncertain smile. 'You're missin' a grand spread, pet,' she whispered.

'I'll make Eva some fresh tea,' cried Letty, jumping up. 'Hughie, pass me the teapot, then.'

'I'll just take off my coat,' Eva called from Roddie's room where she was already rapidly changing out of her best two-piece. *I need never have worn it,* she thought. Nicholas never saw it. Would he ever see it – ever see her again?

She put her hands to her heated face and wondered if her heart would ever stop jumping. Wondered if, when she went back to them, everyone would think she looked strange? Or if only her mother would.

'Come on, Eva!' cried Letty. 'We're waiting for you!'

Eva tried her best to compose herself and went back through to join them.

Thirty-Seven

It was hard for Eva not being able to talk to Letty about Nicholas North. At night, with just the two of them, it had always been so easy to exchange confidences. And to tell Letty would have eased Eva's burden of heartache for Nicholas and guilt that no one in the family knew about him.

But she daren't risk it. The secret was too big; bigger than any she'd kept before. Supposing Bel should be lying awake and overhear?

On the other hand, if she was never to see Nicholas again, why worry if her mother knew? She could just say, 'There's nothing in it, I'm not seeing him again,' and that would be the end of it. Except, of course, that her ma would blow up anyway. And supposing she did see him again?

But no, she wouldn't. It would be stupid. She had her future to consider, and he wasn't – couldn't – be part of it. She had decided they wouldn't meet again. *Save yourself misery*, she thought. *Forget him.*

Round and round ran her thoughts, like something on a treadmill, and there was no hope of sleep until it was almost time to get up again. In fact, when Letty shook her in the morning because they had to put away the bed, Eva felt so weary it was as though she hadn't slept at all.

But at least she had renewed her resolve.

Whatever there was between them, she must put him from her. She would not see Nicholas North again.

Two evenings later, however, when Nicholas came to the college gate and looked down at her with pleading eyes, Katie, watching, wasn't surprised to see Eva put her hand in his.

'Not coming with me?' asked Katie.

'We're just going to walk a bit,' said Nicholas. 'Eva won't be long.'

'So, could you ask Letty to tell Ma I'll be along in a wee while?' Eva murmured, lowering her eyes to avoid the look in Katie's.

'If that's what you want.'

'Please, Katie.'

'No trouble,' she answered, and watched Eva and Nicholas walk away.

Thirty-Eight

On that February evening, as they walked together in the streets, it was agreed that they would meet when they could, in secret. Not too often. Nicholas promised he would not be greedy, not come between Eva and the qualification she wanted so much. But that they must see each other, spend time together, was not to be questioned.

'Because, Eva darling,' Nicholas told her,

standing under a street lamp and ignoring passers-by, 'I love you.'

At the beautiful words she had never thought to hear, she stood quite motionless, until he bent to look into her face.

'Eva, what is it? You're not upset? You feel the same, don't you? I was sure you felt the same.'

'I feel the same,' she said huskily. 'Nicholas, I love you.'

Oh, what a relief it was, to say it. Say what had been in her mind for so long. Perhaps since she was that child at school. For she'd always had this dream, she recognized that now, and it had not played her false. She'd declared her love, but so had he. Nicholas had said he loved her.

Very slowly, they kissed, not minding that they were still under a lamp in a Dundee street; not minding anything at all – not even conscious of anything except themselves and the sweetness of their mouths meeting.

'Oh, God,' Nicholas muttered, as they finally separated. 'How do we say goodbye?'

It was always hard, in the weeks that followed, saying goodbye. Having to ration their meetings. Making do with snatched meals in small cafes. Walks in wet streets. Taking rare trips in the car, when at least they could kiss and caress in privacy, but still in the end had to part, when Nicholas took Eva as far as she would let him on the way to Wish Lane.

She would usually laugh and ask him what on earth he thought the neighbours would say, if they could see that red sports car outside her house? Actually, she was wondering what Bel would say. For her deception of her mother and her family was always in her mind, biting like an acid into her happiness. Nothing could truly spoil the love she shared with Nicholas, but sometimes she would look at Letty, so content and at ease as she planned her wedding, and would wonder what it would be like to be so free.

One evening in March, when she and Letty were walking home from Crindle's, Eva suddenly told her about Nicholas. She hadn't meant to, but out came the words, and it seemed right. She was glad; it was the next best thing to telling Bel.

Letty was transfixed. For a long moment, she stood still on the pavement and stared at Eva with eyes that had become as round as Katie's.

'Mr Nicholas?' she breathed. 'Mr *Nicholas*? I canna believe it. Och, you're pulling ma leg, eh? I mean – how could it've happened?'

'Well, it's not so unbelievable, is it?' Eva answered, rather nettled by Letty's reception of her news; it was exactly what she had expected.

'But look who he is, Eva! How did you ever meet him?'

'At poor Mavis's funeral. But we'd seen each other before. Once at the school, once at the mill.'

'And because o' that, he asked you out?' Letty shook her head as the sisters walked on. 'It's amazing.'

'Thanks.'

'I ken fine you're a lovely lassie, Eva, everybody says so, but he'd know so many o' these rich girls, with good clothes and everything...'

'Why'd he want me, you're meaning?' Eva's face was stiff with hurt. 'It's what I say as well, so I can see why you'd say it, Letty.'

'Ah look, I'm no' wanting to run you down.' Letty took Eva's arm. 'But what's the future in it, then? You have to think o' that, if you go out with somebody, eh?'

'I don't think about the future. Except for qualifying as a teacher.'

'So, you think it'll all just fade away?'

'I expect it will.'

'You'd no' be thinking of ... marriage?'

'I can't get married, if I want to teach.'

Letty's face was filled with sympathy. Not to be able to marry her Hughie – she couldn't bear to think of it. 'Is that why you've no' told Ma?' she asked softly. 'Because it'll no' come to any-thing?'

'Because she'd be so upset.'

'She might be pleased. I mean, going out with the boss's son – that's something to knock everybody in the eye!'

'She'd just think...' Eva hesitated. 'He was playing with me.'

'But he's serious. So why will it fade away?'

Eva looked away. 'Letty, you've made it pretty clear why it would have to.'

'I'm sorry, because I think you're as good as anybody. Honest, I do.'

'We're all as good as anybody,' declared Eva. 'Only, not everybody knows it.'

'I think you should tell Ma, though,' Letty said quietly. 'You'll feel better if you do.'

They both stood gazing at their door, behind which Bel was probably back from work and filling the kettle.

'I wish I could,' Eva whispered.

'You'll have to tell her one day, you ken.'

'Not if it fades away.'

'It might not.' Letty flung her arms around her sister. 'Oh, Evie, I hope it doesnae!'

'Let's talk about your wedding, Letty. That's *really* going to happen.'

'Sometimes I wake up and think I've dreamed the whole thing,' Letty murmured as they went into their home. 'Scares me, I can tell you.'

'I know the feeling,' was all Eva said in reply.

Thirty-Nine

Letty's wedding had been arranged for a Saturday afternoon in April, but in late March Nicholas miserably informed Eva that he had to go south, to England, for a couple of weeks. His father wanted him to meet contacts in London and look into drumming up more business, at the War Office and elsewhere.

'As you know, it's pretty competitive these days,' he explained. 'With the Indian products doing so well, we've to work hard to keep ahead.'

'I understand,' said Eva. 'And it's just as well, in a way, because I've some teaching practice to do. I'll not be able to see you.'

'Just as well? It's not just as well for us to be at the opposite ends of the country!'

'I'm being brave,' she said with a smile, and they held hands over the table in the café where they were having a meal. 'When will you be back, then?'

'Probably on your sister's wedding day. I know you'll be busy enough then.'

'Busy enough now,' Eva replied, thinking not only of all the preparations, but of the shortage of cash to pay for them.

Poor Ma, checking her cocoa tins and juggling savings from one fund to another, but never quite balancing the books, and Hughie saying he'd chip in with what he could, and Dad saying no, that he'd enough to do to find rooms to rent in Edinburgh. Then there was Letty feeling guilty and saying she'd settle for the Registry Office, and Roddie offering to do Saturday work at the mill, and Eva herself trying to find a contribution from her grant.

All she had to do, she knew, was drop a hint to Nicholas and he'd give her anything she needed, but that would never happen. At least, if she was being secretive and deceitful over her love for him, she was not taking money from the mill-owner's son.

'Your sister must be very happy,' he said now, watching her face, and Eva's brow cleared.

'It's all that matters,' she said quietly.

And of course, it was. Money may be short, but wasn't that the case for most of the folk they knew when extra expenses came along? The weekly wage just about got you through, but for anything else ... Well, if you didn't have time to save up, there were the pawnbrokers – which Bel would never use – or you borrowed from friends if any were luckier than you, or you did without whatever it was you wanted. But Letty couldn't do without her wedding. They'd all have to do what they could.

'Dad's cousin in Fife is giving us the wedding cake,' she told Nicholas. 'He's a baker, so it'll be a grand present. Everything's working out, you see.'

'And you'll be bridesmaid?'

'Well, sort of attendant. I've got my outfit made already. It's a rose colour.'

'You'll look beautiful. I wish I could see you.'

'Time to go,' said Eva, looking at his watch again.

'And say goodbye,' sighed Nicholas.

A new worry came into Eva's mind when she arrived home. In all the weeks that had passed since she and Bob Keir had parted, she had never seen him, for of course he was now working in Glasgow and had taken a room there. Embarrassment avoided, then. But Bob was a friend of Hughie's, wasn't he? And now Hughie was getting married.

'Letty,' Eva asked urgently, 'I never thought of this before, but is Bob Keir coming to the wedding?'

'Why, yes. Did I no' say? He's going to be best man – or the nearest thing to it. You're no' worried, Evie?'

'Might be awkward, seeing him again.'

'He'll no' bother you. He kens fine you dinna want him.'

'I hope you're right.'

'Anyway, it's just a tea afterwards, you ken. We're no' having any dancing. Dancing's when you've to watch out, eh? Anybody can come up and ask you.'

'That's a bit of luck,' said Eva. 'No dancing.'

Forty

There had been a shower or two on the morning of Letty's wedding day, but by the time of the ceremony, a cold clear sunlight shone down on the bride arriving at the kirk, and the sky was blue.

'I'm that nervous,' Letty told Frank, who was already running a finger round his stiff collar. 'Will Hughie be there, d'you think?'

'If he's not, I'll give him what for,' said Frank, which was not the reply Letty wanted.

'You think he mightn't be?' she wailed.

'He's there,' Eva told her, smiling. 'I can see him. Look, he's waiting. Away you go with Dad, Letty – you both look lovely!'

'Get on!' cried Frank with a grin.

Eva, who herself looked striking in her new rose-pink costume, did not, of course, show how her own heart was sinking at the sight of

Bob Keir standing next to trembling Hughie. Heavens, he looked stronger than ever, even in his best suit and buttonhole with his unruly hair flattened down. But a tide of colour had risen to his brow and she knew he'd seen her.

How will he be when we meet? she asked herself, but then managed to concentrate on the service. This was Letty's day; Eva would not spend it worrying over Bob.

She soon discovered how he would be, at the café where the wedding tea was held. Very polite, very distant, but the tiger eyes going over her face gave the lie to his lack of interest.

'Eva? How are you, then?'

'Very well, thanks, Bob. But how are you? How's Glasgow?'

'Glasgow's fine. So am I.' He gave a brief smile. 'You getting on well with your course?'

'I think I am. Not too long to go now.'

'And our friend Mr North, how's he?'

Perhaps he'd meant it as a joke, not expecting any reaction, but now it was her turn to flush and the rich bright colour that flooded her face told him all that she didn't want him to know.

For a second or two he stared at her, almost disbelievingly, then he lowered his face to hers.

'Are you seeing him?' he asked in a whisper. 'For God's sake, Eva, are you?'

She couldn't seem to answer, couldn't find the words to lie, as his eyes still held hers, and the moments between them seemed to stretch and stretch - until she heard her mother at her elbow saying they were all going to sit down.

'Come on now, you should be with Letty and Hughie, eh? Canna waste time – they've to be away for the train, you ken.'

Dragging her eyes from Bob's, Eva followed Bel to the table where the radiant newly-weds were sitting, aware with every step she took of Bob's gaze still burning into her back. Thank God, she would soon be away from him, though not from knowing that he had guessed about her and Nicholas.

What would he do? Probably nothing. The truth was she had no idea, but as she tried to eat the food that was placed in front of her, she saw only too clearly that she had been living in a fool's paradise. Somehow, the situation between her and Nicholas must be resolved; they could not go on for much longer, trying to keep their love a secret. If they could not go forward – and they couldn't – they must part.

The table blurred; tears filled her eyes, and as she groped for a handkerchief, Mrs Crindle, sitting at the next table with Katie, called across, kindly.

'Never mind, Eva, Letty's only going to Edinburgh. Though what we're going to do without her, I can't imagine. I feel like crying myself!'

Although for Eva it had seemed to last an eternity, the little reception came to an end at last, with Letty and Hughie leaving in a taxi for the station in a hail of confetti and coppers for the children.

'You'll come to see us off with Mrs Harper, Ma?' Letty cried, as the car door was closed on her. 'You'll all come?'

'No' me,' Bob Keir whispered at Eva's side. 'But can I walk with you to the station?'

'I'll be with the others,' she answered, keeping her face averted.

'All right, I'll no' intrude. But let me just have a word, eh?'

'They're waiting for me, Bob.'

'I'll make it quick. I can see you've no' told your folks about ... I'll no' say who – and that's very wise, because it'll go nowhere. You ken that, Eva? Nowhere.'

She made no reply; could hardly breathe, as she saw her parents and Roddie looking back for her and waving, but Bob still held her arm.

'I canna bear to think of you getting hurt,' he said, close to her face. 'All I'm thinking of is you.'

'I have to go!' she cried, breaking free. 'Oh, God, folk are watching...'

'It's all right, it's all right, they can blame me. Oh, Eva, just take care, eh? I'll no' say anything, no need to worry about that. But just ... take care.'

She pressed his hand quickly, looking at last into his face, then fled along the street after her family, now striding out for the Tay Bridge station.

'Trust Bob Keir to hold you up,' Bel gasped. 'You should've given him short shrift.'

'Think we'd best get the tram,' said Frank. 'Dinna want to be late, eh? For Letty's going away.'

Forty-One

Letty burst into tears when her family came hurrying on to the platform where the Edinburgh train was waiting.

'I thought you weren't coming,' she told them. 'The train's nearly due to go, and I wanted to say goodbye.'

'Oh, what a babby you are, eh?' Bel said fondly. 'Crying, when you're away on honeymoon? Whatever will Hughie think?'

'Och, Letty's just a wee bit worked up,' he said, glancing at his mother, who was shedding a few tears too. 'But I know she's happy.'

'Of course I'm happy!' cried Letty, looking at them all with drenched blue eyes. 'We're staying in a hotel tonight, you ken, before we move in to our rooms.'

'As though you'd no' told us a million times,' said Roddie, laughing. 'Be sure to send us a postcard.'

'The guard's holding his flag,' Frank warned. 'Better take your seats, then. Got your cases?'

'In the guard's van,' said Hughie. 'We're all set.' Suddenly he looked anxious. 'Dinna worry about Letty, now – I'll take care of her.'

'Sure you will,' said Bel, hugging Letty desperately. 'And she'll take care of you.'

'That's right,' whispered Mrs Harper. 'That's

marriage, eh?'

'Evie!' Letty cried, suddenly running to her sister. 'Oh Evie, be happy, eh?'

They clung together for a moment, while Hughie beckoned from the carriage window, then Letty kissed her parents and Roddie, and was pulled into her seat just in time before the train began to move, and waved and waved with Hughie until the train was out of sight.

'Oh dear,' said Mrs Harper into the silence that fell around them on the platform. 'Oh dear, they've gone.'

'Edinburgh's no' so far,' said Frank. 'I mean, you'd think it was China, the way we're going on.'

But everybody knew that although Edinburgh was not China, neither was it Dundee. Things would never be the same for Letty and Hughie, or for those they'd left behind.

'End of an era,' Bel said dramatically as they walked slowly to the end of the station platform. 'When the first one flies the nest.'

'Sure, we'll see her often,' Frank muttered.

'They'll come over,' said Eva.

'That's right,' said Mrs Harper.

A train was arriving beside them as they neared the barrier, and as soon as it came to a screeching halt, streams of passengers began to hurry off.

'From Edinburgh,' said Roddie. 'Must've passed Letty's eh? Be funny without her, Eva. Just you and me.'

Eva sighed and began to walk a little ahead, not paying much attention to her surroundings or the people around her. Some were looking for their tickets, others calling for porters. Only one was looking at her.

'Eva!' Nicholas cried. 'Eva, whatever are you doing here? You didn't come to meet me, did you?'

She stood very still as his smile of surprised joy faded. Of course he could tell by the look on her face that there was trouble ahead. And then there was her mother advancing and standing at her shoulder, and her dad staring. He'd be wondering who this strange fellow was. But her ma already knew.

'Eva,' said Bel tightly, 'what's Mr Nicholas doing here?'

'He's just come back from London, Ma.'

'I mean, what's he doing talking to you?'

Nicholas, looking very pale, very young, gazed at Bel, taking in her fine dark eyes, her likeness to Eva, and put out his hand. 'Mrs Masson – it is Mrs Masson, isn't it? I see you know who I am...'

'Oh, yes, I ken fine who you are.' Bel tossed her head. 'Frank, this is Mr Nicholas, son of Mr North.'

'Of North's Mill?' asked Frank. 'And he knows Eva? What the hell's been going on?'

'Mr Masson, Mrs Masson, I've wanted to meet you for some time...'

'If you've laid a finger on ma girl...' Frank began, when Bel put her hand on his arm.

'We'll have to get off this platform; canna talk here.'

'I agree,' said Nicholas. As passengers from

218

the Edinburgh train continued to weave around them, and porters with barrows almost knocked into them, he picked up his case. 'Let's find a waiting room.'

His serious grey eyes met Eva's. *Courage*, they said, and for a moment a spark lit in her own gaze, then died.

'There'll be people there,' she murmured.

'Maybe not at this hour.'

He led the way off the platform, through the ticket barrier, his tall, well-dressed figure immediately attracting the attention of a porter, but he waved him away and turned to see that the Massons were with him.

'This way,' he told them, and though Bel bridled at his taking charge, she followed him to the first-class waiting room, where he flung open the door and announced that it was empty.

'First class!' Roddie exclaimed, his eyes sparkling, but his mother knocked his arm.

'You take Mrs Harper to her tram,' she told him. 'She'll no' want to listen to this.'

Mrs Harper's eyes were in fact gleaming with interest, and Roddie's face had fallen.

'Ma, I just want to have a look!'

'Away you go. Here's the coppers, and when you get home yourself, see to the stove.'

Forty-Two

So, this is where it will all end, thought Eva, looking at her surroundings. The first-class waiting room had comfortable chairs instead of benches, a Turkish carpet instead of scratched linoleum, and framed watercolours of Scottish scenery around the walls. A pleasant room, in fact, but not a place to lose one's love. Where would such a place be? She'd never allowed herself to think about it.

Her eyes went to her mother, who was perched on a chair, the stern expression on her good-looking face at odds with her wedding hat and costume, a flower still pinned to her lapel. Next to her was Frank. He'd chosen not to take a seat, but to stand with legs apart in a truculent stance, his eyes fixed on Nicholas.

Nicholas too was standing, beside Eva, who had now taken a chair. What he was thinking, she couldn't know, but she remembered the earlier look in his eyes and wished it could have meant something. But there was no hope that it might.

'Now we're here, Eva,' Bel began, 'you can tell your dad and me what's been going on between you and Mr Nicholas. Be quick before somebody comes in.'

'Aye, we're no' washing our dirty linen in public,' said Frank curtly.

'Dirty linen?' cried Eva. 'I don't know what you mean, Dad. Nicholas and me, we met at Mavis's funeral and we remembered seeing each other before, and that's how it began.' She gave a sudden sob. 'There was never anything wrong in it.'

'Never,' declared Nicholas, putting his hand on her shoulder. 'I give you my word on that.'

'Never anything wrong?' cried Bel. 'And ever since that poor lassie's funeral, you've been hiding what you were doing from us, Eva? Meeting in holes and corners, telling lies?'

'I'm sorry, Ma,' Eva said quickly. 'I'm truly sorry. I never wanted to deceive you, but I knew if I told you, you'd have been upset.'

'You're right about that! And why? Because what this fella here's been offering you is nothing. Has he told his folks about you? Has he told 'em your mother works in his dad's own mill?' Bel's eyes flashed fire. 'Of course he's never said a word!'

'Because he's only after one thing,' Frank put in. 'Aye, folks like us know about gentlemen like you, Mr Nicholas, and we have to protect our lassies from you. Like I said, if you've laid a finger on Eva...'

'Dad!' Eva cried. 'Don't talk to him like that!'

'Mr Masson, sir,' Nicholas said evenly, 'I told you just now that there's been nothing wrong between Eva and me, and that is the truth. You have no need to threaten me.' He hesitated. 'The fact is, I love her, and she loves me.'

There was a long, heavy silence. Bel's face grew red and took on a look of scorn, while

Frank seemed nonplussed, as though he couldn't comprehend the word love. Eva's eyes were on the Turkish carpet; Nicholas's on Bel. It had not taken him long to discover which parent must be won over.

'Don't you believe me?' he asked at last.

'I believe that Eva thinks she loves you,' Bel said coolly. 'But I'm no' sure I believe you love her. Love's an easy word to say. What's it mean, then?'

Nicholas looked down at Eva. 'I hope it means we can stay together. I hope we can marry.'

Marry? Eva caught her breath, knowing her mother's eyes were on her. Of course, the idea of marriage had been in her mind, and Nicholas's too, she'd guessed, but never put into words. Love, yes, they could speak of that. But marriage – no. To speak of it would be to face up to the difficulties. Burst the bubble, maybe. Eva knew they'd been too afraid.

But now the word had been said. Whatever it cost, the difficulties would be faced, and Eva, her heart suddenly singing, stood up and took Nicholas's hand. Let her folks see that whatever they believed, she and Nicholas were one. But Frank just stared incredulously at Nicholas.

'You'd get wed?' he asked.

'Eva's going to be a teacher,' Bel said sharply. 'She canna marry. You ken that, Mr Nicholas?'

'I know she wants to work for her qualifications.'

'And then you'd marry her? Think that'll happen?'

'Never will,' Frank muttered.

222

'Never,' Bel agreed. 'Because it's pie in the sky. How can there be a wedding, Mr Nicholas, when you canna even tell your folks about Eva? And without a wedding, how can you two be together?' She turned to Frank. 'Listen, I think we should go home now. No point in talking any more. Eva, come away, we're leaving.'

'Wait – I do intend to tell my parents about Eva!' Nicholas cried as Bel rose and took Frank's arm. 'I made up my mind to tell them on my way back from London. I knew we couldn't go on as we were.'

'I knew that, too,' said Eva, her eyes on Bel and Frank defiant. 'I'm just glad everything's out in the open now.'

'In the open?' Bel was already moving to the door. 'No' till Mr Nicholas does what he says he's going to do. We'll believe that when it happens. Eva, do you hear me? We're going home.'

'I'm staying with Nicholas,' she began, but he shook his head.

'Go with your parents, Eva. I'll get my train home and see you tomorrow.'

She lowered her voice. 'Better not tomorrow. It's Sunday. There'll be things to do.'

'With my people, too. Monday then. I'll come for you at lunch time.' He hesitated, trying to smile. 'Ah, darling, I'm sorry – I should've gone down on one knee to propose. I was planning to.'

Her eyes searched his face. 'As though it mattered. But are you really going to tell your folks about me?'

'I am.'

Was there apprehension in his eyes? Perhaps

only because she was looking for it. Anyway, when he whispered goodbye, it was not there.

She looked back once, when they'd left the waiting room, and saw that a porter had taken his case and that Nicholas was lighting a cigarette, the flame showing his face suddenly weary.

'Train's due out in ten minutes,' she heard the porter say.

So he would soon be home. And talking to his parents. Her imagination would take her no further. She would keep her mind blank.

'Eva!' her mother cried. 'Come away!'

Forty-Three

No one spoke on the way home in the tram. No one spoke in the house at Wish Lane, until they'd all changed out of their wedding clothes and were sitting with the inevitable cups of tea at the table. Roddie was nowhere to be seen, though he'd brought in the coal and fuelled up the stove.

'Out with his pals,' said Frank.

'Just as well,' sighed Bel, setting out bread and cheese. 'Dinna want him listening to all our woes.' She rested tragic eyes on Eva. 'Never did I think we'd end Letty's wedding day like this.'

'Like what?' asked Frank.

'Feeling that sad. Feeling that let down. By our own daughter.' Bel put her hand to her breast. 'I feel it here, you ken; I feel it like a great stone weighing me down. Eva, telling me lies!'

'Ma, I said I was sorry!' Eva cried. 'I always felt bad about it. I always wanted to be honest and tell you about Nicholas.'

'You've been a very foolish lassie,' her father said sternly. 'I thought you'd more sense than to be taken in by a fella like him. I'm no' saying he's as bad as some – mebbe I was wrong about that – but he kens fine he can never offer you anything. His folks'll no' let him.'

'That's right,' Bel put in. 'He says he's going to tell 'em about you, Eva, but even if he gets round to it, and he looked scared as a rabbit when he said he would, it'll be a waste o' time. They're no' going to accept you for him, Eva, so make up your mind to it ... Are you no' wanting some o' this cheese, then?'

'I'm not hungry.' Eva drank her tea and stood up. 'I think I'll get on with my work, if you don't mind.'

'Aye, and that's another thing,' Bel went on. 'There's your studies and all your plans. You promised me you'd never give 'em up, eh? So why get involved with Nicholas North? Where was the future in it, anyway, if you want to teach?'

'I do want to teach, and I will. I never planned to fall in love.' Eva put her hand to her eyes as they filled with tears. 'It just happened.'

Her mother looked at her for a moment, then stood up and put her arm round Eva's shoulders.

'Poor lassie,' she said softly. 'I did warn you, eh? But it was too strong – always is. Now you'll

225

just have to get over it. Stick to your work, that's the cure. And one day you'll be free. Think o' that.'

'Whatever you do,' said Frank, cutting more cheese, 'dinna expect anything from that laddie, eh? He'll have to get over you, just like your ma says you've to get over him.'

'These Cinderella stories – best keep 'em to the books.' Bel poured another cup of tea. 'They never work in real life, you ken.'

'I'll go to Roddie's room,' said Eva, brushing the tears from her eyes. 'I've some things to learn.'

Some time later, Roddie looked in.

'Evie, what happened after I left? I mean in the first-class waiting room?'

'Nothing. Roddie, I'm trying to do some work.'

'Why, you've no' even got your books open-ed!' He came in and sat on the floor by her feet. 'I think Ma was mean, no' letting me stay. I had to take old Mrs Harper to the tram and she walked that slow, I was ready to shoot maself. Listen, was that really Mr North's son we saw at the station? He's handsome, eh?'

Eva opened one of her books and stared at a page. 'He's very handsome.'

'And sweet on you?' Roddie's eyes shone with curiosity. 'Why's Ma no' like him, then?'

'She thinks we're no' right for each other.'

'You look right.'

Eva's expression softened. 'D'you think so?'

'Aye, and he must have pots o' money. Ma

should be pleased about that.'

'I don't care about the money.'

'I thought everybody cared about money.' Roddie studied Eva's averted face. 'You'd be lucky, eh, if you married him?'

'Roddie,' said Eva, 'I wish you'd go.'

Forty-Four

On Monday morning, Katie told Eva she was worried about her. So pale! Such shadows beneath her eyes! What had happened after the wedding, then? She felt sure it was something to do with Bob Keir.

'I saw him holding forth to you, as usual. What was he on about this time?'

'I'll talk to you later,' Eva told her. 'But I have to go out at dinner-time.'

'Meeting Nicholas?' Katie nodded. 'It's all right, I understand.'

She did, too, as far as she could, thought Eva. But nobody who wasn't living through it could know what it was like to be Eva Masson at that time. To count the hours, to live on tenterhooks, to be dependent on the verdict of strangers for her happiness. Thank God the waiting was nearly over. Soon, she would be with Nicholas.

As soon as she saw him, waiting at the gate, she knew he had no good news. It was his eyes, as bleak as the waters of the Tay in winter, that were the giveaway. And then, when she ran to him, he flung his arms around her and held her so close, they might have been alone, instead of the focus of interest from other students leaving for lunch. And if there were any tutors observing – heavens! Even in her strung-up state, Eva could spare a thought for what might happen to her if she were seen being hugged by a man in public.

'Nicholas!' she cried, pulling herself free.

'I'm sorry.' He straightened her hat for her and looked into her face. 'Let's go for lunch. I think, maybe, to my place today.'

By his place, he meant the restaurant where the waiters never left you alone, and she shook her head.

'We'll not be able to talk there. Let's just go to the High Street.'

'Fine. I don't mind.'

Arm in arm, they walked to the café in the High Street, neither speaking, though Eva kept glancing up at Nicholas's profile, wondering when he was going to break the news. Should she tell him she'd guessed it already? She decided to say nothing. Let him take his own time. She was prepared.

When they arrived at the café, they ordered soup and omelettes.

'Only got vegetable soup,' said the waitress. 'Only got plain omelettes.'

'They'll do.' When she'd gone, Nicholas finally turned to Eva.

'I did speak to my parents, Eva. On Sunday. All my father was interested in when I first got

228

home was how I'd made out in London.' Nicholas crumbled one of the rolls the girl had left. 'So, I just told him all about that and he was pleased, thought I'd done well.'

'That's good,' Eva murmured, twisting her hands beneath the table.

'After lunch on Sunday, they usually have rests, Mother and Pa.' Nicholas was now clearing his throat and fiddling with his spoon. 'Thought I'd better wait till they came down. Trouble was, Willow was there too, but then she got a telephone call, and I ... told them.'

'Two soups,' the waitress interrupted.

Oh God, Eva thought. 'Nicholas,' she said aloud, 'will you tell me what they said?'

'Well...' He stared down into his soup. 'They were very understanding.'

'Understanding?' What did that mean? 'Understanding – how?'

'Oh, you know – they appreciated all you'd done – getting the bursary, and that sort of thing. Pa remembered you, in fact, because you were one of the first. Pretty girl, he said, with dark eyes. Highly thought of by your teacher.'

'Fancy,' she said faintly.

'And Mother said you must have worked hard, to be qualifying as a teacher. Then Pa said if you wanted to teach, you wouldn't be able to marry. I told them we'd like to get married when you'd qualified.'

'You told them? Straight out?'

'Had enough?' the waitress asked, snatching at their almost-full soup plates. 'No good, eh?'

'Just a little too much,' said Nicholas.

229

'I've changed my mind about the omelette,' said Eva. 'I'll just have coffee, please. No, make that tea.'

'For me, too,' put in Nicholas.

'Well, hope they've no' started on the omelettes,' the waitress muttered. 'Might hae to make a charge.'

'That's quite all right.'

'You told your folks straight out, that we wanted to wed?' Eva repeated, when they were alone. 'And they were understanding?'

Nicholas stared at her for some moments, his eyes still wintry grey. 'No, they weren't. They weren't understanding at all. I made that up.'

'Made it up?'

'Yes. I made them sound the way I wanted them to be.' He leaned forward and gripped her hand. 'But they weren't like that. They were like stone. Or blocks of wood. They just couldn't make the connection between you and me. In spite of all you've done.' He bent his head. 'It wasn't enough.'

In a way, it was a relief. Eva had spent so much time imagining the axe falling, and now that it had, she felt better. The truth was, she'd never expected good news, and now at least she knew where she stood.

'Nicholas, it's all right,' she said quietly. 'I can see their point of view, you know. They'd be bound to want somebody from the same background for you. I never thought they'd accept me.'

'So why the hell is it all right, then?'

'Well, I mean, we're no worse off than we

were before, are we?'

'I'm not going to give you up,' he said fiercely. 'They know that. What about you, though? Are you going to give me up?'

'I couldn't,' she said simply.

'What if your parents make you? When they hear what mine have done, they're not going to want you to see me again.'

'Nothing will stop me seeing you.'

'I feel the same.' For the first time that day, he smiled. 'You know, if you find your soulmate, you can't let that person go. Ever.'

'Soulmate,' she repeated. 'Nicholas, that's beautiful.'

'Two coffees,' said the waitress. 'Oh, did ye say tea? Sorry aboot that.'

Forty-Five

As they walked slowly back to the Training Centre, they discussed what to do.

'If my father were to cut me off, I could get some other job,' Nicholas said thoughtfully.

'He would cut you off?' Eva cried, astonished.

'He might cut my allowance – I don't know.' Nicholas shrugged. 'But as I say, I can get other work. I've a business qualification.'

'Nicholas, I'd never want you to do that – throw your future away.' Eva's face was troubled. 'I'd never want to come between you and

231

your family, whatever they did. It wouldn't be right.'

'I'd leave Pa's mill for you.'

'No. If I'm going to do my probationary teaching, let's not do anything hasty. Just see how things go.'

'It's not possible, Eva. My father wouldn't stand for it. Neither would your people. We can't continue as we are.'

Nicholas was looking ahead to the gate of the college. They were almost back, and would soon have to part. 'But there's something I haven't told you. Something you won't like, but I think might have to happen.'

'What is it?' she asked fearfully. 'Tell me!'

'I have to go to India.'

It was his father's solution to the problem, he told her as she walked, pale as a lily, towards the college gates, unable to speak for the moment.

'As soon as I mentioned marriage, he came out with it.' Nicholas told her, catching up with her and taking her arm. 'Said he'd been thinking of it, anyway. That it'd be good experience for me, to manage a factory out there, and he could arrange it. Eva darling, please, will you listen to me?'

'I am listening. I hear you say you want to go to India.'

'I do not want to go to India! It's the last thing I want. But the only alternative is for me to part from my family, and you don't think I should.'

'If you go to India, how long would it be for?'

'Two years. Maybe three.'

232

'Three years!'

'I know, I know. But at the end of it, Pa would reconsider the situation. It would be a kind of test. If we still want to marry – well, we'd have passed.'

Their eyes met. Three years – oh, God! How could they stand it?

'You'll be teaching, anyway,' Nicholas murmured. 'And we weren't planning to marry immediately, were we?'

'No.' She was trying to see the good points, but all that was in her mind were those terrible words. Three years ... India...

'And if I agree to go, I'll get my parents' approval,' Nicholas continued. 'The only way I will.'

'What about your mother? She won't want you to go, will she?'

Nicholas looked away. He was remembering his mother's face when he'd told her about Eva. The look of shock in the grey eyes, so like his own. The set of the charming mouth and then the smile she'd put on as his father strode up and down the drawing room, his face turning scarlet. The reasonable way she'd explained that Nicholas could never marry Eva Masson. It would not do.

'She won't,' he agreed. 'But she knows it won't be forever.' And, of course, by the time he came back, he might have forgotten the girl from Wish Lane, his mother would be hoping. She'd put up with something for that.

'What will you do, then?' asked Eva.

'Well, I think I'll have to go.'

233

'When?'

'Pretty soon.'

'I see. Think I'd better say goodbye, Nicholas. I'm going to be late.'

'Eva, listen, you know I love you. If I go to India, it'll be for us. So that we can pass the test. You understand that, don't you?' Nicholas put his hand to his brow, where Eva could see the drops of sweat glistening. 'For God's sake, don't think I want to leave you!'

'No, I don't think that.'

He put his face close to hers. 'Can't you see it's breaking my heart?'

They held each other for long moments, oblivious of passers-by, until Nicholas said he'd see her again soon, that she must look out for him, and they parted.

How did she manage to walk into college? Eva wondered. Collect her books, as though nothing had happened? Smile at people going to the lecture with her? The same way she walked into her home that evening and quietly told Bel and Frank that Nicholas was going to India. His father's idea, so that he could be sure of what he wanted to do.

'Well!' Bel was tying on a fresh apron. 'So they turned you down?'

Her tone was sharp, but Eva had not mistaken the look of relief in her mother's eyes. The boss's son was going to India. That would be the end of that, then. Now Eva could get on with her career.

'Just what we said would happen,' Frank remarked.

234

'Oh, it was no surprise,' Eva agreed. 'But Nicholas says, when he comes back, his father will give us his permission.'

'And how long's he going for?'

'Two years. Well – might be three.'

Frank and Bel exchanged looks. Three years? For people in love, it was a lifetime. How many young men, with all that Nicholas North had to face, would stay faithful for so long?

'Well, you'll have to see what happens,' Bel said cheerfully. 'Meantime, you can get on with your own life. Pass your course, with nobody to hold you back. Get a job.'

'You'll see it'll be for the best.' Frank touched Eva's hand. 'That old North of North's Mill – he's pretty wise, eh?'

'Sit down then, pet, and when Roddie comes in we'll have something to eat,' said Bel, now clattering pans with abandon. 'Think we'll hear from Letty tomorrow? She's sure to send a card, eh?'

'It's grand, the way things've worked out for her,' said Frank. He glanced at Eva. 'They do, you ken.'

Sometimes they do, Eva thought, feeling suddenly rather like an invalid. Making no effort to help her mother, she lay back in her chair and closed her eyes, and Bel, glancing at her from time to time, shook her head at Frank to warn him to be quiet.

'Poor lassie,' he whispered.

Forty-Six

Some weeks later, on a warm summer's afternoon, Eva was sitting between her parents in the hall of the Training Centre, waiting to receive her prize. All around her were brand-new teachers like herself, sitting with proud families, grinning and waving to one another, fanning themselves with programmes, anxious for their special day to begin.

Ahead lay two years of probationary teaching, before they could achieve the parchment that would confirm them as fully qualified teachers, but most believed that the hardest part was over and were already thinking of finding jobs and earning *money*! And, oh Lord, weren't they ready for that!

In the row in front of the Massons sat Katie Crindle and her parents, and several times Katie turned round to smile, the sunlight slanting in through the side windows setting her red hair ablaze.

'She's done well, eh?' Bel whispered to Eva. 'Got the big prize, did you say?'

'That's right.' Eva, wearing the rose-coloured coat and skirt she'd worn for Letty's wedding, waved to a young woman she knew, and then to a couple of young men. She looked very well, her mother thought approvingly. Well, and

236

beautiful. Nobody would suspect her young man was probably in Calcutta by now. But then, Nicholas North wasn't *really* her young man, was he?

'Eva's getting a prize an' all,' said Frank, dabbing his moist brow with a checked handkerchief. 'Katie Crindle's no' the only one.'

'The Flora Stevenson Essay Prize,' Eva murmured. 'Doesn't mean as much as Katie's. Hers is for all-round excellence.'

'Dinna run yourself down,' Bel ordered. 'When I think of all you've come through and how well you've done, I'm that proud I could cry.' She leaned across Eva to knock Frank's arm. 'Has she no' done well, then?'

'I'm the one that's saying so, Bel. Canna get over it, in fact – our daughter a teacher!'

'Just wish Letty and Roddie could've been here. Why did they have to limit guests to two?'

'Ma, this place is crowded enough as it is,' said Eva. She hesitated for a moment. 'Did you see who's presenting the prizes?'

'No, who?' Bel flipped through her programme. 'Havenae had time to look at it yet.'

'Mr North.'

Her parents stared at her, open-mouthed.

'No!' cried Bel. 'Why him?'

'He's an important man in Dundee anyway, and then he's done a lot for education, with his bursaries.' Eva smiled wryly. 'I should know.'

The Massons fell silent, along with the rest of the hall, as the Principal and senior tutors began to file on to the platform, escorting their eminent guest, Mr Joseph North. All having taken their

237

seats, the Principal rose to make his customary end of session speech, and his audience settled down to listen.

Not Eva. Her thoughts were with Nicholas and their last evening together. They'd driven into the country for a wonderful meal they couldn't eat, and wine they'd scarcely touched. Afterwards they had parked the car where they could be alone and held each other without speaking.

'Kiss me,' Nicholas said at last, and for some time they'd kissed with a sad sort of passion that exhausted without giving pleasure, because they couldn't forget they were so soon to part.

'We should have been lovers,' Nicholas murmured. 'But it wouldn't have been right. Not like this, in secret. Before I go away.'

'If you'd asked me, I don't know what I'd have said,' Eva told him, her hand shaking in his.

'I'd never have asked you. Because I want everything to be perfect for you. To give you everything you should have. I don't just mean a wedding ring, but your rights as a person. Do you understand what I'm saying?'

She did. But the way she felt then, when she thought of his leaving her, she still wasn't sure what she might have said. If he had asked her.

They had had to drive back eventually, though neither was worrying about the time. Their parents knew where they were and hadn't said a word. This was the farewell; they were permitting it. Even Bel, who was on pins.

As they approached Dundee, Eva had asked him what he was going to do about his car.

'My car?' He seemed surprised. 'Imagine your

238

thinking of that!'

'Well, I know you'll be sad to leave it.'

'Sad? Leaving the car?' He laughed. 'As though I give a damn. Willow's taking it, as a matter of fact.'

'Your sister? She can drive?'

'Oh yes, she's good. Pa's going to give her a car of her own when she's twenty-one, but for now she's taking mine. Look, don't worry about it. I really don't care.' Suddenly, he pulled in to the side of the road. 'One last kiss, Eva. We can't kiss in the streets.'

When they had clung together in a last embrace and were drawing apart, Eva ran her fingers down his face.

'Is it Southampton tomorrow, then?' she whispered.

'No, London. Mother and Willow are going with me. We're going to stay with some cousins.' His voice shook a little. 'Then they'll all see me off the next day.'

Her face changed, darkened. How well those farewells summed up all that was against her. When only his family – even cousins he probably didn't care about – should be able to say goodbye to him before he sailed.

'I should have been there to see you off, Nicholas.'

'You will be there,' he told her quietly. 'You'll be with me, wherever I go.'

It was those words she was remembering as the Principal's voice sounded over her and she finally brought herself back to the present. Very soon, she would have to shake the hand of the man who had taken Nicholas from her, and how she would do that she wasn't sure.

At least he couldn't take away the memory of those last kisses, those last words, or even of Nicholas parking outside her home in Wish Lane, which she had finally allowed him to do. For it hadn't mattered any longer who had seen them. Two years, or even three, would have to pass before anyone would again see Nicholas North's red sportscar outside her tenement door.

'And now it is my great pleasure to ask Mr Joseph North to present the prizes for us,' she heard the Principal declaring, and as the audience clapped, the first name was called and a young man stepped forward.

'Our turn soon!' Katie whispered from the row in front.

She was right, for the next name they heard was Eva's.

Forty-Seven

Eva knew she was looking her best, and it helped. Helped that for once she had something smart to wear, and that she should feel right and in control. Folk said she was pretty – Nicholas even said beautiful – but she didn't think beauty would weigh in her favour with Mr North. Much more likely to impress would be if she could show she was not overawed by him. If she could show no fear.

Would he even remember her? He'd told Nicholas he did, even from the long ago days of his bursaries. As she approached the platform, she was sure he'd know who she was all right.

'For the Flora Stevenson Essay Prize,' a tutor told Mr North now, as he took the next book from his pile, and looked down at Eva.

'Well done, Miss Masson,' he said in the deep voice she hadn't really heard since she was fourteen years old. His immaculate clothes looked the same, and his large florid face was not much different, but she could see no sign of Nicholas in this man who was his father. Nor, in the brown eyes that met hers only for a second or two, was there any recognition. She knew she hadn't really expected it, and lowered her gaze to look at the hand he had extended. For a moment, she hesitated. Were the tutors raising their eyebrows? Was Mr North? She didn't know, she didn't look at them, but eventually took the large, soft hand held out to her and shook it.

'Thank you,' she murmured and, with her copy of Shakespeare's comedies, left the platform, walking slowly, her back straight, her head held high in its pretty pink cloche. Already, Katie's name was being called.

After the presentations, refreshments were available in the library – tea, coffee, sandwiches, sausage rolls and Madeira cake – all of which was much appreciated, now that they could relax, by the new teachers and their guests.

241

Bel and Frank were with Mr and Mrs Crindle, the four of them so proud, their eyes couldn't keep away from their respective daughters, who were circulating the room, saying goodbye to colleagues they might not meet again.

'Oh, they've both done so well,' sighed Mrs Crindle, taking another sausage roll and frowning over the pastry. 'But now comes the crunch.'

'What crunch?' Bel asked.

'Well, they've to find jobs now, haven't they? And might move away. That's what we're afraid of, aren't we, Bertie?'

'Mr and Mrs Masson already know what that's like,' Mr Crindle replied. 'Their Letty's in Edinburgh – and don't we miss her, eh?'

'Every day!' cried Mrs Crindle. 'We've a young man now, but he's not the help Letty was. I've to tell him things over and over again, and he simply can't get the hang of the typewriters.'

'We miss Letty, all right,' sighed Frank. 'Mind, she's awful happy – we wouldnae change things, eh? And she comes over when she can.'

'Coming this afternoon in fact,' said Bel. 'Especially to see Eva, you ken, as she couldnae get a seat for the prizegiving. She's just as proud of Eva as we are.'

'Our folks look like turkeycocks,' Katie whispered to Eva. 'Honestly, you'd think nobody had ever been teachers before!'

'Means a lot to them,' Eva replied, when she suddenly became aware of a presence at her side. If Mr North came over to you, you would always know he was there.

'Excuse me, Miss Masson,' he said, sending a polite glance towards Katie, at which she immediately melted away. 'May I have a word?'

Setting down her plate, Eva followed him to the side of the room, away from listening ears, though interested eyes still observed the guest of honour talking to Eva Masson.

'I'm pleased to have this chance to speak to you, Miss Masson,' Mr North began at once. 'And first I must congratulate you on your achievement. You've a bright future ahead of you.'

'Thank you, Mr North.'

'The point is, you understand, that my son has a great future, too. At present, he's very young. He's not ready for any serious commitment. It will be years before he is, and then it will probably be with someone who knows his way of life and can...'

'Fit in?' Eva asked.

'I wouldn't put it quite like that, but you're a very intelligent young woman and won't need me to spell things out for you. I'm sure you understand that it wasn't possible for my wife and me to agree to any union between you. We thought it best for Nicholas to spend some time in Calcutta. He agreed himself that it would be best.'

'Because, he said, if we still felt the same way when he came back, you'd know we were serious and accept...' Eva hesitated. 'Accept the situation,' she finished.

Mr North's brown eyes were expressionless. 'I don't know that I made any sort of promise, Miss

Masson.'

Eva's colour rose. 'I can only say what Nicholas told me.'

'Well...' Mr North smiled. 'Perhaps we'd better wait and see what happens. My son may be quite a different person when he returns. Three years is quite a long time. Now, if you'll excuse me, I'll wish you all the best in your future career. As one of the original young people to benefit from my bursary scheme, you've proved it was worth while. Well done!' He turned away. 'Perhaps I'd better have a word with the other prizewinners. Do I see Miss Crindle over there?'

How clever he is, thought Eva, watching Mr North's tall, heavy figure moving towards Katie, whose eyes were widening with pleased surprise. See how he'd just killed all interest in his talk with Eva, by speaking to Katie and the other prizewinners.

Clever, devious and rich. What sort of hope would she have battling against him? It would be like climbing a mountain without footholds, for he was as smooth as he was strong. All the same, she would not be giving Nicholas up for him. In her heart she was sure about that.

'What did he want, then?' Bel whispered, but Eva shook her head. Now was not the time to talk; anyway, they had to make their farewells.

There were hugs all round, and sentimental tears. Tutors were thanked, addresses exchanged, and promises to keep in touch, while Mr North was ushered out to his motor. The Crindles made their goodbyes to the Massons with wishes to be remembered to dear Letty, and Katie and Eva agreed to meet very soon to study job advertisements.

They had already made several applications, but with recent cutbacks in funding and teachers' posts not being so easy to find, they'd probably have to make many more before they were lucky.

'I've lived off my folks for long enough, though,' Katie announced. 'It's essential I make some money now.'

Not half as essential as it is for me, thought Eva, whose grant had come to an end.

Forty-Eight

'What a grand day, eh?' Frank commented on the return to Wish Lane. And it wasn't over yet, for here was Letty jumping up to greet them, while Hughie and Roddie looked on, grinning. There were more hugs and kisses and cries of how well Letty was looking, and Hughie, too. They asked where the prize girl was, and what prize she'd received. Then they admired the Shakespeare book, beautifully bound in leather, with Eva's name in the front along with the Principal's signature.

'Evie, you've done so well,' Letty sighed, then suddenly put her hand to her lips. 'Oh, Hughie, we've forgotten to give her the telegram!'

The word sent shock waves round the room.

245

Telegrams, in the experience of Wish Lane folk, never brought good news.

'It's a cable, really,' said Hughie. 'Came just as we arrived. It's for Eva.'

The colour draining from her face, Eva took the small envelope from Hughie's hand. She knew already that the cable was to do with Nicholas. Something had happened to him on his journey. He'd died on board ship. He'd caught the fever in Calcutta. She would never see him again.

'What's it say?' Roddie cried.

'Give the lassie a chance,' said his father.

'No' bad news, is it?' asked Bel.

Eva's eyes went over and over the pasted words on the slip of paper she'd torn from the envelope. 'It's good news,' she said softly. 'It's from Nicholas. He's arrived and he's well.'

'Thank the Lord for that,' said Frank.

'Let's see it, eh?' said Roddie. 'I've never seen a cablegram.'

But Letty knocked his arm. 'It's private, Roddie. It's like a letter. You canna read other people's post.'

'Of course you canna,' agreed Bel, her eyes never leaving the cable in Eva's hand.

'There's not much in it,' Eva said shakily, but her face was radiant. 'I'll ... just go and change.'

In Roddie's little room, she read the cable again.

Arrived safely Stop So lonely Stop Write
Soon Stop I Love You Stop
Signed Nicholas

For some time, she stood without moving, holding the cable as if it were Nicholas's own hand, making no effort to change from her best suit, hearing none of the talk and laughter coming from the next room.

Finally, she took out a biscuit tin from the cupboard she shared with Roddie, and placed the cable in beside Nicholas's letter and the few other things she kept safe – the programme from her one visit to a pantomime; a ribbon or two from when she'd worn her hair down; Nicholas's photograph.

They'd both exchanged snapshots of each other. Hers, taken by Nicholas himself, showed her sitting on a bench in Baxter's Park, smiling in the sunshine, and was in his wallet, he told her, for all time. His, the one she looked at now, showed him in tennis clothes, standing in the garden at his home. It was her favourite of the pictures he'd shown her, because it reminded her of the time she'd seen him outside the mill. Even then, she'd known he was the one for her. In her heart, she'd known it.

She closed the box and put it back, then stood up and changed from her suit to a cotton dress. Better go next door, she told herself. They'd be wondering what on earth she was doing. But first, for one last time, she took the box from the cupboard and opened it to read the cable again.

'Evie!' came Letty's voice. 'Can I come in?'

Back went the box, and Eva opened the door.

'Ma's been telling me about Nicholas,' Letty said with sympathy. 'Is it true he's to be away for three years, then? Och, that's cruel!'

247

'Might be two.'

'Two – three – I think it's terrible of his folks, sending him all that way away from you. To make him forget you, eh?'

'He isn't going to forget me,' Eva said steadily. 'What's two years, then? What's three? He'll come back to me.'

'Sure he will,' Letty declared.

Forty-Nine

On a chill October morning in 1929, Eva was pouring herself coffee in the staffroom of King Robert's School, Lochee.

What a wonderful idea was break time, she was thinking, for though she enjoyed teaching her class of seven-year-olds, it was true she needed her break, just as they needed their play. And oh, just listen to them and the rest of the school's pupils out in the yard! Hooting and shrieking and calling to the unlucky teachers on patrol duty. And the teachers were shouting that that was enough, and sorting out the scuffling boys and protesting girls, while up in the staffroom their colleagues were pouring tea or coffee, lighting cigarettes, and sighing with relief that it wasn't their turn outside.

Not all schools had staffrooms. One or two places where Eva had worked for teaching practice provided no more than an electric kettle for teachers to make tea at their desks, while their charges were at play.

Staff at King Robert's were lucky, you might say, and in fact Eva did think she was lucky to be working there. Lucky to have a job at all, for the cutbacks she and Katie had heard about two years before were, if anything, likely to get worse. And this job was important to her. It was her lifeline, to keep her going until Nicholas came home.

And if he didn't come home? Or if he didn't come back to her? She never allowed herself to think of that.

It was his parents' hope that he would not, of course, and in spite of all the letters and photographs he'd regularly sent her, neither did Bel and Frank really believe he would ever return to put a ring on her finger.

Just as Bob Keir would never believe it, if he were ever to be asked, and nor would Letty. She might say she would, but then her mind was never fully on anything but her new son, Iain Hugh, and no one could blame her for that.

'Och, Evie, is he no' the best-looking wee laddie you've ever seen, then?' she would croon. 'And the image o' Hughie?'

'Best-looking bairn in the world,' Eva was always glad to agree, and indeed he was a handsome baby, but the important thing for Eva was that Letty was so well herself.

Bel only wished Eva could be so happy and contented, and Eva always felt guilty that though she'd achieved the job her mother wanted her to have, she was not settled. And she'd moved out of Wish Lane, too, to share a flat with Katie, who was also working in Lochee, though at a different school. Well, why not? They had a right to their independence, after all.

Of course, their parents weren't happy about it – that couldn't be expected – but at least Eva had kept up her contribution to her mother's budget, even if Bel had been unwilling at first to accept it.

'Listen, you canna afford it,' she'd sighed. 'You've your rent to pay in Lochee, and we can manage, eh? There's Roddie's money coming in, remember.'

But though Roddie was now wearing his clerk's cuffs and totting up figures in the office at North's Mill, just as he'd predicted, he didn't earn much yet, and Eva told her mother that she wanted to help and that was all there was to it.

'And I'll be the same,' Roddie had promised. 'If ever I get a rise and move out.'

There had been stares and cries from Bel at that, but Frank said they must not hold the laddie back. If he wanted a place of his own – well, he'd have to follow where Eva led.

'And leave us all alone?' Bel whispered.

'Way of the world,' Frank answered.

Poor Ma and Dad, Eva thought now, finishing her coffee. Seeing their chicks leave the nest, and not feeling peace of mind, at least where Eva was concerned. There wasn't much she could do about that, but she decided she'd buy her folks something nice to cheer them up, as she'd often done before. Maybe some material for Ma to make a dress, or some new soft towels to replace the threadbare ones that would scarcely last another washing. A good shirt for Dad, maybe, or some tobacco.

'Hey, is it Christmas?' they'd ask with a laugh, but nothing gave Eva greater pleasure than to make improvements to her parents' life at Wish Lane, though the real improvement would have been to persuade her mother to find a new job. But that, Bel would never do. She couldn't imagine leaving the mill, she said; it was what she knew, part of her life, hard though it was.

'You're just like Letty!' Eva had cried. 'She didn't want to leave the mill, but see how happy she was when she did!'

'Aye, but I'm no' Letty,' her mother retorted. 'I'm too old to change now. Better leave me be, Eva, thanks all the same.'

And Eva had had to admit defeat.

The bell for the end of break rang sharply, interrupting her thoughts, and a refreshed Eva joined the reluctant flow from the staffroom and set off, back to her seven-year-olds.

Fifty

Lochee, Eva's new home, was a suburb of Dundee, with its own schools and public buildings and some pleasant Victorian villas, but very much dominated by the great Camperdown

251

Works belonging to the Cox family. They had originally been bleachers, but had switched to jute manufacture in the nineteenth century, building a huge complex of sheds and workers' housing, over which the giant Cox's Stack, a tower resembling an Italian campanile, looked down.

At first, though not so very far from Dundee itself, Eva had been homesick. She missed the wide expanse of the Tay and the harbour, the parks she knew so well, the familiar streets – the Nethergate, the Overgate, the High Street, Reform Street – even, though she could scarcely admit it, Wish Lane.

And she missed her folks, too, even though she saw them regularly. Her Dad in his chair with his pipe. Bel bustling around. Roddie coming in, eyes dancing over some piece of news. She'd always wanted to get away and here she was, in the nice little ground-floor flat of a detached villa – with a bathroom, and all – but despite all that she had still shed a tear or two in the darkness of the night, when she'd slept in a room of her own for the first time.

Of course, the homesickness passed, and she and Katie settled down to a new routine, sharing the cooking and cleaning, sometimes going out to the cinema, or a concert in a local hall, for Katie was fond of music and Eva was learning about it. But then she also spent a good deal of her time writing to Nicholas and re-reading his letters to her, now stored in a deed box that had replaced the biscuit tin and was kept in her wardrobe.

Nothing made her happier than reading of Nicholas's life in Calcutta and picturing herself there. Though not, as he freely admitted, a talented writer, he still managed to convey what it was like, managing the factory in the great heat, meeting other Dundonians involved in the jute industry, joining in with the social life, but thinking only of her.

About the mills themselves, he was complimentary. They were more spacious than the mills of Dundee, better designed and with specially built housing and jetties, but there was still the dust, still the heat. Though he didn't actually say so, it sounded as though the workers were no better off than their counterparts back home. Wherever they were, it seemed the lot of the jute worker was hard, and so far, Eva would sometimes think sadly, she'd done nothing to try to make it easier.

But then she would read Nicholas's words of love, and drift into a dream – a dream that he was coming home, that they were going to be together – until she came back to reality and put the letters away.

On the evening of that October day, she and Katie arrived home from their different schools together to find letters sitting on the mat.

'Oh no, here's the coal bill!' Katie wailed. 'I was hoping they wouldn't send it yet.'

'Anything else?' asked Eva.

'Of course.' Katie grinned. 'You'd spotted it, hadn't you? Another letter from Nicholas. I must say, it's wonderful, the way he keeps in touch.'

'I'll just take off my hat and coat,' Eva murmured, bearing the letter away to her room to be savoured in private, while Katie called that she would put a match to the fire.

'Might as well use this gold-dust coal, eh?'

But she'd scarcely persuaded the sticks to take light when Eva reappeared in their little sitting room, her face paper white, Nicholas's opened letter in her hand.

'Oh, Katie!' she burst out, but then stopped.

'Eva!' she scrambled up from the hearth. 'Oh God, it's not bad news, is it? What's happened?'

'It's not bad news. It's good news, Katie, wonderful news! He's coming home.'

Fifty-One

Nicholas could not arrive home before December, which meant an eternity of waiting lay ahead, but every day was full of sunshine for Eva, now that she knew he was returning to her. Everyone noticed the change in her. The joy in her face, the lightness of her step, the euphoria that seemed to bubble around her wherever she went.

Some of the young unmarried male teachers, who had never succeeded in attracting her, tried their hand at teasing, but still roused no interest. Even when Greg Campbell, who taught one of the senior classes, asked her if she'd come into money, she only gave a serene smile and shook her head.

'Ah, Little Miss Red, you'd tell me, eh?' he asked, putting his sandy head on one side as he refilled her tea cup one afternoon break. 'Money usually changes political views, you know.'

'I wish you wouldn't call me Miss Red,' she said patiently. 'I may vote Labour, but I'm not a Communist.'

'But you're one for causes. Get worked up about rights and wrongs. Is that not true?'

'You think if I'd come into money, I wouldn't be like that?'

'As I say, it changes things.'

'I have not come into money and I haven't changed at all, Mr Campbell.'

'Oh yes, you've changed,' he said softly. 'You're suddenly very happy. If it's not money, it must be love. Now why didn't I think of that before?'

At that point she took her tea and left him. No one at King Robert's knew about Nicholas, which was the way she wanted it and the way the situation must stay, but as she stood at the window, finishing her tea, she knew Greg Campbell had noticed that she couldn't help smiling.

There were no more letters from Nicholas, but one December evening, after Eva had slithered home on black ice and was about to make a start on cooking, a telegram arrived.

'Any answer?' the delivery boy asked, shivering on the doorstep.

'No answer!' Eva cried, giving him a tip that

255

made his eyes sparkle.

'I take it Nicholas is back?' asked Katie, smiling.

'He's arrived in London from Southampton.' Eva, laughing, hugged Katie hard. 'Oh, can you believe it? He's taking the sleeper north, and I should be seeing him tomorrow!'

'So soon? But won't he have to see his family first?'

A shadow crossed Eva's face and her laughter died. 'Oh yes, of course he'll be going home first. But then he'll be coming straight to me.'

'Tomorrow evening? Looks like I'd better make myself scarce.'

'No, no, we'll have a meal together – I'll cook something nice...'

'With me the big helping of gooseberry? Come on, Eva, you know Nicholas won't want to sit making conversation with me. He hasn't seen you for more than two years, remember.'

'Don't need to remind me of that,' Eva said, her voice suddenly trembling. 'But you could still have something to eat with us, Katie. I'll get some steaks.'

'Take the money out of our box, then. I want to share.'

The following day was an ordeal of anticipation, and Eva wasn't certain how she got through it. But the school bell went at last, and she was gathering her things together before heading home when Miss Yule, the school secretary, put her head round the door of the classroom.

'Ah, Miss Masson, I'm glad you've not left yet. I've a message for you.'

'A message?' Eva stood very still.

'Yes, from a Mr N. who telephoned. That was the only name he gave.' Miss Yule's eyes deliberately showed no curiosity. 'He asked me to tell you that he's had to stay in London overnight and would not be able to come as planned.'

'Not come?'

'As planned. He wanted to speak to you, but I told him our strict rule. No telephone calls unless for an emergency and he had to agree there wasn't one.'

'Did he ... did he say anything else?'

'Yes, he said he would be in touch.'

'In touch. That's all?'

'I'm afraid so.' At the look on Eva's face, the cold Miss Yule relented a little. 'I'm sorry, Miss Masson.'

'That's all right, Miss Yule. Thank you very much.'

'Another day of waiting,' Eva told Katie when she arrived back at the flat, her shoulders drooping. 'I just don't know how I'll survive.'

'Ah, it's a shame.' Katie was so sympathetic, Eva could have burst into tears. 'But, it'll be all right, you'll see. He'll come tomorrow and we can cook the steaks then – they'll keep in the larder.'

'But I've still got to get through another day at school, Katie, and I'm sure the children sense I'm all on edge. They've been far worse than usual.'

'Have you forgotten?' Katie smiled. 'Tomorrow's Saturday.'

'Saturday? Is it?' Eva collapsed into a chair, laughing weakly at herself. 'Oh, doesn't that show what's happened to me? I've lost track of time.'

'Don't worry; I'm sure you'll see Nicholas tomorrow.'

'When, though? When d'you think he'll come?'

In the end it was evening before he came. Eva had spent the day doing things in the flat – any job she could find – because it was quite impossible for her to sit in a chair and wait. Best to fill the interminable hours by cleaning windows, polishing furniture, washing the kitchen floor, while Katie, who was able to leave the house, did the shopping.

'My word!' she cried when she came back, loaded with the messages. 'This place has had a birthday, all right! I've never seen it look so smart.' But as she unpacked vegetables and groceries, she couldn't help laughing.

'What's so funny?' Eva asked wearily.

'Why, I bet when Nicholas arrives, he won't notice a thing! I mean, about the house,' Katie added hastily. 'He'll notice you, all right.'

'Oh, but look at me!' cried Eva, staring at her dusty face in the mirror. 'Katie, supposing he comes now! I'd better get ready – just in case.'

But the afternoon passed and he did not come. Finally, Eva, in her best blouse and new skirt, went to the larder to look at the steaks she'd bought, and was wondering if she'd ever use them, when the doorbell rang.

'Eva!' Katie shrieked. 'I think he's here! Quick, quick, answer the door!'

But Eva was already falling into the arms of the thin bronzed man on the doorstep.

Nicholas North had come home.

Fifty-Two

For some time they simply clung together, not speaking, scarcely breathing, until gradually they moved into the hallway and Eva closed the door.

'Give me your coat,' she whispered. 'It's wet.'

'Sleeting outside,' he murmured. He set down a package he'd been holding. 'Got caught when I left the car.'

'Come near the fire – you must be so cold. After India.'

It was true he looked cold, but then he was so thin. As she studied him in the light of the sitting room, it seemed to her for a moment or two that he was a stranger. His face, which had been so youthful, was hollowed now, the cheekbones high and obvious, and there were little lines by his eyes and his sensitive mouth. But then he smiled and held out his arms, and he was her Nicholas again.

'It's been so long,' he whispered, after they'd kissed passionately over and over again. 'I was dying to get here as soon as possible, and then the sleeper had a fault and I had to come up next day. When some tiresome woman at your school wouldn't let me speak to you, I thought I'd go crazy.'

'It doesn't matter, it doesn't matter, you're here now.'

'Here now.' He began to kiss her again. 'And I can't tell you how often I've dreamed of this moment.'

'Me too.' She ran her hands over his shoulders and down his body under his jacket. 'But you're so thin, my darling. I can feel your bones.'

'That's just the heat. People tend to lose weight.' He held her away from him, his gaze moving slowly over her face. 'But you're just the same, Eva. As beautiful as I've always remembered you.'

'Come, sit down,' she murmured, flushing a little, but he said he must fetch the package he'd left in the hallway.

'Something for you, Eva.'

'For me?'

It was an exquisite silk shawl of rainbow colours that caught the light and shimmered as, speechless, she wrapped it round her shoulders.

'Nicholas, I don't know what to say,' she whispered at last. 'It's beautiful. It's the most beautiful thing I've ever owned.' She kissed him on the lips. 'Thank you.'

'There's something for Katie, too,' he said, gazing at her intently. 'A little scarf.'

'For Katie? Oh, she'll be thrilled! Poor girl, she's keeping out of our way in the kitchen. I'll call her.'

'She's not cooking? There's no need to worry about a meal for me.'

'Nicholas, we've got steaks!'

'Oh, well then, twist my arm and I'll have one.'

After a blushing Katie had been given her scarf and he'd kissed her cheek, they showed him around the flat, which he admired in every way, and left him sitting by the fire while they went to prepare the meal. Everything was surely perfectly relaxed and natural.

Yet Eva was ill at ease. In spite of their passionate meeting and the beautiful shawl he had given her, something wasn't right. He had bad news, she knew it. She could sense it. When they were alone, he would tell her.

What could it be? He'd met someone else? Some girl in Calcutta? One of those daughters or sisters of colleagues Eva had seen in the snapshots he'd sent, wearing white dresses and big hats, sitting under trees? Or maybe an Indian girl in a bright silk sari, with a lovely serene face and a rope of black hair?

What shall I do? Eva asked herself, dropping things in the kitchen with trembling hands. *How shall I bear it?*

'Is everything all right?' Katie asked, picking up a spoon from the floor.

'Yes, why not?' snapped Eva, then apologized. 'I seem to be in a bit of a state.'

'Oh, poor girl, I know! Look, this'll soon be

261

ready and afterwards, don't forget, I'm going out.'

'I feel bad, making you go out on a night like this.'

'It's all arranged. Joan Duffy and I are going to that piano recital I told you about.'

'Thanks, though, Katie. You're very good.'

The meal went off well, with Nicholas praising everything, and talking of his life in Calcutta, where, as he'd told Eva, there were so many Scots, mostly from Dundee because of the jute connection. They'd adjusted well enough, though most were homesick, particularly the wives – and, of course, if there were children to be sent back to be educated, there was heart-break.

'If only India weren't so damned far away,' he muttered, smoking the cigarette he'd asked if he might light. 'I tell you, there were times when I thought I was on the moon.' His eyes rested on Eva, who had been studying him closely for signs of unease and was sure she'd found them. 'On the moon,' he repeated, and at the scarcely concealed resentment in his voice, the two young women exchanged glances.

'I'll just clear up,' Katie said hurriedly, 'before I go out.'

'We'll all clear up,' Nicholas declared, rising. 'Why not? Don't you think I can?'

'We don't know many men who do,' Eva told him. 'P'raps you'd better just stay by the fire.'

As Katie went ahead with the plates, Nicholas grasped Eva's wrist. 'I just want to be with you

262

– if that means washing dishes, I'll wash dishes.'

She stared at him, her spirits rising, as the images of the beautiful girls in India melted from her mind. If there was something he had to tell her, it didn't seem to be anything to do with another woman, and she thanked God for that. Surely nothing else could be as bad? But as his eyes continued to rest on her and she read the anger in their depths, she realized she knew something that might almost be as bad. Something that might take Nicholas from her, just as surely as the smiles of an Indian girl, or someone's sister in a white hat.

'What's happened?' she whispered urgently. 'Tell me.'

'When Katie's gone.' He let go of her wrist. 'Though I think you don't need telling.'

When they were alone, they lay together for some time in the wide old armchair, sometimes kissing and caressing, sometimes just taking comfort in each other's nearness, still not quite believing they could be so close; that no earth and sea were keeping them apart.

Finally they drew apart and faced each other, in the silence of the room that seemed to beat like a drum around them. Then Eva knelt to make up the fire, because she could stand the strain no longer, and Nicholas knelt with her and held her so fiercely, she had to struggle to breathe.

'Nicholas, just tell me what's wrong. Put it into words.'

'Yes ... I'd let myself forget just then, for a little while.' He sank into the chair next to the fire and pulled her to his knee. 'It's my own father,' he said in a low voice. 'My mother. The two people I care most about apart from you. They've gone back on their word. Broken their promise. Broken their promise to me.'

She was silent for a moment, feeling his arms tremble around her. 'When your father spoke to me at the prizegiving, he said he'd never made any promises,' she said at last.

'You never told me that.'

'You'd just gone away. How could I worry you? Anyway, I tried not to think about it. That was the only way to get through.'

'Get through? Yes, that's what we had to do, isn't it? Spend years away from each other, to get through, pass the test. And at the end of it, we were supposed to be rewarded.' Nicholas tightened his grip around her. 'Rewarded, if we still felt the same. Allowed to marry. Eva, he told me so.'

'He actually said that? Your mother, too?'

He hesitated. 'It was what I understood. What I always understood, or I wouldn't have gone out to India. As it was, I couldn't stand three years. I cabled my father that I was coming home and that must be the end of it.'

'Thank God you did,' Eva said with a shudder. 'How would we have faced another year?'

'The fact is,' he said quietly, 'I could have stayed away forever and it wouldn't have made any difference. Their minds are closed.'

'So, when you saw them, they said no?' she asked bravely.

'They said no.'

'That's it, then.' She released herself from his arms, sliding from his knee. 'They've rejected me.'

He leaped to his feet. 'That's *not* it, if you're thinking we're going to say goodbye. I'm not giving you up, Eva. You remember what we said? Once you find your soulmate, you can't let that person go.'

'I remember.'

'Well then.' He took her hands. 'Tomorrow afternoon, I want to take you to Broughty Ferry.'

'To Broughty Ferry? To your home?' Eva had turned pale. 'Oh no, Nicholas, I couldn't. Not after they've turned me down. I couldn't go to your home, don't ask me.'

'It's important, Eva. Vital. The only way they can meet you and understand why I care for you.'

'Your father's met me already.'

'Mother never has, and she must. She must, Eva, because I think she's the one...' He stopped. 'Never mind, I could be wrong...'

'She's the one who doesn't want me in her family?' Eva smiled bitterly. 'And you think when she sees me, she'll be so thrilled that she'll accept me? Nicholas, it will all be a waste of time.'

'Will you come, anyway? Please.'

For some moments, she looked into the fire, then raised her eyes to his. 'All right, I'll come. If it's what you want.'

'It is, it is. Eva, thank you.' He made a move to kiss her, but she turned her head away.

'First, I want to go home. I mean, to Wish

265

Lane, to see my folks.

'To tell them I'm back and I want to marry you?' He gave a short laugh. 'I suppose they'll find it hard to believe. They never trusted me, did they?'

'They have to be told what's happening.'

'Of course. Maybe I should come with you?'

'Not this time.'

'After we get the ring, then.'

'The ring?'

'Didn't you think I'd give you an engagement ring? Eva, we're going to be officially engaged. I always said everything had to be right for you.'

As she went into his arms, tears in her eyes, they heard the sound of Katie's key in the door, and then her voice, calling – warning.

'Hello, I'm back!'

Fifty-Three

'So, he's back?' Bel asked.

It was Sunday morning and she was peeling potatoes for their midday dinner. Frank was cleaning his shoes, heartily brushing away with the blacking brush, while Roddie, who had just got up, was reading a newspaper.

If Roddie'd been a girl, he'd have been peeling the potatoes for Ma, Eva thought, but what was the point in dredging up that old grievance? She'd have to change the world, to get men to do women's chores, and she had enough to worry about at the moment. Besides, she could never be cross with Roddie, the best-natured laddie anybody knew.

'He's back,' she answered, taking off her hat and coat. 'And he hasn't changed his mind.'

'So he says,' Bel said coolly.

'So he *means*,' said Eva. 'Want me to give you a hand?'

'No' in that good dress you've got on.'

Bel's eyes went over Eva's grey woollen dress with its white collar and cuffs, short pleated skirt and low waist.

'You going to a party?' asked Frank, looking up from his brushing.

'I'm going to Broughty Ferry.'

There was a stunned silence. Frank put down his shoes. Roddie put down his paper. Bel threw her knife into the bowl of water with the potatoes and sighed deeply. 'His place?' she asked quietly.

'Yes, I'm going to meet his parents.'

'They invited you?'

Eva hesitated, not meeting her mother's eyes.

'No, it's Nicholas's idea.' She sat down at the table. 'You might as well know; they've not accepted me. Nicholas says they probably never will.'

'So, what the hell is the point in going to Broughty Ferry?' asked Frank, his face reddening, and Bel clicked her tongue.

'Language, Frank. It's Sunday, dinna forget.'

'I dinna care what day it is, I'm no' having ma lassie looked down on by thae Norths, Bel. Eva,

267

you're no' going.'

'Oh, Dad,' she groaned. 'You know you can't stop me. And it's not Nicholas's fault his folks don't want me. He loves me and he wants to marry me. We're going to choose a ring.'

There was another silence as eyes exchanged looks.

'Oh, Lord,' Bel whispered. 'He does seem serious, eh?'

'He's always been serious,' said Eva.

Bel pulled forward a chair and sank into it. 'Oh, Eva, I dinna ken what to say. It's no' that I want to spoil your happiness – you ken that fine – but you're making such a mistake – a terrible mistake.'

'Your ma's right,' Frank muttered, putting his shoe-cleaning brush and polish into a cardboard box. 'No good'll come o' getting wed to one o' thae Norths.'

'If only he'd been an ordinary fella,' Bel moaned. 'Maybe a step up from a working man, you being a teacher an' all – a clerk, say? Or somebody with a little business? Oh, but a jute baron's son – that's asking for trouble.'

'Why?' cried Eva. 'Why is it? All that matters is that we care about each other, and we do!'

'You're no' alone in the world, and neither is he. Everybody has to think o' their families when they wed. And if his family ever do accept you, will they ever accept us? Have you thought about that?'

Eva was silent, staring down at the old scratched table she knew so well, as two great tears welled from her eyes and moved slowly down her cheeks.

'Ah, lassie, you've got yourself into something that's beyond us all,' her mother said gently. 'But believe me, if you could just put that young North out o' your mind, you'd bless the day. When you go to Broughty Ferry, you just remember that.'

'And remember you're as good as they are, as well,' Frank cried. 'All they've got is money.'

'No' much if you say it quick,' said Roddie, his eyes on his sister, full of sympathy. 'I say, if this guy really loves Eva, she should stick with him. She's no' marrying his family, whatever you say, Ma; she's marrying him.'

'As though you know anything about it!' she cried.

Eva, leaning forward, touched Roddie's hand. 'Thanks,' she said quietly.

'Well, are you staying for your dinner?' Bel asked after a pause. 'The wee joint's in and I've just to finish these tatties.'

'I am staying,' Eva told her. 'But lend me one of your aprons, Ma, and I will give you a hand. Nicholas isn't coming for me till half past one.'

'Coming here?' asked Bel with alarm.

'Only to the door.'

'That's all right, then. I'm no' ready to see him here yet.'

'Will he be driving that red sports car of his?' cried Roddie. 'What I'd give for a spin in that!'

'He will be driving it. His sister had it for a while, but now she's got her own.'

Roddie, looking at Frank, laughed and shook his head.

'All they've got is money, I think you said, Dad? Can do plenty with it, though.'

At a little before the allotted time, Eva, in her coat and hat, went out of the house to find the sports car already at the door and Nicholas waiting. She had made a brave farewell to her parents, promising to let them know how she got on, but Roddie had tiptoed down after her, and while she and Nicholas were feverishly embracing, was staring with awe at Nicholas's car.

He was not alone in that, of course, as several children had already gathered, and a number of women were hanging out of windows and calling to others to come see the motor waiting for Bel Masson's girl.

'Nicholas, this is my brother, Roddie,' Eva said quietly, and Nicholas smiled and shook hands.

'How do you like it, then?' he asked, waving a hand towards his car. 'It's a Bugatti Tourer.'

'I've heard of Bugattis,' said Roddie. 'I'm interested in cars. How many cylinders?'

'Eight.' As Roddie looked longingly at the interior, Nicholas asked kindly, 'Like to sit in?'

'Oh, please!' Roddie cried, jumping into the driving seat.

'But have we time?' whispered Eva.

'Plenty. Let him just have a look.'

'It's grand,' Roddie sighed, climbing regretfully from the car when he'd inspected everything in sight. 'First time I've ever sat in anything like it. Wait till I tell ma pals. Thanks very much, Mr North.'

'Another time, you must come for a drive, but

now I'm afraid we have to be on our way.'

As Roddie and the women from the windows waved, and the children screamed with excitement, Nicholas and Eva roared away down Wish Lane in a cloud of dust – but not before Eva had seen Bel's unsmiling face looking down at her from the house, with Frank by her side.

'I know you're not looking forward to this,' Nicholas murmured as they left Dundee. 'But there's no need to worry, Eva.'

'It's pointless to tell me that,' she replied, her hands clutching her bag, her eyes staring straight ahead. The winter sky was steel grey with only a touch of blue, the waters of the Tay looking cold enough to chill the heart.

'Just remember that, whatever happens, we're going to be together,' Nicholas went on. 'I'd like my parents' blessing, but we can do without it.'

'Look, I always said I didn't want you to quarrel with your folks,' she said quickly. 'And then there's your work. What will you do?'

'We've been through all this before. I tell you, there's no need to worry. I have some money of my own – and I could even go back to India, if I liked.'

'India?' She was shocked, completely taken aback. Never had she thought he would come out with such an idea. After he'd told her all about the problems – the heat, the distance, the sending back of children...

'Nicholas, you're not serious? Why ever would you want to go back to India?'

'I could manage a mill again. Why not?' He

271

glanced at her quickly. 'Would you come with me?'

She hesitated. 'If you went, I'd have to.'

'That's all right, then.'

'But I don't want you to have to go. I don't want to be the one who breaks up your family.'

'They're the ones who want to do that.'

For some time they drove in silence, Eva's head whirling. How would it be for her to have to go to India? Leave Ma and all her folks? Be an exile? Perhaps it wouldn't come to that. She prayed it wouldn't. But if Nicholas went, as she'd said, she would have to go with him.

'How soon will we be there?' she asked, feeling more apprehensive than ever about the coming ordeal, now that she knew just what it might involve.

'Pretty soon,' Nicholas answered cheerfully. 'Next stop, Broughty Ferry.'

Fifty-Four

Suddenly, there it was. Garth House. Nicholas's home, built on the slope above the shore, the chosen area for the jute barons' mansions in Broughty Ferry. How well Eva remembered seeing it as a day tripper with her family all those years ago. Suddenly, she was a child of fourteen again, peering through the gates at the towers and balconies and great bay windows of Mr

North's house. Listening to Bel being scornful over it, and Letty wondering about the cleaning, and Roddie telling her she wouldn't have to worry about the cleaning, if she lived there.

But none of them would ever live there, Ma had said, and Eva had daydreamed. One day, maybe...

But no, she knew for certain now that she would never live at Garth House. Even if she married Nicholas, it would never be her home. Even if she didn't have to go to India, she would never live here in his parents' house.

I'd rather live in Wish Lane, she thought with sudden passion, *than where I am not wanted.*

'My grandfather built this place in 1884,' Nicholas was saying as he drove in at the side of the house. 'Can't say I admire it myself, and Willow says it should be pulled down and something modern built on the site. Trust Willow!'

He was talking fast to cover his nervousness, Eva realized as she stepped from the car, looking about her at a large stable block, where a horse's head was peering over a half door. No doubt that was Willow's horse; Nicholas had never talked about riding. But there were garages, too, with a concrete space for turning, on which a man was polishing Mr North's great dark car.

'Want me to put yours away, Mr Nicholas?' he called, and Eva recognized the chauffeur she'd seen outside the mill on the last day she'd worked there.

'Thanks, Angus, I'll leave the keys,' Nicholas answered, taking Eva's arm. 'This way, sweetheart – we'll use the side door.'

Perhaps he'd imagined that using the side entrance might ease her gradually into the magnitude of his home, but of course it couldn't save her from the supercilious smile of the maid who took her coat. Or the eventual sight of the main hall, which seemed to her as big as the Mercat Hall in the Nethergate. Or the drawing room that would have taken all the pupils at King Robert's School and still had room for more.

Beneath the drawing room's vaulted Victorian ceiling, Eva felt dwarfed, but the furniture would have made her feel small anyway, so grand was it. Enormous sofas and easy chairs, vast gilt-framed mirrors and oil paintings, occasional tables almost suitable for dining. And, of course, the piano in the distance – for one had to think of distances in a room like this – had to be a grand.

From the double entrance doors to the plaster chimneypiece where the Norths were seated, the walk was long, and as she moved with Nicholas towards his family, Eva knew their eyes were on her. But though their scrutiny increased her ordeal, she kept her head high and her back straight, and when Nicholas introduced her to his mother, she was rewarded by the slight look of surprise in her cool grey eyes.

'Miss Masson, how do you do?' Mrs North murmured, putting forward a white hand.

How like his mother was Nicholas, thought Eva. The same colouring, the same shape of face – why, she was even as thin, though that was probably by intent. Of course, she was beauti-fully dressed, beautifully made-up and cared for

274

in every way, but something was missing. Warmth? Humanity? She was like everyone's idea of someone grand – and no more real.

'Pa, I believe you've met Eva?' Nicholas asked his father, who rose from his chair and inclined his head.

'And Eva, this is my sister, Willow.'

Nicholas paused in front of the slender blonde girl Eva had last seen at the Post Hotel, wearing a coat with a fur collar and looking so pretty and so bored. Now, she was curled up in one of the huge armchairs, where she might have seemed a waif if she had not been wearing such a perfect blue dress and matching cardigan, silk stockings and elegant shoes, the narrowest Eva had ever seen.

Taking a cigarette in a holder from her darkly made-up lips, Willow North now gave Eva a faint smile.

'How do you do, Miss Masson? You look so cold – come near the fire.'

'Very cold today,' Joseph North murmured. 'Might have snow. Ailsa, my dear, why not ring for tea?'

Tea was served by the supercilious parlour maid – who Eva had already suspected of examining her coat and finding it wanting – and a younger girl, who jumped to follow unspoken orders with anxious sighs.

Eva had thought Mrs North would make the tea herself, using the silver spirit kettle, but she allowed the senior maid to do that, lying back in her chair as though this tea party were all too much and it was not up to her to do anything at all. Her eyes, however, remained active, closely following Eva's management of her scone with butter and hazardous jam, but could have found nothing amiss.

Very little conversation was made, even Nicholas seeming to have given up trying to make small talk, and by the time the maids had removed the tea things and retired, an uneasy silence had fallen.

'Think I have things to do,' Willow remarked, rising at a look from her mother. 'Will you excuse me, Miss Masson?'

When she had slowly made her way from the drawing room, a different atmosphere made itself felt. Down to business, Eva could almost hear Mr North declaring, and immediately gathered her courage together to face whatever was coming.

Fifty-Five

In fact, it was Mrs North who spoke first.

'I'm so sorry, my dear,' she said, leaning forward a little and fixing Eva with her grey stare. 'It's really too bad of Nicholas to have brought you here for no reason.'

'No reason?' Nicholas repeated truculently. 'I brought Eva here for a very good reason, Mother. For you to meet her.'

276

'Yes, well, it's nice that we have, of course, but it doesn't change anything.'

'I'm afraid that's true,' Mr North declared. 'What we've said still stands, Nicholas. There's no point in arguing.'

Nicholas glanced quickly at Eva, who was managing to keep her face impassive, and touched her hand. 'The point I want to make, Pa, is that I agreed to a separation from Eva, so that you could see I was serious about my feelings. You gave me to understand that if I didn't change my mind, when I came home, you would agree to my marriage to Eva.'

'If you understood that, Nicholas, you were wrong. I never promised any such thing.'

'Never,' put in Mrs North. 'The marriage is not possible.' Again, she looked to Eva. 'I'm sorry to be so blunt, Miss Masson, but you are an intelligent young person and I'm sure you understand very well why a union with my son would not be satisfactory.'

'Exactly what I said some time ago, as you probably remember,' Mr North told Eva. 'You've done very well, Miss Masson – no one's denying that – but one day Nicholas will inherit a great business, one begun by his grandfather and carried on by me. And his wife will have to be a very special person, one with a certain background who will be able to support her husband in the life he has to lead. As well as play an important role in the life of the city.' Mr North gave Eva a smile and put his hand on her shoulder. 'You do see, my dear, that your own experience hasn't fitted you for that kind of

277

thing? No one is running you down, just stating what is obvious. You see that, don't you?'

'Of course she doesn't!' cried Nicholas. 'Eva's bright enough to do anything that would be asked of her. Her teachers spotted that years ago, when they recommended her for one of your own bursaries, Pa, and she's gone on from there to be a teacher herself, a professional woman. Don't tell me she couldn't do what Mother does – opening fêtes and subscribing to charities!'

'Thank you so much!' Mrs North cried, her cheeks flushing brightly. 'It's good to know that my work is so appreciated!'

'Well, I'm sorry, Mother, but I'm only saying that all your arguments don't mean a thing. You don't want me to marry Eva because she comes from Wish Lane, and that's the truth of it. Why not be honest?'

'There's no need for us to consider Wish Lane,' Mr North said sharply, turning as red as his wife. 'But I think it's time to bring this discussion to an end. I'm sorry you've had a wasted journey, Miss Masson, but there it is. Some things must be accepted.'

'Not by me,' Nicholas said tightly. 'If you will not give us your blessing to marry, Pa, we'll have to marry anyway. I'll leave the business and find something else. I don't want to. I don't want to make a rift between us, but it looks like I've no choice.'

A terrible silence fell. Mrs North looked stricken, her husband outraged, while Eva, very pale, rose from her chair. 'Perhaps we should go now, Mr North – Mrs North – and discuss this another time?'

'We'll discuss it now!' cried Mr North. 'Just what sort of job do you think you'd do, Nicholas? Times are hard since the Wall Street crash – we're all having to cut back, you know. There'd be no question of my keeping on your allowance.'

'I don't need your allowance, Pa. I've got Grandfather's money.'

'Only the interest from the capital until you're twenty-five. And you know you need a career.'

'Well, I have a business qualification and experience – I don't think I'd have trouble finding something.' Nicholas gave a brief laugh. 'I might even go back to India. Be a jute wallah.'

'Jute wallah?' cried Mrs North. 'Joseph, what is he talking about?'

'He's saying he could run one of the mills out there, as he did before,' Mr North told her angrily. 'And if that's what he wants to do – let him.'

'Joseph!' his wife cried again. 'We can't let him leave us!'

'We can't stop him, my dear.'

Mrs North, her lip trembling, rose to take Nicholas's hand. 'You really mean it?' she whispered. 'You'd leave us for ever?'

'If I have to,' he answered steadily.

'I can't believe it.' Sinking back into her chair, she put a lace handkerchief to her eyes and began to sob. 'I can't believe you'd do this to us, Nicholas.'

As he stood, biting his lips, Eva looked at him worriedly and his father groaned.

'Oh for God's sake, Ailsa, don't cry!'

'What am I expected to do, Joseph, when our son is leaving us? Leaving his country for good? It was bad enough when he went away for two years – I was so happy he wouldn't stay for three – but think what it would be like to say goodbye for ever!'

'People don't stay out there for ever. He'll come back some time.'

'When I'll be dead and gone, probably.' Mrs North lowered her handkerchief and looked at Eva with reddened eyes. 'And what about Miss Masson, Nicholas? Would you take her away from her family, too?'

'I needn't,' he said quietly. 'I needn't go away at all.' A long look passed between his parents as Nicholas moved to stand next to Eva and took her arm. 'Your choice,' Nicholas pressed.

'Joseph,' murmured his mother. 'Couldn't we come to some agreement?'

Joseph North ran his hand over his florid face and groaned again. 'We'll think about it,' he said at last. 'But this is a form of blackmail, isn't it, Nicholas?'

'Not at all, Pa. I'm just saying what the alternatives are. And anyway, how would you describe your threat to stop my allowance?'

His father's hard brown eyes rested on his son's handsome face, then moved to Eva, still so pale, but standing erect in the shelter of Nicholas's arm.

'We'll think about it,' he said again, and put his hand on his wife's shoulder. 'But if you're driving Miss Masson home, Nicholas, you'd better

280

get off. As I said, there could be snow.'

'Her name is Eva,' Nicholas said gently, but to that his father made no response.

'Goodbye, then, Mr North,' Eva murmured. 'Mrs North.'

Ailsa North, regaining her composure with a struggle, put out her hand, which Eva shook. 'We'll be in touch,' she murmured, at which Nicholas smiled and kissed her cheek.

'Well done!' Nicholas said as the car raced through the winter dusk on the way back to Dundee. 'Well done, Eva. I was proud of you.'

'I didn't do anything.'

'You were dignified, composed, everything you should have been. I could tell my people were impressed.'

'They were not impressed.'

'They are going to think again about our marriage. Doesn't that show they were impressed with you?'

'They gave in because of India.' Eva was staring into the darkness. 'Did you know they would do that?'

'How could I know? All I thought was that Mother wouldn't want me to go.'

'Well, you were right, weren't you? Wasn't it a bit hard, making her think you would go?'

'No harder than she was prepared to be.' Nicholas suddenly drew into the side of the road and stopped the car. 'What is this, Eva? Are you accusing me of something?'

'No. It's just that I've never seen you like that before. I was a bit surprised, that's all.'

'I'm my parents' son in some ways,' he said quietly. 'But anything I did, I did for you, Eva. And it worked. They're going to agree to our marriage, I can tell. And whatever you say, I think they were impressed with you.' When she said nothing, he kissed her gently. 'Next thing we do, my darling, is plan the wedding.'

'I'll have to give in my notice.'

'You won't have to work a whole term, will you?'

'Maybe not. There are so many people who'd like my job.'

'I was thinking of a very quiet wedding early next year. Or do you want all the trimmings?'

'Of course not.' Suddenly, she smiled and relaxed. 'The quieter the better, I say.'

They kissed again, more strongly, and then again, until finally Nicholas drew himself away and said they'd better get on and beat the snow. And all the way back to Wish Lane, she could feel his happiness and relief sweeping over her, and very soon forgot everything else, except that she was happy too.

Fifty-Six

No formal acceptance of Eva was ever made by the Norths, and Mrs North never did get in touch. It was simply left to Nicholas to understand that he was to continue working for his father's firm and arrange his marriage as he thought fit. After

Eva had become Mrs Nicholas North, she would be received as one of the family, but his parents would prefer not to attend the wedding. Much easier all round, was the unspoken argument.

'They're no' wanting to meet us,' muttered Frank. 'Aye, well, maybe we dinna want to meet them.'

'But you'll come to the wedding?' Eva asked anxiously. 'It'll be in the Registry Office, and afterwards at the Post Hotel.'

Frank and Bel looked at each other.

'Maybe best if you're just on your own,' said Bel. 'Truth is, we're no more for this wedding than thae Norths.'

Eva gazed down at the five diamonds of her engagement ring and turned it on her finger. 'The truth is, you're just like them. You don't want anybody in the family who isn't the same as you.'

'We're no' stopping you from marrying him,' said Frank. 'It's just that we dinna approve. There's too much against it.'

'All the same, I never thought you wouldn't want to see me wed. Maybe you could come to the reception?'

'We'd no' want to come to something we're no' paying for,' Bel said, shaking her head. 'We're the bride's kin; we should be the ones to foot the bill.'

'Aye, we'd no' be happy,' Frank agreed.

'Look, you can't afford it!' Eva cried. 'Nobody expects you to pay for a lunch at the Post Hotel!'

'Think that makes us feel any better? Just leave it, Eva.'

'It's not fair to turn him down, when he's doing all he can,' Eva said mutinously. 'Why, you've never even asked him here, have you? The man I'm going to marry!'

'As though he'd want to come!' cried Bel.

'I think he should. P'raps at Christmas?'

'Ask him then, if you want to. But dinna forget what happened to Letty.'

'Ma!' Eva stared at Bel, appalled. 'You're never comparing Nicholas to that fellow who upset Letty! After all he's done for me? He knows who I am, Ma. He doesn't care what we've got.'

Bel shrugged. 'Seeing a lassie outside the home is sometimes different from seeing her in it.'

Eva leaped to her feet. 'Well, if he's going to be put off by my home, I'd better find out, eh? I'll ask him over on Boxing Day.'

'Nae bother,' said Bel. 'But if he hurts you, he'll have me to settle with, I'm telling you.'

'And me,' Frank cried fiercely.

Her parents' attitude towards Nicholas was just one more painful burden that had fallen on Eva following her engagement. She'd been so naïve, she supposed ruefully, thinking that everyone would be happy for her. In fact, as she'd quickly found out, the reverse was true.

At school, for instance, when she'd first worn her ring, it seemed it was too grand for her colleagues to believe. When they'd finally accepted that the diamonds were real and had been given to her by one of the North family, the congratulations were slow in coming and the eyes were green.

'Well well, looks like you've changed your coat,' commented Greg Campbell, after he'd made great play of staggering back from the sparkle of the diamonds. 'Little Miss Red should never be wearing a ring like this, eh?'

'I don't know what you mean,' Eva had replied coldly.

'Well, how many bairns could be given hot meals with the cost of these baubles? How many pairs of boots could you buy?'

She had snatched her hand back from his grasp and hurried away, her colour high. *No one else need see this ring*, she thought.

But then there had been Mrs Crindle to show the ring to, and although Katie had been sweet and genuinely pleased over the engagement, her mother, when she heard about Nicholas and looked at the five diamonds, could hardly bring herself to say a word. As plain as though they were written on her brow were the thoughts in her mind. Why should this not have been Katie's ring? Why should it not have been Katie engaged to Mr North's son?

'Isn't it lovely, Mum?' Katie asked cheerfully.

'Oh, lovely,' Mrs Crindle managed to say. 'What a lucky girl you are then, Eva!'

'You're supposed to say the man's lucky, not the girl,' Katie told her, laughing.

'I'm sure he is,' her mother agreed, but for the life of her could not smile.

As for the neighbours, they didn't need to see the ring. They'd already seen the red sports car

285

standing outside Bel's house in Wish Lane, and knew that Bel's lassie had found herself a toff. A grand catch, eh, Mr North's son?

The thought of it was hardly to be borne, although they'd always known that Eva Masson considered herself different from everybody else, and her mother had kept her up in it. In spite of Bel's constant protests that the engagement was nothing to do with her, nobody wanted to talk to her any more, and when she came out to shake her mats, or take in her washing, folk simply faded away. What could you say to a woman whose daughter was marrying a jute baron's son?

It was the same at the mill, where some of the girls treated Bel as though she were from another species, and Berta Loch looked ready to kick the place down with envy, or get into a fight. How had Eva Masson netted Nicholas North, whose father owned the very mill where her mother worked?

Again, Bel would make her protests. She was not in favour; she'd never wanted her daughter to marry the boss's son. Berta and her cronies only jeered. Who did she think she was fooling? Who wouldn't give their eyeteeth to get their lassie married to a North?

'You know something?' Bel asked one Sunday, when Eva had come over for her dinner with the family. 'I'm going to have to leave the mill.'

The others stared.

'You're what?' asked Frank, his jaw dropping.

'I said, I'm going to leave the mill. Find something else.'

'Why? What for?'

'Why do you think?' Bel was close to tears. 'It's because of Eva.'

'Me?' Eva put down her knife and fork. 'You mean my engagement?'

'Aye. Some o' the lassies canna stand the thought o' you marrying Mr North's son and they're taking it out on me.'

'That's ... that's ridiculous!' Eva looked at Roddie, who was staring at his mother, a piece of Yorkshire pudding still poised on his fork. 'Has anybody said anything to you, Roddie?'

'Not a word. Why you, Ma?'

'Because they think I'm putting on airs. Which isnae true.'

'Of course it isnae!' cried Frank. 'Now look, Bel, you've been a spinner at North's nearly all your life, and you're no' going to give it up to please a load o' silly lassies. You stay put and it'll pass. Folk'll forget.'

'With Eva married to that fella? They'll no' forget.' Bel put her hand to her brow. 'It's bad enough with folk giving me the cold shoulder here; I'm no' putting up with it at work as well.'

'I'm sorry, Ma,' Eva said in a low voice. 'I never dreamed this would happen. But it's only some of the girls, isn't it? And they're in the wrong, not us.'

'Aye, Bel, so you stay where you are,' muttered Frank.

'But it might not be a bad thing to move anyway,' Eva went on. 'You know I've thought for a long time that the mill's too much for you, Ma.

You'd do better to find something else.'

'And I suppose that would suit Joseph North!' Bel cried with sudden spirit. 'I dare say he'd like me out o' the mill, so's he needn't say his son's got a spinner for a mother–in-law. If I leave, it'll be for me, no' him.'

'I think you should start looking straight away,' Roddie said eagerly. 'Evie's right, Ma. You could do with an easier job now.'

But Bel, sniffing, gathered plates together and said no more. She did, however, tell Eva as she was leaving that she didn't think she'd have Nicholas North over to the house, after all. She didn't feel up to it and hoped Eva would understand.

'All right, Ma,' said Eva. 'I do understand.'

'I'm sorry, you ken. It's just that everything's that difficult, eh?'

'We can fix it up some other time. Maybe after we're married.'

'Aye, let's say that. After you're married.'

I wish to God I was married now, thought Eva.

Fifty-Seven

Although there had been times when it had seemed as though the wedding day would never come, it arrived at last, and on a damp morning in early February, Eva and Nicholas were married at the Dundee registry office.

Eva wore a two-piece in her favourite dark red,

288

with matching coat and a small hat, while Nicholas was elegant in a dark suit and white carnation. The only guests were Letty and Roddie, who were witnesses, and Katie and Hughie – until Willow North suddenly arrived, wearing a beautiful fawn coat and a spray of gardenias.

'Couldn't miss seeing you married, Nicholas,' she drawled, and kissed his cheek when he and Eva had finished signing the register. 'And don't you both look sweet!'

'How kind of you to come, Miss North,' Eva said politely, and in truth she was surprised that her new sister-in-law had made the effort.

'Please, call me Willow. Won't you introduce me to your guests?'

But the little wedding party was so overcome by Miss North's looks and manner that they were almost speechless when she shook their hands, Eva being the only one to manage a few words.

'Are you coming with us to the Post?' Nicholas asked his sister. 'We've laid on a luncheon.'

'Please come,' Eva said earnestly. 'It's so nice to see you here.'

'The only one on the groom's side,' Nicholas said pointedly. 'Or don't brides and grooms have sides at registry office weddings? Never mind, let's get to the hotel. Where are those cars I ordered?'

As they stood looking out for the taxis, he suddenly turned his head and looked down at Eva.

'Do you realize something?'

She raised her eyes to his. 'Realize what?'

'We're married!'

Their faces were so radiant when the first taxi

arrived that the driver didn't need to be told who they were.

'Bride and groom?' he asked, opening the door. 'Or should I say the happy couple, eh?'

'Post Hotel, please,' Nicholas answered, laughing.

Eva had been in the hotel several times since her first visit with Bob Keir, but she still remembered how nervous she'd been then, and how thrilled to see Nicholas North, though she hadn't admitted so at the time. Now, of course, she came as a very special person – a bride, arriving for her wedding breakfast – and felt wonderfully confident and at ease. But then, in the hotel foyer, she saw her parents.

'Ma!' she cried, scarcely taking in that her mother, dressed in her best coat and hat, was holding Letty's baby, wee Iain. 'And Dad! Oh, you came, you came! Nicholas – they came!'

'So I see,' he said with a somewhat uncertain smile as Eva flung her arms first round her mother, who had hastily handed the baby to Letty, and then her father. 'Mr and Mrs Masson, it's very good to see you.'

'Eva, you're strangling me,' Frank gasped. 'Or else it's ma collar. Lord, how do folk wear these things every day?'

'Letty made us come,' Bel whispered, but her great eyes were tender on her daughter. 'And in the end, I wanted to – I did. I couldnae let you go on your wedding day, without seeing you, eh?'

'I said she'd be glad,' Letty put in, over Iain's wails. 'Did I no' say, Hughie, that Ma would be glad we made her come?'

'Mr Masson, Mrs Masson – may I introduce my sister?' Nicholas asked, as Willow came forward with her small smile. 'Willow, may I present Eva's parents, Mr and Mrs Masson?'

'Grand you could come,' said Bel, recovering from the shock of Willow's elegance more quickly than Frank, who was as speechless as Eva's other guests had been. 'It's nice for folks to have somebody of their own at a wedding, eh?'

'Very nice, indeed,' agreed Willow. 'Shall we all go and freshen up before luncheon?'

Fifty-Eight

The wedding breakfast went off well, with the Massons regaining their nerve enough to enjoy being in the private room Nicholas had reserved, and baby Iain being able to sleep in a small cot the hotel had provided.

At the head of the table, the bride and groom could eat very little, so busy were they smiling and looking at each other and generally behaving like love-birds.

'So difficult to eat when you're floating on a cloud, isn't it?' Willow commented.

'And such a grand meal, an' all,' said Frank. 'Eva, when you come off that cloud, you're going to be hungry, eh?'

'Hush, now,' Bel told him. 'You're drinking

too much wine.'

'No' me, I'm holding back for the champagne.'

Bel frowned. Never in her life had she had champagne, and now it was being served for the toasts at her daughter's wedding, she felt her hold on reality slipping away before she'd even drunk it. Aye, it might be all right for them to sit here in this private room with just Nicholas and his sister from the North family, but how would things be in the future? How would Eva keep a foothold in both worlds – the Norths', and that of her own family?

Bel's eyes met Eva's and she sensed that, for a fleeting moment, her daughter had forgotten Nicholas and was thinking of her. Of her ma, and her dad, and of Wish Lane, and all the life she'd wanted to leave and now felt pulling at her heart. Then Nicholas put his hand over hers and she turned to him, her face radiant again, and the moment was past.

'On your feet, Bel,' Frank said happily. 'Our Roddie's going to propose a toast.'

And there was Roddie, blushing, and waving his champagne about as he stood to make the toast. 'Ladies ... er ... Ladies and gentlemen, I give you ... the bride and groom!'

'Now who taught him to say that?' asked Bel in a whisper, but she was standing with the others and tasting the champagne as they all cried, 'The bride and groom!'

'Long life and happiness!' cried Hughie, and Letty burst into tears.

'Och, they look so happy anyway,' she murmured.

'It's a real fairy tale ending, isn't it?' Katie said, shedding tears too.

'With Nicholas as the handsome prince?' asked Roddie, feeling pleased with himself as he sat down. 'I say Eva's as pretty as a princess, anyway.'

'Quiet,' said Letty. 'Nicholas is going to say a few words.'

His speech was short, and not the usual speech a bridegroom makes, but then this was not a usual wedding. Certainly, there were no witticisms or jokes, but it was what he wanted to say and perhaps all they wanted to hear. He thanked his guests for coming, particularly his parents-in-law and the two witnesses of the marriage. He said how privileged he felt to have married his 'dear wife' – there were smiles at that – and how he looked forward to a wonderful future with her. Very soon, they would be house hunting, and when they'd made a home of their own, he hoped that all their guests would come to visit, when he could promise them a warm welcome.

'And now,' he finished, with a smile, 'may I ask my wife to stand with me and make a toast to you.'

And with Eva at his side, he raised a glass, and so did she.

'To our wedding guests!' they cried, and everyone clapped as they sat down.

'Where's the honeymoon going to be?' asked Willow.

'It's a secret,' Roddie told her.

She fixed him with a long stare. 'How ridiculous! There are only a handful of us here; I think

293

we should be told.'

'London,' Nicholas called down the table.

'London? I thought newly-weds wanted to be on their own?'

'Exactly so. London's the place to be for that. Nobody knows who you are. You go to some tiny little place to be alone and all the residents say, 'Ah, honeymooners!'

'Well, I hope you've booked a good hotel, then.'

'You can be sure of that.' Nicholas touched Eva's arm. 'Mrs North, I think we should be on our way.'

Nicholas had earlier left his car at the rear of the hotel and now drove it to the front entrance, where the doorman stuffed the newly-weds' cases in, and Roddie, aided by Hughie, tied on a tin can.

'Hey, none of that!' cried Nicholas.

'Ah, don't spoil the fun,' called Willow, suddenly animated. 'Has anyone any confetti?'

'I have!' said Katie.

'Me too,' added Letty.

But Eva was hugging her parents, saying good-bye in a cracked voice – not crying, but close to it.

'Thanks for coming to the hotel, Ma, Dad – it meant a lot.'

'Wouldnae have missed it,' said Frank.

'Mr Nicholas put on a good show,' Bel agreed, putting on a good show herself, of not being overcome with tears.

'He's just Nicholas now, Ma,' Eva told him.

'He's your son-in-law.'

'Aye, well he's been very kind, I'll say that for him. But you tell him to take care on thae roads, eh?'

'I take it you're not trying to make London tonight?' Willow asked, sauntering over to the car to give the tin can another knot, and Nicholas shook his head. 'Where are you stopping, then?'

'Aha, that'd be telling! It really is a secret.'

'Good luck then,' she said sincerely, and stood back as he took his seat at the wheel.

'Eva, are you coming?' he called.

'Letty, will you take my flowers to Mavis's grave?' Eva asked quietly as she gave last hugs to Katie, Roddie and Hughie, and kissed wee Iain. 'They'll not last long in this weather, but I'd like them to be there.'

'Sure I will.' Letty gave her sister a little push. 'But you'd better get in that motor, Evie, or Nicholas will be worrying!'

'That's all right.' Eva, taking her place next to Nicholas, waved her hand, as the confetti flew. 'I've not changed my mind about going!'

'Glad to hear it,' said Nicholas as they drove away, but Eva kept on waving even when they'd left the hotel behind, and her family, too.

Fifty-Nine

In the secret location, which turned out to be an inn over the border into Northumberland, Eva and Nicholas spent some time in their room shaking confetti from their clothes before abandoning them completely.

'Oh, Eva!' Nicholas gasped. 'Let's get to bed!'

But she was already there, sinking into the feather mattress, smiling in the darkness as he joined her. For a little while they clung together, murmuring words without much meaning, until Nicholas suddenly whispered, 'Eva? How much do you know?'

'Know?'

He caressed her a little uneasily. 'About first nights?'

'Well ... from living in a tenement, maybe more than some girls would.'

'That's a relief. I've been worrying a bit.'

'No need to worry about me, Nicholas.'

But after they'd made love, Eva was so quiet that Nicholas said he was worrying again.

'Are you all right, darling?'

'Oh, yes! It's just ... well ... I think I didn't know as much as I thought.'

'Eva, I'm sorry. It'll be better next time, I promise.'

'No, I mean I didn't know how much I'd like

it. Folk tell you such things, you see, but they can't have been as lucky as me, that's all I can say.'

'I'm the lucky one,' said Nicholas.

Next day, the lucky ones continued their journey, stopping twice more en route before reaching London, where Eva, who had never seen the city before, was exhilarated by the atmosphere, the people, the number of places to see, and the splendid hotel which was their base.

'This must be costing a lot,' she murmured over dinner one evening. 'Are you sure we can afford it?'

'Always worrying about money,' he said indulgently. 'There's no need, Eva. No need for you to worry about money.'

Imagine anyone saying that to her, she thought as she drank her wine. No need to worry about money! Her heart lifted as she thought of all that could be done with money, the good that could come if it were spread around. If only she could succeed in doing that...

'Any idea where you'd like to live, back in Dundee?' Nicholas asked, breaking into her reverie. 'Remember our house hunting. Don't want to stay too long in that flat we've rented.'

'Not Broughty Ferry,' she said after a pause, and he fervently agreed.

'Dear God, no! And we won't be looking for any Victorian monstrosities anywhere, I can tell you that. There are some quite decent modern houses going up now, I believe, but of course you'll want to choose, won't you? Houses always matter more to women than men.'

'I suppose because they have to spend more time in the home. That'll be me. I won't be going back to work.'

'You'll find plenty to do, knowing you.'

All the same, Eva knew she would miss her teaching. She would never regret leaving it for Nicholas, and perhaps it wouldn't have been fair, if she'd kept someone out of a job when she didn't need the money. Still, it rankled that she'd been forced to go.

Now she must find other things to fill her life. Maybe a family? One day, but not yet. First, she'd like to do what she'd always dreamed of doing, and work for those who needed help. Once she was settled, that's what she would do.

After all, she'd been so lucky, hadn't she? As she and Nicholas left the hotel restaurant, she was reminded again of her luck and her happiness. Hadn't she once said to her father that she was the happiest person in the world? And he'd said in Wish Lane, maybe. No, no, thought Eva as she ran joyfully into Nicholas's arms when they reached the haven of their room. This time, it was true. She was the happiest person in the world.

Sixty

Three months after they returned from honey-moon, Eva and Nicholas found themselves a house. It was not modern, but early Victorian, part of an elegant terrace off Perth Road, one of the finest and longest streets in Dundee, and so charming that Eva thought it could never be hers.

'Look, I can borrow off my inheritance to buy it,' Nicholas told her. 'The house needs a good deal doing to it; not everyone will want it. I may even try an offer.'

Pacing up and down on the pavement, Eva had waited outside their lawyer's offices while nego-tiations were made, and when Nicholas finally appeared she could hardly raise her eyes to his. But, amazingly, her luck had held. Their offer had been accepted. The house would be theirs.

'I feel uneasy,' she murmured as Nicholas went so far as to hug her in the street with their lawyer's clerk watching them from the windows. 'It's all too much.'

'Nonsense! You're just not used to the good life, and that's a shame.' Nicholas laughed. 'When would you ever hear Willow saying she had too much? Or me, for that matter?'

'Nicholas, you don't care about money!'

'Dear Eva, of course I do.'

'No, I know you don't.' She didn't add, 'Because you married me,' though perhaps he knew what was in her mind. In any case, they did not continue the conversation, but went back to their little rented flat, praying that nothing would stop the house purchase going through. But nothing did, and on a beautiful afternoon in May, they were given the keys and and took possession of Number Seventeen Princess Victoria Terrace.

Two-storeyed, with a basement and a small garden to front and rear, it had spacious, well-proportioned rooms and long, elegant windows. Not overpowering in the style of the jute barons' mansions, it was a pretty house, the sort of place where you could quickly feel at home. Even if you'd never been used to anything like it before, thought Eva, walking the bare floors in a dream.

'Never thought I'd live anywhere like this,' she murmured. 'What'll my folks think, then?'

'You've told them about it, haven't you?' Nicholas asked absently as he tapped walls and studied flaking plaster.

'Yes, but they haven't seen it.'

'Bring 'em round, but we've a lot of work to do before we can move in. I'll have to contact a builder.'

'Ma won't know what to make of it. I mean, me in Princess Victoria Terrace!' Eva turned her large eyes on Nicholas. 'And they're in Wish Lane.'

He was silent for a moment. 'You'd like them out? I must admit, I've thought of it.'

'Have you?' Her face lit up. 'Could we do it, Nicholas? Find them something better?'

'To tell you the truth, it's what my parents

would like.'

Of course. Eva knew only too well how the thought of their daughter-in-law's background in Wish Lane must aggravate Joseph and Ailsa North. And then there was Eva's mother, still working as a spinner, for as the weeks had gone by, Bel had changed her mind about leaving the mill.

'Let Berta and company get on with it!' she'd cried. 'I'm staying put.'

And in the end, the troublemakers had got used to the idea of Bel's having a wealthy son-in-law, and as it seemed to have made no difference to her, their protests had died down.

What if Bel were to move to a better house, though? Eva bit her lip. She was not going to give up her idea of improving her parents' lot to please those envious mill girls. *Let them get on with it*, she thought, echoing her mother. *I'll do what's best*.

'Do you think your parents will want to come here?' Eva asked Nicholas, as they inspected the kitchens in the basement.

Since their return from honeymoon, they had only been asked once to Garth House. That had been for dinner, with just his parents and Willow present. A hot meal that might have been served on ice for all the warmth that had been conveyed to the newly-weds, but, as Eva had commented, at least it was a beginning. If there had been no sign as yet of a thaw in relations between herself and the Norths, maybe they could still hope it was on its way.

Nicholas wasn't so sure. 'I suppose we'll have to invite them,' he answered now. 'Might want to see what we've done with the dining table they gave us.'

She knew he minded that his parents hadn't really welcomed her into the family, but then Bel had not kept her promise to ask him to Wish Lane. Though she'd said she was grateful for all Nicholas had done for Eva, she – and Frank too – had given him no more of a welcome than the Norths had given their daughter. Another thing to hope for, it seemed.

'This place needs a complete transformation,' Nicholas commented, looking at the Victorian cooking range, the unpainted shelves and stone floor. 'Could hardly ask a maid to work here, as it is.'

'A maid?' Eva's heart sank a little. 'Do I have to have one?'

'You'd hardly want to spend your time cleaning yourself, surely?' he asked with a laugh.

'No, but I don't like the idea of people having to work for me.'

'You'd soon get used to it. Just tell 'em what to do, and they do it.'

'I'd feel bad, acting the mistress of the house.'

He held her close, still laughing. 'Darling, you *are* the mistress of the house. As long as you pay their wages, they'll do what you say.'

'I'll speak to my folks about a move as soon as I can. It's grand that you're going to help – I do appreciate it.'

'Will they?'

'Of course they will!' she cried.

Sixty-One

The evening when Eva chose to return to Wish Lane was warm and pleasant; the sort of weather to bring everyone out into the open air, put chairs on the tenement pletties, hang out of windows to chat with the neighbours. Children were all at play in the streets, boys whizzing around on their pilers made from old pram wheels and wooden boxes, while the girls chanted rhymes as they skipped, or jumped across tiles on the pavement.

Once, Eva reminded herself, she had been like one of those lassies, not looking forward then to improving herself, just enjoying a lovely evening. And here were her parents, doing that now, sitting by the open window, her dad smoking his pipe, her mother without shoes, resting.

'Anybody home?' Eva called.

'Eva, is that you?' cried Bel.

'Nobody else. Isn't this a grand evening, then? Wish we could be out on a plettie?'

'We're all right. How about you? Left your man?'

'He's got a meeting. I wanted to come and tell you we've got the keys to the house.'

'Fancy.' Her mother's eyes flickered. 'Our Eva in that lovely street, Frank.'

'And got the keys,' he murmured. 'Niver

303

thought you'd buy a house, Eva. Most folk rent.'

'We wanted a place of our own. Will you come and see it? There's a lot to do before we move in, but you could look round.'

'Aye, that'd be nice.' Bel fanned herself with a newspaper. 'I expect you'd like a cup o' tea?'

'Later.' Eva hesitated. 'I was wondering – d'you ever think of moving yourselves?'

'Flitting? From Wish Lane?' They stared, and Frank tapped out his pipe.

'Why'd we want to do that?'

'Well, there are some really nice flats around, you know.'

'What are you on about, Eva? We canna afford the rents o' that sort o' thing.'

'We'd help. Nicholas and me.'

But no one spoke.

Looking round the living room, with the sunbeams dancing in, revealing the shabbiness of everything they touched, Eva could only think how small it was. How cramped and lacking in comfort. Why did it seem so much worse than usual?

'What do you say?' she asked a little impatiently as her mother filled the kettle.

'I thought it'd no' be long before they wanted us out o' here,' Bel answered. 'Thae Norths are dying to change us, eh? And it's no' going to work.'

'You're right there,' said Frank, flinging himself into his chair. 'We're no' going anywhere.'

'This has nothing to do with Mr and Mrs North!' cried Eva. 'It's our idea. Well, mine really, but Nicholas is keen, too. I want you to

304

have a comfortable place to live. Why not? You've worked hard all your lives. Why shouldn't you have somewhere nice, then?'

'What I have, I pay for maself,' Frank answered steadily. 'I dinna take charity.'

'This isn't charity, Dad. Just a bit of help, to make you more comfortable. Make Ma's life easier.' She turned desperately to her mother. 'You'd like it, wouldn't you, Ma? A place with a bathroom and more space – an extra room or two – and maybe even a little garden at the back, not just a drying green.'

'You're a good, sweet girl to think of us,' said Bel. 'But dinna try to be like thae Norths and change us. This is our home, it's what we can afford, and it's where we'll stay.'

The kettle boiled and she made the tea, but Eva hadn't the heart to drink it. A great tide of bitterness engulfed her, as she looked at her parents, so united against her, so unwilling to let her make their lives easier. She'd thought they'd be pleased. Had pictured their eyes lighting up when she suggested helping them to move. Instead, they'd thrown the offer back in her face.

'I never wanted to change you,' she said slowly. 'That wasn't the idea at all. Children often help their parents when they grow up, if they can. I bet Roddie'd like to do the same. There was no question of charity.'

'Let's say no more about it,' her father said, stirring sugar into his tea. 'We appreciate the offer, but we're all right here.'

'I thought you were more like me,' Eva said to Bel in a low voice. 'I thought you wanted more from life than...'

'What I've got? Aye, well I did, at one time. But it'd have had to come through me, no' a son-in-law whose dad doesnae give a damn about his workers. If we took money from your Nicholas, we'd be taking money from the mill folk.' Bel laughed shortly. 'Aye, maybe it'd be our own money we'd be using for this extra rent, eh? Money we never got?'

'Good point,' commented Frank. 'Eva, dinna worry your head about us. You've gone up in the world and if you're happy, that's all that matters. But leave us alone, eh?'

For some time Eva sat without speaking, then she drank her cold tea and stood up.

'I'll go, then. Nicholas will be home by now.'

'Aye, better get home, then,' said Bel.

'Will you still come and look round the new house?'

'When you're settled,' said Bel. 'Oh yes, we'll want to see where you live.' She put her arm round Eva's shoulders. 'And thank Nicholas for the offer, eh? Dinna want him to think we're no' grateful.'

'Tell Roddie I'm sorry I missed him,' Eva murmured from the door. 'Is he out with his pals?'

'Out with somebody. Never says who. That's young men for you, eh?'

Both parents went with her to the street and Eva knew they were sorry for her now, but if she were to make her offer again, they'd refuse it just the same.

'I'll be in touch, then.'

'Aye, we'll look out for you, pet.'

As she walked round the corner from Wish Lane, Eva burst into tears.

Sixty-Two

Never again, Eva vowed, would she try to improve her parents' lives with Nicholas's money. For of course it was the North money that was the problem. When she'd bought them things from her own salary, they'd never refused them, and if she'd been able to help them move herself, they would not have said no.

But to them there was all the difference in the world between her money and North money, and perhaps she should have been more sensitive to that point of view. After all, it was true that Mr North was not one of the more enlightened employers, taking all he could from his workers, and giving the minimum in return. It shouldn't have surprised her that her folks didn't want to be beholden to him, even indirectly.

But where did her parents' views leave her? She was married to a North. She was living on North money. Her new house and almost everything she now owned had been bought with it. Her folks had never blamed her for accepting it, though they'd never wanted Nicholas for a son-in-law, but there'd be plenty that would blame her, she knew. Plenty who would point the finger

– Bob Keir for one.

Well, thank God, she didn't have to answer to him, but she suddenly realized she did have an answer. She'd married Nicholas, not for anything he had, but for himself. The money was an extra, a bonus, something she could hardly refuse. What would her critics have her do? Ask him to live in a tenement? Give up everything he'd been used to all his life?

No, but if she asked him, he would surely agree to share some of the North profits with the workers. Just make their lives fractionally easier. It made her feel a little better to decide to speak to him on this matter, as soon as the house was finished and they had settled into their new life together. Some instinct made her believe it would be better to postpone any discussions until then.

As the summer months progressed, so did the renaissance of Number Seventeen, with Eva throwing herself into supervising the work with all the energy that had once gone into her studies and her job.

It was the first time, of course, that she'd been involved in any such project, and it gave her a particular satisfaction to see her new home returning to its original condition. When the builders, carpenters and painters had completed their work, a firm of specialists transformed the kitchen, providing not only a new range, but an up-to-date gas cooker, as well as cabinets and flooring. After that it was Eva's turn, to choose furniture and curtains, and then, finally, the project was complete.

'It's finished!' she told Nicholas happily. 'We can invite people round.'

First to come were her family and Katie, by which time Eva had acquired a maid. She was a nice, easy-going girl named Cora, reddish-haired and blue-eyed, who said she didn't mind doing a bit of cooking in addition to cleaning, if there was no bossy cook looking on, like in most places she'd worked. And who wouldn't mind cooking in Mrs North's grand kitchen? Cora was in raptures over it.

Though Eva had discovered, when she and Katie were sharing a flat, that she was interested in cooking and quite good at it, she was relieved to find that Cora could help out. Cooking for Nicholas was one thing; cooking for guests and entertaining them at the same time was another. Not that she counted her folks as guests to worry about, but sooner or later there would be Nicholas's parents to invite. Eva put that thought to the back of her mind for the moment.

Everything went remarkably well on the Sunday that her family and Katie came over, with even Bel and Frank joining in the praise from the younger folk, and no comments being made on the fact that Eva now had a maid.

There was, in fact, only one bad moment, when Bel, in Eva's bedroom getting ready to go home, looked at her reflection in the dressing table mirror and sighed.

'Getting older, eh? See thae lines?'

'Ma, you look fine. Always do.' Eva came to

stand at her side. 'But you work too hard. You know I'd like you to find an easier job.'

'Think I'll keep this one as long as I can.' Bel gave her daughter a long, steady look. 'Just as long as you're all right, Eva.'

'Why should I not be all right?'

'Oh, it's all happened so quick, eh? Getting wed, and the house and everything. It's all worked out for you, like they were saying – a fairy story. Do you no' sometimes feel you're in a bubble?'

'A bubble?' Eva stepped back, her eyes beginning to flash. 'You mean you think it's going to burst?'

'No, no.' Bel threw her arms around Eva's shoulders. 'Take no notice o' me. Canna think why I said that. I can see you're very happy with Nicholas, and that's the main thing, eh?'

'It is to me,' Eva answered stiffly. 'Think we'd better go down. Dad'll be waiting.'

'You've a grand home, pet, and I'm very happy for you. Aye, I am.' Bel put her hand on Eva's arm. 'Believe me.'

They were both silent, dark eyes meeting dark eyes, until from below they heard wee Iain begin to cry and, still without speaking, went downstairs.

'Just my people to come now,' Nicholas said that evening, pouring himself a whisky and soda. 'Let's get that over with and then we can relax.'

'Better ask them, then.' Eva, in her chair by the fire, was trying to forget her mother's words. 'Do you no' sometimes feel you're in a bubble?'

The worst of it was, she sometimes did.

'I'll give them a ring tomorrow,' Nicholas said. 'Shall we make it dinner?'

'No, lunch is easier.'

'You could always get yourself a cook, you know.'

Eva rose and said she was tired and she was going to bed. 'I don't want any more than I've got,' she said in a low voice, which Nicholas did not appear to hear.

Sixty-Three

Ailsa and Joseph North did not come to visit Number Seventeen until well into the autumn.

In preparation, Eva and Cora had spent days working on the house, the table and the menu, for Eva was desperate for everything to be so perfect that no criticism could possibly be levelled.

Finally Nicholas was driven to remind her that it was his parents coming, not King George and Queen Mary.

'They'd be easier,' Eva sighed.

'Look, stop worrying. Mother and Pa are not going to complain.'

'I just want them to see the place at its best.'

Looking round at the shining house, with its polished furniture and bowls of flowers, Nicholas told her it was already looking its best. Now Eva could relax.

'Relax? Now I've got to think about the lunch!' she cried, and Nicholas groaned.

On the day itself, however, things at first went very well. The Norths must have been pleasantly surprised by their son's new house and the way in which his new wife had organized it, for everything was praised, even if with lifted brows and exchanged glances between the guests.

'Charming, my dear,' commented Mrs North, sipping sherry before luncheon. 'I can't believe that you worked out all the interior design yourself.'

'Very talented,' her husband remarked. 'And the house is a good choice, Nicholas. Small, of course, but in a good area. Well proportioned rooms, too.'

'Glad you like it, Pa.' Nicholas refilled his father's glass. 'But where's Willow, then? She's called in once or twice when the house was half done, but we wanted her to see it finished.'

'Oh, you know Willow,' Mrs North sighed. 'Always out with somebody. How I wish she'd settle down! When I was her age, I'd been married two years and had already had you, Nicholas.'

'Girls these days are not in a hurry to settle down,' Joseph North muttered. 'Ever since they got the vote, they've been impossible.'

'As though Willow cares a straw for voting!' cried her mother. 'One thing I can tell you, she'd never have been a suffragette.'

'Luncheon is served,' Cora announced, blushing to her white linen cap, and Mrs North gave an indulgent smile.

* * *

Eva had been wise enough not to attempt anything too ambitious for the meal, selecting only soup, lamb cutlets and a Charlotte Russe – a pudding of sponge fingers and cream that Katie had taught her how to make. Though she was on the edge of her chair most of the time, she managed not to show her nerves, and was rewarded when Joseph North said he would send his compliments to the cook.

'We haven't found a cook yet,' Nicholas said quickly. 'Eva's standing in.'

'With some help from Cora,' put in Eva.

'Eva?' Both of Nicholas's parents stared, clearly astonished that their strange daughter-in-law, with help only from a young maid, could have prepared the meal.

'I really must congratulate you, my dear,' Mrs North said quietly. 'You've done well.'

'Indeed.' Her husband finished his wine, still studying Eva, until Nicholas rose and led the way to the drawing room, where Cora had left coffee.

'Last lap,' he whispered to Eva as she poured the coffee. 'You've been wonderful.'

No more to worry about, she thought, smiling as Mrs North murmured something to the effect that she must be so happy in her new home. And then it happened.

'Yes, but I feel so guilty,' Eva heard herself reply.

Why had she said it? As a silence fell around her, she asked herself the question. *Why, oh why, had she admitted to the Norths that she felt*

313

guilty? But she knew it to be true.

'Guilty?' asked Joseph North, pausing in the act of lighting a cigar. 'Why on earth...?'

Glancing desperately at Nicholas, whose face was expressionless, Eva sought the right words. 'I suppose it's because I have so much, when others have so little,' she said at last.

'I'm afraid I can't understand that attitude,' Nicholas's father said flatly. 'No one can expect to have exactly as much as other people. There will always be differences, because there's no equality in this world. People are not equal and never will be.'

'Couldn't more be done to even things out?' asked Eva.

'That's what Communists believe. Doesn't work. It's capital that drives the system. Market forces.' Mr North smoked his cigar, his brown eyes fixed on Eva's face. 'My grandfather started with nothing. There was no silver spoon in his mouth. But he had brains and he understood business. When he'd had experience in the jute industry, he learned enough to start his own firm. Borrowed from the bank, paid it back and went on to be one of the biggest employers in Dundee.'

'Got to hand it to him,' Nicholas murmured, while Mrs North drank her coffee with a weary expression on her face, as though she'd heard all this before.

'Now, Eva,' Mr North went on, 'you probably think that all the workers in the Dundee factories should earn as much as the mill owners...'

'No, of course not!' she cried. 'Just a living

314

wage.'

'A living wage? They were all managing to live on their wages, the last I heard. But if you expect them to get more, you don't understand the way business works. Employers have to make a profit. The more they have to pay their workers, the less profit they make and the more likely they are to go under.' Mr North sat back in his chair. 'Where would the workers be, if the mills had to close?'

Eva was silent. There was no point in this conversation, as it was clear she could never win an argument with Mr North. It would be better to say no more – to him, at least. Her eyes again went to Nicholas, but he was steadfastly not looking at her.

'I do think we've talked business long enough,' Mrs North sighed. 'Joseph, perhaps we should be taking our leave?'

Thanks were made, but farewells were cool, and no future meetings were proposed as the Norths departed. But when they'd been waved off in their motor, Eva turned to Nicholas, hoping that he would understand what had happened. He knew her so well, knew all that mattered to her. Surely, he would?

'Nicholas...' She held out her hands to him, would have gone to him, but the look on his face stopped her.

'For God's sake, Eva!' he cried. 'Why did you have to talk to Pa like that? Why did you have to go and ruin everything?'

Sixty-Four

Her face drained of all colour, Eva went to the kitchen, where Cora was putting away the last of the dishes she'd washed.

'Cora, you go now,' she said quietly. 'It's your afternoon off – I don't want to keep you any longer.'

'Nae bother, Madam, Eh was glad tae give ye a hand.' Cora's blue eyes shone. 'And see your ma-in-law and all. What a lovely lady! Wait till Eh tell Ma aboot her grand dress! Niver made any complaints, eh?'

'No, there were no complaints.'

'I'll away, then, if ye're sure?'

'I'm sure. Away you go.'

But Cora hesitated. 'Ye're that pale, eh? Want me to make a nice cup o' tea?'

'No, no. I'll do that.'

When Cora had finally left for her mother's house, Eva sat down at the kitchen table and stared into space. She thought of putting the kettle on, but it seemed too much of an effort and she made no move. Until a familiar step sounded, when she stood up to look into Nicholas's eyes.

'Oh, Eva,' he murmured, and took her hand.

'I'm not sorry, Nicholas. I'm not sorry I said what I did.'

'Do we have to talk here?'

She shrugged, but allowed herself to be taken up to the drawing room. It still smelled of Joseph North's cigar and she flung open a window as Nicholas watched.

'Have to get rid of that,' she muttered.

'Look, I'm sorry if I was rather sharp just then, but you must admit, it was disappointing. Things had been going so well – I was so pleased – and then you started going on about wages. You might have guessed it wouldn't go down well.'

'I didn't mean to cause trouble, but I only said what I think. And I'm not the only person to believe that the mill-owners should pay their workers more.' Eva bent to add coal to the fire. 'Your father says they can live on what he pays. Would he like to live on it?'

'He explained why it's not possible to pay more. Profits have to be kept up, or the business fails.'

'I know there have to be some profits, but do they have to be so huge?' Eva straightened up from the hearth. 'Can you really think it's right, that people like your father live in mansions, and the workers live in some of the worst housing in the country?'

'Eva...'

'No, hear me out. You've never seen some of the places folk have to live in. Stuffed together into tiny rooms, having to sleep like sardines in a tin, with no decent sanitation, or places to wash. And even in Wish Lane, which is better than some, there isn't a tree to be seen.'

'And now you live here,' he said softly.

'Yes, I live here. That's why I feel guilty.'

'Ah, poor girl.' Nicholas put his arms around her. 'I understand, you know. I can imagine how you must feel.'

'No, you can't, Nicholas. All my life I've wanted to change things for the better for the folk in Dundee.' She gave a sob. 'But I've only changed things for myself.'

'Even if you hadn't married me, you'd have had a good standard of living. You were a professional person, you'd worked hard – why shouldn't you live in a reasonable way?'

'Why shouldn't mill workers live in a reasonable way?' She freed herself from his arms and stared passionately into his face. 'If the mill-owners wanted, they could transform their lives, with only a little extra money. Nicholas, it could be done, it could! Will you say you'll work for that? Try to persuade your father? Promise me you will.'

'I'm sorry, darling, I can't.' His voice was firm. 'I have to agree with Pa. In an ideal world, of course, we'd like to pay the workers more, but it's just not practicable. We're business people; we have to take the long view to keep afloat.'

'You mean, keep up the profits?'

'Exactly. There's a good deal of new machinery coming on the market now, including ideas for dust extraction. You'd want to see improvements in the mill, wouldn't you?'

'Of course.'

'Well, how can we afford them, if we have to pay out more in wages? These are factors you don't think about, you see, because you don't

318

really know the situation.' Nicholas drew her to the sofa, where they sat together and he held her hands, caressing them gently. 'There's something else on the horizon, Eva. I dare say you've read about it in the papers, but we're due for a big recession pretty soon. That American stock market crash has caused trouble all over the world, and our exports are down anyway, with India undercutting us at every turn.' He shook his head. 'Even if we wanted to, we couldn't improve pay, I'm afraid. We'll be lucky to keep going as we are.'

Eva, still very pale, kept her dark gaze on his face. 'We'll be affected?'

'No, no, there's no need to worry about that. We shan't have to leave the Terrace.'

'I didn't really think we'd have to, Nicholas.'

Sensitive to her tone, he flushed a little. 'Eva, don't blame me for things I can't control. Some jobs might have to go – Berry's are planning a three-day week from the new year. We're all in the same boat, you see. Try to understand.'

'Oh, I do.' She stood up. 'Think I'll make a cup of tea. You won't mind a cold supper later on?'

'Of course not.' He gave an uncertain smile. 'Is everything all right between us now? Not cross with each other any more?'

'I'm not cross at all.'

Only sick at heart, she thought, filling the kettle. Sick at heart, to see a side of Nicholas she'd never known was there.

'I'm a businessman,' he'd always said, and so was his father, but she'd never understood before how like Joseph North he was.

It was clear how their arguments for not increasing wages made sense to them. Certain profits had to be made or the business would go under. Paying the workers more wasn't practicable, especially in times of recession. Eva could unwillingly accept that they really believed they couldn't do anything, but what hurt so much, what turned the knife in her heart, was that Nicholas didn't care like she did.

He didn't care about the people involved, that was the thing. She could talk as much as she liked about the way they had to live, but he'd been brought up to believe that that was the way things had to be. Other men might have questioned this, but Nicholas had accepted it, the truth being that he didn't mind. He didn't care. And for the first time, she realized that.

When he came down to have tea with her, she looked at him sadly for a long time. He seemed just the same, her Nicholas, the man she loved. And, of course, she did still love him. Feelings didn't change in a flash. But as she studied the handsome face of her beloved, she knew that something had changed. Something would never be quite the same again.

That night, as they lay together, he asked if she would like to make love.

'I expect you're tired,' he murmured. 'Been a busy day for you.'

'I am a bit tired,' she agreed, with some relief.

And yet, they found themselves making love anyway, taking comfort where they could find it, for both knew – Nicholas as well as Eva – that things were not as they had been between them. Neither would put the knowledge into words, for fear of proving it true, but when Nicholas had turned over, breathing deeply as though he were asleep, Eva was sure he wasn't. Certainly, she couldn't sleep herself, but lay very still, gazing into the darkness.

Is it true? she wondered. *Has the bubble burst? So soon?*

It would seem it had. The honeymoon of her marriage was over.

Sixty-Five

In the weeks that followed, Eva threw herself into what her mother-in-law called Good Works. Indeed, it was Mrs North who suggested them to her, when she and Nicholas were at last invited to Garth House. This time it was for dinner on Christmas Eve, when Willow condescended to put in an appearance and presents were exchanged.

Not the ordeal it might once have been for Eva, as the kind of impression she made on her in-laws was no longer important to her. They knew now what she was like; there seemed little point in trying to present herself differently. In fact, her more relaxed attitude seemed to work better for her, and though she couldn't say the evening was enjoyable, at least it wasn't too uncomfortable.

After dinner, Willow disappeared, as usual, and Mrs North began to tell Eva of some of the charities she might like to work for. There had always been classes available for those mill girls or women from the tenements who were willing to learn to sew, manage their budgets or look after their children, and these always needed volunteers. In addition, help was wanted at the one or two charities that had some funds available for those in dire need, and of course assistance was always needed at the thrift shops and places where the unemployed could be given a hot meal.

'Now, is there anything amongst these that would interest you, my dear?' Mrs North asked. 'I must admit, I tend to organize, rather than actively serve, you know. But one must do what one can, of course.'

Eva expressed her willingness to fit in where she was most needed, adding that she was rather missing her teaching and would be glad of something to do. At which Mrs North seemed pleased and said she would pass Eva's name around after Christmas. Nicholas, glancing across from his conversation with his father, saw her smile, and was, Eva could tell, relieved that no trouble had blown up to spoil the Christmas atmosphere.

'Well done,' he told her as they drove home. 'I can see you're getting into Mother's good books. When do you start your charity work, then?'

'As soon as possible after Christmas.'

First, of course, she had to entertain her family

to their Christmas dinner, which occupied her thoughts wonderfully well.

Of course, Bel's sharp eyes soon noticed the difference in her daughter.

'You're looking rather peaky, Eva. Is anything wrong?'

'No, I'm quite all right. And I'm not in the family way, if you're wondering.'

'Now, I never said a word!' cried Bel. 'It's early days yet for a babby.'

'You'll be the first to know when I have any news.'

'Aye. Girls like to tell their mothers things, eh?'

Despite her mother's significant tone, Eva only said that she would be doing some voluntary work as soon as the holidays were over.

'Voluntary work?' asked Letty. 'What sort o' voluntary work?'

'Oh, maybe helping with those sewing or cookery classes folk run. It's not decided yet.'

'Piece o' nonsense they are,' commented Bel. 'I reckon the lassies know as much as thae ladies doing the teaching. When have they done any cooking and such, eh? I mean, can you see Mrs North handling a sheep's heid?'

'Ssh, Ma,' said Letty. 'Nicholas might hear you.'

Bel stared across at him and said he was out of earshot. 'But he's looking peaky an' all,' she remarked, wondering to herself what was up with the love-birds.

Attention was diverted when Roddie gave the

news that he was moving into a room of his own after Hogmanay. Just a bed-sitter, but in quite a nice little street in Blackness. It was time he was independent, he said.

'Ma, will you be able to manage?' Eva asked at once, but her mother said that she and Frank had been expecting Roddie's move for some time and were prepared.

'Just as long as we keep our own jobs, we'll be all right,' added Frank. 'Did you hear about Berry's going on to a three-day week?'

All eyes went to Nicholas, who made no comment, but Roddie in a whisper told Eva that he would still be giving something to Ma, for her cocoa tins. No need to worry.

'She'll take it from you,' Eva answered. 'But not from me.'

'Fingers crossed, then, for 1931,' said Roddie.

It was a relief to Eva, when the festivities of Christmas and Hogmanay were over, to start on her voluntary work. What an anodyne work was! If you were on your feet and your hands were occupied, your thoughts could be made to switch off. At least the thoughts you didn't want.

Twice a week, she worked at a Salvation Army canteen, serving hot meals to anyone who needed them. One afternoon, she washed and ironed old clothes for a thrift shop, and on another, she did service in the shop itself. And, on one evening a week, she took a cookery class for the girls at the Camperdown Works in Lochee and had supper with Katie afterwards.

'Doesn't Nicholas mind?' Katie had asked. 'I

mean, if you're not at home for him?'

'No, he doesn't mind at all,' Eva had declared so firmly that Katie had opened her round eyes wide, but said nothing.

It wasn't true, of course. Nicholas minded very much when Eva was not at home. In fact, he did eventually ask if she might give up the cookery class and have dinner with him instead of Katie.

'No, I don't think I can do that,' she told him. 'I've agreed to do it and don't want to let them down.'

He fixed her with his grey eyes, which had taken on their wintry look, and she knew he wanted to speak out – was in fact bracing herself for it – when, as usual, he thought better of it. Better not put anything into words, he would be thinking, and she didn't in fact want to put anything into words herself.

Was she being too hard on him? She asked herself that sometimes, because her love for him was still so strong. But it was just that she was so disappointed. He'd said they were soulmates. She'd believed they were. But soulmates agreed on fundamentals, and they didn't.

Well, she'd have to learn to live with her disappointment. It was what people did, when their honeymoons were over and reality set in, and just at the moment, her voluntary work was helping her in that.

She was really managing rather well, she thought, until one Saturday afternoon in D. M. Brown's superior tearooms, she saw Willow North at a window table, laughing with a curly-headed man. And that man was Roddie.

Sixty-Six

For a moment, Eva was so stunned, she sat motionless. But when she looked at the table, she saw that she'd set down her cup with such force that the tea had spilled into the saucer.

'Shall I change that for you, Madam?' asked a waitress, swooping down on her, but Eva shook her head.

'The bill, please,' she whispered, and left the tearoom with her head down and her eyes looking anywhere but at the young couple in the window. Out in the street, buffeted by crowds looking for late bargains, she couldn't think what to do.

For already she knew that this was no chance encounter she was seeing. No single meeting that would lead nowhere. These two knew each other, were at ease together, in a way that could only have come from a long relationship. How long? she wondered, beginning to make her slow way home. How long had this affair been going on? Where could they have met?

And then she remembered. Of course. At her own wedding. They'd been sitting together, must have struck up an acquaintance, with Willow probably making the first move. No doubt she'd been attracted to Roddie, who was an attractive man. Not really handsome, but blue-eyed and tall – for one from Dundee – and with the sort of cheerful, optimistic face that people liked to see. To Willow he must have seemed very different from all the other young men she knew, with their smooth hair and smooth manners, and she must have seemed to him a being from another world. A star, no less, with her soft fair hair and her beautiful skin, her white hands that had never touched a machine. And if she'd showed interest in him, no wonder he'd been bowled over.

But, oh, couldn't he see that he was playing with fire? Courting danger, the deeper he got involved with one of the Norths?

No, he couldn't see. He would have to learn the hard way. Be hurt, be damaged, and Eva couldn't bear to think of it. As soon as she got home, she would write to him at his bed-sitter, asking him to meet her at lunchtime early next week, and then she'd talk to him. She'd spell out his future with Willow, and if he didn't want to listen, at least she'd have done all she could.

But what should she tell Nicholas? Though he was fond of Roddie, she knew he would scarcely welcome the news that her brother was seeing his sister. As to what his parents would think, he probably wouldn't dare even to contemplate it.

I won't tell him, Eva decided. *Not until I've talked to Roddie, anyway. Maybe I'm wrong, maybe he isn't in love with Willow.* But she knew she wasn't wrong. It was written all over him, in his blue eyes dwelling on her face, in his indulgent smile.

Oddly enough, Willow had looked as if she felt the same, but if she did, her feelings wouldn't

327

last. Roddie was a passing fancy, made more exciting because he came from a world she didn't know. Eva had heard about well-to-do people taking up with young folk from poorer backgrounds. They never intended true relationships.

'Had a good day?' asked Nicholas, looking chilled and windblown from an afternoon on the golf course.

'Not too bad,' she murmured, and hurried upstairs to write her letter in the privacy of her bedroom, afterwards slipping out to post it.

There it goes, to Roddie's room, she thought, and guessed it was significant that he'd moved out of Wish Lane. Now he had a place to invite Willow, where they could be alone. Always the problem for lovers, wasn't it, to find somewhere without other people?

'Well, what's all this about?' Roddie asked Eva jauntily as he ate sausage and mash in the café where they'd agreed to meet. He seemed his usual unworried self, except that Eva, who knew him so well, could see that his eyes were wary. An intelligent fellow, he knew she wouldn't have asked to see him alone without good reason, and as he had a secret, he must be wondering if she'd guessed it.

'No beating about the bush,' she answered, starting on her egg salad. 'I saw you with Willow on Saturday.'

'Oh?' He grinned disarmingly. 'No' a crime, is it?'

'How long have you been seeing her, Roddie?

328

I'm not being nosey. It's important.'

'Well, if it's any of your business, since your wedding.'

'I thought so. And you've been seeing her all that time and never said anything?'

'Seem to remember you were the same. Ma and Dad only found out about Nicholas when they met him at the station.'

'Nicholas and Willow can't be compared.'

'I think they're very similar.'

Eva leaned forward and looked seriously into her brother's face. 'Roddie, Nicholas wanted to marry me. You must realize that you could never marry Willow.'

'Why, when you married Nicholas?'

'That was different. He provides for me. You couldn't provide for Willow. Not in the way she'd want.'

'You know I'm studying to be an accountant at night school, Evie. I'm no' planning to stay a clerk all ma life.'

'Yes, I know, but even as an accountant, you'd not be able to pay for all that Willow'd want.'

'She's no' as keen on money as you make out. The way she's been brought up – that doesnae mean a thing to her.'

'So, she wouldn't want to buy expensive clothes, or live in a nice house, or ride her horse?' Eva shook her head. 'Roddie, you're not facing facts. Even if she wanted to marry you, her folks'd never let her. I can't even imagine how you afford to take her out. I mean, who pays?'

'No worries there. We share. Her idea, and I

agreed. Never did see why the fella has to pay for the girl every time.'

'I can't see why, either. But listen, what I'm saying is that at the moment you're a novelty to her. When she gets tired of you, that'll be the end of it. She'll be away and you'll be left grieving.' Eva put her hand to her brow. 'And I don't want to see it, Roddie, I don't! Please, please, don't get involved with the Norths!'

He looked at her curiously. 'Is everything all right, Evie? Between you and Nicholas? Ma said mebbe the gilt'd worn off the gingerbread.'

'Ma's always coming out with things like that. Everything is fine.'

'That's good, then. And I can set your mind at rest about me and Willow. I know I could never marry her and we're neither of us thinking of it. We're just taking things as they come and enjoying what we've got.' Roddie smiled across at his sister. 'And one good thing for me is, she's teaching me to drive.'

'Never! Her sports car?'

'Too right. It's grand. So, you see how we are. As I said, enjoying what we've got. That make you happy?'

'Sounds too sensible by half,' she answered, but managed a smile herself. 'I'll be happy if it's true.'

'It's true. Now, are we sharing this, or are you paying? If you are, could I have some o' that apple pie? And custard?'

By the time she'd reached home, Eva had decided that she did feel happier. Roddie had been more sensible than she'd feared. He might still be in danger of getting hurt, but at least he seemed to understand his own situation. She'd just have to hope things worked out for him and, when the inevitable parting came between him and Willow, that he didn't mind too much. Thank God, she needn't say anything to Nicholas, anyway.

Unfortunately, Nicholas had something to say to her when he returned from the mill.

'Bad news, I'm afraid, Eva.' He stood in the doorway of the drawing room, looking in at her with a tense, drawn face.

'What is it, Nicholas? Tell me!'

'We're having to go to a three-day week, starting on Monday. There will also be some redundancies. Absolutely can't be helped. I'm sorry.'

Sixty-Seven

From the Massons' point of view, there was a piece of good news. Bel's name was not on the redundancy list.

'Last in, first out, is the way we're doing the sackings,' Nicholas told Eva, drawing on a cigarette. 'And of course, it's only a temporary measure. When things pick up, we'll be able to take people back.'

'You think they'll pick up?' Eva asked quietly.

'We're hoping so, of course.'

'Well, it's a relief that Ma's still got her job, because there won't be much going anywhere else now. But how she's going to manage on less money, I don't know.' Eva got to her feet. 'I'll have to go round and see her.'

'Wait till tomorrow. We haven't announced anything yet.' Nicholas studied his cigarette for a moment, then stubbed it out. 'And there's something else I want to talk to you about.'

'More bad news?'

'In a way, but the plan is that I try to do something about it. You remember I told you our exports were down?'

'I remember.'

'Well, that's more to do with the competition from India than the slump. So what Pa and I've decided is that I and Tim MacFee should go abroad for a time to push our products. Try to recoup lost ground.' Nicholas smiled wearily. 'I doubt if I can do much, but we have to try to do something. The only way we can get back to full production is if we can get the orders coming in again.'

'Abroad?' Of all that Nicholas had said, this was the word that Eva seemed to have heard the clearest. He was going abroad. She didn't know what she felt, which was an indication of how far she and Nicholas had come in the last few weeks. At one time, to lose him for a day would have meant desolation of the spirit. Now, maybe she would welcome time alone. She realized he was watching her closely.

'You might come with me, if you liked,' he said with an attempt at lightness. 'Tim wouldn't mind and you've never been abroad, have you?'

'Go with you?'

'Well, you'd see Europe – parts of it, anyway. Not Germany – that's still in a mess. But we used to do well with other countries and I could show them to you.'

For a moment she hesitated, thinking how she would once have been over the moon at the thought of travelling with Nicholas. Now, she turned away.

'I think I'd better not, Nicholas. I mean, there's Ma to worry about, with these cutbacks and everything, and then I've got my work.'

'Work?' he repeated coldly.

'My voluntary work. I do have commitments. And it sounds as though you'll be away for some time.' She managed to look into his face. 'I think it'd be best if I just stayed here.'

'As you please.' Nicholas took out another cigarette and lit it. 'Now, if you'll excuse me, I've some letters to write.

'You're smoking too much,' she called after him. 'I'm sure it's not good for you.'

'Do you care?' he asked, and let the door of the room bang behind him.

'So, he's going away and you're no' going with him?' Bel asked, with the searching gaze she'd begun turning on Eva lately. 'Thought you'd jump at the chance.'

'I've a lot to keep me here, Ma. Worrying about you, for a start.'

'No need to worry about me. There's just your dad and me now, and we can get by, three-day

333

week or no three-day week.'

'There's still the rent to find, and the coal and messages.'

'Aye, well I might take a lodger.'

'Ma, you wouldn't!'

Bel shrugged. 'Or, I might try for a couple o' days at the jam factory. They're still doing well, folk say.'

'If you need help, you know where to come.'

'I'm wondering if you're the one needs help.' Bel put her work-worn hand on Eva's. 'You'd tell me, eh, if there was anything wrong at home?'

'There's nothing wrong. Why d'you keep asking?'

'When a wife doesnae want to go with her man, there's usually something wrong, is all I can say.'

Eva said she had to go. There was Nicholas's packing to do.

'Keep in touch, pet,' her mother said softly.

'Don't I always?' Eva replied.

That night – Nicholas's last before his departure – they made love, then lay without speaking, each feeling the loss that was to come, aware of loss already suffered. Maybe it was, in fact, too late to say anything. Tomorrow, they must begin their new temporary lives apart.

In the morning Nicholas left by taxi for his train south, refusing to let Eva come to see him off.

'Hate station farewells,' he told her. 'I'll ring you before I sail.'

'And write?'

'When I can. But you have my itinerary and I'll send details of poste restante addresses where you can write to me.'

'It's not as if you're going to India,' she said, trying to be cheerful.

'I'll be back by summer, I expect. Have to see how things go.'

As the taxi driver stood with his door open, they embraced for the last time, then without a backward look, Nicholas climbed into the taxi, the door was shut, and he was driven away.

'Ah, Madam, dinna cry,' Cora whispered when Eva drifted into the kitchen like someone lost. 'I'll make you some tea.'

'It's all right, I'm not crying,' said Eva, though she felt like it. Felt like crying over many things.

Eventually, she went slowly up to her bureau and checked over her various appointments and jobs she'd lined up to keep her busy. Even her old Labour Party membership card revealed itself, as she sorted through, and she turned it in her fingers and felt bad that she'd forgotten about it. Though Greg Campbell at King Robert's might have called her little Miss Red, she'd never really been involved with the party, but she had paid her dues.

Maybe she'd call in some time and renew her sub. Needn't tell Nicholas, who wasn't there to be told. In any case, they never discussed politics.

Days, she decided, wouldn't be too bad to get through, since she had so many calls on her time. Nights, though, would be different. Nights were the time when words and deeds came back to haunt, and there was no remedy but to wait for the dawn.

Lying awake on that first night without Nicholas, however, she was clear on where her disenchantment lay. It was he who'd burst the bubble, not she, but if she could have changed that, what would she have given?

Everything.

Sixty-Eight

One afternoon, after she'd been working at the thrift shop, Eva did call in at the Labour Party rooms. It was not the best time. After working with old clothes all afternoon – even though most had been washed before sale – she usually felt so grubby she just wanted to get home to bath and change. Still, she decided she might as well renew her subscription and get it over with, as she was passing. What she hadn't bargained for was meeting Bob Keir.

He was in conversation with two other men, standing in the centre of a long room lined with trestle tables, where some women were sorting papers and others were looking after a hissing tea urn. Bob, in a brown sweater and corduroy trousers, and holding forth in his usual way, did not at first see Eva. It was only when she was turning to the door, intending to sidle away, that she heard his familiar voice call her name, and halted.

'Eva!'

'Hello, Bob.'

As she slowly came back, the two men who'd been talking to Bob turned aside, and Bob himself took a step towards her.

'Is it really you?' he asked, without smiling.

He'd put on a little weight, she noted, but otherwise was the same as she remembered him. Tiger eyes, untidy dark hair, truculent expression – he hadn't changed. But then it hadn't been so very long since they'd met. Just seemed so.

'Why so surprised?' She kept her tone light as they shook hands. 'I live in Dundee. I thought you lived in Glasgow.'

'I know you live in Dundee, but why would I expect to see Nick North's wife in the Labour Party HQ?' As his gaze went over her, he still did not smile. 'And I left Glasgow six months ago. I work here now.'

'On another paper?'

'No. I'm an organizer for the party now. Full time. The *Monitor* folded, just like the *Key*.'

'I'm sorry to hear that. You're a good journalist.'

'Aye, well, I was offered this and it suits me fine. There's a lot to do here, you ken, even if we have got a so-called Labour government. And what brings you here, then?'

She laughed a little. 'As a matter of fact, I came in to renew my subscription.'

'Eva!' His eyes brightened. 'I canna believe it! He's letting you do that?'

'Letting me? I don't have to get permission for what I want to do, Bob.'

'No? Well, that's grand. Come this way. I'll renew it for you. Got your old card, then?'

When she had gone through the formalities of renewing her subscription and paid what was required, Bob introduced her to one or two of the women and offered her a cup of tea.

'Urn behaving itself, Joan?'

'Aye, Bob. Is it milk and sugar, hen?'

'Take a seat for a minute,' Bob told Eva when she'd been given her mug of tea. 'You look tired, if you dinna mind me saying so.'

And when they'd taken a couple of chairs away from the party workers, he looked at her more closely and asked if everything was all right.

'Of course. Why shouldn't it be? I've just been working at the thrift shop, that's all. Usually makes me feel like a rag and bone man – woman, I mean.'

'Thrift shop?' Bob was really smiling at last. 'Well, you've no' changed altogether, then. Or is this what the Norths do to make themselves feel better?'

She drank her tea without replying and he briefly touched her hand.

'Sorry, that was unfair. It's good of you to do what you can.' He sat back on his flimsy chair. 'So, how's the Lord and Master, then?'

'If you mean Nicholas, he's in Europe. Trying to boost export orders.'

'Europe, eh? Well, I'll wish him luck. I've heard about the three-day week. How's your ma

338

managing?'

'Managing is the word. Getting by.'

'No' letting you help her, eh?'

'My folks like to be independent.'

'And dinna want North money.' Bob set down his mug. 'Are you happy?' he asked quietly. 'Is it working out for you?'

'Yes, of course. I'm very happy.'

For some time, he kept his eyes on her face, then glanced at the darkening windows. Dusk came early in January; already, it seemed like night outside.

'Come on, I'll walk you home,' he said, rising. 'Where do you live these days?'

'There's no need, Bob.'

'I'd like to – I'll just get ma coat. What's the address, then?'

When she told him, he smiled. 'Just where I'd have picked for you maself. Let's away, then.'

As there was no point in arguing with him, she let him lead her out into the icy streets filled with workers going home, where he walked strongly beside her as in the old days. He did not, however, put her arm in his, for which she was grateful. Though there was no reason at all for her to feel guilty, walking again with Bob Keir made her hope she didn't meet anyone she knew.

'Weren't you planning to be a local councillor?' she asked, since he made no move to speak himself.

'I was a local councillor for a bit. In Glasgow.'

'Well done, you.'

'Aye, and I plan to stand for the council here eventually. As I told you, there's a hell of a lot to be done in Dundee.' He glanced at her quickly. 'Housing problem's as bad as ever it was.'

'I know.'

'Trouble is a lot of mill workers and such canna pay council house rents. There's always grand plans for slum clearance, but before you can move folk out of the slums, you have to build places they can afford.' In the light of a street lamp, he gave a grin. 'Think I'm on ma orange box? Giving you a try out of one o' ma speeches?'

Eva laughed and suddenly felt at ease with him. She knew it was because his views were the same as her own, and there was something comforting in that.

Outside Number Seventeen, they stopped and both looked up at the attractive façade, Eva seeing it as he would be seeing it, for the first time. She felt pride, mixed with guilt, knowing what his feelings would be.

'Grand, eh?' he murmured. 'Got what you wanted, then.'

'Is there anything wrong with that?'

He shrugged. 'Used to think you wanted different things from this.'

'You always used to say I wanted to leave Wish Lane.'

'But not all we worked for.'

'I still remember.'

He put his hand on her arm. 'Like to come delivering leaflets with me? There's a meeting coming up with our MP. We want a good turn out.'

'I don't want to get involved in meetings, Bob.'

'OK, but you could deliver the leaflets, eh? Need help, you know.'

She hesitated. 'I'm already doing quite a lot.'

'If you want something done, ask a busy person, is what they say. Shall I collect you here, or at the HQ?'

'The HQ,' she found herself saying. 'Just the one time, Bob, and that's all.'

'When would suit? Friday afternoon?'

She couldn't understand it. In seconds, it was all arranged, and he was touching his hat and walking away with a wave of his hand, and she was at her door, putting in the key. How had it happened? She was going out delivering leaflets with Bob Keir? Was she crazy?

Still, she didn't call him back, and when she was inside her home, she found her diary in the bureau and wrote, under the date for Friday, *Six thirty – Labour Party HQ – Bob Keir*.

It looked quite matter of fact, like that. Just another of her many appointments.

Sixty-Nine

Although she had once been a part of it, returning to the land of the poor was harrowing for Eva. She had not forgotten what conditions were like in the crowded tenements, but time away had blunted the memories. And some of the places where she went with Bob on that Friday afternoon, when they went out delivering leaflets, were a good deal worse than Wish Lane.

It didn't help that the January day provided so little light, and that everywhere in Bob's choice of area seemed blackened and grim, the pletties greenish with mould, the steps damp and greasy. Smoke from the mills filled the air, and looking up, past the rows of chimney pots, it seemed that the sky was a long way away and that the sun was nowhere.

'Och, yes, the sun's up there somewhere,' said Bob. 'It comes out, all right. Only problem is, things look worse in the sun, you ken. Shows up every flaw.'

'You're right.' Eva looked down at her remaining leaflets announcing the Labour candidate's next meeting. 'Not many more to deliver, thank God.'

'Lucky everybody's at work, else we'd have been caught for chats and cups of tea.'

'I wouldn't say no to a cup of tea.'

'I'll take you for one, soon as we finish.'

'At the Labour HQ?'

'No!' Bob grinned. 'At D. M. Brown's, eh? That'd be just up your street.'

'Not Brown's,' Eva said quickly. 'If you don't mind.'

'Afraid you'll see somebody you know?'

Well, she had, of course, seen Roddie and Willow only the other week and was still thinking of them.

'It's not your sort of place, Bob. Some little café will do.'

'I see. That's me, is it? Some little café?'

'You know what I mean.'

Later, when they were having tea and cakes in just such a café, Eva raised her eyes to Bob and gave a wry smile.

'It wasn't chance you picked on one of the worst parts of town, was it, Bob? You wanted to remind me of what life's like for some, in case I'd forgotten.'

'Did remind you, eh?'

'I hadn't really forgotten – but it's true, I've moved away from tenement life.'

He took another iced cake. 'And of course it's wonderful, being away. Especially living with a man who's never been there in the first place. Tell me, Eva, what's Nick's view on the poor, then?'

'I wish you wouldn't call him Nick. No one calls him Nick.'

'Sorry, what's Nicholas's view on how the other ninety per cent live, then?'

Eva looked down at her plate. 'As you say, he's no experience of them.'

'And no imagination, either? Canna put himself in their place? He should be able to do that, seeing as it's his dad who keeps them in it.'

'I don't want to talk about Nicholas, Bob.'

His eyes were sharp with understanding. 'Think maybe you dinna need to,' he said quietly and finished his cake.

'Poor lassie,' he murmured as they made their way down Perth Road towards Princess Victoria Terrace. 'Life's no' easy for you, eh?'

'How can you say that, Bob? When we've been where we've been.'

'Sure, you're well off in some ways.'

'Nicholas gives me everything I want!'

'Except understanding.'

'Bob, I said I didn't want to talk about him. He's my husband and I love him. I won't have you talk against him.'

'All I'm saying is, he canna share your views. Or doesnae, anyway. You've no' said, but I can tell.'

They had reached the top of her street and she put out her hand. 'Goodnight, Bob. Thanks for coming back with me.'

He held the hand she had offered. 'Shall I see you again, Eva? Will you look in at the HQ?'

'I don't think so. I've a lot to do.'

'There's a lot I'd like you to do. Maybe we could have a meal some time?'

She shook her head. 'I can't, Bob. I'm sorry.'

'OK. Goodnight, then.' He released her hand.

344

'Thanks for your help today.'

'That's all right.' She began to walk away, aware he was watching.

'Nice to see you again!' he called, but when she reached her door and looked round, he had gone.

Some days later, however, when she was serving at the thrift shop, she heard a deep voice say, 'Got any cheap shirts, Missus?'

And there he was, at her counter, grinning.

'Sixteen and a half inch collar, eh? And I like a nice stripe, if you've got one.'

'Oh, Bob! What are you doing here? Not actually buying shirts?'

'I just came to see if I could interest you in an initiative for sick bairns. I know you've got a lot on, but this'd mean you could do a bit of teaching. Can I tell you about it?'

'You know I can't teach. I'm married.'

'As a volunteer, you could.'

Standing at the counter amongst a crowd of women keenly turning over clothes, he was serious as he looked down at her. 'Just let me tell you about it, Eva.'

'Laddie, will ye just shift yourself?' a shrill voice cried, and several hands thumped his broad back.

'Please?' cried Bob.

'All right, all right,' Eva said hastily. 'I'll come to the HQ. But better go now, or we'll all be in trouble.'

Relaxed and smiling, as she'd seen him look so often in the past when he got his own way, he said he'd watch out for her.

Seventy

So began her second relationship with Bob, or as she saw it, second friendship, into which she slipped so easily, so naturally, she almost ceased to worry about it.

There was never a hint of anything romantic about it – certainly no sign of secret love from him, as there might once have been – that was all over. All he asked was that she helped out on the 'initiatives', as he called them, which he'd thought up to get her back to teaching, and her time seemed so elastic, she could stretch it to anything and was glad to do so.

Mainly it was the sick children she helped; those confined to bed with TB, rheumatic fever or other illnesses. But occasionally she'd teach adults, who'd slipped through the net at school and could do no more than put a cross for their names.

'Aye, and I swear I'm no' thinking of ballot papers,' he'd added with a grin. 'Though with an election coming up, it'd be handy to call on some more Labour voters.'

'What election?' Eva asked.

'There'll be one eventually, mark ma word. Ramsay MacDonald's making such a piece of nonsense of everything, there'll have to be. Nearly three million unemployed and the government losing money like water down a drain? Canna keep going like that.'

'Well, don't ask me to go canvassing,' said Eva. 'I don't have a minute to myself as it is.'

Neither of them made the point that by the time of the next election, Nicholas might be back, and Eva would not be going canvassing anyway.

She wrote to Nicholas regularly, telling him of her various voluntary enterprises – though not, of course, mentioning Bob's name – and he wrote back when he could, usually on picture postcards of the cities where he'd stayed. News of his success, or otherwise, in promoting the North's jute was sparse, but Eva had the feeling his mission was not going well. The prospects of an end to three-day working seemed remote.

'World recession,' Bob commented. 'Canna expect too much.'

'No one expects much in Dundee,' Eva retorted, but at least there was one piece of good news. Her mother had managed to get an extra day's work at the jam factory and said she was quite enjoying it.

'As long as I'm no' next for the chop,' said Frank glumly, but Bel told him roundly that he needn't always think the worst. It might never come.

'Did you tell your ma you'd met up with me again?' Bob asked Eva.

'Yes, and she was interested,' Eva reported, not adding that her mother had pursed her lips and and shaken her head, as though Bob's return was nothing to cheer about. 'Of course, she's not one for getting involved in politics.'

'Just as long as she marks that ballot paper the right way when the time comes,' said Bob. 'No need to get involved with politics, as long as you vote.'

It was not possible, of course, for Eva to invite Bob to her home, but now and again she did agree to have a meal with him, after he'd come to collect her from one or other of her duties. Usually they kept clear of the centre of town, just in case people they knew might see them and get the wrong idea – though this fear was never put into words – and Eva always insisted on paying for her share of the bill. That way, she could be clear in her mind that they were, in truth, just two friends dining together.

One evening in June, they had supper in an inexpensive restaurant, one some way out of town, as usual. Eva had been spending time with a small girl suffering from a bone disease and was feeling rather depressed, while Bob, who had arranged to meet her, was depressed anyway by news of further government cuts.

'Sometimes, I feel like losing heart,' he muttered. 'But that's just what I canna afford to do.'

'I feel the same,' said Eva. 'We're all in the same boat – Nicholas, too.'

'What's he got to do with anything?'

'Well, he may have had no luck abroad, Bob. And he's due home soon.'

'Due home?' Bob asked, staring at her.

'Yes. You knew he'd be coming back some time.'

'But no' so soon. I thought it was late summer.'

'No, no. This month.'

Bob pushed aside his plate, his eyes taking on that glitter Eva knew meant he was feeling strongly about something. She lowered her own gaze and pretended to be concentrating on her pudding, until Bob's hand went over hers and held it fast.

'So, that's the end for us, is it? Him coming home?'

'He is my husband, Bob.'

'He's no' made you happy.'

'Let's not go into that.'

After a moment or two, he withdrew his hand from hers. 'Want coffee? Or tea?'

'I don't think so, thanks.'

'I'll get the bill, then.'

'Wait, let me pay my share, Bob.'

'My treat,' he said sourly. 'Seeing as there'll no' be many more chances.'

Having paid and tipped the waitress, they were moving towards the door, Eva's spirits by now as low as Bob's, when a woman's voice called sweetly, 'Goodnight, Mrs North!'

Shocked as though by a blow Eva shrank back, but couldn't avoid seeing Berta Loch's face smiling up at her from a corner table, where she was sitting with her husband and an older man.

'Enjoyed your supper, Eva?' asked Berta. 'You and Mr Keir? Art and me often come here, you ken, with his Uncle Dan. We couldnae afford it, could we, Art, if it wasnae for Uncle Dan?'

Arthur Loch nodded agreement, as the grey-haired man who was his uncle gave Berta a fond smile and patted her hand.

'That's all right, Berta – ma pleasure, eh?'

Berta, her eyes like dark pebbles, turned back to Eva. 'Aye, money's short these days. Specially since I lost ma job at North's. Last in, first oot, they says, but me that's been there for years gets the sack anyway. Just for speakin' ma mind!'

'I'm really sorry,' Eva said with stiff lips. 'Bob, you remember Mrs Loch? We've just been visiting a sick child, Berta. Called in here for a meal afterwards.'

'Visiting a sick child?' Berta, staring past Eva to Bob, looked as though she could have laughed in their faces. 'Is that no' good o' them, Art? Mebbe I'll take up good works, seein' as I'm out of a job?'

'Maybe you should,' Bob said curtly. 'Will you excuse us? We have to leave now.'

Seventy-One

Outside in the evening air, Eva felt quite faint, but refused to take Bob's arm as they waited at the tram stop.

'Eva, what is it?' he asked with concern. 'That damned Berta woman? Forget her. She's nothing to worry about.'

'She saw me with you.'

'What of it?' His eyes were glittering. 'Think she'll tell your Nicholas? That'd be the best

x

thing she could do.'

'Bob, the tram's coming. Please don't say any more.'

He shrugged, but in the tram he was silent, folding their tickets in his large fingers and staring into space, while Eva slumped beside him, feeling as battered as though she'd been involved in a fight.

Talking to Berta had done that, of course, for it was always her style to stir up aggression. And even though she'd appeared friendly in the restaurant, she was quite able to convey to Eva that she could expect trouble. Oh yes, Berta had been given a wonderful weapon, as soon as she'd set eyes on Mrs Nicholas North and Bob Keir together. She was certainly going to use it.

Beads of sweat broke on Eva's brow as she tried to imagine how, but Bob's heavy shoulder moving next to hers reminded her that Berta was not her only problem.

She glanced at his profile and instantly felt the full force of his own gaze on her, and his hand searching for hers.

'Shall we walk for a bit before you go home? It's a nice evening.'

'If you like.'

'Surely, if we're no' going to meet any more, you can spare me some time?'

'Why, yes. I said we could walk. Where shall we go?'

'Down by the Tay.'

The tram had rattled to its stop in the centre of Dundee, and with Bob's hand on her elbow, holding her as though she were a fugitive who might run away, they stepped out on to the pavement.

'All right?' he asked.

'There'll be people, down by the Tay.'

'To hell with worrying about people. I'm tired of living this hole and corner life with you.'

'You seem to forget, I'm married.'

As they walked through the streets in the soft warm air of the June evening, he deliberately took her arm. 'I ken fine you're married. But you made a mistake, Eva. Admit it. You made a terrible mistake when you married Nicholas North. He was never right for you.'

'I thought he was.'

'Aye, I know. But you've found out since that he's no' got your humanity. He canna understand what you want from life. Thinks a smart car and a grand house'll be enough, but you know that's no' the case, eh? I can see in your eyes that you do.'

She would not answer until they had reached the Esplanade, where it was true there were people strolling, admiring the bridge and its lights reflected in the water; gazing across to Fife through the blue dusk, where more lights shone.

Sitting on a bench the farthest they could find from any other, she said, reluctantly, 'I have been disappointed, it's true. Because I've learned I can't do what I'd hoped to do.'

'You see, I was right.' Bob's voice was soft, even consoling, as he smoothed her hand in his. 'You made a mistake, Eva. I dinna blame you – you were dazzled. But it's no' too late to do something about it.'

She took her hand away from his. 'No. It's not possible.'

'You think you have to say that, but it's no disgrace to admit you've made a mistake.' As she said nothing, he went on earnestly. 'We've always been right for each other, you ken. Got the same background, got the same views. I knew that from the start, from the time we were at school. Remember Miss Balfour's class? I wanted to be cleverer than you, so's you admire me, but you just thought me bigheaded, like everybody else.'

'I did admire you, Bob. I still do.'

'Aye, well, when we met up again and you were at college, I used to wonder what would happen between us. Because you were so set on a career and didnae want marriage – couldnae get married and stay a teacher, in fact. I thought, we'll sort it out somehow.' He laughed a little. 'And then, look what happened.'

'You despised me, didn't you? For being dazzled?'

'Aye. I thought you were giving up all we'd believed in, for a fella who could never understand what mattered to us. And still doesnae understand – is that no' right?'

'Why are you even here with me now, then?' cried Eva. 'If that's the way you think of me?'

'Because, when I met you again, I found you'd no' changed,' he said softly. 'You were the same Eva I'd always loved. Only sadder and wiser. Full of regrets.'

He took back her hand, looking at her now with eyes that had lost their glitter. He seemed quieter, more vulnerable, as though he'd grown weary in his battle for love, yet must go on – was driven to go on.

'If you'd seemed happy when we met again,' he said carefully, 'I swear I'd have left you alone. But I could tell that your marriage was wrong and you knew it. You'd made a mistake and couldn't see any way out. I was the way out, Eva. I'm offering it to you now.'

She was struck by his words. She had not been happy, and had let him see. In effect, she'd brought this on them both. Hers was the blame, and as its force held her, she was glad in a way, to feel as bad as Bob. Still, she had to speak.

'I can't leave Nicholas,' she told Bob quietly. 'He's my husband. I still love him.'

'Eva, he's no' what you thought. You admitted it.'

'I know. He isn't. But maybe I expected too much.' She put out a hand, which Bob did not take. 'I'm sorry, Bob. He's coming home. I'll have to be there.'

He stood up, not looking at her. 'Seems like all I've done is remind you of what you feel for him. Why the hell did you have to come in that day to renew your party card?'

The dusk had deepened, was turning to night, and as they walked back to Princess Victoria Terrace, Eva had no need to worry in case people should see them. But she'd wounded Bob so badly, she couldn't think of others and what they might think, only of the bitter taste of her own guilt.

354

At her door, he turned to her. 'Is this where I say I wish you all the best? I'm no' sure I can.'

'I don't deserve good wishes.'

'Well, I will say this.' He fixed her with expressionless eyes. No tiger light now, she noticed sadly. 'If you ever need me – and you might, whatever you think – I want you to remember you can call on me. I mean it, Eva. Any time, I'll be there for you.'

She couldn't speak, but lifted her face to his and kissed his cheek, at which, without a word of goodbye, he left her, walking fast as he always did, up the terrace and away.

For several minutes, she remained where she was, calming herself, wiping her eyes, straightening her hair, until finally she let herself in.

'Oh, Madam!' Cora cried, hurrying up from the basement. 'There's a telegram come for you. Eh put it on the chest. Hope it's no' bad news.'

'Good news.' The letters of the message were dancing before Eva's eyes. 'Mr North is coming back on Saturday – that's only two days away.'

'Is that no' grand?' cried Cora. 'Oh, Madam, you'll be that pleased to have him back, eh? What'll we get for his dinner?'

Seventy-Two

That night, Eva scarcely slept, which did not surprise her. Hour after hour passed, with the same faces succeeding one another in ghostly procession – Bob's, Nicholas's, Berta Loch's – until she was at screaming point and got up to make tea.

'Madam, you should've called me,' cried Cora, seeing the evidence next morning of Eva's cup and saucer and a pot half full of cold tea. 'Are you no' well, then? Better no' go to the Salvation Army today.'

'I'm all right – too excited to sleep, that's all.' Eva buttered some toast and tried to eat it. 'But I'll go to the canteen; I won't let them down.'

'Well, you have a nice rest when you come back, eh? Got to look your best for Mr North.'

There was, however, no possibility of a rest for Eva when she returned home from the Salvation Army canteen. She'd only just taken off her coat and hat when the doorbell rang and Cora came in, looking dubious.

'Someone to see you, Madam. Said she was a friend.'

'Did she give her name?' asked Eva, her heart beginning to pound.

'Aye.' Cora raised her eyebrows. 'Mrs Arthur Loch.'

After a long moment, Eva gathered herself together. 'Show her in then, please.'

'Shall I bring tea?'

'Yes.' Eva put her handkerchief to her lips. 'Yes, we'll have tea.'

Berta, wearing a black jacket and short skirt, with a white hat tilted over her dark hair, took her time about approaching Eva in the drawing room. It was plain she wanted to see everything and sent her eyes darting round as though taking an inventory, finally allowing her gaze to come to rest on Eva's pale, unmade-up face. And then she smiled.

'No' so well today, Eva? What's up, then?'

Eva, making no answer, waved Berta to a seat, from where she continued to look all around the room.

'My, you've come a long way, eh? When I remember you as a wee shifter at North's, wearin' your sister's hand-me-doons, I can hardly believe ma eyes to see where you've ended up.'

'Did you have something to say to me?' Eva asked, breathing deeply to calm her nerves.

'Just being neighbourly. Thought I'd see how you were.'

'Tea, Madam,' announced Cora, entering with a tray, and Berta's dark eyes snapped.

'And here's the wee maid, wi' tea and all! What a grand life you must lead, Eva!'

'Will that be all, Madam?' asked Cora, casting a look of scorn at Berta, and giving the impression that she thought she ought to stay.

'That's all, thank you.'

When Cora had left them, Eva poured Berta tea and handed her a plate of cakes, over which she hesitated for some time before selecting a macaroon.

'Almond!' she cried. 'My favourite!'

'Just say what you've come for,' Eva said shortly, sipping her own tea. 'I know it's not to ask after my health.'

'No, it isnae.' Berta bit into her cake with relish. 'It's just I think I should speak to Mr Nicholas.'

A cold hand squeezed Eva's heart. What she'd heard was only what she might have expected, but now that the threat had come, been put into words, she was terrified. Not least by the fear that she might show her feelings to Berta. Summoning up all her courage, she said evenly, 'My husband is not here. He's abroad.'

'Aye, but he'll be back soon, eh? The word at North's is any time.'

'I thought you'd left North's?'

'Still got ma pals.' Berta dabbed at crumbs round her scarlet mouth. 'Mind if I have another o' thae cakes, Eva?'

'Help yourself.' Eva filled up Berta's teacup. 'And what do you think you'd tell my husband, anyway?'

'Why, about Mr Keir! I mean, it's no' right, is it? You seeing him when your man's away?'

'There is nothing between Mr Keir and me. We are just friends.'

'He's a man.' Berta's lip curled. 'You canna be friends with a man, Eva. Ony husband'll tell you that.'

'You don't care about my husband, Berta. You just want to hurt me. Why? What have I ever done to you?'

Berta shrugged. 'You've aye had it so easy. All your life, things've dropped intae your lap, when the rest of us've had tae work oor fingers to the bone. It's time somebody took you doon a peg or two, and it's going tae be me.'

'I suppose you want money?' Eva asked bitterly.

'Niver said so. Though we've the two bairns noo, you ken, and life's no' easy. But I jist wint to speak to Mr North.'

'Why tell me first, then?'

Berta grinned and stood up, straightening her short skirt and sauntering over to a wall mirror to look at herself. 'Give you something tae think aboot, eh?'

Eva rose and took her bag from a chair. 'Berta, I'm going to give you some money, anyway. For the bairns.' She opened her purse and took out two ten shilling notes. 'Here, take these. I don't like to think of children going short.' She looked Berta up and down. 'Though you don't look as though you're going short yourself, if you don't mind my saying so.'

'All second-hand,' Berta said airily as her fingers closed over the notes. 'This is verra kind of you, Eva, I really appreciate it. But it'll no' stop me speaking to Mr North when he gets back, I may as well tell you.'

'That's all right.' Eva opened the drawing room door and held it wide. 'But there'll be no need for you to say anything about Mr Keir to my husband when he comes back. I'll be speaking to him myself.'

'You'd niver!' cried Berta, a flush rising to her cheekbones.

'Shouldn't have warned me, should you?' Eva smiled. 'But you wanted to watch me take the news, didn't you? Goodbye, Berta. I'll see you out, shall I?'

'Mrs Loch gone?' asked Cora, coming to clear the tea things. 'Should've let me show her oot.'

'No,' said Eva. 'I wanted to do that.'

Seventy-Three

All day long on Friday, Eva waited for Nicholas, just as she had waited for him on his return from India. In some ways this waiting was worse, because there had been the coldness between them. And then, in the background of their reunion, would be Bob Keir. But she wouldn't talk about Bob until she and Nicholas had celebrated his homecoming; nothing must be allowed to intrude on that special reunion.

Everything was ready for his arrival, with the whole house spring cleaned from top to bottom, as though his mother was coming to visit – as though he'd even notice! But it made Eva feel better that she and Cora had made Nicholas's home look its best.

Then there had been his dinner to consider, for Cora was very serious about gentlemen's meals – they needed so much more than ladies, she said. And as the day turned to evening, a large chicken was made ready for the oven, vegetables were prepared, Nicholas's favourite pudding was in the larder, and the dining table was made to look splendid with candles and flowers.

'A triumph,' Eva told Cora, who smiled.

'Aye, it looks grand, eh? Now, we just want the master to arrive.'

'Must be soon.' Eva, at the drawing-room window, was shivering in her light dress, though the evening was warm. 'Oh, I hope there's no delay!'

'Madam, I think he's here,' whispered Cora. 'I hear a motor.'

'The taxi!' cried Eva, and ran to fling open the front door.

He was there, paying the driver, a tall thin figure in casual clothes, a raincoat over his arm, and as he heard the door, he turned. Their eyes met. She called his name, but he did not smile, and she knew he was uncertain of his welcome. Not for long, though, not for long.

'Nicholas!' she cried again and ran to fling herself into his arms. 'Oh, thank God you're back!'

'Have you really missed me?' he murmered as they stood kissing in the hall, while Cora tactfully disappeared upstairs with his two small cases – his only luggage, as his portmanteau would be arriving later.

'Oh, I have, I have!' Eva told him. 'But did you miss me?'

'Did I not? I thought of you all the time.'

He pulled her into the drawing room, kicking the door to behind them, so that he needn't release Eva from his embrace.

'All the time, my darling, I promise you.'

'I thought you were supposed to be meeting people?'

'Oh, yes, but even when I was trying to sell our damned jute, I was wondering what you were doing and thinking I was wasting my life away from you.'

'I've been pretty busy, trying to fill my days, you know.'

'Doing what?' he asked fondly as he ran his fingers down her face. 'That charity work Mother wanted you to do?'

'Mostly, but let's not talk about that, let's talk about you. All the places you've seen, what you did – I want to hear everything.'

'First, I think I should go and unpack. Want to come with me? I've some presents for you. Some French scent and a silk dressing gown – or would you call it a negligée? Hope it fits.'

'Don't worry about presents,' she said breathlessly. 'We can look at them later.'

They climbed the stairs together, arms wound round each other, eyes fixed on each other's faces, until they were in their bedroom, where Cora had left the cases, but was, thank heaven, nowhere to be seen.

'She'll be cooking the chicken,' Eva whispered. 'You'll be wanting your dinner soon, I expect.'

'Are you joking?' Nicholas was already slipping her dress from her shoulders. 'You know quite well what I want.'

It felt like their honeymoon time all over again, only better than their honeymoon, for there were no constraints in this love-making, no uncertainties, as they met in bliss with all the coolnesses and sadnesses of the past forgotten. Time, too, was forgotten, until Eva, leaping up from the bed, cried, 'Oh, Nicholas, the chicken! I'm sure it's been done for ages – how long have we been here?'

He smiled lazily and would have drawn her back to him, but she insisted they must go down for the meal. Poor Cora would be so disappointed if they didn't.

'Only you would think about Cora at a time like this,' Nicholas said, laughing, but when he and Eva had taken a quick bath together, he announced that he was in fact ravenous.

'Me, too,' said Eva. 'You'd think if you were happy, you wouldn't think about food.'

'I always eat when I'm happy. That's why I'm so thin – I haven't been happy away from you.'

Downstairs, Cora, with a knowing smile, said not to worry about the chicken, she'd kept it hot, and as everything else was ready, asked if she should serve dinner now?

'Oh, please,' groaned Nicholas. 'I can't tell you how much I'm looking forward to some Scottish cooking again.'

'We've got your favourite pudding, too,' said Eva. 'Everything needed for your homecoming, dearest.'

'My homecoming.' He was suddenly serious, and when they were alone at table, added, 'I wasn't sure what sort of a homecoming it would be, you know.'

Eva looked down at her plate. 'You knew I'd miss you.'

'No, I didn't know anything. I seem to remember when I left, you weren't happy with me.'

'Let's not talk about it.'

'Are you happy with me, Eva?'

She looked into his face, shadowed in the candlelight. 'I love you, Nicholas.'

He put down his knife and fork and for a moment rested his head on his hand. 'Eva, that's all I want to hear.'

She rose and poured more wine for him. 'Come on, sweetheart, finish your dinner.'

'I will.' He gave her a radiant smile. 'And then ... I feel so tired ... may we have an early night?'

Seventy-Four

The following morning, wearing her new silk negligée, Eva looked at herself in her mirror. She thought she looked different. Like the cat who'd swallowed the cream. Like a woman who'd spent the night making love.

'Shocking,' she told the beautiful face looking back at her, but the face seemed to answer, No, no, you're married, you're entitled.

And then Eva's expression darkened, for she'd remembered what she must do.

It would be all right, she told herself. Nicholas would understand about Bob. She'd surely proved to him since his return that he was the one she loved? Maybe she needn't tell him?

But the memory of Berta's pebble-dark eyes was enough to strengthen her resolve. Better that he heard about Bob from Eva herself, than from Berta Loch. After all, there would be nothing really to confess. Only a few meals and talks. Bob had never even kissed her. Nicholas would understand.

He'd just finished telephoning his parents when she called him to breakfast, and came in frowning.

'Anything wrong?' she asked as he began on his eggs and bacon.

'No, they're thrilled I'm back, but I'm just thinking I'll have to get my reports together for Pa and they're not as good as they might be.'

'Sorry about that.' Eva hesitated, as she took some toast. 'I was wondering ... could I have a word, Nicholas?'

'A word?' He smiled. 'Do you have to ask permission?'

'No, but it's just something I want to tell you. Maybe after breakfast would be best, then we won't be interrupted.'

'Eva, you're not...?' His eyes were shining.

'No, no.' She laughed a little. 'Heavens, I'd have told you the minute you came in, if there was a baby on the way.'

'Oh well, plenty of time, I suppose.'

'Plenty of time.'

After breakfast, they met in Nicholas's study upstairs.

'Won't take long, will it, Eva? I really do want to get down to my reports.'

'Not long.'

He sat down and looked at her expectantly, and for a moment or two, she couldn't begin. Finally, she cleared her throat and said, 'It's just that, when you were away, I met up with an old friend. Bob Keir, as a matter of fact. You remember him?'

'Bob Keir?' Nicholas drew himself upright in his chair. 'Of course I remember him. What about him?'

'Well, he was very good about suggesting I did some voluntary teaching. He knew these poor sick children – and others – who needed help, and we started going round – you know – just to see them and teach them...' Eva's voice trailed away. 'But there was nothing in it.'

'Nothing in it?' Nicholas had gone rather pale. 'Why should I think there might be something in it?'

'Oh, you shouldn't at all. It was just seeing these folk – and teaching – and then occasionally we'd have a meal...'

He was very still, his face losing all expression, as though he'd put on a mask.

'Eva, what are you saying? While I've been away, you've been seeing Bob Keir?'

'Not in the way that sounds, Nicholas. It's as I

said, we just visited people – or I did – and then he'd meet me and we'd have something to eat.'

'I don't know what way you think that sounds, but to me it sounds as though you were seeing another man.' Nicholas got to his feet. He walked to his window, drew aside the lace curtain and looked out at the spring morning.

A pain formed in her chest; she felt she couldn't breathe and took deep breaths. He didn't believe her. He was imagining something that hadn't happened. An affair with another man. Bob Keir. Someone who'd once entered his life for a fleeting moment, but had not been forgotten by Nicholas. Because he'd seen at once what she'd missed in these last few weeks: that Bob was in love with her.

'Nicholas,' she said, gasping a little, 'please look at me. You're taking all this the wrong way. Bob Keir means nothing to me. All we had were some talks and meals...'

'Talks and meals?' Nicholas swung round and fixed her with eyes so cold they pierced her heart. 'Talks and meals, Eva? That's what lovers like to have. They meet, they talk, they have meals. And then what?'

'Nothing!' she cried. 'There was nothing else between Bob and me. We were just old friends – we went to school together. It's natural we should have just liked to talk, have a meal, and I always paid my own way.'

'And this fellow who let you pay for yourself, he's not in love with you?'

Before his look, her own gaze fell. *Deny it*, she told herself, *just say no*. But she'd never been any good at lying, and Nicholas nodded.

'I know he is in love with you,' he said quietly. 'I saw it in the few minutes we talked years ago. And it seems he hasn't changed. As soon as he meets you, finds I'm away, he begins to think of ways of seeing you – having, as you put it, talks and meals – and you say there's nothing in it? Nothing between you?'

'Nothing, Nicholas. Can't you believe me? Trust me?'

'I thought I could,' he said quietly. 'Now ... I don't know any more. All I know is that when Bob Keir wanted you to see him, you saw him. When I was away from you, you went out with him.'

'Nicholas...' She went to him, putting out her hands to him, but he turned aside.

'I'll have to think about this, Eva. Decide what to do.'

'Do?' she asked, trembling. 'What is there to do?'

'Everything is spoiled,' he murmured, as though to himself. 'I was so happy when I came back. So surprised that things were all right. That you wanted me...'

'I do want you, Nicholas. Couldn't you tell, the way we made love?'

'I tell you, that's all spoiled. All I can see now is Bob Keir. You and Bob Keir, having talks and meals...' Nicholas walked to the door. 'I think I'll go out for a bit. Walk. Clear my head.'

'I'll come with you!'

'No, I'm going alone.'

When she heard the front door bang behind

him, Eva sank into a chair. She didn't cry – she was past tears – but simply sat still, too numbed to move.

'Is everything all right, madam?' she heard Cora ask some time later, and must have answered something, for Cora went away.

And then Nicholas came back and said he'd decided what to do.

Seventy-Five

This time, they sat in the drawing room and drank the coffee Cora brought them. No, they didn't want anything to eat. Neither could imagine eating again.

'I've decided it would be best if I moved out for a while,' Nicholas announced.

'Moved out?' Eva's voice was hoarse, her fingers around the handle of her cup cold and white. 'You want to move out?'

'Yes. It will give us a chance to think about things.'

'Where will you go?'

'That's not important.'

She looked around the beautiful room she had furnished with such care, which now seemed like a pack of cards closing in on her. Was it Alice in Wonderland whose world had fallen about her? Eva remembered reading the book Miss Balfour had given her long ago. But Alice was living a dream, and this was no dream.

This was a nightmare.

'Nicholas, won't you believe me?' she asked after a long silence. 'I swear there was nothing between Bob Keir and me.'

'I think I do believe you. It only makes things worse. He meant nothing to you, but you still went out with him. You must have realized you were playing with fire.'

'I didn't, I was stupid. I didn't think at all.'

'When you knew how much your seeing him would hurt me,' he went on quietly. 'And hurt him, too, in the end.'

There seemed no more to be said. Both set down their coffee cups and stood up.

'What are you going to do now?' asked Eva.

'I'll see my parents. Give my reports to my father. It's Saturday, he'll be at home, and I can pick up my car at the same time. I left it at Garth House, if you remember.'

'And then?'

'Then I'll come back, pack a bag and get out of your life for a while.'

His face, averted from hers, was mask-like again, as though he'd made himself a stranger. But she was the one who had made him into a stranger when she'd told him about Bob.

'You'll be all right for money,' he said. 'You have the joint account at the bank, and you can send my post and all bills care of the mill. If you need me, of course, you can also reach me at the mill.'

'I'll try not to do that.'

His grey eyes rested on her face for several

moments. 'Well, no need to say goodbye yet; I'll see you when I return.'

'You'll be telling your parents what's happened?'

He hesitated. 'Not sure about that.'

'I'll say goodbye, anyway,' she said.

Some time later, she found herself at the station, with a porter in attendance and two large suitcases on his barrow. Letters to Bel and Frank and the various charities that would have been expecting her had been posted, and a note left for Nicholas on the chest in the hall. Cora, sobbing, had promised to look after him, and Eva had said she'd keep in touch. With Cora, she meant.

Her note to Nicholas had been very short.

Dear Nicholas,

There's no need for you to go away. I'm the one who should go, and you're right, it will give us the chance to think about things.

With all my love, Eva.

It seemed cold, and she could have written more, but what was the point?

'Where to, Madam?' asked the booking office clerk.

'Edinburgh,' she told him. 'Third Class.'

'Single, or return?'

'Single, please.'

There was no way of knowing when, or if, she would be coming back.

Seventy-Six

Letty had taken her in. Wonderful, sweet Letty. All she'd said was, 'Pay off the taxi,' as Eva had stood on her doorstep. And Eva had paid off the cab she'd kept waiting in case she'd had to move on, carried in her cases, and for the first time had allowed herself to shed a few tears.

Two weeks had passed since then, and in that time, Bel had already come hurrying over to see her in Letty's Comely Bank flat, and Eva had an interview arranged in July for a teaching job. Not permanent, and in one of the industrial parts of Edinburgh, but she was desperate to get it, and constantly rehearsing in her mind what she would have to say to be successful.

Naturally, her mother and sister had been devastated by the news that she'd moved, alone, out of her lovely home. How could such a thing have happened?

Well, they knew, of course. What man was going to accept that his wife had been seeing another man, even if in all innocence, when he'd been away? Whatever had Eva been thinking of, to meet Bob Keir in the first place?

'I don't know,' Eva said desolately. 'I suppose I was still upset, because Nicholas wouldn't try to do something to help the workers. And when I met Bob, it seemed good, at first, being with someone who agreed with me.'

'Oh, Evie,' Letty had sighed. 'Wasnae right to get involved for that.'

'Aye, but understandable, you ken,' said Bel. 'I always said...'

'What did you always say?' asked Evie. 'No, don't tell me. I know.'

'I always said there'd be trouble if you married Nicholas North, and your dad said the same. Things were against you from the start, Eva.'

'We were very happy, Ma.'

Bel pursed her lips. 'Until you found he'd got feet o' clay.'

'I still loved him.'

'But didnae mind going around with Bob Keir.'

'I shouldn't have done that and I'm sorry I did.'

'I blame Berta Loch,' declared Letty. 'She's the one who caused all the trouble.'

'Aye, a bad lot, and that's all you can say,' agreed Bel, but Eva shook her head.

'She couldn't have caused any trouble, if I hadn't given her the chance.'

'Maybe Nicholas will come seeking you,' Letty had suggested hopefully, after no one had thought of a reply to that.

'No,' Eva said firmly, 'he won't. And I don't want him to, anyway. If he doesn't want me, I'd rather not see him.'

'Oh, what a mess!' cried Bel. 'What are you going to do, then? You canna stay here for ever.'

'I'm going to find a room of my own and get a teaching job.'

'You're married; they'll no' take you.'

'They needn't know I'm married.'

Bel and Letty stared.

'That's no' right, Eva,' Bel said slowly. 'I'm no' happy about that.'

'Blame their hard rules, then. Anyway, I'm not being supported by a husband, am I? I'm not using Nicholas's money. I've every right to a job.'

'Oh, Evie,' whispered Letty. 'Will you have to take off your wedding ring?'

Looking down at the ring Nicholas had put on her finger on the happiest day of her life, Eva realized she hadn't thought of ever having to remove it. It would be a sign, she felt, when she did, of the great abyss that stretched between her and Nicholas now, with no means of crossing. And as she strained in her imagination to see him, Nicholas's figure, on the opposite side from her own, seemed to grow smaller and smaller, until she couldn't see it at all.

'If he did come looking for me, I think it'd be too late,' she said quietly. 'We're too far apart.'

'Never say that!' cried Letty. 'Ma, tell Evie no' to talk like that.'

'She's no' a bairn,' Bel retorted. 'She'll have to work things out for herself. How about putting the kettle on, then?'

'I'll just see if Iain's woken from his nap first.' But Letty paused in the doorway and looked back. 'Evie, it's just so sad. I could bawl ma head off, so I could.'

'And that never did any good at all,' said Bel.

* * *

374

A day or two later, Eva was dressing carefully in a dark jacket and skirt for her interview at Lockhart School. As the position was only a temporary one, she would be seeing only the headmaster, which might be easier than having to face a full board from the Corporation Education Department. On the other hand, it might not.

'Oh, wish me luck!' she cried to Letty and Hughie when she was ready, and they kissed her and hugged her and wished her all the luck in the world.

'If I get it, I'll be out of your hair,' she told Hughie, who had lifted up young Iain to give his auntie a kiss as well.

'As though we mind you staying,' said Hughie, who had certainly been very understanding about Eva's troubles, and never mentioned Bob Keir once.

'There might no' be a lot in for it,' Letty told Eva encouragingly. 'I mean, it's only temporary.'

'The way things are, there are plenty in for every job.' Eva gave a last look at herself in the mirror in the hallway, and tweaked her hat into position. 'I'll just have to hope for the best.' She gave the watching family a gallant smile. 'I'm away for the tram, then.'

'Good luck!' Hughie called, and Iain waved his plump little hand, while Letty, leaning against Hughie's shoulder, again said she felt like bawling her head off.

'Ma poor sister, eh? Left her man and having to go back to work again – after she had so much.'

'Let's hope she does get back to work,' said Hughie.

Seventy-Seven

Lockhart School, built in the nineteenth century on a site beyond the Haymarket, was surrounded by railway yards, depots, breweries, warehouses and gaunt Victorian tenements. The other face of Edinburgh, Eva reflected, from the parts the tourists saw – but then every city had its working areas, and Edinburgh's were no worse than others. Wouldn't make any difference, she was convinced, to the number of candidates wanting this job.

'May I help you?' asked a young, dark-haired woman approaching down the corridor. 'Is it Miss Masson?'

'Yes, that's correct,' Eva answered, feeling already self-conscious at the use of her maiden name. 'I'm here for interview with Mr Torrance.'

'Would you like to come this way?' The young woman gave a brief smile. 'I'm his secretary, Miss Leys. I'll show you straight in.'

'Not late, am I?'

'No, no, but you're the last. The others have gone.'

The others ... Eva sighed inwardly as she followed the secretary down the corridor. Well, as she'd told Letty, she'd known she wouldn't be the only candidate. Only one with a secret, probably. But that was a thought best put to the back of her mind. She must not go into the interview looking guilty.

The man rising from the chair behind a large, littered desk was about forty; tall, with hair as red as Katie Crindle's, but his brown eyes were harder than hers. He smiled at Eva, however, and shook her hand with a firm, dry grip.

'Like to take a seat, Miss Masson?'

'Thank you.'

He glanced down at her application form on his desk.

'Now, it says here you're from Dundee. Why Edinburgh, then?'

'I wanted to be near my sister, who's moved here. She's married, but wasn't well at one time. Could do with support.'

Oh, Letty, forgive me, prayed Eva, crossing her fingers.

'I see. Now, I have the details of your education, Miss Masson. Seems you were a bright girl. And have some excellent experience.' Mr Torrance glanced at the attached sheets of the old references she'd supplied. 'And your references are good, except that there appears to have been a gap. Weren't you teaching after you left your practice schools?'

Eva looked down at her hands folded on her lap, at the finger on her left hand that looked so naked, except for the mark where her wedding ring had been. She covered the mark with a glove.

'There were family reasons,' she said at last, forcing herself to look at Mr Torrance. 'I was always keen to continue my career, but I had to delay things for a while.'

It sounded weak, she knew. Told him nothing, and he would realize that. See how his eyes were riveted on her face...

Her heart beating fast, she looked away, then back again, and read in his eyes that had appeared so hard and now were not, that he was attracted to her. Perhaps it shouldn't have been surprising – she was young, considered pretty, even beautiful. But she'd been through so much, felt nothing about her looks, or how they might affect a man. Especially not one who was the headmaster who held it in his power to give her a job.

Long moments passed, until Mr Torrance looked down at the papers on his desk again, and Eva, with a confidence of which she was rather ashamed, waited for him to speak.

'Well, as you know, Miss Masson, this post is just a temporary appointment,' he said at last. 'Initially for six months. One of our staff members is unfortunately seriously ill and at the moment we can't predict what the situation will be in the future.'

'I understand.'

'We'll be closing for the holidays this week, but would like someone to start mid August, for the autumn term. Would you be willing to do that?'

'Oh, yes, quite willing.'

He doodled a little with his fountain pen.

'Miss Masson, mind if I ask, is there any particular reason why you shouldn't be applying now for a permanent post?'

'No – not really. I just thought this might be a good place to...'

As she hesitated, he finished the sentence for her.

'Start again?'

'Yes, I suppose so.'

'And the fact that this is a somewhat deprived area doesn't worry you? The children here are not from middle-class backgrounds.'

Eva smiled. 'I was brought up in a tenement in Dundee. I think I know enough about deprived backgrounds not to mind working in another.'

'That's good.' He stood up and again put out his hand to her. 'Thank you for coming to Lockhart, Miss Masson. You'll be informed in the next few days of the name of the succesful candidate for the post. Good afternoon.'

'Good afternoon, Mr Torrance, and thank you.'

She thought he would return to his office when he'd seen her out, but he walked with her down the corridor to the main door.

'Not a bad school, really,' he told her, as they looked together into the street, where the smell of the brewery wafted over them, and the noise of the traffic made him raise his voice. 'We do our best.'

'I'm sure you do, Mr Torrance.'

As she walked away towards a tram stop, she was aware of his watching her, but when she turned her head, he had gone.

Quite soon afterwords, she received a letter informing her that she had been successful in applying for the temporary post at Lockhart

School, and if able to comply with all the necessary formalities, would be required to start in mid August at the beginning of the autumn term.

'Evie, that's grand!' cried Letty. 'What now, then?'

'I find a room somewhere.'

'You could stay here. We've got the spare room.'

'No, no, you and Hughie don't need me hanging about. I'll look for something small and cheap around the Haymarket.'

'Small and cheap,' sighed Letty.

'I'm paying my own way, Letty. Small and cheap it has to be.'

And a small, cheap room was found in a tenement with rooms to let in Dalry, beyond the Haymarket. Hughie and Letty lent crockery and bed linen, until Eva could choose her own, and on a day in late July, she moved in.

Looks like I've come full circle, she thought as she looked round her room on her first night. From a tenement in Wish Lane to a tenement in Dalry.

But the tears she wept when she was in her bed were not for being in Dalry, but for not being in Dundee. Whether for Wish Lane or Princess Victoria Terrace didn't matter; she was just homesick for what she knew, and must endure it.

Seventy-Eight

Eva slipped so smoothly back into teaching, it made up to a certain extent for being away from home. Of course, it helped that her class consisted of seven-year-olds, the age she liked best, and that her colleagues were so friendly and welcoming. If they wondered about her circumstances, they never asked about them, and were able to tell her all she needed to know about her predecessor, Jane Robson, and Gregor Torrance, the headmaster.

Poor Jane was in a sanatorium for TB, and everybody knew what that meant. She'd be there for years – if she ever came out. So, it was a chance for Eva, eh?

'Oh, don't speak of it,' said Eva.

Dead women's shoes – or even a sick woman's shoes – did not appeal.

Well, wait and see, her new friends advised. It didn't do to turn down jobs, the way things were. Especially the way Ramsay MacDonald was handling things. But talking politics reminded Eva of Bob Keir and she could only back away.

As for Mr Torrance – he was apparently fine. Strict, but fair. You knew where you were with him. He was a widower. Poor man, his wife had died of the Spanish influenza when they'd only been married a year. He'd just come back from the war, it was said, and was only in his twenties. And only thirty-nine now – young for a head.

For some time after she'd heard this, Eva brooded on Mr Torrance's troubles. Poor fellow, twelve years he'd grieved for his wife. It seemed to put her own grief for her lost life into perspective, even though it was real enough.

Was he grieving still? She didn't think so, and in fact hoped not, as long as she'd been mistaken over his interest in herself. One thing she did not want was to be the cause of anything like that again, and sometimes she managed to believe that she'd seen something that wasn't there.

Until there would come a chance encounter in the corridor, or a staff meeting she would have to attend, and his eyes would find her and rest on her again, and she knew she was not mistaken. Luckily, he never put anything into words. All situations could be managed, if nothing was said.

As she had prophesied, Nicholas never came seeking her. She'd been certain he wouldn't, for he'd been too badly hurt just to come looking and hoping they could start again. She knew how he felt, for she felt the same, and was gradually beginning to believe what Bel had said – that there'd been too much against them from the start.

Nor did she ever hear anything from Bob Keir, which was a relief. He'd said if things went wrong for her, if she ever needed him, she could count on him, but she knew she would never do that. And of course, he didn't know what had happened, didn't know that she'd left Nicholas.

'I do see him now and again,' Hughie told her, 'but I've never said anything. The truth is, we never speak of you.'

'Thank God for that.'

'The point is, though, he will hear eventually, about the break. Word gets around. What'll I do if he asks me straight out, where you are?'

'Don't tell him where I am,' she said fervently. 'Never tell him.'

And Hughie said he never would.

Since she'd moved to Edinburgh, Eva had seen nothing of Roddie, though she'd thought of him often and worried about his continuing affair with Willow. What had passed between them concerning Nicholas and herself? Had he heard how the Norths had taken the separation?

She longed to write and ask, but didn't dare, and in the end it was Roddie who wrote and asked if he could see her. Bad news, she thought at once. Willow has ended their affair. He will be devastated.

In fact, when they met in Princes Street Gardens – her suggestion – he said no, nothing had changed between him and Willow. His news was for Eva.

'News? For me?'

His tone, so unusually serious, made her turn pale.

'Aye. Nicholas has gone back to India.'

She was surprised at the strength of the pain. All along, she'd said Nicholas would not come looking for her and that she didn't want him to, but

383

now that she knew for sure that he would not, the pain was bad. So bad, she could have held her side and cried aloud, but of course she didn't.

'Oh, Evie,' he whispered, watching her, his blue eyes distressed. 'I hate to see you look so sad. It's all right, he'll be coming back.'

'Who told you?' she asked, staring unseeingly at people passing by.

'He did.'

'Nicholas himself?'

'Came into the office, asked for a word in private. Looked pretty ill.'

'Did he ... mention me?'

'Aye. He said, as he didn't know where you were, would I tell you he was going back to India? No' for years this time – just some months, to look into things.' Roddie smiled faintly. 'He'd no need – we all know how the jute industry's doing in Calcutta, putting us out of business. Willow said it was his dad's idea, to get him out of the way. Cut down the scandal.'

'Scandal?' Eva caught her breath. 'His folks are saying I've caused a scandal?'

'No, but when a couple separate, some call it that, you ken, and Willow says her mother's in a state. Mr North and all.'

'So, they've sent Nicholas away again. And he didn't mind going.'

'Seemingly he's got a pal in the army going out to join his regiment – he was travelling with him.'

'And when will he come back?'

'February, maybe. Willow wasnae sure. In the meantime, they've got your wee maid coming in

384

as a daily to keep your house going.'

'Cora's so good. I got her to pack up the rest of my clothes, you know, and send them to Letty's. But I feel bad I've never been back to see her.'

Roddie took Eva's arm.

'Come on, let's have tea, eh? You need something and there's Logie's right over there.'

'I can't face all those Edinburgh ladies, gossiping away.'

'Never mind 'em.' Roddie hauled her to her feet. 'We'll have tea and cakes – my treat – then I'll see you to your tram. Afterwards, I might look in on Letty, as you're no' going to show me your room.'

'It's not much of a room to show, Roddie.'

He made no answer, only shepherded her across the street as though she was an invalid. She knew he was thinking of the house she had left, but she put the thought of it from her mind, as she had trained herself to do.

Over tea and cakes, she told him she was reminded of seeing him with Willow, in a tearoom such as this.

'I never thought you'd still be going out with her, Roddie.'

He shrugged. 'She likes to see me, Evie. Sees other fellas, too.'

Eva's eyes widened. 'And you don't mind?'

'No. I'm happy about it. Stops things getting too intense, you ken.'

'Well! That's amazing. How can you be so easy-going?'

'We're no' so involved as some folk are.'

'Not married, Roddie, that's the thing.'

'Foot loose and fancy free, that's me.'

Was he really as casual about Willow as he pretended? Eva studied her brother for a moment or two, but knew she'd never be sure of his feelings. He'd always been good at hiding those.

When he'd paid the bill and they were back in Princes Street, looking up at the castle, its flags hanging limply in the summer heat, she smiled a little.

'When we were bairns, would you ever have believed we'd have tea at a place like Logie's?'

'I'd never have believed a lot o' things that have happened to us. Me in accounts at North's, for instance.'

'Wish we could do more for Ma and Dad.'

'Maybe one day, eh?'

At the tram stop, they quickly hugged.

'You take care now, Evie, and keep in touch.'

'You too.' She pressed his hand. 'Thanks for telling me about Nicholas.'

'He did want you to know he was going abroad again.'

She looked away. 'Here's my tram, Roddie. Bye, now.'

As he blew her a kiss, she boarded the tram, marvelling over the cheerful spirit that was his great attraction. Lucky Roddie. With the news he'd brought her, she couldn't summon up much cheerfulness herself.

Seventy-Nine

It was hard to make a show of being cheerful anyway, loaded down as she was by keeping secrets. For her marriage was not her only secret.

Another, so worrying she could only keep hoping it would go away, had begun to occupy her mind. But every day that passed only reminded her it was still with her, and she had to renew her efforts to appear what people thought her – a young, carefree, un-married woman.

In fact, these were not carefree times for anyone. The government Ramsay MacDonald had put together to solve the economic crisis had achieved very little. There had been cuts in public services, and proposals to cut unemployment benefit, while MacDonald himself had been expelled from the Labour Party for joining in with the Conservatives. There were riots from the unemployed, mutiny from unpaid troops, and everywhere depression.

'What a mess, eh?' Eva's staffroom colleagues groaned, all feeling the cold wind that was whistling round their heads, all desperate to keep their jobs, while Eva herself shivered more than most. For hers was the most real fear of getting the sack – a fear that was becoming stronger and stronger every time she looked at the calendar.

I'm still well, she told herself. *It could just be a false alarm.* Loads of women were late. Wasn't it everybody's worry? As a child, she'd heard neighbours talking in whispers to her mother, then later perhaps coming in beaming – there wasn't going to be another mouth to feed, after all. Few of the folk from Wish Lane could afford to be as happy as Letty had been, over having a baby.

As for Eva, she had to admit, something she would once have welcomed would now be a disaster. So awful to think about, she refused to contemplate it. Until, one September morning, she was sick.

'Oh, Letty, d'you think it can be true?' she wailed, having hurried round to her sister's for support. 'D'you think I'm expecting?'

'Evie, how can I say?' asked Letty, worriedly. 'I mean, you'll have to see the doctor.'

'No, no, I couldn't face it.' Eva put her hand to her mouth. 'Supposing he says I am?'

'If you are, it'll be best to know now. Then you can plan what to do.'

'I've got no plan, that's the trouble. I just don't know what I'd do.'

'Well, Dr MacIver's very nice and he doesnae charge much. You go and see him, Evie, and see what he says. Then we'll work something out.' Letty hesitated. 'You'd have to tell Nicholas, you ken.'

Eva was silent, not meeting Letty's eyes.

'He'd have a right to be told,' Letty pressed. 'You could write to India. Roddie could get his address.'

'I'm not telling him,' said Eva. 'We must have started this baby when he came home from Europe. Now I don't want him coming back because of the baby and not for me.'

'You'll need him, Evie. If you have to give up your job, what'll you do for money?'

'I've got some savings, from when I was working in Lochee. I could manage for a while.'

'And then there's Ma. You'd surely tell her? Oh, Evie, you'll have to tell her, eh?'

'Later, maybe.' Eva gave a long, shuddering sigh. 'Just think what it's been like for her, anyway, Letty. With all the neighbours and the lassies at North's knowing I've fallen flat on my face? Up with the rocket, down with the stick, they'll have been saying, and laughing.'

'Oh, Evie, that's no' true! No' everybody's like Berta and her pals. Some were pleased for you, they were.'

'Were they?' Eva shrugged. 'I don't really care what folk think, apart from Ma. But don't ask me to tell her yet if there's a baby coming and no husband around. That'd be too much.'

'Go and see the doctor,' Letty said, after a pause. 'There's no point talking, is there? Until you know?'

Two weeks later, after Eva had found the courage to go to the doctor's, she knew.

Sitting in Dr MacIver's consulting room, wearing her wedding ring again and known to him as Mrs North, she somehow had to look pleased when he gave her the news she'd been dreading.

'The twentieth of February is the date, my dear, I'm happy to tell you – though as you probably know, that's not exact, just something to work on.' The doctor – a cheerful, middle-aged Edinburgh man with a florid face and dark hair turning grey – was smiling. 'Some good news to tell your husband abroad, then?'

'Oh, yes,' Eva agreed. 'It's very good news.'

'Be sure to see your own doctor on your return home after your visit here, and follow all his instructions. Take a little peppermint if you have any more sickness, and rest every afternoon.'

'Thank you, Doctor.' Eva rose. 'I just wanted to make sure I wasn't ill with something else, you know.'

'Of course, of course, but don't regard pregnancy as an illness, my dear. It's the most natural thing in the world, and something we know more about than we used to.' The doctor put his hand on Eva's shoulder. 'I wish you the very best, Mrs North. Take care, now.'

'And your bill?' she asked hesitantly.

'Don't worry about it now. I'll send it care of Mrs Harper's address. Good afternoon, Mrs North.'

'Good afternoon, Dr MacIver, and thank you.'

Walking back to the school in the autumn sunshine, Eva felt numb. Sometimes, when you feared something and it didn't happen, then you could breathe again. But when you feared something and it still happened, you felt worse, because you were so disappointed you hadn't been wrong.

What was she going to do? She couldn't begin at that moment to think. One thing was for sure, she wouldn't be able to stay at Lockhart, her haven of a school in the centre of industrial noise and fumes and sweet-sour smells from the brewery.

At least she wasn't showing yet, but how long might she be able to conceal her secret? Everyone said women were different. Some showed almost from the beginning; others not for months.

I might be lucky, thought Eva, but as she entered the front entrance of the school, she had no hopes of it. Luck had been with her in getting a job; why should she expect more?

She'd arranged to visit the doctor's at a time when her class joined another for Physical Training, and now might just have time to snatch a cup of tea in the staffroom before she must collect her pupils. But in the corridor, close to the headmaster's office, she met the man himself, and her heart sank.

He was going to ask her how she was, she could tell; could see the concern in his eyes and his uncertain smile as he halted before her.

'Miss Masson, how are you? I was sorry to hear that you'd had to go to the doctor's. Is everything all right?'

'Yes, thank you, Mr Torrance. It was nothing important.'

Nothing important ... But she had to say something to put off his questions, so that she could get away, make for the staffroom, think what she must do.

'That's good.' The headmaster seemed genuinely relieved, but made no move to go into his office. 'I had been thinking lately that you'd been looking rather pale. I was hoping there was nothing wrong.'

'No, no, nothing wrong.'

'You're doing so well here, Miss Masson. I've been meaning to tell you, I'm very pleased with your work.'

'That's very kind of you, Mr Torrance.'

Eva put her hand to her brow, pushing back the brim of her hat, for a headache was forming, like thunder in the distance. Beat, beat, beat. She was beginning to think she would like to lie down, when she noticed that Gregor Torrance, a dark red colour staining his cheekbones, was staring at her left hand.

Mystified, she looked down at the hand herself and saw, as the thunder gathered round her head, that she had forgotten to take off her wedding ring.

Eighty

He had asked her to come into his office, had closed his door and placed a chair, where she waited, as though calm, for his wrath.

In fact, he too appeared calm as he faced her across his desk, but as her hands trembled on her lap, his eyes revealed his pain.

'I take it that is a wedding ring on your finger?' he asked quietly.

'Yes, I'm married.'

'And your married name is...?'

'North. My husband's name is Nicholas North. But we are separated.'

'Separated? Your husband's in Dundee, is he?'

'No, in India.'

'So, you're on your own, and that's why you needed a job. Was it necessary to tell lies to get one?'

Flushing deeply, Eva bravely kept her eyes on his. 'It's not easy to get any job just now, and I wanted to get back to teaching. I didn't see why I shouldn't be able to do the work I was trained for.'

'You knew the rules, though. I agree that they seem unfair on married women, but you can't just disregard them. They apply to almost all professions.'

'I was very sorry to have to deceive you,' she said in a low voice. 'I hated not being honest. But I was alone and needed the money.'

'Your husband left you no means of support?'

'He did.' Eva looked down at her folded hands. 'I didn't want to take it.'

'If you'd taken it, you realize someone else could have had your job?'

She bit her lip. 'I know. I'm sorry. I just wanted to be independent again.'

'I can understand that,' he said after a silence. 'But if you didn't want to lie to me, why didn't you tell me your situation? I might have been able to arrange something.'

'You think the Board would have let you employ a woman separated from her husband? The next thing to being divorced?' Eva smiled wryly. 'With so many people after every job, what chance would I have stood?'

Again he was silent, then stood up and began to pace his room, turning at last to look at her.

'I wish there was something I could do.'

'It's all right, Mr Torrance, I don't expect you to do anything.' She stood up. 'If you'll excuse me, I have to collect my class from PT now. But I'll put my notice in tomorrow.'

'There's no reason why you shouldn't stay until the end of term,' he said quickly. 'I needn't inform the Board of your reason for leaving.'

'You're very kind, and I appreciate it, but I think I'd like to go as soon as possible.' She had no wish to tell him that by the end of term her condition would be obvious and, as a supposedly unmarried woman, considered shocking. 'I think maybe I've had enough of pretending.'

'It's not long to half-term. You could leave then – make some excuse?'

'That would be best.'

He gave her a long sorrowful look and put out his hand. 'Look, if I can think of anything to help, I will. You'll let me do that?'

'You're very kind,' she said again. 'Thank you, Mr Torrance.'

As she went to collect her pupils, she knew that she had been let off lightly and should have been glad. But a dull sadness for the way her life had gone, for the damage she had caused, made her heart heavy. And even, for a little while, allowed her to forget the date she'd felt was carved on her brow.

February the twentieth. It soon came back.

That evening, Eva went round to give the date to Letty. Hughie was there and it could have been embarrassing, but they were both so kind, they made it easy.

Of course, they insisted, when the time came to leave the school, she must give up her room and come and stay with them.

'No, I mean it,' Letty told her earnestly. 'We both do, eh, Hughie? You're family. Think we're going to leave you to manage on your own?'

'Of course not,' put in Hughie. 'We'll take care of you, Eva.'

'You're so good to me,' she whispered, with tears ready to fall. 'I don't know what to say. But I haven't decided what to do yet. I might even go back to Dundee. I don't know.'

'You've got your lovely house there,' said Hughie. 'Why no'...?'

He stopped and the sisters looked at him.

'Why no' what?' asked Letty.

'Just give in?' murmured Eva. 'Sometimes I'm tempted. Ah, let's leave it. I can't really see myself back in the Terrace, but I'll think about it.'

'You'll have to make arrangements about having the babby,' said Letty, as Eva prepared to go back to her bed-sitter. 'I mean – hospital, or at home, you ken.'

Home? Eva wondered where that would be.

She knew she wouldn't be taking advantage of Letty's offer, or be returning to Dundee, but she'd work something out. She'd have to, wouldn't she?

Eighty-One

Only two weeks later, Eva said goodbye to Lockhart School. Even after so short a time, her class seemed sorry to lose her, some of the little girls even bursting into tears, because Miss Masson never lost her temper and wasn't too handy with the ruler, like some others they'd known. And who would they be going to get now? Some awful supply teacher, so they'd heard.

'Family reasons' was her vague excuse, which she'd thought might be harder for her colleagues to believe, but such was her reputation for being nice, they'd accepted it without question and showered her with sympathy.

They said it was a shame she had to go back to Dundee so soon, when she had just settled and was doing so well. Maybe she'd come back to visit some time, though? And in the meantime there were hugs and good wishes, and even a bouquet of flowers.

'I feel so bad,' she told Gregor Torrance when she saw him privately to say goodbye. 'Telling lies again.'

'All over now,' he said comfortingly. 'But what

will you do? I was thinking you might care to try for some private tuition work. You could do that as a married woman.'

'Yes, that's a good idea,' she agreed, knowing it was out of the question until she'd had her baby. What parents would pay for extra tuition from a tutor in the family way? Working women often had to keep going almost until the baby's birth, but folk such as lady teachers were supposed to stay at home and keep out of sight.

'I worry about you,' Gregor was saying. 'Is it not possible for your husband to return, to be with you?'

'I don't think so.'

'Well, it's not my place to tell you what to do, but you're so young to be separated – are you sure you've given your marriage every chance?'

'I was in the wrong to begin with,' she said painfully. 'And I wasn't forgiven. So, I've been unforgiving too. Now, I think we can't go back to what we were.'

'We only have one life, you know, Eva. And when it's over, it's over. Nothing can ever be said again. No word of forgiveness, no reconciliation.'

As she turned to go, her shoulders drooping, he caught at her hand and said he was sorry.

'Such sad talk for your farewell; I just want to wish you all the best. Is it possible for us to keep in touch? I'd like to know how you get on. I still want to help.'

'I'll try to let you know,' she told him, which was as honest as she could be. 'And I'll never forget your kindness.'

'If your name really had been Miss Masson, things might have been different for us, do you think?'

She smiled and made no answer. There was no way of knowing how she would have felt, if there had never been any Nicholas North.

They shook hands and parted, and a little while afterwards, Eva left the school, carrying her flowers and her teacher's bag of books and papers, and went back to her bed-sitter. To another new phase in her life.

Eighty-Two

At first, after leaving work, her small world appeared darker than ever. With unemployment as high as it was, there was no prospect of finding another job, even of a temporary nature. And now that she was putting on weight fast and having to wear dreary maternity clothes, who would want to take her on anyway?

She'd worked out that the savings she still had from her Lochee salary would just about tide her over until after the baby was born. Beyond that, she hadn't thought – and indeed she sometimes felt like giving in. Moving back to the Terrace and using the money Nicholas had made available. Well, why not?

Because it was the last thing she wanted to do. Go back to Dundee, with a baby on the way and her husband nowhere near? No, she couldn't face it and, like her mother, didn't want to take North money anyway.

Did she still love Nicholas? She'd told Bob she did, but that was before. Before the balloon had gone up, the bombshell had exploded, her world had collapsed. Now she didn't know what she felt, but she had to admit that there were times when the thought of Bob himself was comforting. And he would be willing to be comforting. 'If you ever need me,' he'd said, 'I'll be there.'

Perhaps it was true what he'd always claimed, that he was right for her. If anyone was her soulmate, it should have been Bob, for there was so much between them that Nicholas could never share. They knew each other's background and schooling. They had the same ideals, dreamed of the same sort of social change that Nicholas would never want to make.

On the other hand, Bob might say he loved her, but he didn't even know her situation. How would he feel when he saw her carrying Nicholas's child?

And what were her feelings for him anyway? Or what might they be?

At the moment, all she wanted was to have her baby and sort herself out. But the way things were looking, she wasn't even sure if she could do that. If only she could tell her ma what was happening. She vowed she would, and soon – as soon as she felt more confident. As soon as her luck turned.

Out of the blue, her luck did turn, and for the

better. She couldn't believe it.

First, Letty volunteered to look after the baby so that Eva could go back to work. 'Think I'd let you send ma nephew or niece to a child minder? You're family, eh? And I've only got Iain and no' much hope of any more. I tell you, I'd be glad to do it.'

'Oh, Letty, are you sure?' cried Eva. 'No, it's too much.'

'Look, I've just said I want to do it. And I'll no' need paying, either.'

'Of course I'll pay you, Letty. From my wages, eh? Oh, what a grand thing it'll be, not to have to worry about the bairn!'

'Next thing is to get you to come and stay with us. You canna have the babby in that bed-sitter, Evie.'

This was a perennial argument and one that Eva shelved again, but she had to admit that Letty was right when she told Eva she must book in with a doctor and arrange for her confinement.

'No good thinking it'll all go away, Evie. You'll have to get on with things.'

'I know,' Eva sighed. 'But your doctor thinks I've gone back to Dundee and I don't really want to see him and try to explain. Where can I find someone else?'

'I'm sure I dinna ken,' Letty said worriedly. 'But you'll have to do something soon.'

But what?

This was where the second piece of luck came in. On a chance walk in George Street, window-shopping for the want of something better to do, she had caught sight of a tall young woman with a freckled face and short fair hair that used to be thin little plaits. Could it be? Yes, it was Ada MacGill, once a fellow pupil at Toll Road School, now, as it turned out, a midwife at a private nursing home, and tenant of a small flat in Marchmont.

'A midwife?' echoed Eva, her eyes shining with wild hope.

'Do you want one?' asked Ada, smiling, but sending her experienced eye over Eva's bulky figure nevertheless.

'Oh, Ada, if you only knew!'

Over tea in a department store Ada, her long face sympathetic but detached, as nurses' faces have to be, soon knew all that she needed to, and without hesitation said she'd be glad to look after Eva. Not in the tiny bed-sitter that sounded so unsuitable, and not in 'Heather Lee' where Ada worked, because that was far too pricey, but in her own flat, where a colleague had just vacated the small spare room to go to Canada.

'I can't believe this is happening,' Eva said faintly as she took another slice of cake, for she was always hungry these days. 'Do I hear my guardian angel's wings beating? Must be your wings, Ada. And have you got a halo?'

'Oh, come,' said Ada, embarrassed. 'We're friends, eh? Even if we'd lost touch. But Ma always sent me news of you and your folks, and I've always been meaning to look up Letty since she moved here.'

'Wait till I tell her what you've offered me, Ada!' Eva wiped her sticky fingers. 'But tell me the rent; I don't want you to be out of pocket.

401

And then I'll want to pay you for what you do for me.'

'Look, you pay me what you can for the rent, and don't worry about anything else for now. Let's get you settled first. Who's your doctor?'

When Eva admitted that she had no doctor, Ada looked grave, and said she'd organize one as soon as possible.

'Time's getting on, Eva. It'll soon be December, and if the baby comes early, you'll be in trouble.'

'I never thought of that.' Eva looked stricken. 'I suppose I've been a bit foolish, eh?'

'Foolhardy, more like. But some women do take risks.' Ada buttoned on her coat and called for the bill. 'We'll make sure you're all right, though. I'll get a doctor friend of mine to see you.' She gave a smile that suddenly transformed her face, and Eva knew that the 'friend' was rather special. 'But when are you coming up to see the flat? From the sound of your bed-sitter, I think you should move in as soon as you can.'

Eva, her hand closing on the bill the waitress had brought, said, 'Ada, if you could see my bed-sitter, you'd say tomorrow.'

Eighty-Three

The flat – which turned out to be the conversion of the ground floor of a stone-built terraced house – reminded Eva of the place she'd shared with Katie in Lochee. Carefree days then, when she'd had a job she loved and Nicholas had been coming home to her. It hurt, as it always did, to remember the past, so it was better not remember it. At least the present had taken a turn for the better.

If not free from anxiety – she could scarcely say that – she was as much at ease as she could hope to be. Ada's friend, young Doctor Barrie Lennox, had assured her that all was going well, while Ada herself was able to give Eva regular checks and said she was going to sail through the birth – no question.

'You think I'll be all right to have the baby here, then?' asked Eva.

'Of course. It's what we agreed, eh? I'll have everything prepared, no need to worry.'

'Supposing you're on duty, when it comes?'

'It'll no' be in a hurry. First babies never are.' Ada gave Eva's shoulder a confident pat. 'I'm just up the road at the home and I've got a phone here. All you need to do is give me a ring.'

The time had come to invite Bel over, and Frank

403

with her, for at least Eva was confident now and had had the good luck she needed. Even so, when her folks arrived one Sunday, there were tears from Bel and a long face from Frank, even though they admired Ada's flat, as well as Ada herself.

'We're that grateful for what you're doing for Eva,' Bel told her, sniffing. 'Oh, the poor lassie! Fancy falling for a babby and her man away. Aye, and keeping it all to herself, when she should've told me. Letty, why did you no' tell me what was going on?'

'Ah, Ma, it was Eva's business, eh? She didnae want to tell you till she was organized.'

'Organized, in Edinburgh?' groaned Frank. 'Should be at home in Dundee.'

'No, no, she's right to be away,' Bel told him. 'She'd no want to come to us, or stay in the Terrace, with all the neighbours buzzing.'

'It's all out in the open now anyway, Ma,' said Eva. 'And I hope you'll come over whenever you can.'

'Try to stop me!' cried Bel, swooping up Iain and setting him on her knee, whether he liked it or not. 'And you let me know the minute that bairn is born, eh? It'll be grand to have another grandchild. No hope at the moment from Roddie, you ken.'

'Ma, he's got plenty o' time,' said Letty. 'He's got his studies to think about.'

'No' even got a lady friend,' her mother sighed. 'At least, no' one he tells me about.'

'I'd better check the roast,' said Eva, carefully not looking at Letty, who'd been told of Roddie's affair with Willow.

'Roast, eh?' asked Frank. 'I'll be looking forward to that!'

'Not more than me,' Eva told him. 'Nobody tells you how hungry you get.'

'Is it true you have to eat for two?' asked Hughie.

'Just another old wives' tale,' Ada said firmly. 'It's no' wise to put too much weight on.'

'All I'm worrying about is taking it off,' said Eva.

But that would be when she'd had the baby, and she really couldn't think as far ahead as that. Would there ever be a time when she was herself again? Fitting into her clothes? Looking in the paper for jobs?

'Cheer up, pet,' said Bel, hugging her on parting. 'No' too long to go now, eh?'

'I wish the baby could come tomorrow, Ma.'

'Aye, but dinna forget, your whole life'll change when it does come.' Bel's face sagged a little as she turned away, adding in a low voice, 'Just wish you hadnae been on your own.'

Eighty-Four

Just before Christmas, Katie came over with presents, and treated Eva to lunch in a smart Edinburgh restaurant, where only the lucky few would be able to eat. Heaven knew what the families of the unemployed did for food. Some people preferred not to worry about it, and Eva herself had decided not to spoil Katie's day by bringing up the subject. Oddly enough, it was Katie herself who remarked on the latest figures, as they studied the menus.

'Terrible, isn't it, Eva, all these folk out of work? Bob says this National Government is a disgrace, doing so little to help. And they're even talking of having a means test before the poor souls get any benefits!'

'Bob?' repeated Eva.

'Bob Keir.' Katie's serene expression seemed to be giving the impression it was not surprising to hear his name on her lips. 'I've seen him a few times lately.'

'Oh? Where?'

'Well, the first time was in the Nethergate. I'd gone over to Mum's for the weekend and was doing a bit of shopping. We bumped into each other. Ended up having a coffee.' Looking so flushed and pretty as she raised her hand for the waitress, Katie made Eva feel quite drained. 'Shall we order? They say the fish is very good here.'

Never mind the fish, thought Eva. 'So, you had a coffee together?' she asked, agreeing to Katie's choice for the meal. 'You never had much time for Bob in the old days.'

'What's a coffee, then? Well, that day I just thought he was looking so down, he needed cheering up, and I let him talk. And what he had to say was really very sensible – and interesting.'

'Fancy.' Eva hesitated. 'Did he ask about me at all?'

It was Katie's turn to hesitate. 'No, he didn't.'

'Said something, then?'

'Well – only that he knew you didn't want to see him, or you'd have told him where you were.'

'You didn't tell him about the baby?'

'No, of course not!'

They were silent as their orders were brought, then Eva quietly said, 'So Bob arranged to see you again?'

'Yes. He suggested I might like to go to a meeting.'

'A meeting?' Eva smiled. 'At the Mercat Hall?'

'Well, it was a political meeting – they're often held there. The Labour man was speaking.' Katie drank some water. 'Spoke very well, too.'

'Whatever do your folks think of you going to a Labour Party meeting?'

Katie shrugged. 'They know I have to have my own views. And Bob and I don't just go to meetings.'

'No?'

'We've been to the pictures a couple of times. The films seem so strange with the sound, don't they? I used to think I'd never get used to it.'

'And you have meals, I suppose?'

And talks, of course. Talks and meals, Nicholas had said, were what lovers liked to have. Finishing her sole, Eva carefully laid her knife and fork together. Her head was spinning. Bob and Katie having talks and meals? She felt she'd taken a step that wasn't there.

Not that they'd be lovers, of course – just friends. Friends having talks and meals.

'Pudding?' asked Katie brightly.

They settled on treacle tart, with coffee to follow.

'That was grand, Katie, thank you,' Eva said, rising. 'Now you must come back to Ada's – we've some presents for you.'

'Such a relief that you're with Ada,' Katie murmured as they left the café. 'I'm sure Bob would have been pleased to know that too. He does care about you, you know.'

'Used to.'

'Well, it's been some months, hasn't it, since he saw you? I think he's finally come to terms with the situation.'

'My situation?'

'I mean, that you could never feel the same for him as he felt for you. When you split with Nicholas, he must have thought there was a chance for him, but now he knows there's not, he's had to accept it.'

'You seem to have thought about this quite a lot,' Eva observed, still feeling her colour fading beside Katie's bright, flushed face. 'If it's true what you say, I'm glad. I'd like him to be happy.'

'Me too, poor Bob.' Katie's step was jaunty as she took Eva's arm to cross a road. 'So much bluster, but he has a good heart, hasn't he? I always admired him at school, you know, even if we did call him Big Head.'

'Seems we all admired one another when we were at school,' Eva said rather acidly. 'You never had a good word for him when he used to call for me at college, though.'

'Didn't I?' Katie was looking into the distance, smiling faintly. 'Eva, would you say he has got tiger eyes?'

After Katie had gone, Eva lay on the sofa for a while, trying to settle her thoughts.

Bob taking Katie out, and Katie willing to go? Surely a turn of the wheel she could never have expected? They'd never got on, whatever Katie said. Unless Katie's aversion had been only the other side of an attraction? She'd always been willing to talk about him, now that Eva remembered. And it was no wonder that he'd been willing to be cheered up by such a pretty girl. Have his wounded spirit soothed. His self-respect restored.

But wasn't I a fool, to think I might call on him for comfort, Eva mused, holding her hands to her aching head. Poor old Bob. Always there for her, he'd said so himself. But who could blame him, as the months had passed, for growing tired of waiting to be needed?

Eva didn't blame him. No, it was true what she'd said, she wanted him to be happy, while she could look for comfort elsewhere. Or do without it.

That was it. She could manage. She didn't need anyone at all.

Eighty-Five

After Christmas and Hogmanay spent with Letty and Hughie, Eva gave herself up to the quiet life of waiting and preparation. It was worrying at first, when Ada announced that she would be moving on to the night shift at the maternity home, but she soon lulled Eva's fears.

'It's all right; there are always three of us on. If I get the call from you, I'll be there by the time you need me.'

'Are you sure, Ada?'

'Aye, I'm sure. Now stop worrying. It's bad for you.'

'Everything is,' sighed Eva.

Towards the end of January, she had a call from Roddie. Just to ask how she was, he told her, but then his news came out.

First, Nicholas hadn't arrived back yet.

'I never asked you if he had,' said Eva.

'Well, I thought you'd like to know.'

Secondly, Roddie had passed some intermediate accountancy exams. When he finished his course, he would have to find a firm to take him on, so that he could become chartered. He rather fancied moving away.

'Not too far, I hope.'

'Edinburgh, maybe.'

'That would be grand!'

410

'Aye, but it's no' easy these days, getting taken on. I'll have to hope for the best.'

Thirdly, he and Willow had come to the final parting of the ways.

'Oh, Roddie!'

'Nae bother. It's been winding down for some time. We're both fine about it. But I'll miss her, I'm no' saying I won't. She's added a lot to ma life, you ken.'

'Driving, you mean?'

'Ah, now, no' just that. We had a damn' good farewell dinner and promised we'd never lose touch.' Roddie laughed. 'Of course we will, but it was a nice way to say goodbye.'

'I'm sorry, Roddie, I really am. But it was never going to last, was it?'

'All good things come to an end, they say. But, Evie, are you truly all right? Everything going according to plan?'

'As far as there is a plan, yes, I'm well. How about you? Are you lonely, without Willow?'

'As a matter of fact, I'm getting to know a very pretty typist at North's. Miss Hanna's replacement. She's called Marigold. We're going to the talkies tomorrow.'

'Roddie, you're like a rubber ball, aren't you?' cried Eva. 'When you're down, you bounce right back up.'

'Who says I was down?' Roddie asked.

That night was bitterly cold and when Eva went to bed, after Ada had gone to work, she took a hot-water bottle to hug, but still couldn't get warm. A little after midnight, she got up and made herself tea, for the air in her room was so chill, she couldn't sleep.

The tea seemed to do her good, but back in bed, she felt the faintest little pain. Not a pain, really, just a sort of squeeze. Even so, she froze.

Was this it? The start?

No, it couldn't be. The sensation was too small. Besides, it was too early. But there came another one, another little squeeze. Was it, or wasn't it? If only Ada had been at home, she would have known. Better not ring her at work, though. At least, not yet. Wait and see.

Nothing much seemed to be happening, and Eva relaxed. She would try to sleep.

In fact, she did sleep, and dreamed and dreamed. Mainly of Nicholas. He was looking for her door but couldn't find it. 'Eva!' he was calling, but then he turned into Roddie, and Roddie said, 'Nicholas isn't back yet, I thought you'd like to know,' and with a great start, Eva sat up. And knew, without needing Ada to tell her, that it had started, all right. Without any doubt at all. She must ring the nursing home at once.

'You're all right, Eva,' came Ada's comforting voice. 'Remember I told you the first stage could take some time. Try to rest till I get back.'

'But when will you come?'

'Don't worry. I'll be with you when things really start happening.'

'They're happening now,' Eva told her with conviction. 'I don't think I can wait.'

'You canna have progressed so fast, Eva. Sometimes folk imagine things, you know. It's a nervous thing.'

'Ada, I'm not imagining things. The contractions – they're really strong.'

'All right, I'll get away as soon as I can.'

'Thank you,' Eva gasped.

An age seemed to pass before she heard the key in the front door, but finally Ada was there, in cape and starched uniform and a cloud of disinfectant, hurrying to her side.

'Eva, I'm here! Quick, let's have a look at you, then.'

Oh, the relief, to be in Ada's capable hands, to know she was no longer alone!

'Well!' exclaimed Ada, when she had finished her examination. 'Looks like you're going to be lucky, Eva. A very short labour. Happens sometimes, you ken.'

'I don't feel very lucky,' Eva whispered.

'Aye, well, I think I should warn you, these quickies are no' always straightforward. You might need stitches.' Ada stood, looking down at Eva and frowning. 'I'm afraid we're going to have to move you. Be on the safe side, eh? As the baby's a wee bit early and all.'

'Move me where?'

'The Royal. Ah, now, no need to look like that. You'll be in good hands.'

'But I wanted you to deliver the baby, Ada! All along, it was going to be you!'

'Canna be helped, Eva. You just stay there and try no' to worry. I'm going to phone for an ambulance.' At the door, Ada turned and gave a quick smile. 'Before you know it, you'll be looking at your baby. Just think of that, eh?'

* * *

Before she knew it? Eva would not have agreed with that, but it was true enough that she didn't have too long to wait before she saw her baby. By eight o'clock in the morning, she was in bed in a ward, washed, stitched, and gazing, awe struck, at the bundle the nurse had just placed in her arms.

'There you are, Mrs North, your lovely daughter, all six pounds of her. What a fighter, eh? No complications at all.'

'I can't believe it.' As she looked at the small, wrinkled face and the tiny hands, Eva's eyes were wet. 'She's really here? It's all over?'

'All over, dear, but I'm going to whisk her away now to the nursery and let you have a cup of tea. We'll be along soon to help you with feeding, eh?'

As she picked up the baby, who let out a loud wail, the nurse patted Eva's shoulder. 'Well done, dear. Got a name for her, have you? Or is Dad going to have his say?'

'My husband's abroad,' Eva replied quickly. 'But I've chosen the names anyway. Isabel after my mother, and Frances because I like it.'

'Very nice, dear, very nice indeed. Let's hope hubby approves, eh?'

'Oh, yes,' Eva murmured, suddenly feeling extraordinarily tired. When her tea came, she could only drink half of it before she fell asleep. And this time, she did not dream.

Eighty-Six

The following days were the easiest Eva had spent for a very long time. Apart from feeding and admiring Isabel, she had nothing to do but rest, talk to the other patients, and receive her visitors.

'As though I were royalty, no less,' she told Letty. 'To tell you the truth I feel an awful fraud. Now I've had the stitches out, I'm sure I'm well enough to go home, but they make you stay on, just in case. Just in case of what, then?'

'They say all kinds o' things can go wrong,' said Letty. 'I dinna ken what. Just have to do what they say, eh?' Her gaze was soft on her sister. 'Oh, but it's grand it's all over, Evie, eh? And you've got the sweetest wee girl! Iain's disappointed, he wanted a laddie to play with, but I says, you'll play with Isabel just as well. Wait and see!'

They laughed at the thought of that tiny baby playing at all, but Eva was sure that the nurse who'd called her a fighter was right. Already she seemed to be showing signs of strength of character – and of course she was the best-looking baby ever seen. No argument there.

Bel agreed, when she came one Saturday afternoon, and declared herself thrilled to death that such a beautiful child had been called after her. She'd brought snowdrops bought at a market stall, and a batch of her own queen cakes, because everybody knew what hospital food was like.

'I'm enjoying it,' Eva told her. 'I eat like a horse, and I'm as hungry as ever, but how am I going to get into my clothes? If and when I get out of here.'

Bel hugged Eva hard. 'Never mind, what's it matter? Oh, I'm just that relieved, I canna tell you! Just like I was with Letty, eh? If there's one thing worse than having bairns yourself, it's going through it with your daughters!'

'Where's Dad, then?' asked Eva, eagerly biting into a cake. 'And Roddie?'

'And Hughie,' said Letty. 'Ah, these men – canna stand hospitals!'

'Well, no' women's wards, anyway,' put in Bel. 'Course no' many in Wish Lane ever get to hospital – well, you ken they all have the bairns at home, and everybody sits out on the steps till it's over. But your dad's just worried that this place'll be full o' women in nightgowns, and he's too scared to show his face.'

'Same with Hughie, but he's sent some magazines, Evie.'

'And Roddie's sent some sweeties,' said Bel. 'Is it no' grand he's doing so well with his studies? He'll make a grand accountant.'

'Fancies a move, Ma,' said Letty. 'Might come to Edinburgh.

'Does all ma family have to live in Edinburgh?' Bel cried. But she sat back easily on her flimsy chair and looked round with interest at the other patients and their visitors, the banked flowers on the central table, the nurses hurrying about.

'Very nice,' she whispered. 'But will you have to pay?'

'I think if you can, you pay something. If you can't, it's free. Suppose I could make a contribution.'

Letty and Bel were silent, no doubt thinking of the North money, as Eva was too.

'You've no' told Nicholas?' Bel asked at last.

Eva shook her head. 'I don't even know where he is, exactly.'

'And what about his folks?' Bel pursed her lips. 'They are the grandparents, eh?'

'I haven't told them either.'

'Mebbe you should?' ventured Letty, and Eva shrugged.

'Now that Isabel's born, yes, I could tell them. No hurry.'

'Aye, dinna put yourself out,' Bel advised. 'They never did for you.'

But I didn't marry them, thought Eva.

As soon as Bel and Letty had left that Saturday, Katie took their place, bringing daffodils from herself, and a large bunch of dark red chrysanthemums from the staff and pupils of King Robert's School.

'Oh, did they send these?' cried Eva, touched at the thought. 'Katie, how kind! Ah, that's so nice, eh? That they remember me.'

'Of course they remember you! Soon as I gave 'em the news about your baby, they started having a whip round. And your old class sent special love, as well. They still miss you.' Katie's gaze on Eva was admiring. 'But you know, Eva, you're looking really well! Quite your old self. So much better than when I last saw you. Not that you didn't look very nice, of course,' she added hastily.

'Oh, come, I looked like a ghost, I know. Don't remind me! Some women bloom, they say, and some don't, and I was one who didn't.' Eva, noting that Katie herself was as radiant as before, knew she didn't need to ask if she was still seeing Bob. All the same, she had a question.

'Have you told Bob, Katie? About my daughter?'

'"My daughter ..." Oh, that sounds so sweet.' Katie lowered her eyes. 'As a matter of fact, I have. I thought you'd want me to, now that the baby's here.'

'You're right, I do.' Eva touched the curled petals of the chrysanthemums. 'And what did he say?'

'He was astonished. Couldn't believe it. I think all he wants now is for you to be happy.'

'You can tell him that I am.'

'Is that true, Eva? I hope it is.'

'Well, at the moment, of course, I'm over the moon, because I've got Isabel. And then I've found out that I can run my own life – not be dependent. So I think I can say I'm happy enough.'

That little word, 'enough', hung between them, until Katie asked worriedly, 'But what are you going to do, Eva? You'll need to find a job, and can't go back to teaching.'

'Ada thinks she might be able to get me clerical work at Heather Lee. If she can, I'll find myself another place to live. Somewhere near Letty, so that she can take Isabel. Ada's been wonderful, but I don't think I should stay on with her. Not with a new baby. She deserves a rest when she comes home.'

'But it sounds like things are working out for you, Eva.'

'Except I'm not in Dundee.'

'You miss it?'

'I miss it.'

'It's a sad place at the moment, you know. There've never been so many folk on poor relief. The council's built some new houses, but the rents are too high for most folk. I mean, they would be, wouldn't they? If so many are out of work?'

It might have been Bob talking on his soapbox, thought Eva. What a convert he'd found in Katie! And as Katie blushed at the look in Eva's eye and began to gather up the flowers, Eva revised her view of this new friendship. Maybe it wasn't a friendship at all. More like a love affair. Well, time would tell.

'I'll just find some vases for the flowers,' Katie said. 'And then have a peep at the baby in the nursery. I bet she looks just like you, Eva!'

In fact, it was hard to say if Isabel looked like anyone, although by the time Eva took her back to Ada's flat, her blue eyes were already turning grey.

Eighty-Seven

Everyone said Eva should take a long rest before she took on work, but she didn't need a rest, she needed money, and was soon making enquiries about the nursing home post. Going back to work would mean bottle-feeding Isabel, of course, and leaving her every day with Letty, which would be a terrible wrench, but Eva couldn't see that she had much choice.

'It's only what the women in the mills do all the time, anyway,' she told Letty. 'There's no rest for them. They go back to work straight away.'

'No' ideal for them, and no' ideal for you,' said Letty. 'I feel bad you have to do it, Evie.'

'I've my bills to pay and my rent for my own place, when I find it, apart from all the other expenses. It's just not possible for me to manage without some wages.'

'Well, come and stay with me till you get a wee flat of your own,' Letty offered. 'That'll make things easier all round, for you and me, and Ada.'

'This time, I think I'll take you up on that. I couldn't be more grateful.'

'No more o' that. We'll be glad to have you.'

'As long as you get some sleep at nights. Ada says Isabel's got the strongest cries she's ever heard, and night is when you hear 'em!'

* * *

The clerical post at the Heather Lee Nursing Home, though not as interesting or as satisfying as teaching, was not too badly paid and one Eva thought she could easily do. When it was offered to her, she accepted, and arranged to start on a date in late February.

'It's mainly keeping patients' files, sending out bills, looking after the office generally,' Mr Wheatley, the owner of the home, explained. 'There's an assistant and a typist already on the staff, so you won't be too overworked, and we hope you'll be very happy with us.'

'I'm sure I shall,' Eva answered. 'Thank you for appointing me.'

And thank heaven there was still a job she could take, even if officially a married woman. Though if the truth were known, as time went by, she was beginning to feel less and less married. More like a woman on her own.

As soon as she got the nursing home job, she found herself a cheap little flat near Letty's, before making a fond goodbye to Ada and presenting her with a fine table lamp she couldn't afford but was determined to give her anyway.

'Oh, Eva, this wasn't necessary!' Ada had cried. 'I did very little.'

'Rescued me, that's all. I'm not even going to try to thank you.'

'Just as long as you come to ma wedding,' Ada told her, taking pleasure in Eva's delighted surprise. 'Aye, Barrie Lennox and me are tying the knot. Some time in the summer. But I'm no' giving up nursing – not at first, anyway.'

'Ada! I couldn't be happier for you! What a dark horse you are, though, never to say a word!'

'Did I need to?'

'No, maybe you didn't,' Eva said with a smile.

'What do you think?' Eva asked Letty and Hughie when they came round to view her new home.

'Well, it's better than that bed-sitter you had,' said Hughie cheerfully, but Letty was looking doubtful.

'It's close to me and that's good, but the furniture's awful shabby, Eva.'

'Can't expect a lot for what I'm paying.'

'Auntie Evie, your baby's crying!' Iain shouted.

'I know, I know.' As though they couldn't all hear Isabel roaring from the bedroom next door. 'I'll pick her up in a minute.'

'Maybe you could bring over some o' thae nice pieces from your other house?' Hughie suggested, testing the springs of the battered settee before sitting on it. 'They'd make a difference, eh?'

'Bring furniture over from the Terrace?' Eva asked slowly. 'What are you talking about, Hughie? I could never do that.'

'Well, I just thought, as you're no' going back, you might as well use some o' the stuff.'

Not going back ... The words were an arrow, turning in her heart. Not going back. Well, she wasn't, of course. Hughie'd had a right to say so. But to hear the words said like that, so matter-of-factly, as though there could be no doubt, had caused pain she'd not known was still there. The scar was healed, surely? But Hughie had opened the wound.

'I'll get Isabel,' she said quickly, and turned away, but Letty was with her, putting her arms round her.

'Oh, Evie, dinna look like that! Hughie was just talking – he didnae mean anything...'

'No, no, I didnae,' he said, stricken. 'I'm sorry – I'm really sorry; I wouldnae upset you for the world, Eva!'

'I know you wouldn't.' Eva shook her head. 'Don't worry, Hughie. I'm just being foolish.'

But as she went into the bedroom to pick up Isabel, accompanied by Iain, dancing at her side, she heard her sister whisper, 'She's no' over it, Hughie. In spite of all she says.'

'I'm the foolish one, eh?' Hughie said. 'Ever to believe she was.'

Eighty-Eight

Ever since Hughie had said what he did, Eva couldn't get her old home out of her mind. Though she'd been in touch with Cora, she'd never been back to the house, and up till now had tried not to think about it. But there it was, back in her thoughts, and gradually it came to her that she must return there. See it, and then forget it. She decided to go, anyway and on a chilly day in late March, she asked Letty to look after Isabel on her day off, and took the train home.

'You're sure you'll be all right?' Letty had asked anxiously, and Eva had laughed.

'I'm not sure at all, Letty. This is just something I want to do.'

Had to do, in truth.

As she looked down on the Tay from the train as it crossed the high bridge, Eva felt such a fluttering in her heart she had to tell herself that this was just her home town she was seeing, this was just dear old Dundee.

As she came out of the station, however, and felt all the old atmosphere, and smelled all the old smells of steam and smoke from the mills and factories, she was still trembling, inside if not outside, and had to go back into the buffet to buy a coffee to calm her nerves.

When she felt a little better, she set off to walk down the familiar streets towards the Terrace. She had no desire to look in at North's Mill, even to see Ma or Roddie, when she would have to meet so many curious eyes. No, she would stick to her goal, which was to return to her home. Or what had once been her home. See it and forget it. Put it from her mind.

As she reached the top of her street, a pale sunlight came through the clouds and caught the windows of her house, seeming to distinguish it and illuminate it especially for her. As she stood still and let her eyes go over it, she felt as weak as water again, but took a deep breath and straightened her shoulders.

'It's only a house,' she murmured. 'There's no

need to be afraid.'

But the house had stirred deep emotion, which might in itself cause her some sort of fear – of what might lay hidden, of what she might not want to face.

She walked on, down the Terrace and through her own gate. Up the path between the small front lawns, all in good order as she noticed, just as the brass doorbell and letterbox were wonderfully bright.

Very slowly, Eva raised her hand and rang the bell, for though she still had her key, she would not use it and give Cora, if she was there, a fright.

And Cora was there, for it was she who opened the door and stared at Eva, as though she were a stranger. Then she gave a cry.

'Why, Madam, it's you! Oh, mey God, Eh canna believe it! After all this time! And you've just missed him, eh? What a shame!'

'Missed him?' Eva's voice was faint.

'The master, Madam. He's just gone. Dinna ken where.'

'Mr North is back?'

'Aye, yisterday. Went stright oot last evenin', dinna ken where, then this mornin', he says to me, niver mind about meals today, Eh'm no' sure where Eh'll be. And away he's off again. Oh, but it's good tae see you, Madam! Shall Eh make you some tea?'

Eva had the tea in the kitchen and made Cora have some with her, for it helped to talk in a normal way, and pretend everything was normal, too. As though it were quite the usual thing for a wife to come back to her home after months away, and not even know her husband had returned.

'And how was the master looking?' she asked casually, as Cora kept passing her biscuits and filling up her cup.

'Oh, jist the same, Ma'am. Very thin, o' course, and tanned, but rushin' roond the place like he'd a million things tae dae. He did say Eh'd kept iverything very nice, though. Eh must say, he's aye polite and kind.'

'Yes, well he's right, everything's looking nice, Cora. You've worked so well, and all on your own. I feel bad about not seeing you.'

'You kept in touch, Madam, and that was fine by me.' Cora's eyes searched Eva's face. 'But how are you, then? You're a wee bit pale.'

'That's just today. I'm very well, thanks.' Eva hesitated. 'I've got a baby now, Cora, a sweet wee girl. I've called her Isabel.'

'A babby? Niver!' Cora leaped up and poured more tea, as though there must be a celebration. 'Oh, that's grand news, that is! Why'd you niver say, though? Eh could've knitted a matinee coat or something.'

'I've been meaning to write and tell you, but you know how it is with a baby – there's no time.'

'Eh wish ye'd brought her today, Madam. Does she look like you?'

'To be honest, I think she looks more like Mr North.' Eva rose and walked round the kitchen. 'You say you've no idea where he's gone?'

'Maybe his folks, eh? He'd be sure to want to see 'em, now he's back.'

'Yes, I expect you're right.'

'You could give 'em a ring on the telephone?' Cora asked hopefully, though Eva was sure she very well knew she would not be phoning her in-laws.

'Maybe later. I think I'd just like to look around, Cora. See if there's anything I need.'

'Mind if Eh ask, then – will you no' be stayin' a while, now you're back?'

'I'm afraid not, Cora. I just came for the day.'

'What a shame you missed the master, then!'

'A terrible shame,' Eva agreed, leaving the kitchen. 'That's the way things go.'

'You'll be wanting some lunch, though?' cried Cora as Eva stood looking about her in the hall. 'Eh can get you a nice wee chop – or a bit o' haddie?'

'Anything will be nice, but then I'll have to go.'

'Oh, Madam! When you've just come!'

'I'm sorry,' was all Eva could say.

Eighty-Nine

Moving round her old home was almost unbearably sad. Even the public rooms, as the Scots liked to call their reception rooms, were filled with memories – of decorating and furnishing,

427

and being so happy, with no cloud darkening her own private sky.

Upstairs, though, the anguish deepened. There was the bed where they'd made love. There were Nicholas's cases, most still unopened where he'd left them. On the chest in his dressing room were his brushes and comb, a pile of coins; on the back of a chair, a jacket dangled. It was as though she'd stepped back in time, and at any moment would hear his step on the stairs, his voice calling her name.

What had she done? she asked herself. By coming back here, she'd destroyed all she'd tried to do to protect herself. Just like Hughie, she'd opened up old wounds, forced herself to feel again.

'Mrs North!' Cora called. 'Eh'm away to the butcher's – no' be a minute, eh?'

'Cora, wait!' Eva went running down the stairs. 'Cora, I've changed my mind – won't wait for lunch – I've got to go – collect my baby – thanks all the same.'

'Oh, Madam, Eh'm that disappointed! Eh was lookin' forward to doin' some cookin' for you, and noo you're away! Are you sure you couldnae stay?'

Eva shook her head. 'I'd like to, Cora. I'd like to stay and talk to you, but I'm worried about the time. Listen, are you all right for money and everything? Does Mrs North keep an eye on things?'

'Sends her hoosekeeper,' Cora answered, making a face. 'Real old devil she is and all! But I'm fine, Madam, 'specially noo the master's back.'

Eva carefully buttoned up her coat and tied her scarf. 'Cora, you needn't tell him I called, you know. He might wonder why I did.'

'Why'd he do that, Madam? This is your home.'

'Well, I think it might be best if you didn't say anything.'

She did not explain, of course, that if Nicholas were to come seeking her, it must not be because he'd thought she'd already come seeking him. It must be his wish to find her. If that weren't so ... well, she'd tell him about Isabel, but that would be all. Until now, it was all she'd expected anyway. It was only seeing their house again – their rooms, their bed – that had unsettled her. The sooner she returned to Edinburgh, away from what she'd once had, the better.

Cora, studying her face with sympathy, seemed to have read something of her mind, for she said softly, 'Mr North might still come over to Edinburgh, eh? To see you, Madam, and the babby?'

'He doesn't know about the baby yet.'

'Eh'll no' say anything, then.'

'No, I'll be telling him myself.'

'When he comes over?'

'He can't come; he doesn't know where I live.'

'Oh, Madam, and eh've got your address! Your sister's, anyway. Remember, that's where eh sent your box o' clothes?'

Eva took a deep breath. 'Did you tell Mr North?'

'Why, no, Madam. He niver asked me.'

There was no more to say. When she'd moved to the front door, Eva suddenly turned and put her arms round Cora's small frame. 'Thank you, Cora. Thank you for everything. I'll be in touch.'

'You'll be back again, eh? You'll let me see the babby?'

'Well ... maybe. Yes, I'll try, I will.'

With a wave of her hand, she walked back down the garden path, away from her house, and thought it best not to look back.

It was evening when she reached Edinburgh and made her way to Letty's to collect Isabel. She couldn't deny the tiny, momentary hope that when Letty opened her door she might see her eyes round with excitement, might hear her say, 'Evie, he's here! He's waiting for you!'

But Letty's face was just as usual, and she only asked if Evie was all right.

'No' too upsetting at the house, eh?'

'It was pretty upsetting, but I'm glad I went. How's Isabel been?'

'Good as gold. No trouble at all.'

'Auntie Evie, she cried!' said Iain. 'She cried a lot.'

'Now you ken fine you shouldnae contradict your ma,' Letty told him hastily. 'She did cry, but it wasnae much, Evie. Anyway, she's all ready for you. Do you want a cup o' tea before you go?'

'No, thanks, I'd better get back.'

For some time, Evie held her daughter, putting her face close to the smooth little cheek, looking into the wondering grey eyes.

'I didn't tell you,' she called to Letty, finally lowering the baby into Iain's old pram, which

430

she'd borrowed. 'Nicholas is back.'

Letty's mouth opened in shock.

'Back? Nicholas is back? Evie, did you see him?'

'No, he was out somewhere. Cora told me. He came back yesterday.'

'Oh, Evie, that means...'

'What?'

'Well, he might come over.'

'He doesn't know where to come.'

'He could find out, eh?'

Eva shrugged. 'He could. Look, I'll away and get this one to her bed. Letty, a million thanks, eh? I'm sorry you had to take Isabel on my day off, when you have her so often, anyway.'

'Ah, I love to have her. She's the wee girl I never had.'

'Ma, I'm your wee boy!' cried Iain, and Letty swept him up and hugged him.

'Of course you are, and I'd niver change you for anything!'

But when Iain had wriggled from her arms and run off, Letty said quietly, 'Just wish you wouldnae keep giving me money, Evie. You've no need, you ken.'

'It's the least I can do. What would I do without you?'

Eva manoeuvered the pram into the street and gave a last smile as Isabel, who had been alert and watching her, suddenly closed her eyes, put her thumb in her mouth, and fell asleep.

'Quick, I'll away,' Eva cried. 'Bye, Letty!'

Minutes later, she halted. Outside her flat, one of a stone-faced block round the corner from

Letty's, was a car. A sports car – not red, but dark green. Very like the red sports car she used to know. And itself familiar.

'Willow's car?' she whispered.

But the driver who climbed out and turned round was Nicholas.

Ninety

As he stood beside the car, sweeping off his cap, he did not speak. Nor did she. But just as when they'd met years before, outside Toll Road School, their eyes spoke for them. Grey eyes, dark eyes, facing across the years and the abyss they had created, until Nicholas took a step forward.

'Eva?' he asked, as though to confirm to himself that she was really there before him. And she, not forgetting to put the brake on the pram, went to him.

For a long moment, they stood in the street and held each other, not kissing, just holding, until Eva drew back and took his hand.

'Come and see Isabel,' she said quietly.

'Isabel?' He looked in at the sleeping child. 'Is this Letty's baby?'

'Letty's baby? Nicholas, she's yours.'

It was a moment Eva savoured. To see the wonder on his face, his colour come and go. To see his gaze wildly moving between herself and

Isabel, and hear the words he could hardly form tremble on his lips.

'You're not serious?'

'I've never been more serious.'

'Eva, why didn't you tell me?' He put his hand to his brow. 'Why didn't your mother tell me?'

'My mother?' Eva's enjoyment faded and her eyes grew large. 'You saw Ma? When? When did you see her?'

'Last night. How d'you think I found out your address?'

'You went to Wish Lane?'

'As soon as I got back. I thought your people would be the most likely to tell me where you were. And I had to know.'

'And they did tell you? I never thought they would.'

'They said it was time. Time I was told. Eva, you don't mind?' His eyes were pleading. 'You know I had to find you. I was thinking of nothing else all the way home.'

'No, I don't mind. They were right; it's time.' She touched his hand. 'You know, Nicholas, I always wanted you to see my home, but Ma would never invite you.'

'Well, she invited me in last night. I think she was glad I'd come. Your father too.'

'I'm glad, too, that you went. It's a part of me, you see, Wish Lane. You had to see it. You had to know about our lives. All our lives.'

'I was impressed, to be honest.'

'By Wish Lane?' She laughed. 'I never thought to hear you say that.'

'Not by what it is, but the way your mother

433

keeps it. Against all the odds – Eva, she's a heroine.'

'Has to be. Like a lot of women in Dundee.'

For a time, they were silent, trying to take in that they were together again, in that quiet Edinburgh street. A husband and wife, meeting again, their baby in her pram. A commonplace scene, yet unbelievable.

At last, Nicholas made a move and bent his head to look in again at Isabel, who was stirring a little, though her eyes were still closed.

'So small,' he whispered. 'So perfect. I can't believe how perfect.'

Suddenly, the baby's eyelids flew open and as a pair of solemn grey eyes met his, Nicholas gave a cry.

'Eva, look there! Oh, my God, she's got Mother's eyes!'

'Your eyes, Nicholas,' said Eva.

Soon he was carrying the pram up the stairs to her flat, and she was holding Isabel and watching, as he looked around.

'This is where you live, Eva?'

His gaze took in the sagging armchairs, the springs sticking up from the sofa, the deal table and tiny fireplace where sticks and paper were waiting for a match.

'It's all I can afford,' she said a little coldly.

'You haven't been using the money in the account?'

'I preferred to manage on my own.'

'But why, Eva? Why?'

'Look, I can't talk now. I have to make Isabel's bottle and put her to bed.' As she left the living room, she said over her shoulder, 'You can light the fire, if you like. The matches are on the mantelpiece.'

It was some time later before they could sit in the uncomfortable chairs by the fire and exchange looks again. The baby had been fed, washed, changed, and put down in her crib, where she was asleep, at least for the time being.

'No going out to dinner, of course,' Nicholas whispered.

'Leaving my baby? I should say not.'

'Our baby, Eva.'

Her eyes softened, filled with tears. 'Oh, Nicholas, I can't believe this is happening. That you're here and know about Isabel. I could never even imagine it.'

'Our being together?' He drew her to his knee. 'Are we, Eva? Is it what you want?'

'It's what I want.' She ran her fingers down his lean cheek. 'It wasn't always.'

'I blame myself.' His eyes were bitter as he held her. 'I was a fool. Couldn't see straight. Couldn't see anything but Bob Keir.'

'I don't blame you for minding about Bob, Nicholas. I was a fool, too.' She smiled a little. 'No need to worry about him now. He has a new love.'

'A new love? No, tell me, who is it? Do you know her?'

'Oh, yes. It's Katie.'

Nicholas stared, then laughed aloud. 'The pretty redhead? So much for his grand passion, then!'

'To be fair, it didn't happen at once. They met, he was depressed, Katie comforted him. Now she's a convert to his politics and very happy. And I'm happy, too, for both of them.'

'And for us, Eva?'

She slipped from his knee, and made up the fire. 'I'm not sure I dare to say, Nicholas.'

'You just said you wanted us to be together!'

'I do, but maybe we should take it slowly. So much has happened. We're different people, aren't we? From those newly-weds?'

'You've been through too much,' he said after a silence. 'I know, without your telling me. I never wanted you to suffer, Eva.' He stooped to hold her close again. 'For God's sake, why did you have to run away?'

'I didn't run away. I left. Just as you said you were going to do.'

'I was crazy. I'd have come back. I still loved you more than anything in the world, but you'd found me lacking, hadn't you? You didn't believe I was right for you, and then you told me about Bob ... I just thought I had to get away.'

'I felt the same. Everything had fallen around me. I needed to start again.'

As he made to kiss her, she moved her face. 'Looks like we got everything wrong, didn't we?'

'But we've got the chance to get things right.' He added, carefully, 'For Isabel, too.'

'Yes.' She took his hands. 'Nicholas, would you like something to eat? I could make you an omelette. And there's cheese.'

'Sounds wonderful.' He laughed ruefully. 'I

436

don't think I've eaten all day.'

'Nor have I. Except for a sandwich at the station buffet.'

'What station?'

'I went to Dundee today. Don't ask me why, but I wanted to see the house. I wanted to see the Terrace.'

'And we missed each other?' He groaned. 'Why do these things happen?'

'Let me go and start the omelettes. We'll feel better when we've eaten.' At the door to her little kitchenette, she looked back and smiled. 'Fingers crossed, Isabel doesn't wake up!'

Ninety-One

Over the simple meal, she told him of her life in Edinburgh. The job at the school which she'd had to give up, the dreary bed-sitter she'd been glad to leave to share a flat with her good school friend, Ada. How Ada had looked after her and would have delivered the baby, only things had gone a bit wrong...

'Don't tell me, don't tell me.' Nicholas winced. 'It's terrible to think of you on your own at a time like that, when I should have been with you.'

'I wasn't alone; I had Ada. Anyway, I was all right. Lucky, really – didn't have too bad a time at all. And everybody was so kind, Nicholas.

437

Made me feel so good'

'Everybody except me. If only you'd told me, Eva!'

'I didn't know where you were. And would you have come back from India, anyway?'

'I wanted to come back a long time before I did.' Nicholas cut some cheese, but only stared at it on his plate. 'Didn't take me long to realize what an idiot I'd been. But I thought ... well, you know what I thought.'

'Tell me.'

'That you didn't want me anyway.'

'If you'd written to me, Nicholas...'

'I wrote you dozens of letters. Never sent one.'

She sliced some crusty bread for his cheese and passed a crock of butter.

'But when you did come home, you must have changed your mind about me, Nicholas. Because you came to find me.'

'Well, I'd decided by then that I'd try my luck. See if I could find you. See if you still cared.' He raised his eyes. 'You do, don't you?'

'I still care.'

'Even if you think we've changed?'

'I think it might take time to get back to where we were.'

He reached out for her hand. 'But you'll come home with me? Come home to Dundee?'

Home to Dundee...

'Oh, yes, Nicholas, yes! I'll come home with you.'

'Tomorrow?'

'Not tomorrow. I've a clerical job at a nursing home. Ada found it for me. I can't just walk out.'

438

'Who has Isabel?'

'Dear Letty takes Isabel. She's been such a rock, Nicholas, such a support. When I used to be the one who had to support her.'

'I'll go round and thank her. I'll thank Ada, and everybody who's helped you.' He shook his head. 'Done my job for me. So, when can you leave this nursing home, then? How much notice will they need?'

'Maybe only a week, as I get paid weekly. I'll feel bad about leaving, though.'

'Same old Eva. Worrying about other people.'

She jumped up to put the kettle on the little gas stove. 'Like some tea? Sorry, I've no coffee.'

'Who wants coffee? Shall we wash up first?'

'If you're offering.' Eva gave a wry smile. 'Whatever would Cora say if she could see the master washing up?'

'Everybody should at some time or other do the washing-up,' he said with a grin. 'And this is my time.'

Later, when they were drinking their tea by the fire, he asked her if she'd told his parents about the baby.

'No. I haven't seen them at all. I knew what they'd think of me.'

'You don't know what they think of you.'

'Yes, I do. They'll say it's just what they said would happen – that I'd let you down, bring disgrace on the family.'

'No, they never said that. I think they blamed us both, to be honest. Said we'd been foolish – which we say ourselves, anyway.'

439

'How are they, then?' she asked after a pause. 'I suppose you've seen them since you got back?'

'Yesterday morning. They're just as usual, thanks.

'And Willow?'

'Oh, Willow's the same, too. But she kindly let me take her car, seeing as mine wouldn't start. Angus has been looking after it, but it probably needs work.' He glanced at his watch. 'I suppose now you're wanting me to go?'

'Well, Isabel will wake up soon. She usually does about now and has a crying fit.' Eva gave an apologetic smile. 'Ada says she's just exercising her lungs.'

'I don't mind her crying.'

'You haven't heard her!'

'I'll need to get used to it.' He stood up. 'But I'll go back now. If you don't want me to stay.'

She hesitated for so long, he was resigned to leaving anyway, but then she stretched out her hand and touched his.

'No, Nicholas,' she whispered. 'Stay.'

Ninety-Two

As Eva had predicted, Isabel did wake up and, after demonstrating her lung power and being given a feed, took some time to settle.

'You could have a practice walking the floor

440

with her,' Eva told Nicholas. 'Let me put something over your shoulder, though – don't want to
mark your jacket if she's sick.'

'Lord, never knew there was so much to
looking after a baby. No wonder people employ
nannies.'

'No nannies,' Eva said firmly. 'I'm going to
enjoy taking care of Isabel myself.'

When, finally, the baby's eyes closed again and
she was put back into her crib, Nicholas, having
claimed all credit for having got her off, touched
Eva's arm.

'Tell me where I can sleep,' he said quietly, and
at the expression on her face, shook his head.
'Doesn't have to be with you. I'm not expecting
that.'

'I've only the one bed.' She gave a nervous
laugh. 'It has as many lumps as burnt porridge.'

'I can sleep on the floor, if you give me a
blanket. Of course, I've no pyjamas.' He finger-
ed his chin. 'And no razor. I'm going to look like
a fellow on the run tomorrow.'

'Oh, Nicholas!' She caught his thin frame to
her. 'Come to bed.'

It was strange, making love again. Less frantic
than the lovemaking that had followed Nicholas's return from Europe, yet in a way more
significant. A marker, they felt, of their new
beginning, of their future together.

Afterwards, they couldn't sleep, perhaps because they were so conscious of Isabel's snuf-
fling breathing so close; perhaps because their
day had been too long, too significant. Eva didn't

441

mind lying awake anyway, now that she was with Nicholas again. She felt at peace, wonderfully serene, all her battles over.

But Nicholas was restless. 'Eva,' he said into the darkness, 'have you forgiven me?'

She turned, trying to make out his face, but could only sense an anxiety in him that seemed to have flared up again from nowhere.

'Look,' she answered patiently, 'I thought we'd agreed that we both made mistakes. We can forgive each other.'

'I'm not talking about what happened over Bob Keir. I mean that time when you were – you know – disappointed in me.' He moved uneasily against her. 'When I said I had to agree with Pa, that we couldn't do anything more to help the workers.'

'There doesn't seem much I can say about that. You've your views, and I've mine.'

'Well, I've changed mine, Eva.' He put his hands behind his head and lay back against his pillow. 'I suppose I couldn't have a cigarette?'

'No, you couldn't! Smoking in bed – what next? And Isabel's here.' She raised herself against her own pillow. 'What do you mean, you've changed your views?'

'It happened in India. You were in my mind most of the time while I was there, you know. I kept going over and over everything that had gone wrong between us, and I kept telling myself that Pa and I were right. We might want to increase wages, but it just wasn't possible.'

'So, where was the change, then?'

'Came after I'd done another stint in one of the

mills. I was looking at the workers one day, and it was so damned hot and they were working so hard, and I got to thinking of our own workers back in Dundee, in heat and dust as well, and earning a pittance, and I suddenly thought, why the hell should people have to live like that? Why should things have to be that way?'

'Market forces,' Eva whispered. 'And firms have to have profit.'

'I know, I know. Pa's views. My views. But then I thought of your views, Eva, and it came to me – maybe we should look at the whole set-up again. Work with the unions. Try to do something, to even things out.'

'That's all we ask, Nicholas. But it's not easy, is it? And the thing is, dearest, it's not for you to say.'

'No.' He heaved a long sigh. 'It's not my mill. Even if Pa were to see my point of view, and it's not likely, but even if he did, there's the world situation. The recession. We'd still have to wait until things improved.'

'But if the will is there, Nicholas, change can follow. It can. You just have to want it enough.'

'Easy for me to say that the will is there, when I can't do anything.'

She flung her arms around him and fiercely kissed him. 'No, Nicholas, it's not easy for you to say. It goes against all that you've been brought up to believe. But you do say it, and that's what matters.'

'What matters is that I mean it, Eva. But it shouldn't have taken a trip abroad for me to see what was on my own doorstep. Until last night,

I'd never even been inside a tenement – can you believe it?'

'Well, I'm glad Ma asked you in at last. It makes us more of a family, somehow, that my folks wanted you to see the house.'

'And wanted me to find you. I'd have had a hard job without them.'

'I think you'd have found me, anyway.'

'I know I would.' Nicholas turned on his side. 'Guess what, I think I might sleep now.'

'Too late,' cried Eva, as a piercing wail rent the air. 'Isabel's woken up.'

Ninety-Three

It was a relief to Eva that Mr Wheatley said he quite understood why she must leave Heather Lee. The family must come first and though he would be sorry to lose her, he wished her all the best, back in Dundee.

Back in Dundee... The words thrilled her, and now that her return was so close she was impatient to be away.

For their drive home, they had to pack Mr North's great car, which Nicholas had brought over because the Bugatti didn't have the space. All the possessions Eva had accumulated while in Edinburgh, as well as the equpiment for Isabel, were stowed in somewhere, and they were about to make ready to leave when a man

444

passing by stopped and touched his hat.

'Is it Miss Masson – I mean, Mrs North? Yes, of course it is – how are you?'

Eva, standing at the open car door with Isabel in her arms, gave a small cry of recognition.

'Mr Torrance! I didn't know you lived round here!'

'Yes, I have a house next to the sports ground.' He was smiling uncertainly, his eyes going from Eva to Isabel, from Nicholas to the handsome motor, and back to Eva. 'I didn't know you lived here, either, Mrs North, but it looks as though you are leaving, anyway.'

'Oh, please, let me introduce my husband, Nicholas North,' she said quickly. 'Nicholas, this is Mr Torrance, headmaster of Lockhart School. He's been very kind to me, very kind indeed.'

As the two men shook hands, Eva could see Mr Torrance's eyes flickering over Nicholas's handsome face, and knew he was recognizing from her husband's looks and manner all that was in his background. If he was surprised, he did not show it, but turned to smile at Isabel, who was giving him one of her long grey stares.

'And who is this?' he murmured. 'I had no idea, Mrs North, that you had a baby. Such a beautiful one, too.'

'She was something of a surprise to me,' Eva said with a laugh. 'A wonderful surprise, though.'

'I'm sure.' Gregor Torrance's eyes rested on her face for a moment. 'May I say, I'm very glad. About everything.'

'Thank you.'

445

She could say no more, but they both knew he was referring to her reconciliation with Nicholas. 'We're going back to Dundee,' she told him. 'Back to our home.'

Again he touched his hat. 'I wish you all the very best of luck. It was nice knowing you, Mrs North.

'And you, Mr Torrance. I'll never forget your understanding.'

'I must get on then. Safe journey.'

They watched him progress slowly up the hill, then Nicholas said they might as well go.

'Door locked? Got the keys for Letty to hand back?'

'Door's locked and yes, I've got the keys for Letty.'

'Right, we'll drop them in, then, and be on our way.'

Letty and Iain were waiting for them at the door to their flat, and there were emotional goodbyes as Eva thanked Letty again for all her support, while Nicholas slipped five shillings to Iain who couldn't believe it.

'Oh, Letty, you'll come over often, won't you?' Eva called, taking her seat in the back of the car with Isabel. 'I'm going to miss you!'

'And I'll miss you!'

'Maybe Roddie'll be coming to work in Edinburgh one of these days.'

'He's a grand laddie, but no' the same as you, Evie. When'd he want to go shopping wi' me?'

'Never, if he were me,' Nicholas said with a grin. 'Have to go, then.'

446

'Don't forget – you're coming over!' cried Eva, and then they were away, the great car purring through the outskirts of the city, carrying them home.

'Seemed a nice fellow, your Mr Torrance,' Nicholas remarked once they were on their way.

'He is. When he found out I was married, he didn't tell the authorities, which saved me getting into trouble.'

'That was decent of him.'

Yes, and when he found out we were separated, he gave me some advice.'

'We were never officially separated.'

'No, but you were in India and I was in Edinburgh – I'd say we were separated.'

'All right, what was his advice?'

'To be reconciled with you.'

Nicholas frowned. 'And he didn't even know me?'

'No, but he was saying not to leave it too late. In case it couldn't happen at all.'

'No need to tell us that.'

'Not now,' Eva agreed.

Eva's return to the Terrace was very different from her previous visit. This time, Nicholas and Isabel were with her. This time, there was no anguish, no regret, only a singing heart and a resolution never to leave home again.

In fact, hers was not the only heart to be affected, for Nicholas said he felt his was practically beating out of his chest with joy, and Cora couldn't believe her luck. Mr and Mrs North home again, and their wonderful baby with them! Now the dark days were over.

Not for the world, of course, with the recession biting ever deeper, but Eva said maybe they should be allowed to enjoy their own private happiness, for a little while.

'Of course we should,' Nicholas told her fondly. 'Everyone's entitled to happiness – if they can get it.'

Sooner or later, of course, other matters had to intrude, and on their second day back, Nicholas reminded Eva that they should be thinking about going to Garth House. His parents and Willow now knew about Isabel and were, of course, anxious to see her. And Eva, too, he'd added quickly.

'I'd like to go round to my folks first,' Eva said, thinking about the Norths with some unease.

'Of course. Would you like me to come with you?'

'No need,' she told him hastily, for she was looking forward to a chat with her mother. 'You can come another time.'

'Now that I've been allowed in.'

'You'll be very welcome,' she told him.

But would she be welcome at Garth House? With a sinking heart she agreed that they should go over to Broughty Ferry the following day.

Ninety-Four

Bel said she supposed it was only right that Eva should finally take the baby round to see the Norths. They were the grandparents, after all. And you had to let grandparents see their grandchildren.

'I haven't said I wouldn't go,' Eva told her. 'It's all arranged.'

'Mind you, I'm just being kindhearted,' Bel said, gazing down into the sleeping face of Isabel, who was on her knee. 'I dinna really want to share this bairn with anybody. It's a funny thing about grandchildren, I've found – you sort of enjoy 'em more. Your dad says the same.'

'Aye,' agreed Frank. 'I'm that looking forward to takin' Letty's laddie to the footba', you ken.'

'No' something Isabel'll want to do,' said Bel with a laugh. Her eyes moved to Eva. 'But it's grand to have you back, pet. It was a long pull, eh?'

'It was, Ma.'

'And I did right to tell Nicholas where you were?'

'Oh, yes!' Eva cried fervently. 'Yes, you did right. We had to be together, somehow; we had to be.'

'And you say he's brightened his ideas up, eh?' asked Frank. 'I mean, about North's doing more for their workers?'

'He wants to, Dad, and that's the main thing. But he's not in charge, remember. He doesn't own the mill.'

'What caused the grand change?' asked Bel, taking Isabel up into her arms.

'He said it happened in India, when he looked at the workers and thought of people at home. Why should they have to work so hard for so little? He came to see it wasn't fair.'

'Hmm? That's what he says, is it?'

'What's the matter? Don't you think it's true?' asked Eva, frowning.

'Partly. But I think what gave that laddie a change o' heart was coming in here.'

'Here? What do you mean?'

'Well, when I invited him into ma house, it was the first time he'd ever been in a tenement. He told me so. And I could see his eyes opening like saucers as he looked all round, and I could tell he was knocked sideways. Is that no' right, Frank?'

'Sideways,' Frank agreed, drawing on his pipe.

'Ma, he told me he thought you kept the place really neat and clean!' cried Eva. 'He said you were a heroine.'

'Now does that no' prove ma point? He thinks me a heroine for managing a place like this, though he's no idea what some houses are like, eh?'

'No idea,' said Frank.

'Aye,' Bel went on, 'if he could see the rooms where folk roll out o' bed and others roll in, and the bairns ha' no beds at all, but sleep on coats. And the wives need to go to the pawnshop till

450

they get their wages at the end o' the week, and sometimes ha' only a cup o' water to go to work on. What he saw here is no' so bad, but t'was bad enough for him, seemingly, to see the light.'

'You think it was Wish Lane made him begin to agree with me?' Eva asked slowly. 'He didn't say so.'

'Didnae want to hurt your feelings. Though it's true, thae folk in India might have helped his views along. Their lives'll no' be any beds o' roses, eh?'

'Just glad to get the work, I expect,' put in Frank. 'And that's nothing new, eh?'

'And talking o' work, hasn't that wretched Berta Loch turned up at the jam factory!' cried Bel. 'Canna get away from that lassie, eh?'

But Eva would not speak of Berta Loch. Even to think of her sent the knives into her heart again, and she leaped to her feet saying she must prepare Isabel's bottle, desperate to change the subject.

'What a shame you couldnae carry on nursing Isabel, eh?' asked Bel. 'It's a tragedy for women here, you ken, if they've to find the money for babby food. Still, that'll no' be your worry, eh?'

'Finding money needn't be yours, either,' Eva said pointedly, but the shuttered looks came down on her parents' faces and she said no more.

Still, when the time came to leave, Bel patted Eva's shoulder and said to tell the truth she'd had a change of heart of her own.

'Aye, I've taken to that laddie o' yours, Eva. When he came here the other night, I could see what you see in him, and it wasnae his money.

451

So nice, you ken, so anxious to please. And that fond o' you.'

'No feet of clay after all, then?' Eva asked gently.

'You've had your disagreements. Who hasnae? But you'll be all right with him now.'

'Took a lot o' notice o' what I said, too,' said Frank. 'And your ma's no' the only one with opinions, though you might no' think it.'

'Oh, Dad!' Eva said, laughing as she put Isabel into her pram. She added that she'd let them know how she got on at Garth House.

'Might find they've had a change o' heart, and all,' said Bel.

But nobody really believed that.

Ninety-Five

The following afternoon at Garth House, the Norths received Eva and Nicholas in the drawing room, as they had on Eva's first visit. She remembered with crystal clarity how she'd felt then, and how the visit had ended, but now, of course, she had a wedding ring on her finger and the Norths' granddaughter with her, sleeping in her new Moses basket. If there hadn't been the separation between herself and Nicholas, she might have felt better. As it was, she couldn't be sure of her welcome. Nicholas had said his people didn't blame her; she was sure they did.

All went well, however, when the little family arrived. Nothing was said to indicate that there had been any problems between the Norths' son and the woman they'd never wanted him to marry. In fact, it was as though there had been no problems at all, and that the Norths had seen Eva only the other day. How strange!

Perhaps they'd decided the situation would be easier to handle if no one spoke of it, which suited Eva just fine. Or perhaps the presence of the new little member of the North family had smoothed everything over. Isabel, even asleep, was certainly the centre of attention.

'Oh, what a poppet!' Mrs North cried, bending over the Moses basket. 'Eva, may I hold her?'

'Shouldn't do that, Ailsa,' Mr North hastily advised. 'When was the last time you held a baby, then?'

'Mummy, supposing you dropped her?' cried Willow.

'It's easy, holding babies,' Nicholas declared, picking up Isabel himself. 'Watch me!'

While Willow squeaked with alarm and her parents smiled, Isabel opened her eyes in her father's arms, at which Willow cried, 'Oh, look, Mummy, she's got your eyes. Why, she's your image!'

'Is she?' asked Mrs North, immediately interested. 'You know, I think you're right. Those are my eyes – and Nicholas's, too. What a wonderful thing a baby is, then! Willow, do ring for tea.'

Over tea, served by the same two maids Eva had seen on her first visit, Mrs North asked about plans for the baby's christening.

'Now, I don't want to interfere, if your parents have made arrangements, Eva, but if it's possible, Mr North and I would like to hold the christening party here.'

Eva, taken by surprise, at once turned to Nicholas, who gave a small shrug.

'We've not thought about the christening yet,' he told his mother.

'And my mother's made no arrangements,' added Eva. There weren't many christening parties held in Wish Lane. On the other hand, it would be very suitable to hold one in Princess Victoria Terrace.

For a moment, Eva pondered over what she wanted to do. Might it not be better, after all, to sweeten her mother-in-law a little and go along with her plans? 'I'm sure it would be very nice to have the christening here, Mrs North. Nicholas and I would like that.'

'You're sure?' Mrs North smiled as Isabel, who'd been fed, lay gurgling in her basket. 'And would you mind if the ceremony was held in our local church? It's Episcopalian, not Church of Scotland.'

'If you've strong views, please say,' Mr North ordered. 'Don't want to upset anyone.'

'I'd be happy to have the ceremony in Nicholas's church,' Eva told him. 'I like to go to the kirk sometimes, but we've no strong views – as a family.'

'We can go ahead with the arrangements, then,' said Mrs North. 'Wonderful. I have some beautiful family robes you might like to look at, Eva. And then you must think about the god-

454

parents.'

Nicholas and Eva again exchanged glances.

'Needn't decide now, need we?' asked Nicholas. 'Haven't had time to think of any of this.'

'Mustn't leave it too late, dear, or Isabel will be too big to fit into any of the christening robes. What about your sister for one, Eva?'

'Yes, I should like Letty. And Willow.' Eva turned a smile on her sister-in-law. 'If that's all right?'

'Oh, of course!' Willow's eyes were shining. 'I should love to be a fairy godmother! Heavens, what can I give? I must think of something really special.'

'And the godfather, Nicholas?' asked Mrs North. 'Any suggestions?'

'I've one or two friends I might think about,' Nicholas began, when Willow had an idea.

'Why not your brother, Eva?' she suggested casually. 'That nice young man who's going to be an accountant?'

'Eva's brother is going to be an accountant?' asked Mrs North. 'I'd no idea. But how do you know him, Willow?'

'Oh, I met him at the wedding,' she answered carelessly, which seemed to satisfy her mother, but Eva could see Nicholas's eyes resting on his sister with some surprise.

Should he have been told about Willow's affair with Roddie? Eva herself wanted no secrets kept from him, yet she could say nothing about this one, for it was Willow's. No doubt she had not wanted to speak of it, for it was all over, anyway. Just as well. The Norths would have been even

455

less happy about Roddie as a son-in-law than Eva herself as a daughter-in-law.

In the end, it had to be admitted, the Norths had been surprisingly friendly to Eva that day. On the way home in Nicholas's now repaired car, after polite farewells and promises to keep in touch over the christening, Eva couldn't help remarking on this to Nicholas.

'Why do you think they were so nice?' she asked. 'They never said a word about what happened.'

'Don't want any difficulties,' Nicholas answered, after some thought.

'Well, they made plenty of difficulties before. I think it's Isabel who's made the difference. Perhaps it's simply that they can't cut me off, when I have Isabel.'

'Of course they're not going to cut you off. Especially when Mother can have all the fun of planning a christening. Next best thing to Willow's wedding.'

'Willow is getting married?'

'No, but Mother would like her to.' Nicholas cast a sideways glance at Eva. 'What was all that about Roddie, then?'

'You'd better ask Willow.'

'There's something between them, then?'

Eva settled Isabel on her knee and shifted in her narrow seat. 'I think we do need to have a more suitable car than this, Nicholas. It's really not safe, carrying a baby in this seat.'

'I'll have to have a word with Willow. Find out what she's playing at.'

'It's her business, Nicholas, but if it will set your mind at rest, I can tell you it's all over. And Roddie's thinking of moving to Edinburgh eventually.'

'Willow wanted him to be godfather, though.'

'That's because they're still friends.'

'This christening could be tricky, all the same.'

'Just as long as my folks are invited.' Eva set her chin. 'Maybe I should have made that plain.'

'Mother would never miss out the other grandparents, Eva!'

She'd have to miss out me as well, if she did, Eva thought, but wisely said no more.

Ninety-Six

As soon as Eva had told her family that they were to be invited to Garth House for the christening party, consternation reigned.

First, Letty said no, that she couldn't face being godmother, not in front of the Norths and their friends. She'd be in such a state, she said, she might drop the baby at the font. And besides, she'd nothing to wear.

'Willow could be the one to hold Isabel at the font, if you like,' Eva suggested, but at that idea, Letty's face clouded.

'I think it should be me really, Evie. I mean, I'm older than she is, and she's as scatty as they

457

come, eh?'

'You just said you didn't want to be godmother at all, Letty.'

'Well, perhaps I should be. I mean, it is an honour to be asked. And I wouldnae mind seeing the inside o' Garth House. Might be nice to buy something new to wear, though? If I'm to be godmother?'

Although Roddie seemed quite happy to be Isabel's godfather, persuading Bel and Frank to agree to attend the christening proved just as difficult for Eva as organizing Letty.

'Us, visit Mr North's house?' cried Bel. 'You must be joking, Eva!'

'I'm no' going there,' Frank declared. 'And that's that.'

'But it's the reception for Isabel's christening!' Eva cried. 'And Letty's going to be a godmother and Roddie the godfather. You'd surely not want to miss it?'

'Might go to the ceremony,' said Bel. 'But to the Norths' place, no.'

'It's all over now and we just want to be friendly,' Eva said desperately. 'This invitation's a sort of olive branch, and I think we should take it.' As her mother's expression appeared to be softening, she added, 'And Nicholas is very keen for you both to come, you know. I think you should consider it.'

There was a silence as Bel and Frank appeared to think about it. Then Frank said slowly, 'If I go, I'm no' telling anybody, eh? I'd never hear the last of it, if the lads knew I was going visiting to a jute baron's palace.'

'Same for me,' said Bel. 'I'd never live it down.'

'You'll come, then?' Eva's face was bright. 'And don't worry over what to wear. Dad, you can hire a suit again, the same as you did for my wedding reception. And Ma, don't argue, I'm going to get you something smart, and I needn't pay for it with Nicholas's money. I've still got some of my own savings left.'

'I wasnae goin' to argue,' Bel answered graciously. 'I'd no' mind something new. If I'm visiting at Broughty Ferry, I'm going to have to look good.'

'All arranged,' Eva told Nicholas later, as they sat together in his study. 'They're all coming – Ma and Dad, Letty and Hughie, and Roddie. Letty made a fuss, and so did Ma and Dad, but I'm pretty sure they meant to come all along. Couldn't resist seeing Garth House.'

'Mother will be pleased,' said Nicholas, pouring himself a whisky. 'Might take her mind off Dad's worries.'

'I know things are no better,' Eva murmured. 'Feel guilty, spending so much.'

'A drop in the ocean of what it's costing us to keep going,' Nicholas said as he drank his whisky. 'To tell you the truth, the only thing that might save us is another war.'

'Don't speak of it!'

'Well, they say these Nazis in Germany are pretty belligerent. Can't get over losing in 1918.'

'I don't see how a war would help us, Nicholas.'

He gave a crooked smile. 'Sandbags, darling, sandbags. Made from jute, right? And there'd be plenty needed in a war.'

'I hope it doesn't come, all the same!' Eva shuddered. 'Oh, think of it – so much loss of life and misery to go through all over again.'

'Don't worry, it may never happen. Let's change the subject. Got the rest of your invitation list sorted out, then?'

'Yes, everyone's accepted. Ada and Barrie, and Miss Balfour. Did I tell you I met her in the street the other day? She was my teacher long ago. And then there's Mr and Mrs Crindle, and Katie...'

As Eva hesitated on Katie's name, Nicholas drank more of his whisky.

'And Bob Keir?'

'I had to ask him, Nicholas, as he and Katie are practically engaged.'

'And is he coming?'

'No. He told Katie to tell me he had to go to a conference in Aberdeen.'

'Tactful,' Nicholas remarked, stifling his disdain.

'It might be true.'

'He's not coming, anyway. I don't mind telling you, I'm relieved. I know he's no threat now, but I just don't want to see him.'

'We'll have to go to his wedding one day, I expect.'

'I'd be happy to make an exception for that,' said Nicholas with a grin.

Ninety-Seven

At four o'clock on the day of the christening, the guests arrived at Garth House for tea, champagne and cake, following the ceremony at the Broughty Ferry church.

All had gone well. Letty had not dropped Isabel, resplendent in a robe of silk and lace, while Roddie and Willow had provided perfect support, and Bel and Frank had amazed themselves by enjoying everything.

It was true that Mr North had been only polite when he shook their worn hands, even though impressed by Bel's dark and beautiful eyes and her likeness to her daughter. His wife, however, had been most charming, throwing a velvet cloak over all past neglect, and quite bowling over Frank, if not Bel.

'I'll say this for her,' he murmured when they'd taken their seats in the church, 'Mrs North's made us welcome, eh?'

'Seeing as we're grandparents, same as her, you might say that's the least she could do,' Bel snapped.

Ailsa North had certainly done a lot, and both Eva and Nicholas warmed to her and heaved sighs of relief that Isabel's day appeared to be free of disasters. In fact, by the time they reached Garth House they were as relaxed as their guests,

461

especially when Isabel, worn out with all the struggle of being put into that christening robe, fell peacefully asleep.

Stunned by the splendour of the drawing room, the exquisite flower arrangements, the tables laden with elegant food and towering christening cake, Eva's guests could hardly speak.

Even Mrs Crindle, who was rarely lost for a word, only pulled herself together enough to say, 'Katie, would you look at that?' While Mr Crindle kept on shaking his head, and Iain for once kept close to his parents and confided to Letty that he didn't think the great iced cake could be real.

'Sure, it's real,' she told him. 'Everything here is real.'

'Specially the presents,' Hughie murmured, eyeing the splendid display of mugs, napkin rings, spoons, bracelets and necklaces on a corner table. 'Every one guaranteed hallmarked, you bet, even our wee chain and cross and Roddie's bangle.'

'Eva'd never have wanted you to spend a lot o' money on presents,' Bel said firmly. 'There's better things to do wi' cash, if you've got it, eh?'

'Just what Bob would have said if he'd been here,' Katie declared.

'Just as well he isn't,' her mother snapped, who was not in favour of Bob Keir as a son-in-law, but had been allowed no say in the matter.

'Can we no' go and have some o' thae sandwiches?' asked Frank. 'I'm starving.'

'You're going to need an awful lot to fill you

up, then,' said Bel. 'They're only the size o' postage stamps. And be careful wi' the champagne. Might go to your head, eh?'

'Just where I want it!' Frank retorted.

Circulating the room, Eva, meanwhile, had met up with Miss Balfour again, who looked not a day older and was now working at Dundee High School. Almost at once, they were joined by Katie and Ada, who wanted to introduce Barrie, and then Hughie had to be brought across to shake his ex-teacher's hand. Which left only George, in Africa, and Bob, in Aberdeen, missing from the special little group who'd gained Mr North's first bursaries.

'How well you've all done!' cried Miss Balfour. 'Of course, I always knew you would, but you've proved me so right. You're perfect examples of how education can change lives.'

'I suppose we should be grateful to Mr North, then,' said Ada. 'He set us on our way.'

'Shouldnae have to be dependent on the Mr Norths of the world, though,' Hughie put in. 'Secondary education should be available to all.'

'Oh, you sound so like Bob!' cried Katie. 'Miss Balfour, did you know that Bob and I are getting engaged?'

'No need to look so surprised,' Ada laughed. 'Katie's turned into a disciple.'

'I'm very happy for you, Katie,' Miss Balfour said diplomatically. 'For you all. But I must thank you, Eva, for inviting me here today – it's been wonderful.'

'Come and meet Nicholas,' Eva cried, but,

after making the introductions, was waylaid by Willow, looking rather flushed in a pretty silk two-piece and enormous hat.

'Oh, Eva dear,' she murmured, putting a slender hand on Eva's arm. 'Hasn't it all gone well, then? Didn't you think that Roddie and I made a wonderful couple as godparents? Heavens, you must be so proud of him!'

'Roddie?'

'Well, he's so bright, isn't he? He's going to do really well, even Pa says so.'

'Yes, he's going places.'

'My point exactly.' Willow's flush was fading, as her eyes searched the throng of guests but seemed not to find what she was looking for. 'I do miss him, you know, Eva. He was the best companion I ever had.'

'Was he, Willow?' Eva asked wonderingly. 'But these things come to an end, don't they?'

'His idea,' said Willow. 'He was the one who said we'd no future.' She laughed. 'I'd have eloped!'

'I'm sorry. I never knew how you felt.'

'Not brought up to say. But I expect I'll find someone else. In fact, there are one or two on the horizon.'

'I bet there are. We'll dance at your wedding yet.'

'Poor Mummy can't wait to get the invites out. She's had such fun organizing this christening, you know. Oh, there's Daddy wanting to make a toast if I'm not mistaken – let's charge our glasses!'

* * *

A silence had fallen on the room, as all eyes went to Mr North standing with his wife and Nicholas by the christening cake. But he appeared to be making no move. As a waiter approached to fill up his glass, Ailsa North glanced at her husband's face, then touched Nicholas's arm, and Nicholas at once bent closer to his father.

The silence deepened as the guests waited, then Nicholas signalled to a waiter to bring a chair, and Mr North, looking grey and sweating heavily, sat down. He did not speak.

'Ladies and gentlemen, please raise your glasses for a toast to my daughter, Isabel Frances North,' said Nicholas, still glancing down at Joseph, and Eva, who had left Isabel sleeping in the care of one of the maids, moved to his side.

'Long life and good health to Isabel!' someone cried, and the glasses were raised, the toast made, and everyone drank. Except Joseph North, who had closed his eyes and was quietly, slowly, falling from his chair to the ground.

As great cries of alarm moved through the drawing room like a rolling wave, Mrs North and Willow screamed, and Nicholas dropped to his knees beside his father. But the people who knew what to do were already on their way.

'Please, Nicholas, let us see him,' said Barrie Lennox, and as Nicholas stepped aside to put his arm round his mother, Ada loosened Mr North's collar and tie and Barrie began to examine him. A moment later, he looked up at Nicholas.

'We have to get your father to hospital now – no point waiting for an ambulance; we'll take him by car. Help me to get him out of here.'

'We'll take Pa's own car,' Nicholas gasped. 'I'll call Angus now. Can we go with him?'

'Ada and I will go with him. You and your family follow. Hurry, there's no time to lose.'

As willing helpers carried Mr North from the room, Ailsa clung to Willow. 'Oh, what is it? What is it?' she wailed, while Eva stood, white-faced, wondering what she could possibly do to help.

'I'm afraid it looks like a heart attack, Ailsa,' said a distinguished-looking man, who was John Berry, another jute baron and friend of the North family. 'Let Willow get your coat. You must try to get to the hospital as soon as possible.'

'A heart attack? He's had a few little pains – nothing at all, he said.' Ailsa's face was twisting and her hands were at her mouth. 'Nothing at all, he said – oh, God!'

'Your coat, Madam,' whispered the little maid who always seemed nervous. 'Mr Nicholas wants you to come now.'

'We're ready,' cried Willow, throwing aside her great hat. 'Eva – come with us.'

'Ma, will you and Letty look after Isabel?' Eva asked her mother hurriedly. 'Daisy, one of the maids, has her in the room next to this and her bottle and things are in the kitchen.'

'Leave her to us, pet, dinna worry,' Bel said. 'Letty, we'll away to find the babby, eh?'

'Oh, what a terrible thing,' cried Letty as Eva ran after Willow and her mother, and shocked guests slowly began to leave.

What had been a scene of joyous celebration only brief moments before was now quiet and desolate, with maids and waiters beginning to clear away food, glasses, and champagne bottles. Standing in pride of place, never cut, was the magnificent christening cake.

Ninety-Eight

Outside, the spring evening was still light, but Eva felt it should surely be dark. Everything felt dark, anyway, as Nicholas's new family car hurtled on towards Dundee, with no one speaking, only thinking. For what could anyone say?

It was Mrs North who broke the silence at last, but only to ask where the doctor was taking her husband.

'The Infirmary,' Nicholas told her. 'He'll get the best care there.

'But what about Rivermead? We always go to Rivermead, Nicholas. Your father knows it and will be comfortable there.'

'Rivermead's a nursing home, Mother. Pa needs a hospital.'

'But will it be right for him? I mean, will he have a private room?'

'What is she on about?' Willow muttered to Eva in the back seat. 'All that matters is if the doctors can save him.'

'Your mother knows that,' Eva whispered back. 'But it's natural for her to try to get the best for your father.'

'Of course he'll have a private room,' Nicholas said placatingly. 'There's no need to worry about comfort, Mother.'

'No need at all,' Willow added.

When they arrived at the hospital, Nicholas led the way, running, into the reception area where they found Barrie and Ada waiting for them.

'Well done, Nicholas,' Barrie said, trying to look cheerful. 'Your father's with the doctors now. There's a place where you can wait. Mrs North, would you like us to show you?'

'Is he in a private room?' Ailsa whispered as they moved through the corridors. 'He would never tolerate being in a public ward.'

'At present, he's being treated,' Barrie told her gently. 'Time to think about his room later.'

'Here's the waiting room,' said Ada. 'I'll see about finding some tea, shall I?'

'Quite pleasant,' Willow observed, looking round at the room's pale walls, pale carpet and easy chairs. 'Is it for private patients?'

'I'm not sure, but everyone has to pay something if they can,' said Barrie. 'Hospitals are partly funded by voluntary contributions – they need as much as they can get.'

'I've done my share of fund-raising for hospitals,' Ailsa murmured, sinking into a chair and sighing. 'I never thought poor Joseph would end up in one.'

'He's getting the best of care, Mrs North. Be assured of that.'

'If you say so.'

'Someone's bringing tea,' Willow announced.

'The first essential, isn't it, a cup of tea?'

'Nicholas, are you all right?' Eva asked in a low voice as he came to sit near her. 'I know that's a foolish question, but I'm here with you. I'll do anything I can.'

'We can't do anything, Eva.' His grey eyes were at their bleakest. 'Pa's in the doctors' hands.'

'I suppose we could pray?' asked Willow. 'But we've never been much of a family for praying.

'We go to church!' Ailsa cried.

'Not always the same thing, Mother.'

Eva was anxious to speak to Ada, who put her arm around her for a moment and gave her a sympathetic smile.

'Poor wee Isabel,' she said softly. 'What a christening day, eh?'

'Already seems a long time ago. But thank God you and Barrie were there, Ada.'

'We did what we could.'

Eva looked around to see if anyone could overhear, but no one appeared to be listening.

'Listen, can you tell me – is Mr North going to pull through?'

Ada hesitated. 'I can't say at this stage, but he was unconscious when we brought him in. I wouldn't say the prognosis was good.' At the distraught look on Eva's face, she added quickly, 'They'll be doing everything they can. But, to be frank, that isn't a lot. Until somebody comes up with some new techniques, we're in the hands of the gods.'

'Oh, Ada!'

'We'll see. Maybe I'm looking on the dark

side. Mr North's not that old and seems strong. He might make it.'

But only a short time later, a senior doctor, still in a white coat with a stethoscope round his neck, appeared in the waiting room and asked to speak to Mrs North. She stood up and walked towards him, but he took her hand and guided her back to her seat.

'I'm so sorry, Mrs North. So very sorry.'

She did not speak, only gazed up at him with a blank grey stare.

'We did everything we could, but your husband had suffered a massive heart attack before arrival – I'm afraid he did not respond to treatment.'

'There was never any hope?' Nicholas asked baldly.

'He was unconscious when he was admitted and died shortly afterwards. I'm sorry.' The doctor turned to Ailsa. 'Would you like to see him?' he asked gently.

She nodded and, on the arm of her son with her daughter holding her hand, she left the waiting room.

'Eva?' Barrie whispered, but she shook her head.

'They're family, Barrie. They should see him alone.'

'You're family, too,' Ada murmured.

'No, not today. I'll wait here for Nicholas.'

They drove back to Garth House, just the two of them, for Ailsa and Willow were being driven home by Angus in Mr North's car. And somehow, it was the thought of that – his wife and daughter travelling in the car he would never use again – that brought the tears to Eva's eyes.

While he had not been the most sympathetic of employers, and had never wanted Eva to marry his son, he had nonetheless been her husband's father and must therefore matter, to her as well as to Nicholas. She felt she should not deny him her tears.

'Hard to believe,' Nicholas said as they swung into the drive of Garth House. 'My father will never come here again. We've come back, but he has not.'

'Nothing is ever so final,' Mr Torrance had said, talking about death, and on that April evening his words had never seemed so true.

Ninety-Nine

As was expected of a jute baron's farewell, Joseph North's funeral was a grand affair, attended by everyone who was anyone in Dundee, if only by a handful of his workers. Though deeply hurt by that, Nicholas made no comment, perhaps knowing in his heart that his father had not been well loved. *How different it would be for him*, Eva thought loyally, *if he should come to run the mill himself.* But only when the will was read could he be sure of doing that.

* * *

Two days after the funeral, Nicholas told Eva that a meeting had been arranged with the lawyers. 'For the reading of the will,' he explained, gazing at her with shadowed eyes. 'You must come, too.'

Though he had not wept for his father's death, those darkened eyes and the strained lines on his face were signs enough of his grief. In some ways, Eva thought, it would have been easier for him to cry, together with his mother and Willow, but as a man he had been brought up not to shed tears.

'I don't think I should come to the lawyers,' she replied. 'Reading the will is a family matter.'

'You still don't think of yourself as family?' Nicholas shook his head. 'I'd be sorry to believe that. As my wife, you are family – let no one say any different.'

'Coming into a family by marriage, it's never quite the same. Especially where money's concerned.'

'There is no need to worry about the money. As you know, Pa told us all some time ago how the estate would be divided. Today is just a formality.'

Eva kissed his cheek. 'Sounds as though you don't need me, anyway. I'll stay here and you can tell me about the will when you get back.'

'As I say, there's no need to worry.'

'Very well.' She smiled a little. 'I'm not worrying.'

Not about the money, anyway. In her view, the Norths scarcely needed any more. Even Isabel, it appeared, was to have her own trust fund, while for Ailsa, Willow and Nicholas himself, generous provision had been made. Ailsa was also to have Garth House, which she intended to sell, and Nicholas had been promised he could have what he most wanted, and that was the mill.

Just as long as that promise had been kept, Eva thought, after Nicholas had gone, for everyone knew that promises and actual terms of a will could be quite different. She would have to wait and see.

The front door banged, and then came the sound of Nicholas's step and Cora's voice as she took his coat and hat.

'Like some tea, sir?'

'I'll just speak to Mrs North.'

'Nicholas!' Eva cried, running to him. 'How did you get on? Quick, tell me!

'Shall I bring tea, Madam?' asked Cora. Eva nodded and turned back to Nicholas.

'You haven't said what happened, Nicholas. You haven't told me about the will.'

His still sad eyes met hers, yet he was trying to smile. 'It's all right, Eva. Pa was satisfied with me, after all.'

'He's left you the mill?' she whispered.

'He's left me the mill.'

One Hundred

'Without strings?' Eva went on fearfully.

'Without strings. I'm to be running it as Pa did, with the aid of a board of management. But just as all key decisions were his, now they'll be mine.'

All key decisions. That meant the way ahead lay clear. She opened her mouth to speak, but Nicholas had something else to say.

'Everything in the will was just as Pa had said it would be. Bequests to us, bequests to charities, legacies to the servants, and so on. There was just one surprise.'

'A surprise?'

'Yes, for you.'

'Me?' she asked, incredulous.

'He left you five hundred pounds.'

'Five hundred pounds?' She was stunned. 'I can't believe it!'

'To spend on yourself, he hoped.' Nicholas smiled wryly. 'I guess he knew you'd spend it on the mill girls, or your family. But you see, he did appreciate you, Eva. Whatever you thought of him, he knew your worth.'

'I've always been grateful to him for my bursary, that's true.'

'Yes, that was good, but he was never going to do what you wanted him to do for the workers.

He was a businessman first, second – all the time. He couldn't change.'

'Maybe a part of him thought I was right, but he couldn't admit it?'

'Maybe.' Nicholas drew Eva to his knee, where she lay against him, in the favourite way she had, and they quietly kissed.

'You know things are no better?' he murmured after a while. 'I mean, there's no sign of trade picking up. No sign of the recession lessening.'

'I know.'

'I can only promise to do what I can with what we make from the firm, Eva.'

'I know,' she said again.

'But a start can be made. Money can be found from our own resources, if you're willing?

'Willing?' She widened her eyes. 'Are you asking?'

'All right, we can go for the new equipment – dust clearers, better machines, high-speed spinning frames, that sort of thing. We will turn the corner eventually, and when we do, we'll be ready. North's will be stronger than ever.'

'Stronger than ever,' she repeated thoughtfully.

'I know you're thinking of the wages, Eva. As I say, I'll do what I can. Speak to the unions. The main thing is, there will be change. Maybe not just for us, either. I have the feeling that if we come though this slump, things will be different all round in Dundee.'

'With you leading the way. Oh, Nicholas, you're wonderful.'

'Of course I am.' He gave his first real smile in days. 'I'm your soulmate – I'd have to be.'

'Soulmate ... What did you once say? That if you once find your soulmate, you can't let that person go.'

'Ever,' he said solemnly. 'You can't let that person go, ever. Haven't we learned that lesson by now?'

'We've learned a lot of lessons, Nicholas.'

That night they made love for the first time since Nicholas's father had died, and afterwards, Nicholas fell into a deep and peaceful sleep. But Eva couldn't sleep and rose to look out from her window over the quiet city.

Across the roofs, not very far away, was Wish Lane. Not very far, but a thousand miles, and Eva had travelled every one of them, yet still carried it with her. Her mother had made it home, and Eva would never forget it, but one day, as she'd already vowed to try to make happen, folk would live differently.

Oh yes, change would come for Wish Lane, for Dundee. One day, there would be a better city, where bairns needn't be brought up in slums, and their parents needn't toil at work for a pittance. It would take time and money to achieve, but Eva knew she was not alone in wanting it. Somehow, it would come.

Just as long as I live long enough to see it, she thought, glancing back at the sleeping Nicholas, who suddenly stirred and called her name.

'Eva, where are you?'

'Coming.'

But first she checked on Isabel in her little nursery next door. Isabel, who should see an

476

even brighter future than her parents'. Isabel, who was sleeping like an angel, breathing so quietly that Eva had to bend her head to hear her.

'Whatever are you up to?' Nicholas asked sleepily, as Eva slipped into bed.

'Only counting my blessings,' she replied.

Afterword

Eva turned out to be right. After the long depression of the 1930s, followed by a horrific world war, change did come to Dundee. A new generation was not prepared to live as their parents had lived. Something, they declared, must be done. Slums were cleared, and housing estates, roads, schools, and a splendid hospital were built. A new face was given to a city that was no longer dependent on jute. After years of battling against foreign competition, the industry, though it didn't die, went into decline. Some mills closed. Others – including North's – experimented with new materials and found different things to make. Outside companies moved into the city and made different products, and as the jute barons retired, their palaces becoming schools or nursing homes or falling into decay, a final end came to the great divide between rich and poor in Dundee.

And what of Eva's childhood home, Wish Lane?

That disappeared in the massive housing clearance, and even where it had once been was very hard to find. Sometimes, Eva and Nicholas would walk round the new Dundee with their grown-up children – Isabel, a lawyer and Christopher, an engineer – and Eva would try to point out where she'd once lived. But the old tenements of Dundee were a vanished world, and all one could cling on to were the people who had been part of it:

Bel and Frank were now retired and living in a bungalow with a garden, much to Eva's delight and relief. Roddie had married Marigold and was doing well as an accountant in Edinburgh. Letty had her Hughie, a successful newspaper editor, and her Iain, a chemist. Bob Keir was married to Katie, of course, and had become a Labour MP, still fighting for a perfect world.

A perfect world might not have been achieved, but even the privileged, such as Ailsa and Willow North, agreed that the new Dundee was better than the old. 'So good to see the children with shoes,' Ailsa, who now lived in apartments in the Berrys' old mansion, would remark. And Willow, who had married a banker, said it was wonderful not to feel guilty any more.

Had she ever felt guilty? Eva wondered. You could never tell with Willow. She still occasionally asked after Roddie, and smiled at his name.

'Aye, you canna believe it, eh?' was Bel's verdict on the changing times. 'No more Wish Lane. No more dust in North's Mill, and everything's that

clean and quiet. Is it no' sad that folk like poor
Mavis couldn't be living now?'

'Well, Berta Loch's still around, from what I
hear,' said Letty. 'What does she find to complain about these days?'

'Oh, plenty,' said Bel. 'You know Berta. Says
she misses the hingy oots she used to have from
her windows – as though they were something to
miss!'

'I think Nicholas worries that we might one
day have another slump,' said Eva. 'But even if
we do, things will never be as bad as they used
to be.'

'Thank God for that,' Bel said with feeling.

The years had been kind to Eva and Nicholas.
Though Eva's dark hair was now greying, and
Nicholas had at last put on some weight, they
were still attractive people, still leading busy
lives, full of plans and hopes, and still, as Eva
said, counting their blessings.

'Aren't you glad we've lived long enough to
see what we wanted to see?' Eva asked one evening as they returned from a walk by the Tay. But
Nicholas smiled, and said he wasn't sure he liked
to think how long he'd lived.

'Why, we're only middle-aged!' cried Eva,
taking out her key, for no maid would now open
the door. Cora had long ago left to be married,
and Eva, content not to be waited on, had never
replaced her. 'In fact, we're young – young at
heart, anyway.'

'And still in love,' said Nicholas, kissing her in
the hall. 'Still soulmates. Some things don't
479

change, you know. Shall I put the kettle on?'

'As though that's not a change in itself, you putting the kettle on,' Eva said, laughing.

But she knew what he meant.

29
34
29
26
7